FAITH ALONE

- The Heart of Everything -

FAITH ALONE

- The Heart of Everything -

Bo Giertz

TRANSLATED BY
BROR ERICKSON

Faith Alone, the Heart of Everything

Published by:
1517 Publishing
PO Box 54032
Irvine, CA 92619-4032

Publisher's Cataloging-In-Publication Data
(Prepared by The Donohue Group, Inc.)

Names: Giertz, Bo, 1905–1998, author. | Erickson, Bror, translator.
Title: Faith alone : the heart of everything / Bo Giertz ; translated by Bror Erickson.
Other Titles: Tron allena. English
Description: Irvine, CA : 1517 Publishing, [2020] | Translation of: Tron allena. Stockholm : Svenska kyrkans diakonistyrelses bokförlag, 1943.
Identifiers: ISBN 9781948969345 (hardcover) | ISBN 9781948969352 (softcover) | ISBN 9781948969369 (ebook)
Subjects: LCSH: Brothers—Sweden—16th century—Fiction. | Reformation—Sweden—16th century—Fiction. | Faith—Fiction.
Classification: LCC PT9875.G53 T7613 2020 (print) | LCC PT9875.G53 (ebook) | DDC 839.7/72—dc23

Printed in the United States of America

Cover art by Brenton Clarke Little

CONTENTS

Map of Sweden during the time of the Reformation

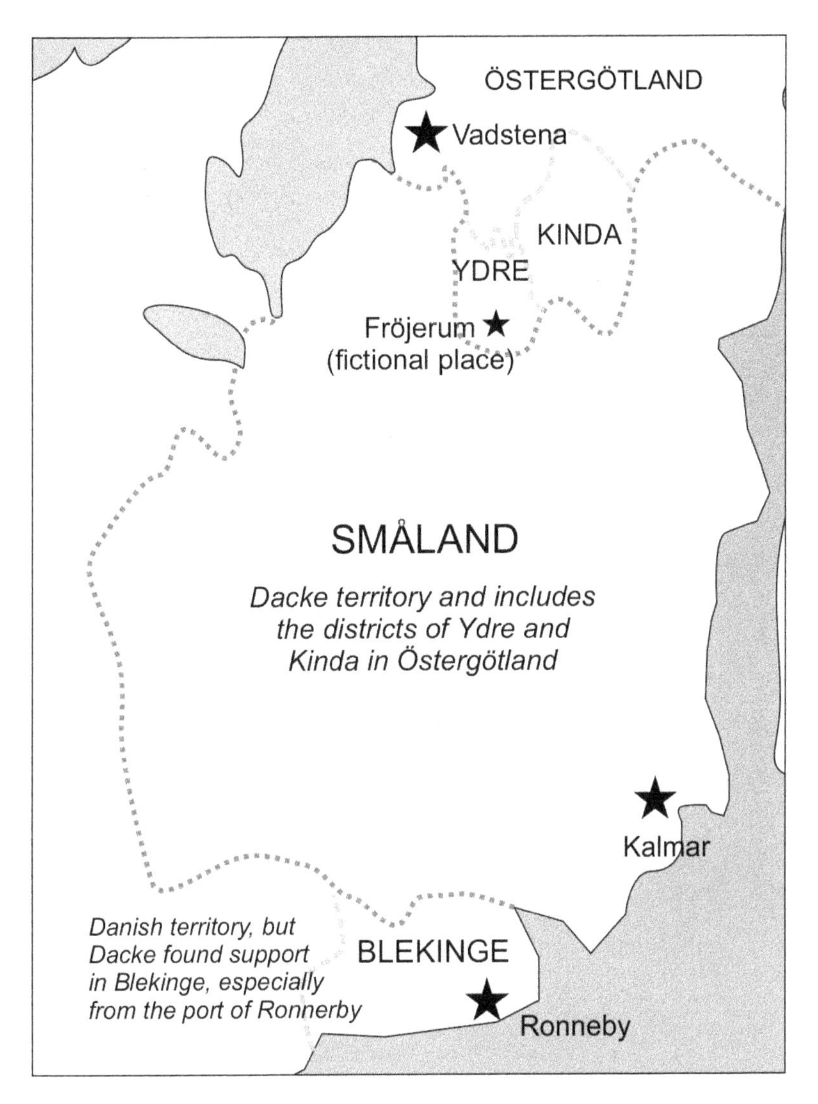

Territories in southern Sweden affected by Dacke's Rebellion

HISTORICAL INTRODUCTION

Mark Granquist

Many times, when history is written, it is from a perspective that is too far removed from the subject itself. This is not just the time difference, often hundreds of years later, but also from a perspective that knows the final outcome and cannot help but be shaped by such knowledge. This history-from-beyond inevitably shapes the narrative in light of the final outcome, which seems even in the course of that narrative to be almost foreordained. History is also often too "clean," where events seem quite obvious, and little confusion is manifested. But, of course, this is not at all how things work out in reality. At the time when events are actually happening, there is often a fog about them, and participants are rightly confused and unclear about not only what events are taking place, but also (and more importantly) what those events actually mean. Rarely is it a history that can bring to life the complexities, ambiguities, and confusions of those who were actually living and participating at the time of any particular historical event. This is why historical novels such as *Faith Alone, the Heart of Everything* by Bo Giertz are so important. In his work about the Protestant Reformation in Sweden in the sixteenth century, Giertz skillfully narrates the very human confusions and ambiguities of this age, and how personally and socially wrenching these changes were for so many people. This is a vivid and masterful work.

The events of Swedish history, especially the introduction of Protestant Christianity in the sixteenth century, are not well known, so this introduction will provide a brief background. This is a key period of time in Sweden, for the establishment of an independent Sweden and the introduction of Protestantism go hand-in-hand. It is important first to understand the political history of Sweden, and then to look closely at the religious changes brought to Sweden during the sixteenth century.

The character of medieval Sweden was shaped by its roots in pre-Christian tribalism, and by the feudalism of Europe during the middle ages. Local political and military leaders were spread over the territory that is now Sweden, and conflict between them for power and prestige were a constant feature of life. Slowly during the thirteenth century, a form of national unity and political centralization was achieved through the initial consolidation of the Swedish monarchy. The Swedish king had limited power and resources and was mainly dependent on his ability to persuade other powerful individuals and groups to support him in order to balance their competing aims. The local and regional nobility were the key power brokers, but there were many others who also wielded power. Unlike their counterparts in many other areas of Europe, the Swedish peasants retained their freedom and their traditional rights, which they guarded jealously. Led by regional leaders, these peasants would regularly revolt against both the king and the nobles (this will play a big role in the novel itself). The leaders of the growing towns were another force, as was the medieval Catholic Church, and the large population of German traders within the country.

In the fourteenth century, political instability and warfare resulted in the triumph of the Danish monarchy, and the establishment in 1389 of the Union of Kalmar, where the three Scandinavian kingdoms were brought together under the rule of a single, Danish monarch. This worked for a time in Sweden, but as could be expected, there was an eventual reaction against this. Members of the Sture family consolidated their position as leaders within Sweden, which brought them into conflict with the Danish kings, who sought to maintain their control over the country. In 1520, the Danish army defeated the Swedes, and the Danish king ordered the execution of eighty-two leaders of the resistance, the so-called "Stockholm bloodbath." This caused the Swedes to unite behind a young noble, Gustav Eriksson Vasa, who began to successfully repel the Danish armies with considerable financial help from the German city of Lübeck. In 1523, the Swedish assembly, the *Riksdag*, proclaimed Gustav Vasa as the King of Sweden.

Being proclaimed king was only a first step for Gustav Vasa, for his political situation was in constant jeopardy for most of the first twenty years of his reign, not only from the Danes but also from the many different power blocs within Sweden. Because of his movement to bring the Church in Sweden under his own royal control, Gustav Vasa has often been compared with King Henry VIII in England, and this is in part a reasonable comparison; they both brought the Church under their personal control to consolidate their political and financial power. But Gustav Vasa was in a far more perilous situation than was Henry, who had a strong tradition of monarchy behind him. Gustav Vasa faced resistance and revolts from the nobles, the regional peasants, and the leaders of the Church, along with crippling debts to the city of Lübeck. There were a number of times where it seemed that Gustav Vasa would be forced out of office, and it was only through his application of military might and his skillful rhetorical powers that he managed to survive. He did more than just survive, however. He established the modern Swedish monarchy, and his reign marked the beginning of the nation-state of Sweden itself.

One significant, yet controversial element of his push toward monarchy was his dependence on foreign aid and advisors, mainly from the new Protestant states in Germany. Through trade and the Hanseatic League, there had been a long-standing and influential presence of Germans in Sweden, especially in the major towns. German advisors and financiers were an important presence in Sweden, although many Swedes (especially those in positions of leadership) came to resent their power. Gustav Vasa had important German Protestant advisors and significant financial debts to German bankers. That Gustav Vasa needed significant taxes and the "loans" of money from nobles, towns, peasants, and the Church to pay off these loans was a major factor in the popular resentment of German influence in Sweden.

Sweden was one of the last areas in Europe to accept Christianity, and the adoption of this new faith proceeded slowly in the countryside. Although missionaries came to Sweden from Germany and England as early as the ninth century, the formal establishment of Christianity in Sweden has generally been recognized with the establishment of an archbishop in Uppsala in 1164. The power of the medieval papacy upon the Swedish church was limited, although a number of monasteries and convents were established, notably the community of St. Bridget in Vadstena during the fourteenth century. Christianity existed in the rural areas in parallel with many of the practices of the pre-Christian religion, which either slowly died out or were absorbed into the life of the Christian parishes. By the beginning of the sixteenth century, medieval Christian faith and practices were firmly implanted in Sweden, even among the rural peasants, and began spreading to Swedish-ruled Finland. The Catholic bishops of Sweden became an important political bloc as well, and the Church amassed great wealth, owning or controlling up to twenty percent of the territory of the Kingdom.

The ideals of the Protestant reformation came into Sweden in the 1520s, from Germany and Denmark, and by means of Swedish students who went to study in Wittenberg. One of these students, Olavus Petri, returned to Sweden and became an ordained priest and preacher in Stockholm, where he would begin to influence King Gustav Vasa. During the 1520s, Petri began to break with Rome. He married in 1525 and introduced a Swedish-language New Testament in 1526. A number of others in the church began to adopt the new Protestantism into their congregations at the same time. As these new "evangelical" preachers were supported by the King and by some of the leading nobles, the Swedish Catholic bishops were hesitant to move too openly against them. In 1524, the king formally dissolved papal control over the Church in Sweden and took control of its institutions under the advice of an influential Swedish church leader named Laurentius Andrae. A number of the older bishops resisted this for a time, but as they either died or went into exile, they were replaced by new "evangelical" Bishops. In 1531, this process led to the appointment of Laurentius Petri as the Archbishop of Uppsala, the titular head of the Swedish Church, which was preceded by the nationalization of the Church and elevation of the king as its head.

Part of this transition on the part of Gustav Vasa was for him to obtain the power and wealth of the church. Not only did he move against the monasteries, convents, and cathedral chapters, he also demanded the "surplus" wealth of the parish churches. After 1530, this included a deposit of one bell from each church for the royal treasury. Gustav Vasa desperately needed to raise money for troops to fight the Danes and put down local rebellions but also to pay off his debts to Lübeck. The parish confiscations, especially, created hard feelings among the peasants, which led to further outbreaks of local revolts.

By the early 1530s, the evangelical position of the Petri brothers was firmly in place within the royal administration, and their influence peaked. However, by the mid-1530s, Gustav Vasa seemed to feel that he had achieved his aims in controlling the Church and its assets. So, he began to "put on the brakes" for further reforms along evangelical or Protestant lines. Olavus Petri and Laurentius Andrae fell from the king's favor, and in 1540 they were tried and convicted of treason, though they were not executed and were soon restored to positions of prominence. In their place, Gustav Vasa turned to advisors from Germany, who suggested that the king consolidate his control over the Swedish Church even further. These measures occasioned the last serious revolt against the king during the period 1542–43 (this is the immediate backdrop for the novel itself). The rebellion was serious enough to threaten the rule of the king. After putting down the rebellion, Gustav Vasa took steps to moderate his demands and distanced himself from his German advisors. In 1544, the *Riksdag* responded by reaffirming the evangelical nature of the Swedish church and the power of the king by making the monarchy hereditary. The modern religious and political character of Sweden was thus set into place.

One of the great elements of this novel is its vivid and detailed description of the confusion and turmoil of the first twenty years of Gustav Vasa's reign. This was a traumatic and chaotic period, and the lives of many Swedes were deeply disrupted by these religious changes. Sweden was then essentially conservative; many considered the old ways as best, and religious changes like those of this time were deeply troubling to many. Not only did these changes threaten the stability of their faith and the persistence of their religious practices, many also resented the intrusion of royal power into their own local religious communities. To be sure, the events of 1523 to 1543 were deeply disruptive and divisive, as individuals and local communities struggled to make sense of the new evangelical practices and teachings. Certainly, in many areas, the change-over to the new evangelical system took time and was slow to make its way into the hearts and minds of individuals. But the new teachings also brought with them a new hope and a new and liberating way of understanding the grace of God. This new message was eventually widely adopted by the Swedes, and the country became firmly Protestant. This is not, however, to undercut the very difficult transition that many people underwent, which is at the heart of this thoughtful and insightful novel.

Mark Granquist
February 2020

GOD AND CAESAR

January 1540

. . . Saint Anne, the 5th Day of January A.D. 1540
Andreas Ragvaldi, parish priest in Fröierum

The old shepherd of souls signed his name to the letter with endless bitterness. He would rather have stood up and torn the paper into shreds before throwing the entire miserable mess into the fire. But he sat there instead, his arms laying on the table motionless and heavy.

Of all the humiliation that had befallen his church during these unhappy years, this was the most shameful. He had been compelled to drink deeply from the cup of degradation since the very beginning. Now the cup was empty. He could taste the dregs in his teeth as he sat there.

Reminiscing, he had anticipated that it would all spin out of control the very day canon Martin came back from Västerås appalled and reported on the ill-fated recess.[1] At that time, Andreas was seventeen and a regular and permanent scholar at the cathedral school in Linköping. He stood there listening among the other priests in

[1] Västerås recess of 1527 was the resolution of the Swedish Parliament (or *Riksdagen*) which was called to deal with rebellion in Dalecarlia, and in which it was decided that the church should be subject to the King. The nobles could reclaim all property sold or donated to the church since 1454 and the King could claim whatever castles belonging to the bishops that he wanted.

training on the cold and damp stone floor of the landing outside the cathedral. They had just sung Sext and were on the way back to the schoolroom. As usual, old Magnus Laurentii, the rector, had taken the lead with slow steps, his bare head bent forward in thought. At the door, he had almost collided with the large dean Martin, who was hurrying in from the castle, followed by two other canons. In distraught Latin sentences, intertwined with outcries of Swedish, Herr Martin reported the incredible news concerning the blow that King Gustavus had now given to the church's freedom: The bishops' palaces were to be handed over, the possessions of the canons stripped, the monastic estates plundered—the entire spiritual entourage was a bruised reed.

Anders remembered how everything turned to black before his eyes as he stood there with his ears on alert. Half in a haze, he walked out into the sunlight. In the extreme excitement, Rector Magnus gave the students leave to do what they wanted for the rest of the day, before making his way up to the bishop's castle. So Anders walked listlessly along the Stångån River, and it seemed to him that the elm seeds fluttered down like dead leaves, and nature was preparing to die even though it was barely a week past the Feast of St. John. The terrible truth began to sink in for him slowly: the king's heavy hands would also lay claim to Askanäs where he had played as a child under the rowans,[2] where his dead father had built the farm-house, and his mother had sung hymns to Mary at dusk.

His mother, Bothild, was a pious woman. She was from a free-born family, though she married the rich farmer in Askanäs. Even in childhood, she had a zeal for the catholic faith and concern for the church's welfare that suited a woman of nobility. She had always wanted her two youngest boys to go out into the world and become priests. So she had set it up for both of them to attend the Latin school in Linköping. Then came the year of misery when she was widowed and lost her oldest son, who was supposed to inherit the farm. From that day on, she lived in the cloister. Then she finally decided to donate Askanäs to the nuns in Vadstena. Because the farmer at Askanäs had been the last of his family, there was no one

---

2 Ash trees.

to claim the family's entitlement to the land. Martin, his younger brother, had perhaps made a little fuss, but as always, he finally bowed to his mother's will. As for himself, he was the one who had the strongest claim to inheriting the farm, but he only rejoiced. He had already learned to love the holy song over and above everything else on earth. He lived in the devotionally saturated world of the daily hours. In his common poverty, he found a revelation of the heavenly city on the mountain whose walls always radiated with light. The sincerity of shy responses and the infinite pure beauty in the tone of the antiphons always filled him with immense joy. He could not wish for anything more than that the rye from his father's tilled land on the beaches of Fröjerum should be converted to hymns that would forever blend with clouds of smoke in the cool, dim light of the Blåkyrkan.[3]

So, everything came together. His mother had kept the two small fields up at the edge of Ödesjö and arranged that a certain portion of the rent from the main farm would be allocated to both of her sons so long as they needed it for their studies. In the two years since the farm and been handed over to the cloister, a stranger had taken over as the farmer and made himself at home in the large cottage.

He felt nothing but great joy when it was all finished. It was perhaps a bit painful when, for the first time, he could not swing in between the lindens[4] for the holidays like before and see mother Bothild walking on the large courtyard below the granaries. But feelings of joy won out again as he continued up the hill toward the forest. There lay the gray square yard of the family estate. It was set apart for God, like himself, and the only thing he could feel was a sixteen-year-old's complete and indescribable joy to live for the Lord, to be one of those who followed the gospel's counsel, forsook the world, chose poverty as his bride and became a companion of the saints.

And now the king, that insatiable silver-bellied devourer of homes, would lay his slimy hands on Askanäs too! His innermost

---

[3] Blåkyrkan (pronounced blow-shirken), or the Blue Church, is also known as the Cloister Church in Vadstena.

[4] Linden, a deciduous tree with heart-shaped leaves and fragrant yellowish blossoms.

sense of justice revolted. From that very day, he had been a sworn enemy of the new government with its wanton demand to sacrifice everything in service to king and country.

His bitterness only increased on account of his helpless impotence. The king's bailiffs took Askanäs. The poor boys of Linköping were not even able to keep their meager maintenance. The bailiff laughed at him when he attempted to reclaim the farm. Such could be the case for nobility, but not for a bastard![5] What would he want the farm for anyway if he was still going to become a priest?

At home, the soldiers now kept a fortified camp in the yard. They came every year in March. They stayed a few weeks and consumed everything there was to consume. They carved in the benches and puked on the tables. Then they went off to spread the French disease[6] in the village. Incense and hymns did not ascend from mother Bothild's pious gifts, but vapor from the king's brewing vats and jody calls marking cadence in his fully manned fähnleins.[7]

Herr Andreas straightened up where he sat by the parsonage's unvarnished oak table in a high, turned stool. He shivered in the cold. It was particularly unpleasant to sit still for so long in the drafty cottage. Neither was it any good to allow bitterness to stiffen him. He had to get up.

He rose, rubbed his thin frozen hands together, and looked around. Embers were still glowing in the dim light of the great open hearth under the oven. The gray and lifeless winter days fell in through the oiled skins of the ceiling windows. There were some worn pelts of black sheepskin on the coarsely woven floor beds. The bed behind the bedposts in the corner had not yet been made today, the skins and rugs were thrown in a pile. There was a wooden plate on the table with the remains of a dried fish and black breadcrumbs. The only valuables in the room were three books bound in silver-gray

---

[5] Though the two characters, Martin and Anders, were born to married parents and knew their father, the fact that their father was a peasant man married to a noblewoman gave them the same status of a bastard—no legal right to the property under the current conditions.

[6] Venereal disease.

[7] A medieval Swedish infantry unit.

parchment, which found their place on a shelf set particularly high in the gable where they were kept safe from rats.

He was almost ashamed of the untidiness and went over to make the bed. Then he took the wooden plate out from the little cottage and threw the scraps in the snow outside the backdoor. He went back in again and put a couple of logs in the embers. They hissed and steamed as he leaned against the vault of the oven and cooled his feverish forehead against the cool mortar.

Complete tranquility ruled here on the parsonage property. Saint Anne's chapel in Fröjerum was really just a little circuit rider's preaching station, and the parsonage was just a storm shelter where the priest could turn in when he came riding to mass on holy days. He was the priest in Ravelunda, but he would never have asked for it at this time if it had not meant that he would also be the priest of Fröjerum where he could lead mass in the little wooden church of his fathers. He thrived the best up here in the woods and often resided for many days in a row at the deserted parsonage. One of the peasant farmers in the church-village[8] had managed the farm for a long time. Animals no longer bleated in the gray barn, and he had never found himself a housekeeper either here or in Ravelunda because he had determined once and for all not to feed the popular and offensive stories concerning the lifestyles of rural priests. So it was no surprise that idyllic peace reigned here among the old logs.

Herr Andreas sat down at the desk again and hastily looked at the letter he had just finished writing. His chest flared up again. The fire had caught on in the hearth where lusty flames licked the logs. The delicate manner in which the fiery tongues danced tempted him, something about it all jerked him by the arm and gave him the wild desire to throw the paper in among the logs.

But he controlled himself. He had already fought the fight to the end and admitted defeat. The letter would not burn in the fire but go to Stockholm. The King's bailiffs would note that Ravelunda and Fröjerum had also added themselves and signed the letter of

[8] "Church-Village." Not all villages in this area would have a church, and the villagers in the surrounding area would be expected to attend the church in this village, which grew up around the church.

enslavement. The free church and the free parish had compromised. The last position of justice was lost.

Really, how could it have continued so long? As Anders looked back on the past twenty years, he thought about the demonic consequences of the king's actions. The tyrant's plan must have been clear from the beginning; he had only come to show what he did behind the shield. So the jousting tournament had begun, first good words, then some careful thrusts, then a bold grip and a well-calculated parade with the breaking wheel for the reluctant, and slippery assurances for the indulgent—and the whole time with the hateful stubbornness and cold-hearted calculation of a fox.

It began just a year after the war of independence with the great treasury of silver. Herr Andreas[9] was only a schoolboy at the time but could remember well the anxious disputes on the stairs of the chapter house. Then the king had only spoken about a loan; he would pay everything back readily. It did not sound so dangerous. Such things had happened before. Herr Svante had already borrowed from the Saints of Kalmar. There was good reason too: the creditors of Lübeck were merciless, and it was necessary to expatriate the foreign mercenaries at any price. So they made an exception to save the land from her distress, and King Gustavus had sworn his life and blood to preserve the holy church and her privileges.

But the very next year, his fingers groped for the money collected for the coffers of Saint Karin at Vadstena, one hundred and fifteen solitary marks. This time there was a storm of wrath throughout the whole region of Östergötland because the money was given to the saint and not to the king's unfortunate Gotland expedition. The resentment was so strong that there was an end to the robbing of the church for

[9] The title *Herr* could be translated in many ways, sometimes "Sir," sometimes "Lord," or simply as "Mister." However, I decided, for the most part, to just leave it as *Herr* throughout the text. It was used for both priests and nobility, and we do not have a good translation that can convey that range of use in English. Though in Lutheran circles, the term *Herr Pastor* is still used, often in a pejorative manner to refer to pastors who feel a sense of entitlement, it does not have that connotation here. Where multiple men are addressed as Herrs, or where they are called Herr without their surname, I have translated the word simply as *lord*.

some years afterward. Instead, the priests were caught in the middle as the tithe from which they received their income was taxed arbitrarily and harshly, but at least the sacred vessels stood untouched.

Then the king began to catch his wind by breathing in the Lutheran heresy, and so the deathblow came in 1527. The old revered bishop gave up the game and fled from the country. The diocese was like a flock without a shepherd. The bailiffs began to confiscate properties belonging to the bishop and monasteries, and as soon as a priest or a canon went out of turn, they were there with their demands and threats. Pure sacrilege followed. A letter came to Askeby and another to Vadstena with orders to quietly send the church's silver up to Stockholm. The king thundered as usual and threatened the most terrible evils if even a whisper of the matter made it to the villages. But naturally, he could not stop people from guessing what had happened to the golden processional cross or St. Martin's reliquary. Then came the bell tax—now, this at least was done legally. In Fröjerum, they ransomed their great bell with silver; it was twice as precious since that day.

When it went that far, every man knew that the debt to the creditors of Lübeck had been paid, the country was in good standing once again, and King Gustavus was considered the richest prince north of the Alps. He could relish going into Herr Eskil's treasury where it was said, he often stood before crates of silver and would dig in them like grain bags, and then take a midafternoon nap surrounded by all Mammon's glory.

So, this last encroachment was twice as upsetting. Ever since the new German advisors had come to Stockholm, it seemed that all rights and freedoms were doomed and trampled underfoot. A request had come from the dean a few days before Christmas. Herr Andreas had quickly ridden to Näs, and the dean had delivered the memorandum the Diocese had written under the direction of the king. At the risk of his harsh indignation, all the gold, and silver, all the treasures, the money and vestments, which up to now had been abused in unchristian fashion in service to the true God, should be documented. Priests would confirm these lists and at least three trustworthy parishioners who also would vouch for the trustworthiness of the information with their life and blood. Then the documents would be sent to the chapter before St. Knut Day, or the pastor in concern would forward them to Stockholm at his own expense. Regarding this last bit, the dean had comforted his brothers in the office by telling them that they did not need to send letters to Linköping because he understood that at New Years', a royal scrivener would be traveling through the county to gather the documents and thereby also check their correctness. As if that was any comfort at this time!

What these documents would contribute to was something every man could see for himself. Members of the congregation were not any less wise to it either. They knew what was happening. Upon his return, Herr Andreas gathered the elders and the churchwardens and filled them in on the situation. They could hardly believe him. They knew very well that the church had been built by the donations of parishioners who gave all they owned. Did the law of the land not say that neither king nor individuals could own the church, but only those who enjoyed respite for the soul there? What then had the king to do with their church and her silver treasures? Their fathers had paid for them honestly. They, too, had gathered before the gilded monstrance with the pictures of the apostles currently stored behind double locks in the sacristy. And they had given it to their church and not to Herr Eskil's treasury. The king had no more right to it than he did to their fields. But perhaps that was the meaning, that the whole kingdom would be regarded as the king's storehouse and every Swede as his dependent tenant?

After a long deliberation with many bitter words, they realized that there was nothing to do but submit. They hid their little treasury of good Danish silver and some of the clippings with it. They would rather have done the same with the golden monstrance that was the pride of the parish, but it was all too well known outside the parish boundaries for anyone to make such a foolish attempt. Then they broke up and left the priest to write the letter.

Herr Andreas never thought that it could be so hard. He had thrown the pen from his hand many times. Everything he had seen since he was a child, and now that he had been ordained as God's presbyter,[10] he held them in his hands. There was the paten, from which he had received the sacrament for the first time as a little

[10] Priest. In Swedish, the word *priest* is related to the New Testament word *presbyter* often translated as "elder" in English.

seven-year-old boy. There was the cope with its silver weave. He could remember it from days long past when the procession approached Askanäs in the brilliant May sunshine and he joined the assembly that would follow it over the fields. His short legs made him run barefoot as he tried to keep up, singing the litany's refrain at the top of his lungs: *Te rogamus, audi nos!*[11]

But now it was still done. It remained for the king's scrivener to receive the document and snoop about in the sacristy.

Once again, he clenched his fists. What did King Gustavus's scrivener have to do with the sacristy in Fröjerum? The church owned the land it was built upon free and clear. Free men had given all that they had of their own free will. It was given and consecrated to God's glory. Did not the sun have to darken, and the mountains split when the princes plundered the Lord's altar with impunity? Why did Bishop Johannes not stay in the country? Brask[12] could have been enough to call all honorable men to make a stand all by himself. Now everything was plotted away. The Dalecarlians had alerted their side and had their bloody heads impaled. Peder Sunnanväder and Master Knut were forced to drink the duskål[13] with the executioner and then given the breaking wheel, even though they were prelates. The lords of West Gothland had to escape the country. Now, if a wretched farmer dared defend his rights against the bailiffs, he lost ears and hand.

Herr Andreas began to walk back and forth over the worn and creaky planks. Then he stood at the low front door and peeked at the sun through the gaps. It moved toward Nones. Soon, it would be three. It was time to go up to the church. He exhaled. At least there was still this comfort, a divine resting place among the thistles.

---

[11] We implore you, hear us.

[12] Bishop Johannes Brask (1464–1538), bishop of Linköping, was a vocal opponent of the Lutheran faith but fled to Danzig after the Recess of Västerås.

[13] "To drink the duskål" references being stripped of your title, which then meant you could be executed like a common criminal—that is, with the breaking wheel, a form of punishment common for highwaymen. *Du* is an informal address in Swedish used when addressing close friends and those of a lower class than you, and *skål* is a toast—the idea being that by drinking to this toast, you are acknowledging your new position in society.

He pushed the creaking door open and stood for a moment, almost blinded by the daylight that suddenly fell in through the door of the half-dark cottage. Everything was white on white. Only the gray felled-timber shed drew dark lines over the white table, and a few dried thistle or yarrow stuck up like a dark contour from the blanket of snow.

He went down over the gently sloping yard and took the path out between the sheep shed and the feed barn. His long coat fell to his feet and swept the thin layer of snow on the ground. Frost crystals fastened like a white brim to the black homespun wool. The sun broke through for a moment at the horizon in the west, drawing a band of light across the meadows. The clear evening light swept across the church-village up on the hill. The gray stock houses with their white edges of snow in the foreground lit up for a moment, the church's high, black tarred gable contrasted even sharper and more noticeably against the clouds. Then the sunlight faded again. Low, heavy gray snow clouds rode the wind, and the countryside once again sank into the tired twilight of the colorless and quiet winter.

Herr Andreas pulled his hat down on his head and wrapped his coat tighter around him. He looked at the church-village with despair. Complete tranquility ruled there, but the smoke that whirled away in the wind said that the farms were still inhabited. It was, of course, the Eve of Epiphany. He didn't see a soul heading to the church.

Well, if he was alone during these smaller hours, it did not make them any less meaningful. He knew someone would at least come to hear vespers.

He left the village to his right and walked up the church hill. The wind bit through the gate and swept snow through the churchyard. He went over to the little wooden door on the south side, took hold of the rusty iron ring, and opened it. A heavy whiff of smoke blended with the comfortable smell of chilled and damp wood smacked his face. It was almost dark inside, only the small window apertures high up on the south side allowed the gray daylight in, and the eternal flame glowed like a golden star in the darkness before the altar.

He stretched out his hand and let his fingertips rub over the ice in the font holding the holy water. He crossed himself and fell to his knee. He hardly prayed with words. A great calm filled him. God lived here. The saints stood watch here like a motley crew of silent and solemn squires with unfathomably tranquil smiles on their faces. The pictures here reflected the Savior's bloody suffering and his glorious victory. Songs of praise had caressed every plank and every joist of this immense timber galley roof for centuries, drenching them with holy memories.

He looked up and then quietly rose to his feet. The great beam that bore the heavy triumphal crucifix could be just barely seen in the dim light. To the left stood the side altar at which the women were blessed and received back into the congregation after childbirth,[14] and the offering chest held up on a pedestal. Along the wall were three wooden pictures with heavy colors and shiny gold frames, the floor occupied the expanse in between, open and bare, with an occasional stone slab set between the oak planks.

The pastor opened the wooden gates in the choir screen and approached the altar, he genuflected again, lit the candle and exited into the dark sacristy on the left. The wardrobe, with its pointed gothic gable, cast a fluttering shadow against the coarse stone surface of the arch. Herr Andreas took the surplice from the hanger and put it on over his coat, which he left on because of the cold. Then he went into the choir again and lit both of the coiled candles that were set in the heavy, three-footed bronze holders on the altar and genuflected toward the south corner of the altar where the breviary lay open. The candle that he moved right up to the cover illuminated the dense black print where great multi-colored letters and brick red crosses lit up the dark columns.

When he had prayed the Paternoster, Ave Maria, and the Creed, he began to sing with a dampened voice. Singing the hours here in the church was actually quite superfluous when he could just as well read them at home in the parsonage, but he had his own thoughts on the matter. As so many times before, he looked up to the patron saint of his church, the holy Anna, with her mysterious smile. She sat enthroned above the altar with the Jesus Child held on the Mother of God's knee. The gold moldings in the altar reflected the flames like glimmering stars. Mary's blue coat billowed in conical folds, and in

[14] Kakaltare. This custom was based on Leviticus 12. If the practice is retained at all today, it is in the form of a blessing to new mothers.

the shadow behind the saint's elbow, just before the gold crown on the Jesus Child, a little angel poked out with full cheeks and rounded lips that seemed to hold an infinitely long tone of jubilation. Herr Andreas had always felt he could relate to the angel. It was carved with infinite care, though no one could ever see it from the nave, and it sang and sang, assiduously though no one heard it, but Saint Anna and the holy mother of God with her blessed Son. So he wanted to stay here and sing his hours with care and dignity though no one heard it, except for God and his saints. It felt like a courtly tribute to the glory of the Holy Virgin. Perhaps it would even be counted to the credit of one of the dead citizens of Fröjerum that he stood here and sang God's praises with the same care as if he had been versicularius[15] in the cathedral and the whole sanctuary was packed with people like Easter morning.

It was at the cathedral school that he learned to love the holy chorales. They were the hourly prayers in the church, the merciful balm that healed the wounds in his hands and back. The school was an unheated stone room with benches that had no back. He had to sit there relentlessly straight and still, as he read Remigio's feared *Quepars*, the old grammar with black and white pages and endless rules. He suffered the despairing homesickness of a teenager in the evenings with the lonely tears of an abandoned child in the deacon's barn where both the Fröjerum boys had their humble hostel. He would never have toughed it out if it were not for the hourly prayers. Here he learned the love of Latin, which crept in like flowers nestled among the tendrils of the music's wickerwork. He learned to understand the deep meaning of these melodies that were always chaste and sober but which in their zeal could hold and endless joy or a suppressed suffering. They could be majestically exalted like an autumn sky over his childhood's bronze-red oaks and, at the same time, spiritual and merciful like the hand of mother Borthild when she caressed the bump on an eight-year-old child's forehead. So he lived in this world of heavenly beauty and comfort. Every morning, he rejoiced in the praise of God with Laudes. He saw Christ as a ray of the dawning sun upon the new day. He was borne through these

[15] A medieval cantor in charge of singing prestigious parts in the Daily Hours.

hours by the strong spirit of the psalms, until he finally laid his soul to rest with compline like a tired chick under the wide wings of the Merciful One, while two individual flames of light fluttered at the high altar and the dark cathedral stood like a troll's forest of stone tree trunks.

Herr Andreas had sung both the hymn and the psalm. Now he raised the affectionate tone of the response: *viderunt omnes fines terrae / salutare Dei nosti.*[16] The finale rang out like a playful child's jubilation: Alleluia! Alle-eluia. He hadn't even realized that he had raised his voice so that the whole frosted wood roof reverberated. His agitated soul had been calmed and attentive like one of the calm flames on the altar. He felt an unreflective assurance that God would finally save his church, even from this extreme humiliation. And come what may: apart from all earthly injustice, the light of God's holy city always shined. No worldly king could ever reach it with his rough hand. Songs of praise would continue to be heard there even when the last daily hour had been sung on earth.

He began to pray—at first the prescribed Latin prayers, then in Swedish with his own words. He prayed to Saint Anna. He cried to the Mother of God and Saint Martin and Saint Barbara, whose immovable figure stood in a gold hemmed coat at the altar's toe-board. He prayed for the salvation of his church, for her renewal and rehabilitation and rescue from the violent powers of this world.

He finally dared to raise his eyes to the Jesus Child. He always did it with a certain trembling. The little one held a scepter in his hand, the iron scepter with which he would crush the disobedient with his immutable judgment. The child's hand was in a tight fist. There was something unfathomably distant in his gaze. He was the strict Judge who kept the final fate of the soul hidden, but with his holy demand for chastity and poverty opened a narrow way for those who had the courage and strength to deny themselves.

Herr Andreas bowed his head deeply, kissed the altar cloth, and began to pray again to the Holy Mother, with the burning and confidence of a son to his mother and like a man in distress to the earthly manifestation of divine mercy. Then he got up, smoothed the altar

[16] All the ends of the earth have seen / the salvation of God.

cloth out, brushed away some rat turds, lowered the eternal lamp on its noisy iron chain, and refilled it with oil. Then he busied himself with a few small things, moved the bookmarker to the right place in the breviary, extinguished the candles, genuflected for the last time, and went back out into the blizzard singing to himself: Alleluia, alle-eluia.

* * *

Sundown approached. Sunlight permeated the low hanging snow clouds that just would not deliver but floated in space like a golden day illuminating the whole landscape with a new light. The cold gray hardwood grove took on a softer tone resembling that of a squirrel's coat, and the old houses in the village looked alive and warm, where they gathered in gray flocks like pastured sheep in the first snows of winter.

Martin Ragnvaldsson departed from the forest path and turned toward the open country. He rode a good deal ahead of the servant boy, partly because his horse had the lighter load, and partly because he traveled upon the familiar paths of home territory. But mostly it was because he was driven forward by the same mysterious power that always made the last mile so short for his tired feet when he turned toward home from the school in Linköping as a boy.

He had seen this same view a million times. The parish opened itself like a flat pan in the great forest. The hills and hillocks of the forest's dark carpet encircled it, a little lake barely visible in the middle, split in two by large bays now covered in black ice crisscrossed with streaks of white snow. A brownish-gray thicket of willow and hardwoods interspersed with long white stripes skirted the shoreline.

Martin whistled cheerfully and once again jabbed his dull iron spurs into his tired horse. He was as cheerful as a schoolboy on holiday. He had not set his foot in Fröjerum for many years, but tonight he would sleep in Askanäs again.

Askanäs—yes, it was crown land now. He was still bitter that at the eleventh hour his old mother would have let it go to the prowling gray brothers. Not that he blamed her for anything. On the contrary, he idolized her. She had been a veritable saint of God. But had she only waited two or three years, she would have withheld the donation letter. And who knows if she would not have been won, her too, for the new faith, and ignored purgatory, squeamish nuns and all that papist nonsense. Then maybe she would have left the estate to her own Martin instead.

Well, perhaps he still would not have used it. Now he was the royal scrivener, Martinus Ravaldi, barely 28 years old, and yet entrusted with many difficult tasks. The miserable Latin that he had learned through tenacity and tears from the monks at Linköping had become useful in the end. But it was the German that brought him greater joy. He was glad the old furrier from Rostock that provided lodging for him and his brother had taken time to teach him. If only he had known Italian or Polish too, then he would have climbed high in the ranks. The king had a lack and sore need for literate men.

The king! Scrivener Martin slapped his frozen hands together and laughed, a red-cheeked laugh with a boyish glint in his eyes and delighted wrinkles on his nose. It surprised him, but he was glad to be 240 miles away from His Grace again. He served a strict and moody lord. No one within a thirty-mile radius was ever safe from his thunderbolt. And yet he served him with all of his heart. He loved and marveled at this grim lord who roared and raved, brooding dark like a stormy night on the great Sommen[17] one minute, and in the next could smile and joke like the glittering sunshine of May.

Scrivener Martin became serious again as memories of the past returned. His first memories of the school sat like the mark of a brand in his soul. At eight years old, he followed his brother Anders to the Latin School. It was at New Year's. They had come to the city amidst gusty weather with heavy gray clouds over the hillside. Long before the toll booth, they had already heard that King Christian himself stayed with the bishop on his way back to Denmark. Inside, the city was full of soldiers who swore oaths and carried on loudly outside the taverns. Otherwise, everything was eerily quiet. He felt completely lost in the crowd, the sled squeaked as it made its way down the alley, and suddenly it was stuck fast in the crowd occupying a large open square. He looked up and was startled to see a large wheel with a boot that outlined itself against the gray sky. Curiously

---

[17] A large lake in the Swedish highlands bordering Östergötland and Småland.

he had looked at it and to his horror realized that a dismembered leg with a bloody pant leg stuck out of the boot. There next to it was an impaled hand and further up on the wheel, a spiked head with squinting eyes and an outstretched tongue. He hid down in the sleigh and heard the sleigh driver ask what had happened. A coarse voice let it be known that they had been rebels who had led the siege of the bishop at Munkeboda and were now punished by His Grace. But in the evening at the hostel, Nils, the driver, had whispered to him that they were two peasants from the parish of Risinge, upright Swedish men who had signed on with Sture's men and now received Christian's[18] revenge.

Never would he forget those foggy January days when the heavy atmosphere lay like a dead hand over the city. Everyone seemed to fear informants and bloody convictions. Neither would he ever forget the rainy summer day when Arvid Västgöte came to the city with the peasant army. He had escaped from the school to stand by the road to Vreta and wait. He ran in road mud that was spattered by horse hooves and screamed and rejoiced and cried viva like the others. Never had he been so wet, never had he gotten such a beating and never had he been as happy as on that evening.

So the years passed with Latin and discipline and in between beautiful evenings on the river or secret outings to the forbidden apprentice quarter with funny songs and drinking kirsch. Then gradually, a defiant decision matured within him: I will never be a priest. He had quickly picked up the new doctrines from the journeymen of Söderköping. He had heard that the pope was the anti-Christ and Rome the great whore, that God never instituted any cloisters or commanded any monks to be silent. One day he got his hands on one of the forbidden German books, but Master Gottschalk, the furrier they lived with, found him out when he asked about a few of the glosses. In the childish belief that he would now be burned at the

[18] Christian II of Denmark (1481–1559), monarch under the Kalmar Union, ruled Denmark and Norway from 1513–23 and Sweden from 1520–21. He was hated in Sweden, where he was known as Christian the Tyrant because of the Stockholm Bloodbath. He eventually lost control of Denmark also and died a prisoner after a failed attempt to retake Denmark and Norway in 1531.

stake, he escaped from the school that very night and made his way to Stockholm.

A completely new era began for him there. As if bewitched, he sat under the pulpit in the Storkyrkan[19] and heard the new proclamation. Through the help of Master Olaus, he came into a writing apprenticeship. Three years later, he had already begun copying documents in the king's office. It was now ten years later. He had learned a lot in those years.

Above all, he had gained an unconditional admiration for King Gustavus. He was a Gideon sent from the Lord, a man of wonder crowned by God, sent to save and establish the fatherland. Who else would have been able to start with two empty hands and a knapsack up in the snow of the Norwegian border-mountains, and three years later sit as the King of Sweden? He must have been crowned by the Lord, who alone was able to establish the fallen kingdom simply by the power of his word and his sword.

Scrivener Martin knew the power of the king's word. He had seen the whole chancellery explode into laughter when His Grace hilariously dictated letters. He had seen the lords huddle together in fear of his thunder. At the Disting,[20] he had seen how the skinny and reluctant Upland peasants were defeated by his eloquence and released the greedy grip from their purses, ready to offer both their last penny and their church bells.

The king could certainly be very hard. For sure, he directed the whole kingdom as if it was one great royal estate. And he sure did love money. But behind the harsh thoughts concerning the treasury, everything else was marked by suffering for the kingdom, for the reestablished kingdom, and its future power and glory.

Scrivener Martin suddenly reined in his horse. Did he hear right? Yes, he really did hear church bells down in the village. It must be ringing for a holy day. Yes, of course, it was the Eve of Epiphany.

He stayed and listened, not without emotion. How far away had the bells been heard in the winter sky of Askanäs when mother Bothild always finished her work and sang Ave Maria Stella. He could

---

[19] Stockholm's cathedral.

[20] An annual winter market held in Uppsala.

still hear the beautiful refraction of the bell tolls over the snowy landscape and the song from within the sanctuary.

This evening there were even two bells. So both bells remained. The peasants must have ransomed them from the bell tax. It made him glad despite all he had said about the great sacrifice of bells being justified and needed. If he was his king's dutiful servant, seized by the thought of a new kingdom, he was also still the old boy from Fröjerum inside his leather shirt.

It had now become so dark that it would have been hard to find the path if he had not known every field and cottage so well. The closer he came to the church-village, the harder his heartbeat. It had been ten years since he had last been here. At first, he had planned to ride to Askanäs and find lodging. Then he would hear if it was possible for his brother Anders—Herr Andreas—as he was now called, to come up and celebrate mass for the holy day. And then he would find Jon of Flodlycke or some of the other old men who came in and out of his parent's home as his father's best friends.

Now the church estate opened before him. It was almost dark, but he could still see the village of Återbol to the left, down by the lake. The terrain rose straight out in front of him, and there the contours of the snow against the fences contrasted against the darkness. He saw the broad white bands of the roofs in the church-village. Behind them rose a pointy, acute corner, sharp and white-faced against the night sky. It was the gable end of the church.

Scrivener Martin wiped the snow from his face to see better. He caught a glimpse of a single light up there. When he came a little closer so that the church clearly separated itself from the accumulation of sheds and church stalls along the churchyard wall, he saw that there was light within the church. So there was worship tonight. He jerked the bridle so that the horse lifted its hanging head and took a few more lively steps before immediately falling back into a slow gait. The rider did not notice. He kept his eyes glued to the small glimmering windows up ahead. Perhaps even now, his brother Anders stood before them. In such a case, they would meet this evening for the first time in many long years.

He slid out of the saddle and walked up the steep hill with stiff legs. He looked up at the crest the whole time. There was light, and then it went out.

He had a deep respect for his brother Anders—strangely enough even though Martin had always been the stronger of the two. But Anders had within his unworldly and compassionate being something of authority and the gift of leadership—and a stubbornness, which like a red-hot spike bored itself through all obstacles. They had only exchanged a few short letters since Martin had escaped from school, mostly concerning Martin's share in the royalties from Askanäs. Anders had been consciously fair and friendly in tone, but it had still not been really good between them.

The scrivener was warm and out of breath when he finally reached the crest of the church hill. He had tied his horse in the lee of the churchyard wall, shook the snow out of his fur coat, and looked yet again with wonder at the church whose edifice now looked immense and strong as it rose above the leafless trees. Then he walked the path between the stone borders of the family graves to the wrought iron church doors. He caught his breath a minute and then opened them.

A warm waft of smoke, melted wax, and damp wool slapped him in the face. He stood still at the door. Some gray figures genuflected right to the floor. Others huddled together off to the side in the dim light. Further up lay the little choir in clear gold light from all the lamps on the altar and in candelabras. Facing the altar stood a tall, lean figure, broad-shouldered but slightly bent, and dressed in the old cope. It had to be his brother.

Martin had a hard time holding his emotions back. The song and the blue velvet vestments brought back childhood memories. The priest had stood there like that on Easter morning when they had come up to the church-village in the day's first light parading through fields that smelled of willow and the running spring rivulets. The light had glittered on the cope's silver buckles just like that, and the chanting had sounded just like that under the high wooden ceiling: monotone, soothing and slow-paced, far away from the uneasiness and striving of this world.

Now the figure up by the altar turned. A long, lean face with a high and pale forehead turned to the congregation. The dark eyes looked absent and far-sighted in the dim light. The light of the altar must have blinded them, Martin thought. Now they only saw empty darkness. Anders was a little paler and thinner than before. Other than that, he was the same.

Now he lifted his hands, and the whole congregation fell to their knees to receive the blessing. The scrivener put his right knee to the floor, crossed himself, and bowed his head devoutly. When he lifted it again, the priest had already disappeared into the sacristy.

The servant boy stood out on the church hill holding the two horses by the reigns. He had crept in between them to find shelter from the wind, which had gotten colder. Some of the churchgoers watched Martin, wondering who this curious stranger could be. A little reserved, they stood in the path of the door as they wondered.

At the same moment, Herr Andreas came walking up. The men at the wall went to meet him. The priest stood and looked in disbelief at the two horses. Martin stepped out onto the platform before the front steps.

"Anders," he said gently, "do you recognize me?"

"Martinus! Brother! It has been a while. Welcome to Fröjerum!"

He put out his hand.

"Thank you, brother!"

The men at the wall had come forward. They greeted him full of surprise and joy. It was the churchwarden and sexton, old Petrus of Bortistorp.

"No, look... Martin of Askanäs! The royal scrivener, I mean..." the sexton corrected himself.

The scrivener laughed.

"Call me Martin as before, old man, and grab me by the hair like before when I stole your apples..."

They both laughed. The pastor spoke.

"Follow me home to the parsonage, Martinus. And keep us company..." he gestured to the others with his hand. "I don't have much at home, but tonight I will bring out what little there is. It is the Eve of Epiphany!"

Scrivener Martin lifted the bag from the pommel and threw the straps over his shoulder. He gave his orders quickly. The boy would go straight to Askanäs with the horses. Svinnetorp's widow would show the way.

Another couple of parishioners arrived, and he gave them a loud and jovial greeting. Then they turned down toward the meadows. Two lonely stars shined through a break in the clouds. Off to the west, one could make out the moon hunted by the clouds above the treetops. Otherwise, everything was dark; only a path of thinly packed snow led the way.

The scrivener walked, tossing his bag over his shoulder and talking loudly.

"Do you remember, Anders, the Eve of Epiphany, when the snowstorm buried the entire barn? It was winter back then. This year there is hardly enough to sled down the roads once. Father drove over the pasture fence with a load of firewood back then. Do you remember the toboggan run we had on the roof of the cottage? There was a jump down to the drift below. We would fly in an arch resembling the tail of a crapping cow and land in the snow like a down pillow."

He turned to the churchwarden.

"I am the one who is supposed to visit Årtebol and Flodlycke tomorrow. No, not tomorrow, tomorrow is still a holy day, but on Monday. Then I will return to my shitty life. Yeah, yeah, you can laugh, old man. But he who scribbles with the quill year after year always yearns for a trusty shit shovel. In Stockholm, you walk with your nose hanging in the gutter. There it just smells of rotten cabbage and untanned leather. Then one yearns for the glorious smell of a sack of manure."

He had put his arm around the churchwarden. They followed the path to the parsonage right on by the bell tower. Martin Ragnvaldsson joked with the old man the whole way.

At the parsonage, Herr Andreas lit a piece of fatwood in the oven and went out to the storehouse. He sat with the crackling stick between his teeth, lifted the stone from the salt barrel, and opened the lid. Down below the crust that looked like half-frozen slush, he found a piece of beef with the tip of his knife. It was green like hair cap moss inside the bone and safely salted. It would taste old, and he knew that the old men would like that. He pulled the wood pin on the keg and let the beer run down in a big cask.

Meanwhile, he took out two cakes of black pudding and a dried leg of mutton from the rafters. Then he found a little bit of cheese with a six-pointed star pattern on the label before returning, heavy laden, to the cottage with the flame still between his teeth.

"Tonight is the feast of the three kings," he said. "Now we will drink and rejoice. First for the sake of the star and then for you, my brother Martinus. Jon, would you put some more wood on the fire. A Christian soul should not sit in the dark this evening."

The churchwarden put all the goods in order on the table and got some firewood from the nook above the fireplace. Martin had already looked in the cupboard at the end of the bed and found a couple of round cakes of barley bread and a few apples. He looked questioningly at his brother.

"Butter? Anders?"

The pastor gave an embarrassed grunt.

"It only goes rancid for me," he said.

"And yet it is so very salted! So you gave it away even though it would have been good for another year," the brother laughed. "You are the same as ever, Anders. In Linköping, you never ate more than half your ration. When my ration of butter was gone, you still had half as much left. And so you gave the rest to me. It hasn't made you any richer."

"On the other hand, you beat the smith's laborers up for me. For that, you have many thanks," the priest said dryly. He went to the table, put his hands together for prayer, and recited the Latin table prayer, *Oculi omnium*.[21] They all crossed themselves and began to eat. The men grabbed their knives and cut for themselves. Martin was still missing his butter.

"And I thought that the country pastors sat in butter up to their chins this year," he said. "It speaks well of you, brother, that you are not like the other stuffed sausages full of lard. But you could at least have half a pound of butter at home to invite a hungry wayfarer. For the rest, you can live like a crofter. Bare timber walls, not even habitable. We had it better in Askanäs."

"I am not compelling you to stay here," the priest said calmly. "But it is not certain that the good Göran will give you lodging in Askanäs tonight. He is a bit chafed at the bailiff in Bocksholmen and has to pay out so much money for a guest that he is hardly happy to have one. It might happen, though, since you were born on the

[21] All eyes (from Psalm 145:15, "The eyes of all look to you, and you give them their food in due season").

estate. But first, let's drink a toast to the three holy kings, to Gaspar, Melchior, and Balthasar . . ."

He had already lifted the tankard, but the scrivener hurried to register a protest:

"In Askanäs, I would be received like the king himself. Askanäs is a royal estate now, and I travel on behalf of the royal majesty, on the crown's errand."

The priest still held the raised tankard in his hand.

"What errand?" he asked, surprised.

"To make an account of the church's silver and treasure on behalf of the king. I believe that that should be good enough for both room and board."

There was dead silence. Herr Andreas slammed his stein on the table with a bang, spilling the foam.

"No! Now you ride for the damn Devil himself, Martin! Do you come to us tonight as the black Judas? Do you betray your home church?"

The scrivener turned toward his brother with amazement.

"Watch your words, Anders. I am no traitor. I am your king's faithful servant."

"And your old mother's most unworthy son! Do you believe she gave the chalice veil of damask so the king could make it into trousers for a little prince? Do you believe father gave the silver bell so that the king could use it to call his little friends when he wants his evening beer? Whenever did the king have a right to the peasant's silver? Will you collect our spoons too? And our rings? And our belt buckles?"

The scrivener stayed calm.

"Don't say stupid things, Anders. You know, of course, what was determined by the council of the realm in Västerås . . ."

"Yes, that the cloisters and cathedrals would be robbed of their estates, and the bishop should lose his fortified house! But of the parish churches, nothing was said. They belong to the people of the parish, and no one has the right to touch them."

"Because they belong to the people, so the King in the best interest of the people might collect their superfluous possessions . . ."

"The best interest of the people? Lübeck has already received payment in full, the kingdom has not been so free in living memory, the king is as rich as Solomon—and he still fleeces his people worse than Christian did. He is the crudest plunderer and abuser of peasants . . ."

Now the scrivener was enraged. He leaned forward and pounded both fists on the table.

"Damn your impudence, Anders! Have you been walking around with your hat over your nose for twenty years? Do you not know that the king saved the kingdom and land for us? Do you not know that we would have been scum to everyone, beaten black and blue by the Jutes, and left destitute by the Lübeckers if King Gustavus had not gone to the woods like a hunted animal and risked his neck to get the Dalecarlians to resist the Jutes?"

"Sture's men did that too! But they did not plunder God's Church for it."

The priest had regained his composure. The scrivener continued just as heatedly as before.

"So, the work was left half done. We were never able to afford a proper military, the navy was a complete fraud, and the Jutes came back as soon as the farmers ran home to make hay. Is that the way you would have it?"

"A kingdom should be supported with honorable weapons, not with goods stolen from the church."

"See for yourself how the prelates and great men of the Holy Spirit have carried themselves! Did not Gustavus Trolle come home from Rome with four hundred soldiers and then allow them to kill as many Swedish men as it took for his Grace to get back Almare-Stäk. Did he not carry the shield against his own country and arrange soldiers for Christian? Where did he get the money for that? Did it not come from the church's treasury? And the tithe? Was it better used to make war against us, than that the king makes use of it to create a free land for us?"

"Do not bother with Trolle. He was a traitor against both Sweden and the Holy Church! But the one treachery does not excuse the other. One may not steal from the church just because there have been priests who have done it. This Gustav Erickson is a church thief, a defiler of monasteries, a mugger of saints . . ."

"Hold your mouth, Anders, and watch your neck! There are witnesses to what you are saying!"

The pastor snorted with contempt.

"Yes, it has gone so far. Everywhere you look, you find eavesdroppers and spies. You have to look around twice on the church hill before anyone tells the truth. He fosters misery and bondage, your king of freedom. But in Fröjerum's parsonage, there sits no traitor this evening—except perhaps for you!"

Scrivener Martin burned red as he looked around. Then he saw the others. He had almost forgotten they were there. They sat quietly, chewing their bread. In the uneven firelight, the melting snow glittered like pearls on their gray coats. Peter, the sexton, sat with his back to the fire. His toothless old jaw ground slowly and steadily in a warped rotation. He gazed at the oil jar, but the whole of his facial expression betrayed that he listened attentively on the edge of his seat. The two others sat opposite with their weathered and bearded faces colored red by the firelight. They were both a little past middle-aged. Their facial expressions were powerful and eccentric; the lines around their mouths were deeper than normal. The eyes were half shut, and the gaze distant. Martin, the scrivener, recognized the expression from town hall meetings. This was the way a peasant looked when he didn't really agree but was not ready to answer either.

The scrivener felt a little unsure. That the peasants could not keep up with everything the king did, that was obvious. Added to that, King Gustavus was far ahead of his time. But that one could count on their faithful loyalty and their absolute trust in the monarch, that he knew from experience. He turned to appeal to Jon of Flodlycke, the churchwarden that sat next to him.

"Old man, you can't agree with what the rector has said tonight. None of us want to have a different regime in the country?"

The peasant was silent, and the scrivener continued:

"If that happened, then we would all leave our houses and have to protect our freedom again."

Now the churchwarden nodded his head without lifting his eyes.

"Were that to happen."

The scrivener continued:

"Do you all remember when they dug the trenches in Holaveden and trapped the Jutlanders? You were there yourselves, right?"

"Yes, of course."

"Do you remember when Christian demanded that the peasants turn in their crossbows and sent the bailiffs to confiscate them? They certainly didn't need to go further than to the counties. There the farmers waited with their crossbows and shot the Jutlanders like hedgehogs. True?"

"Yes, of course. We cut a lot of bolts in Flodlycke that winter."

"And the people have not lost their honor, am I right?"

"No," said the peasant loudly. "I do not believe so."

Now, he looked at the scrivener with two inscrutable eyes. The others had nodded in agreement. Martin turned to his brother again, excited.

"Anders, there you have it. I understand full well that all of this is hard and new for you in the beginning. Never before has there been an ordered regiment and an orderly police force here in the kingdom. Now the king is setting up a completely new council . . ."

"With foreign fortune-hunters. Yes, I have heard the talk about that."

"You mean the chancellor?"

"Yes, that Pyhy or Peutinger or whatever his name is. Does he not travel around with a concubine, since he abandoned his legal wife in Bavaria? And then this Norman? What sort of cuckoo is he?"

"Magister Norman is an honorable man! A learned Pomeranian. He has the best recommendations from Wittenberg."

"I can believe it! Typical kraut, Lutheran, royal bootlicker, milquetoast, and schooled in the art of stealing the church's silver, a rare bird. What shall he do now?"

"He is the superintendent."

"He's what?"

"Superintendent. It is the church's highest dignity if you must know. All over Germany, the princes have appointed superintendents after the bishops have gone. They visit the congregations and see to it that the priests preach God's pure word and teach his people the catechism."

The pastor burst out into a bitter laugh.

"Super-intend-ant! Isn't that neat! And since the new teaching is so excessively biblical, perhaps you can tell us where in the Holy Scriptures it talks about such a fine lord? I have read about bishops in Scripture. That Paul and the holy apostles appointed the first bishops, you know that as well as me. But some super-intend-ant neither you nor the king can find in the Bible. By the way, isn't there already an archbishop in Uppsala, appointed by the king? What will he do with Archbishop Lars now?"

Martin was quiet. He really did not know what the king planned to do with the old bishops. Naturally, King Gustavus also had a plan for this, and, of course, it would one day be seen that he had done the right thing.

The sexton turned around to throw wood on the fire during the brief and awkward silence that followed. Then wind whistled down the chimney, blowing ash and smoke throughout the room. Snowmelt fell into the hearth and snarled. Apparently, it had turned into a real snowstorm outside.

Martin was the first to break the silence.

"You do not need to be bitter, Anders," he said conciliatorily. "Archbishop Lars was not appointed by the King. He is chosen and consecrated in a canonical order that not even you can comment against. Was it not Petrus Magni of Västerås that ordained him? And had he not been ordained in Rome? King Gustavus is no tyrant . . ."

"He *is* a tyrant," said Herr Andreas with resolute force and slammed his fist on the table again. Silence fell over the table again.

"In any case, tonight we drink to the three holy kings," Martin said with another attempt to broker peace. He lifted the beer to his mouth. The three peasants had chewed on their dry bread quite long enough and followed the admonition willingly. They drank deeply. Then Herr Andreas said:

"Yes, would to God that all earthly princes were like the three holy kings. They brought gold to the Christ Child. They did not steal it from him."

"That would have been rather difficult as both the Lord and his holy apostles at the time were poor and not rich like our bishops and abbots."

"Nonetheless, it was the Holy Virgin that received the gold, frankincense, and myrrh—with joy for the pious hearts that gave these gifts. It was Christ who received the treasure and not Herod!"

The priest suddenly let go of his defiant tone.

"Martin, brother, he said, I know well enough that this holy church needs reformation from head to foot. You remember that

Master Knut had already spoken with us about this in Linköping. And all the bishops we have had in my time, except old Ingemar in Växjö, would probably have agreed with that. But it is *one* thing to reform the church. It is another to deform her, and still, another to raze her to the ground! The bishops want to reform the church, Luther wants to deform her, and the king wants to raze her altogether so that he can lay his hands on the church lands and tithes and create a national community school instead, where he can teach peasants and nobility alike to fear God a little and the government all the more."

Scrivener Martin's hunger was palpable, and for a minute, he sat eating quietly.

"Martin," the priest said again. "Think for yourself where this goes. Here comes a foreign magistrate to us Swedes. Since the days of Saint Sigfrid, we have had properly consecrated bishops, as there have always been in the church. We have had deacons and priests according to ancient orders. Neither prince nor parliament has ever disturbed this. Rome fell to the barbarians, but the church stood fast. The Hunnish hordes and Vandals burned cities and laid waste to countries, but the church could not be overthrown. She kept bishops. She ordained new priests, and prayers continued to be prayed. Everything went on as it had before. The daily hours were sung, and the mass remained. For fifteen hundred years, the holy ministry continued. And now here comes a German magistrate who is not even properly ordained, but the king receives him and immediately makes him the almighty bailiff over the whole of our church. Does any church authority even have the right to speak? It used to be that one asked for a council of bishops or called the priests to a synod before one decided something that touched upon the church's most pressing concerns. Now the king speaks for forty-five minutes with his German chancellor, and then he hands down a new order from his royal authority and turns the structure of the church on its head, the structure that not even the Huns and barbarians were able to dislodge. The sultan doesn't even operate so badly. And what shall come of it, if one fine day there is a manifest heathen and blasphemer on the throne, and he writes laws for God's church on his own authority."

"You imagine things," Martin said, annoyed. "King Gustavus may well be a good Christian though he does not suffer the lazy friars with their senseless roaring and moaning. In any case, he is a better Christian than any bishop that we have ever had because he is the first to have ensured that God's pure word is preached to His glory."

The priest shook his head.

"The King does not concern himself with the pure preaching of God's word any more than you concern yourself with the singing of the daily hours. If someone uses God's word on him, he chops his head off. You can be sure of that."

The wind came in again through the wide mouth of the chimney. The fire flickered so that the shadows danced over the whole cottage. The men could hear how the snow-covered the window. Over at the door and here and there along the way, the wind whistled through the cracks.

"Drink, good men," said the scrivener. "Now, we drink to the star that shined above the kings."

"Yes," said the priest, "it was a good star. She led the men away from Herod so that they would serve Christ. Now people run from both monasteries and orders to serve Herod instead—and from the schools for the rest," he added, looking at his brother.

The scrivener thought about answering but was never able to get it out. The front door flew open and slammed hard against the wall. The wind blew in, leaving a white strip of snow on the floor. An oversized man entered into the firelight from the gaping darkness of the door. He took off his hat and dried the snowmelt from his forehead and eyes with that back of his hands and looked cautiously around the room.

"God's peace!" said Herr Andreas with surprise. "Where do you come from?"

"Good evening," the man greeted leisurely in the dialect of the district. "We come from Örebro with the pastor from Vi. He is on the hill behind because his mare is tired. And now I must ask for lodging for the night. Herr Peder is frozen, you see," he added by way of clarification.

The pastor rose from the table. All the others quit eating and turned around on the benches. Herr Andreas still held the tankard in his hand, when he answered.

"Tell Herr Peder that he is welcome at my house. There is room here at this table for a heretic!"

The stranger disappeared again. He closed the door behind him, but the snow was compressed hard on the threshold and prevented it from shutting properly again. After a brief moment, the door opened again, and the storm roared into the cottage. A draft of air forced its way into the hearth, ripping the flames from the burning embers and roaring up the chimney. Jon of Flodlycke got up. He scraped the threshold clean with his hands, threw the snow out, and pushed his broad shoulders against the door. For security's sake, he pulled the boom.

The pastor had seated himself again. He looked quite pensive. "It will make me happy to meet the man—the first heretic among the priesthood in this district. May he be the last!"

"Is it Peder Knutsson, the priest in Vi, you mean?" asked the brother.

"So, you know him?"

"By pure chance. I helped him with the king's compilation of his benefice. He was there to pick it up."

"And paid a tidy sum for the office, it is said. Is that true?"

"Almost everyone does that nowadays."

"In earlier days that was called Simony,[22] and was considered sinful and shameful."

"But when the Pope dickered with the bishoprics and sold them for expensive annates, was that perhaps canonical and edifying?"

"No, that was sinful and shameful too. But we would have changed it ourselves if only the king did not get involved."

Suddenly, Herr Andreas changed his mind. His mocking grin flattened out, and he laughed gently.

"Yes, here we sit and talk the night away, just like the evenings at the student hostel," he said. "Now it is better that we prepare ourselves to receive Herr Peder. If his body has the chills, he will need to drink something warm."

---

[22] *Simony* was the pejorative term given to the practice of paying someone for a church office such as bishop rather than earning the office through service. This was widespread in the middle ages because the office gave one access to huge amounts of wealth and prestige. It would often pay for itself over time. It was called Simony after Simon the Magician, who tried to purchase the Holy Spirit from Peter in Acts 8.

He pushed forward a three-footed pot toward the fire and poured beer into it. He grabbed some small bags with spices from behind a hatch in the wall.

"Petrus, you can mix it," he said to the sexton as he threw him the pouches. "But no homespun hexes, even if you know a couple!"

"And you, Jon, can you help them with the horses when they come? There are some hardwood branches in the path. Watch yourself for the krummholz[23] between the stalls."

The churchwarden bowed. He brushed the crumbs out of his beard with his hands, wiped his fingers on his coat, and put the knife back in its sheath. Then he sat there and waited. Now and then, he looked at the scrivener with a wise and watchful eye.

Martin savored the food. The exchange of words did not weigh heavily on his mind. He was accustomed to taking abuse for the sake of the king and accustomed to always being right in the end. So he could afford to take the piss from time to time without getting bent out of shape. That he would now receive news from the parliament, put him in even better humor.

There was a knock, and the churchwarden immediately opened the door. Two men wearing crude homespun and carrying another in snow-covered fur stumbled in.

"God's peace, Herr Peder," greeted the pastor. "I wish you a blessed feast, and even more, I wish you a better faith than the one you have had so far."

Herr Peder did not answer. He had sunk into a chamber pot chair carved from a log as his servants removed his hat and mittens. Herr Andreas stared at his face in amazement. It was wet and shiny from melting snow and dark red from fever. His eyes were bloodshot and watery as if he were drunk.

"It was high time we got him under a roof," said one of the strangers. "We meant to get to Ravelunda, but he became so miserable in the forest that we had to stop here in the village. And then this blasted storm . . ."

---

[23] Gnarled brushwood stunted by the elements in subarctic and mountain terrain, which often poses a tripping hazard.

"We will take care of the right reverend now," said Herr Andreas harshly. "You men, go out and see to it that the nags get under shelter."

The churchwarden was already at the door, and the servants disappeared with him. The storm roared through and shook the whole cottage. The sexton poured the steaming mulled beer into a tankard. The others removed the furs from Herr Peder. He was slumped and motionless with his arms flat on the table.

Herr Andreas handed him the beer.

"*Domine Petre*," he yelled in the sick man's ear, "drink! You must warm yourself!"

The sick man looked indifferently ahead of him with feverish red eyes. Then the priest held the mug under his nose. The strong waft of spices got him to react. He sipped on the drink, took another gulp, and then took hold of the tankard and brought it to his mouth. The scrivener stayed on the other side the whole time, holding the carved wood handle for the sake of safety.

"Slurp with dignity, lord!" he said good-naturedly. "Slurp but do not spill. It's supposed to go down the throat, not on the ruffles."

The sick man looked up and blinked. Then he smiled helplessly and nodded. The other handed him the ale again, and he drank.

After a while, he began to talk a little. He seemed to understand where he was. He recognized Herr Andreas, and even the scrivener, though he could not fit them together. He drank again.

"Now, let's go to bed, right reverend," said Martin irreverently, yet with good-nature. He took the sick man under his arm. His brother helped. Herr Peder walked across the floor rather steadily and sat heavily on the edge of the bed. They removed his shoes, and instantly he laid down in the furs. The priest sat next to him, leaning against the bedpost, with the folded bed curtain to his back. Martin sat beneath him on the bed, holding the tankard of beer.

Herr Peder had his senses about him now.

"You must not have done this for nothing."

Herr Andreas nodded.

"Rest now, dear lord and brother. Get your strength back, and we can talk later. I'm not letting you leave Fröjerum without trying to win you back for the Holy Catholic faith."

The sick man reached his hand out and took hold of a fold in the priest's dark frock.

"There is less separating us than you believe," he said. "I want to be a son of Christ's true and catholic church just as much as you do. For just that reason, I must be truly evangelical. But now is not the time to quarrel but to stay together. Now Herod's soldiers ride again through the night to murder the baby Jesus."

The other two looked puzzled. Over by the hearth, the sexton and churchwarden had piqued their ears and were listening attentively. The sick man raised himself on his elbow. His feverish eyes shined in the firelight when he looked up at Herr Andreas. Then he whispered with a hoarse voice:

"The king has sentenced Master Olaus to death!"

Now it was Martin's turn to slam his beer down with a bang that echoed through the cottage. The churchwarden and sexton came closer.

"You're delirious," Andreas answered. "You are delirious. Master Olaus is the king's henchman. He is the point of the spear he wants to run through the heart of the church."

"I tell the truth," said the sick man and shut his eyes. "Master Olaus is condemned to death and Laurentius Andrae, the archdeacon too. The king is wild and crazy. He rages against everyone and everything that dares to think or speak according to his conscience. Master Olaus is God's witness. He has preached repentance without consideration of the person. He has chastened the king for his sins. He has dared to speak against his gruesome oaths and his boundless abuse of God's name. He has dared to say that it would be better to turn the church estates into schools and hospitals than that the king and lords should make themselves rich from them. For this, he shall be executed. His blood shall flow on the block. God's prophets may not speak in this land. They shall be silenced with the sword. God shall be quiet, and the king shall be the only majesty."

He opened his eyes again.

"They were pardoned in the end. The others risked their necks for them. It was disgusting. In court, the king paced back and forth like a caged animal, shouting and swearing and grabbing the hilt of his sword. It was not easy to try to say a reasonable word. Archbishop Lars sat there pale as a corpse and stared out in front of him with dead eyes. Pyhy sat there, twisting his mustache, and drinking Rhinish wine while he sneered at the bishops. The soldiers stood there by the door with their battleaxes and stopped everyone going in or out. For three days, there was the sentence of death—and then mercy. Mercy was the worst. Royal mercy—for Master Olaus! Should Herod have mercy on John the Baptist? Shall the guilty pardon the righteous?"

Herr Peder shut his eyes again. The pastor sat completely still. In the dim light under the roof of the bed, his pale face glimmered with unnaturally big eyes and tightly pursed lips. Martin collapsed at the foot of the bed with arms between his knees. The large puddles of beer glistened on the table and floor where it had spilled. He looked up and shyly observed the sick man. What if it was all just a feverish fantasy?

At the same time, the servants came back in. The churchwarden already had them in hand as if they had served in the Flodlycke estate for years. He set them up at the table and got them something to drink and then cut their portion of the food for dinner with the practiced view of a farmhand. Then he sat next to the sexton on the bench along the wall by the hearth.

Martin rose and sat down with the men. He began to talk to them, though his cheerfulness was strained. He learned the route they had taken, broached the subject of Örebro and asked about the parliament, and soon received confirmation concerning the inconceivable: Master Olaus had received the death sentence. He and the archdeacon were convicted of some major crime that the servants couldn't quite explain. They received mercy in the end, but they would pay grievous penalties.

The wind howled and screamed from the window in the roof, the snow pushed in like flour through knots in the logs, and the whole house seemed to be in danger of blowing away. The servants ate. Martin cut an extra portion of meat for them and refilled their tankards with beer. His hand trembled.

He collapsed again into the chamber pot chair, completely incapable of sorting out what had really happened, or what would happen. He was irritated by the presence of the others. Otherwise, he would have gone on his way. But the sick priest kept him there. Herr Peder from Vi was the only one here who might be able to sort out the mess. He at least belonged to the clearly evangelical and had always been considered faithful to the king.

The scrivener sat still for a long time. Then he turned to the churchwarden.

"It will be hard for my brother to take care of Herr Peder by himself tonight. I think I will stay here. But then there is hardly enough furs for everyone to stay the night. You, old man, have to take these boys here with you to the church-village and find them lodging. Send them here early tomorrow morning to see to the horses. They will have breakfast here."

Jon of Flodlycke nodded. His face was not so closed any longer when he looked at the scrivener. There was a glimmer of appreciation in his eye. He wished him God's peace and took the others with him. Martin set the boom after them since he pushed the snow out with a little effort. Now he was alone with his brother and the sick priest of Vi.

Herr Andreas had gone back to the sick man as soon as he said good night. He sat completely still by the bed at the headboard, leaning against the cabinet wall. He crossed his arms, and his face, which was shaped by the dark shadows behind the bed board, was pale and hollow-eyed. He looked at his brother for a long time.

"Well, what do you say now, Martinus?"

"Brother, what shall a poor man say? I don't understand anything."

His voice was so childishly helpless that the priest lost all desire to argue.

"I believe we will soon have to choose between God and Caesar," was all he said.

"Now he sleeps," he added after a minute and drew the furs over the sick man.

"We should keep the beer warm," said Martin. He lifted the tankard from the bench by the bed and poured the remainder into the pot. Then he put more wood on the fire and began to clean off the table.

"You have to eat, Anders," he said. "Your beer is almost untouched. And you have tasted neither meat nor cheese."

The priest obeyed and went to the table. He ate silently, while the scrivener thoughtfully tended to the fire. He brushed his hands through his hair and was sitting hunched forward, supporting his head with spread-out fingers through which blond tufts of hair fell.

He tried hard to sort out his thoughts. Why had this happened? And what would happen now?

That the king had not been completely satisfied with Master Olaus, he had known for a long time. That there had been serious disagreements between the archbishop and Pyhy was no secret either. That when it came to foreign policy, the king didn't trust the evangelical princes of Germany and began to cozy up to the French king, he had also been able to overhear in the chancellery. But none of that could explain why now, the king who had long squashed papism in the land, considered it necessary to begin the process with the reformers. It must be because here he also sensed some danger to the kingdom's cohesion and strength.

But in that case, did he not have the right?

Scrivener Martin removed his hands from his hair and began to beat on the fireplace. King Gustavus *must* be right. Had not the Swedes been defenseless and at the mercy of Jutes and Lübeckers for two hundred years? Had it not been because of the unfortunate discord between the church and the crown? Had not these two gentlemen, who could not fit under the same roof, humiliated the kingdom and rendered her impotent, until finally now a new day began to dawn with a united kingdom and a close-knit people?

The scrivener stretched. His face was calm once again; only one wrinkle between the eyebrows revealed that there was a little tension behind the calm. Now or never! If Sweden should be saved, then there must be something to it. Then the walls must be built from the ground up, without a single crevice where strife could set its crowbar. But then the king was also right when he relentlessly took every head that tried to lift itself so high that it no longer needed to bow before His Grace's will.

His thoughts went further.

Must it not be for an evangelical people that the church is part of the state once and for all? The church—it could well never be anything but the people itself—then mustn't the church have the same head as the people and the same lawgiver as the people? And mustn't she now be a part of the kingdom's possession as well? Must not church property be crown property? And was it not obvious that the silver that was no longer needed by the parish churches was deposited directly into the king's treasury? So King Gustavus must have thought about the matter, and he could well enough be right, now as always. But the death sentence for Master Olaus was bitter. This man had been Martin's benefactor. And he had preached with authority and power that must have come from God. Not because Martin could always understand the new doctrine, where he sat behind his column in the Storkyrkan.[24] When Master Olaus explained the letter of Romans and talked about sin in our evil nature, then it was not easy to follow him. But when he defended the Swedish mass and said that even we Swedes belong to God and that our language can be as good as any other, then Martin had hardly been able to turn without wanting to rejoice and clap hands in God's house.

The priest set his beer in front of him. Martin turned around and was almost terrified by what he saw. Herr Andreas had the face of an old man tonight. But he said nothing.

The sick man turned about in bed and groaned. The priest returned and sat down. After a minute, he hunched forward and loosed the sick man's cloak. His shirt was soaked through with sweat. They helped to undress him and covered him in an old ratty linen sheet that the priest scrounged up. Then they laid him down again and hung the clothes to dry by the fire. The whole time the snow pushed in under the window in the roof, and the flames blazed endlessly in the storm.

The brothers agreed to take turns waking to watch the fire and the sick man. The scrivener would go to bed first: he had spent eight hours in the saddle today.

The priest picked up two of the sheepskins from the floor and laid them on the bench fastened to the wall closest to the fireplace. Martin opened the top of his coat, rolled it together with his cap for a pillow, took off his shoes, and covered himself in a fur coat. He turned to face the wall and went to sleep.

---

[24] Storkyrkan (*store* + *sheerkan*) is a reference to Sankt Nicolai kyrka (St. Nicholas). *Storkyrkan* means "the great church" or "large church," and Sankt Nicolai kyrka is named thus not because it is a big church, but because of a painting, *The Sun Dogs*, that Olaus Petri (Sweden's reformer) commissioned in which the church dwarfs the king's castle next to it. In reality, the king's castle was much larger, and the king did not appreciate the implications of the painting. The painting is still on display in the church.

The pastor sat in his place in the bed by the sick man's head. He felt apathetic and broken. He began to wonder why this news met him so unmercifully hard. Deep down, he still had a secret hope that he did not want to admit to himself. He had now borne an unbroken anguish for his church for fifteen years. He saw how everything withered away before his eyes. The bishopric broke down. The cloisters were smashed, the priests betrayed. Still, he dared to believe that the church that remained since the days of the Savior would be able to overturn it all. He had searched for signs of renewal in this chaos. Even as a schoolboy, he had imbibed reforming principles from the days of the great councils. Piety would be restored from its decadence. The Bible would be read by all, the cloisters would be renewed, and the bishops would be apostolic shepherds rather than rulers with princely incomes and princely burdens.

For a minute, he asked himself if God had perhaps sent this Martin Luther to carry out the work. But then he had seen Luther break with Erasmus and turn his back on all the cultured friends of the reformation, and then he received confirmation that Luther's fruits among the unabashed German people and the undisciplined soldiers whose new faith consisted in stuffing themselves with meat during a fast and sleeping it off on Sunday morning. Then he understood that the church's renewal would never be able to come from anywhere but the church herself. But when he noticed how dreadfully the curia treated their northern province, how the bishops faltered, how Bishop Brask fled, and the cathedral chapter gave up the fight, then in his despair, he began once again to look for signs of renewal in other areas. Perhaps he had still hoped for something from Master Olaus and his powerful preaching. At least Master Olaus was not such a beer belly and coarse brawler as Luther. There was something honest and serious about him amid all the heresies.

Now even this last hope was extinguished. God's wrath had hit the heretics. The beast that they had helped attack the church had devoured them. Now only the beast had any power in the land.

What would happen now?

That the king did not intend to restore relations with Rome, that was easy to assume, no. The fox would continue with his program. First, he had used Master Olaus as a battering ram against the church. Now the spiritual power was in ruin. Now he threw the battering ram away, and the king alone was left to collect the plunder from Eskil's chambers. The renewed church he dreamed of as a boy would never come to be.

Why had all this been allowed to happen?

Why were so many passionate prayers to the holy Virgin so completely powerless? Was it all a fearful punishment? Yes, truly, the church's servants deserved punishment. Neither popes nor clerks had measured up.

He went to put more wood on the fire. It seemed his brother had already fallen asleep. The pastor went again to the cupboard in the headboard. There he bent his knees against the stool in the corner and began to pray Compline, the last of the daily hours. He mumbled the words quietly to himself in order not to wake the others. He had been able to recite the Latin text from memory for many years now. He had always had a particular love for Compline. It was so wonderfully peaceful, only a single thought in artful development, the most comforting of all thoughts: to sink into God, to come to rest in his heart, to lay aside the day's sins and worries, to be surrounded by light and mercy, to sleep in such infinite comfort that it would only be a joy if this evening were the last.

Even on this heavy Epiphany Eve peace returned, while he heard the storm whistle and force its way through gaps in the log cabin wall at his side, as he recited the artfully sculptured Latin. The whole time he heard within him an echo of the evensong sung in Linköping, in Vadstena and Askeby at this very hour. Somewhere above him, he saw the star, the sign that God set in the darkness of time, the light that he would praise in mass tomorrow.

Hurriedly he went to the fireplace and put more wood on the fire. The storm continued to blow just as wildly outside. He wanted to see how much snow had fallen in the last few hours, but because the parsonage walls did not have any windows and the door might not shut again if he opened it to look outside, he just let things be. He swept the coat about him and pulled his hat down over his head.

* * *

It was not easy to say how many of the night's hours had passed. The storm screamed just as wildly, and the snow stressed and rattled along the roof and the log cabin walls. It was as if the whole house stood in a swirl of ice crystals.

The coals glowed in the hearth now, and when the wind slammed in and blew life into it, red reflections were cast far out into the room.

Scrivener Martin had woken on his bench and saw them fluttering on the roof. He heard heavy breathing from the bed over in the corner and looked in on his brother. He sat leaning forward against the table, with his head resting in his arms, and the black cap drawn down over his forehead. He had fallen asleep.

Martin crept up without shoes and put some more wood on the fire. Then he looked over the sick man for a minute and sat down again on the bench. The snow that was stuck to the bedding had begun to melt, and the cold moisture helped wake him. Now, heavy and sleep drunk, he clumsily tried to sort out his thoughts.

He suddenly wanted to wake his brother. Here he had living proof of all that which he wanted to say this evening. Here they had been driven together by the power of fate. They were in opposition to each other. Anders was a papist, he and Herr Peder were evangelical. But on the other side, he was in opposition to both the others, for he was faithful to the king, and for them, King Gustavus was a tyrant. All that tore Europe apart at this very hour was forced together under this clogged turf roof: Rome and Luther, Church and the power of the princes, rural freedom, and concern for the kingdom. And still, they had been able to help each other and stood by each other. Quite simply, a more powerful will than their own had forced them together.

Was it not in the same way with the Swedes? Did they not sit like a handful of insects in the vast wilderness with dangers and downfall lurking all around? Was then not cohesion the most needed and obvious thing of all? Must not all else be small and insignificant when it came to living or dying?

Was His Grace not right again with his nationalism?

Herr Andreas jumped up over at the table and righted himself.

"Are you awake, Martin?" he said, confused.

"Yes, it is time to switch."

The scrivener put on his shoes, and, for the sake of appearance, he walked over to check on the sick man. He had lost all desire to talk anymore.

"He is sleeping well," he said. "Go and lay down."

The priest went over to the bench and laid himself out where it was still warm. Martin had sat in the chamber pot chair and poked the fire. The storm still fought with the flames.

When he had been sitting a long time, the priest suddenly began to speak over on the bench.

"Martin"

He startled. He thought his brother was sleeping.

"Yes?"

"Do you remember the evening after St. Bartholomew's Day, when we rowed the skiff across the lake, and the storm came upon us?"

"Yeah, of course . . ."

"Do you remember how it felt: first only dull angst, then a little black cloud wall with gold on the edges that rose in an arch just as if a giant cat was stretching . . ."

"Yes, it was almost eerie. And then it began."

The pastor was silent a moment and then slowly said:

"Martin, I saw that wall of cloud on the horizon this evening."

"What are you talking about?"

"Yes, I saw it behind John of Flodlycke and Peter the sexton. You did not understand them. You spoke about a man leaving his house and cutting shafts and fighting for freedom, and they meant well when they nodded. But you thought the whole time about following the king and going against the enemies of the realm. The boys thought of something else."

Now Scrivener Martin was wide awake.

"What do you mean?"

"I mean nothing. But I saw a storm cloud this evening that I have not seen before, Martin. Does the king ever hear what someone like you says?"

"Not often . . ." Martin grinned. "He only speaks to us small scriveners when he is scolding us, and then it is best to bow and hold your tongue. But if he is in good humor, a man can dare approach with a little something."

"Then, Martin, it is your duty to tell the king that there may be a storm here the likes of which he has not yet seen. The farmers tolerate a lot, but if one pokes them in the eye, they react wildly in the end. And then it is best to keep out of the way."

"What do you mean?"

"That if the king takes our silver and forbids our old way of worship and violates our most sacred faith, then it can become serious enough that a man leaves his house."

Anders sat himself up, very straight and pale.

"Martin, by the Holy Mother of God and by the memory of our own mother, I swear to you: Do not trust the king in everything. Even he makes mistakes from time to time. If he tries to destroy God's church, then there *must* be war—for life and death."

He took a deep breath as if he hesitated. Then he said in almost a whisper:

"I was ready to despair. But then I read the nineteenth psalm in Compline. You know: *Consulcabis leonem et draconem.*[25] Now I know that no devil can overthrow the church. And therefore, there must be strife if the King sets himself up against God. Then I pray that you will not ride with Herod but stand on the right side."

The scrivener watched the fire silently. The priest continued even more seriously.

"Martin, you must see what this means. The Holy Church alone shall remain, in the power of God's commission, whether she suits the powerful of the world or not—even if our poor people are handed over to serve Mammon and the powers and the glory of princes."

Now Scrivener Martin turned and looked at his brother.

"Andreas . . . It is *you* who must understand what it means. Here we finally have our own kingdom. It was hanging by a thread, and everything could have been lost. It can hang by a thread again. There are a thousand fighting wills to tame before we Swedes can keep peace in our own house. It can very well happen that there is strife once again, then I pray you stay on the right side, think about the future, about freedom, about the land's strength and success. You must use all the authority you have over the farmers to get them to understand that the king fights for our common interest. You must understand that we betray ourselves and our children and our people if we do not now gather as one man around the king and his kingdom building."

---

[25] "You will tread on the lion and the adder" (Psalm 91:13).

The priest looked at his brother for a long time. Then he said:

"Martin, do you remember that I was the one who wanted us to turn around that time when the black cloud rose above us?"

"Yeah, I remember that."

"But you wanted to check on the nets first. Then it came upon us all together. We lost both the net and the boat and almost lost our lives too. Now, I only say: go to land before it is too late!"

The other was quiet.

The pastor laid down again. The storm beat harder than ever on the roof, and the black smoke from the birch bark billowed and left soot everywhere in the cottage.

The scrivener rearranged the logs in the hearth to bring the fires together in the back corner and sat to the right at the table again. He felt depressed and wanted to say something. But then he noticed that his brother was sleeping against the wall. He sat for a moment, silently. He went over to him and pulled the pelts over his shoulders. Then he said, slowly and authoritatively:

"Yet, you can't stop us from sticking together."

HIS OWN WAY

September 1542

The scratching and scraping inside the bedside cabinet by his pillow woke Herr Andreas, who still half asleep, banged his fist on the worm-eaten cabinet varnished in grease. The scratching ceased. A heavy thud on the floor and a quick rattle followed when the scared vole shuffled away along the planks and disappeared in the hole by the fireplace.

The priest sat up in the bed. The first pale rays of daylight fell through the stretched membranes used for the ceiling window. It was very cold. It had certainly frosted last night. He crawled back into bed and pulled the warm sheepskins over him. But he could no longer sleep. The day's worries crept up on him and set themselves like black leeches on his heart. Like so many times before, they began to drain the strength and joy of life from him before the day even began. He turned heavily in the bed a couple of times. Finally, he decided to get up. He dressed in seconds and opened the upper half of the cabin door and yawned.

It was a foggy and cold September morning. The endless rain had quit. A damp haze hung in the air, and steam rose from the ground. Every blade of grass was heavy with cold dew. Pregnant water beads lined the split log roofs of the cowshed, where they constantly flowed together and split apart again. The old apple trees by the granaries glittered in the fog with shiny wet leaves, among which the dark red apples looked like frozen lingonberries. A steamy wet mist rose up out of the meadows and swept the whole yard in a haze. It was only half daylight.

Herr Andreas walked straight through the wet grass down across the meadow and up to the church. He wanted to finish Matins and Lauds as early as possible so that he could ride to Askanäs and reason with the soldiers.

He had made it partway up the hill to the church-village when he suddenly stopped and listened. In the still of the morning, he only heard the heavy rattle of drops that a solitary breeze shook down from the aspen leaves.

No, there it was again: the clear sound of a walking horse slowly lifting its hooves from the wet mud. The sound came down from the great path that crossed over the churchyard. A stranger coming to the village had to go straight here. And these days, a stranger often meant important news.

Herr Andreas stood still and watched the saplings down by the stream. They rose up out of the fog like gray heaps of half-sleeping, rain-heavy peasants at a morning market. The sun had just come up, and a group of travelers appeared in the glittering fog. They seemed to have come straight out of the holy history. First, a single man with his peaked hat pulled deep over his face, and his damp coat tightly wrapped about his waist. Behind him walked an old mare with tired steps. A woman sat in the saddle with a bundle in her arms that could not be anything but a child. Truly, this must have been what it looked like when St. Joseph fled to Egypt with God's mother. It was easy to confuse the furry horse for a donkey as she let her tired head hang down toward the ground.

To the priest's surprise, the entourage did not continue up to the church-village but turned off toward the parsonage. He understood what this meant and sighed a moment over the fate that forced the priest to be the village innkeeper. Now he had to forsake the silence of the church and fetch beer instead. Unwillingly, he returned to the parsonage.

The strangers stopped when they caught sight of Anders. The man took a few steps to meet him and removed his hat with a tired movement. The priest cried with amazement. It was Herr Peder, his brother in the office at Vi. Happily surprised, he hurried to him. It had been almost three years since that stormy Eve of Epiphany when Peder took refuge in his home. He had met him only a couple of times after that, always with bitter clashes concerning doctrine, but not without a certain reciprocal friendship and understanding. In any case, Herr Peder was a thinking man with whom one could converse. There were not too many birds of that sort up here in the forested wilderness. But who was the woman?

Suddenly the priest of Fröjerum felt a shiver run through his body as if all the ice water in the folds of the hat had run down his back. Of course! The woman was Herr Peder's wife. Now it made sense. He remembered that the old heretic had married just over a year ago.

Herr Andreas stood completely stunned. His brother in the office came up to him and offered him his hand. He took it and was finally able to speak.

"What in all the world are you doing here, Peder?"

"There's time enough for you to learn that. But first, get us under your roof. We have been on the road since yesterday morning, my Margareta is dead tired, and the boy's back will be stiff and sore if he can't lay down soon."

"But why in all the world do you travel about in the wild forest at night? You look like St. Joseph on the way to Egypt!"

"It is not so different, as you shall see. I want to get my wife and child to safety."

"To safety—from what?"

"From Dacke's horde of thieves and rapists! Have you not heard that they are on their way toward us?"

The priest was silent. Naturally, he knew what the whole village had been talking about for ten days. But he had completely different feelings concerning the peasant uprising than Herr Peder. So instead, he asked:

"Where do you plan on hiding then?"

"I do not plan on hiding myself at all!" Answered Herr Peder heatedly. "If I can only get Margareta to safety, I shall return. If these forest thieves come as wolves over my flock, then I will be like a shepherd among them. But my Margareta should escape the worst. Dacke is a powerful fighter for everything old and ancient. You know how it sounds: The mass in Latin, otherwise you lose your nose! Parade with the cross and banner around the cemetery, or you end up in the marsh. Separate from your wife, or we burn the parsonage! That is his gospel. But when he comes to Vi, he shall seek the priest's wife in vain."

When they came to the yard, Herr Peder helped his wife out of the saddle and loosed the strap, and the priest hobbled the horse. It could just as well graze here on the turf as out in the pasture.

They went in. The woman laid the boy down on the bed and collapsed in the chamber pot chair. Herr Andreas observed her shyly. For him, a priest's wife was anathema, a living revelation of the sin with which the devil tempted St. Anthony in the desert. But Mother Margareta truly did not look seductive where she sat, awake too long, guarded and with a paleness under her sunburn that gave the homely and robust face the faded hint of dirty yellow.

He served his guests beer, bread, and cold cuts. When they had pacified the worst of their hunger, they put the boy to bed in the furs. The priest took a mattress off the bed, and the woman stretched out on the bench, shrouded in Herr Peder's coat. Her husband sat down again at the table.

"Andreas," he said. "Now, it is serious. You showed yourself to be a merciful Samaritan that night when the cold was killing me. So I am here again."

The priest looked at his guest, inquisitively. Then Herr Peder bowed forward and whispered:

"Have you heard what mad Joen has done?"

"Joen of Brohult?"

The pastor looked doubly inquisitive. Herr Joen of Brohult was their brother in the office, an older man, perhaps a bit litigious but incessantly dedicated to the old faith. Herr Andreas had always liked him.

"What has Joen done?"

"He has preached rebellion! And that was not enough. He has sent around a bloody board with a ring of brass and a ring of iron in each corner. On the board, he has scrawled with a burning iron: 'One hand and one foot and one belt buckle.' And this is supposed to circulate in the whole of Ydre, in North and South Vedbo—the meaning is: Come quickly citizens of Kinda to help, for the anti-Christian king has sent a mighty host against Kisa, pure mercenaries and bloodthirsty soldiers and they have orders to mercilessly hack hand and foot off every man in Småland and shamefully abuse every woman."

Herr Andreas looked at his brother in the office steadily. His face was hard, and he rubbed his chin so that the stubble rasped.

"When did the bidding stick go out?" he asked.

"It came to Vi the day before yesterday."

"Ah . . . and how did the peasants react?"

"They waffle."

It was quiet for a moment. Herr Andreas tried to remember what he had heard and seen over the last two days. But he could not find anything that indicated a muster. He would not have been kept from such an important matter either. Or did one fear that he would dissuade them?

The silence lingered.

"What will you do, Peder?"

"I will do my duty."

"What then is your duty?"

"To obey the authorities."

"But if the authorities are godless?"

"One should obey them anyway."

"That's a pleasant teaching."

"No more pleasant than that I can expect to be killed for it if Dacke comes to Vi."

"Do you really plan to die for King Gustavus—the church thief?"

"It is not for the king that I risk my life but for the authority, for justice and order in the kingdom. There have always been godless men in authority. But if the district judge takes bribes, one cannot repeal national law. If the king acts arbitrarily and hard with church property, one may not steal and plunder for it. The authority is from God."

"What should we then do?"

Herr Peder stared out into space.

"I don't know . . . But I pray to God. *He* knows."

"But one can't just sit with their arms crossed while the church and peasants are plundered of everything but the shirt on their back?"

"No, but one can seek legal redress."

"But if it doesn't help?"

"Then one might think on the word: If anyone would sue you and take your tunic, let him have your cloak as well! We keep God's kingdom."

The pastor looked at his colleague, thoughtfully.

"You still have some sort of faith, brother heretic. But now think of the peasants. Everything intensifies for them. Interest and the land tax, quarter charges, and food prices—everything! No one knows when it will increase or how much it will increase. Soon they will have to give every fifth pig as tax for the acorns. No one can sell a pair of oxen for more than sixteen marks. They are not allowed to drive them south either, though a person can get twenty-five for them in Ronneby—only because the residences of Norrköping and Stockholm should earn more! And the king's bailiffs go around and threaten to take everything into account: oxen and sheep, sheaves and butter churns, chemises and canvas. And the plundering of the church! Have you heard what the peasants say: 'Soon it will be as sweet to walk in the empty forest as in a church.' It no more resembles the Lord's temple than a tithe barn. When the king finishes plundering the mice will be all we have left."

Now Herr Peder laughed a pale and tired laugh.

"But, Andreas, the altar remains—and the chalice? The baptismal font and missal? You can still baptize children and hold mass like before, right? The church does not need silver for the salvation of souls. If you can still distribute the holy sacrament and freely proclaim God's word, can you not do without the rest?"

"But if you cannot even preach according to God's Law? Do you remember how it went for Master Olaus when he preached against oaths?"

"Then, one can still preach and risk their necks. If it goes so far, one may entrust the matter to God's hands and then do like the holy martyrs."

Herr Peder was quiet, and his host continued, heatedly and insistently as if he fought with something inside of himself:

"Is it not, on the contrary, better to put an end to the evil before it manages to destroy everything for us? What did Engelbrekt do? What did Sture's men do? What did king Gustavus himself do when he drove Christian out of the land?"

Herr Peder was still silent, and the pastor continued almost whispering. His voice trembled with zeal.

"Peder, you called the peasants forest thieves just now. What did you think Jösse Eriksson and Didrik Slagheck and Gustaf Trolle called the Dalecarlians when they came out of their forests? They were also called insurrectionists, snipers, highwaymen, and robbers. But they were the ones who saved freedom for us. Do you not believe God could have called small people to do the work this time?"

Herr Peder was quiet.

"Peder, if one shall always listen to the authorities, then should King Gustavus have given himself to Christian, and then Didrik Slagheck would still be a bishop in Skara."

Herr Peder had shut his eyes. Now he looked up again with his rapid and fiery eyes.

"No amount of human thought can untie that knot," he said. "There are enough tyrants that have pushed their way into authority. They can very well be driven away with Gideon's sword or Jephthath's. But I do not believe this concerning King Gustavus. We have elected him as our king, according to the law. So I tell the peasants: Compose a complaint letter, I will write it out for you. I will take it to Stockholm, but do not rebel."

Now it was Herr Andreas who shut his eyes and supported his forehead on knotted fists. He slammed the pale blue knuckles hard against his head.

"No," he said. "No thought of man sorts this out. Have mercy on us, Holy Mother of God!"

There was another silence. Then the rector straightened himself up.

"Now, where are you going? Where is your Egypt?"

"In Fröjerum."

"What do you mean?"

"Andreas . . . You once showed yourself to be a merciful Samaritan. Now I stand here again just as helpless, seeking shelter from the storm. I cannot hide Margareta anywhere in Vi or Brohult if Dacke comes. But no one will look for her up here in the woods. Is there any place where she can find shelter until the storm is over?"

Herr Andreas was silent. When he didn't answer. His guest continued hesitantly:

"Could you not use a housekeeper here in the parsonage?"

Herr Andreas quickly answered.

"A petticoat shall never stay overnight in this house. I have sworn before St. Laurentii's picture up there in the church!"

"Well, then do you maybe know of an upright peasant that will take her into his home? She will gladly help in the fields."

The Pastor was quiet for a while.

"It won't do," he finally said. "Of course, they will take her in both at Flodlycke and Årtebol. And no one would be perverse with her, though no one here is happy that you married. But if the peasant hordes come here with foreigners, then I dare not take responsibility. Can you not bring her to Vadstena or Linköping?"

Herr Peder made a helpless hand gesture.

"I cannot run away from my post, least of all now when it is humming in the villages like a hive. If she could only find a safe travel companion, then I could not ask for anything more than to get her and the boy down the hill."

Now Herr Andreas got up.

"Perhaps God will find you a travel companion before this evening," he said. "I just received an errand in that direction. But first, I want to go up to the church and sing Matins. You can sleep through it—like a true evangelical priest," he added mockingly.

The other lifted his pale head. His large eyes rejoiced.

"I'll come with you," he said quickly. He glanced at his wife and the little boy sleeping soundly. The priest was already out the door.

The morning sun had broken through the fog. There were still silver veils hanging over the tufts of grass in the meadow, and there was steam at the edge of the forest. Up above the sun shone, and the skies were blue. It was a clear and warm day. The mild weather came up over the village from the west.

On the way up to the church, Herr Andreas gave a few words of explanation about what he meant. There were soldiers in Askanäs, German mercenaries, about thirty men. Then young Herr Tönjes and six armed men from the district summoned by the King were added to these. Essentially, they were to take up residence in Jönköping with Lars Siggesson, but because the peasants are able to overrun the forest trails to the south over Holaveden at any time, they have not dared to depart until they receive better news from the South. They had been bivouacked there for weeks now. In Askanäs, their rations began to run out, so they had taken to demanding hospitality from the farmers. The only reasonable thing for them to do was to march north and join the king's troops in Vadstena or Herr Mån's muster, which had gathered somewhere in the east. It was high time that they give up the field if the peasants are not to lose patience. Three swine and two sheep had already disappeared and if anyone in

Askanäs inquired about it, the soldiers would just grin and dry the drippings from their mustaches.

They had made it up to the church. When Herr Andreas stepped into the dim interior wafting of incense, he paid furtive attention to his guest. Peder did not take the holy water but crossed himself and bent his knee like any other Christian. Up in the choir, he prayed the Apostle's Creed and the Our Father, just like Herr Andreas. Then he voluntarily sat in the chair to the right, and when Andreas began to sing the Venite, he joined in at the invitatory. He would soon be a forty-year-old man, Herr Peder, and he must have gone to school during the good old days. Thus he was not completely ignorant of the Holy Office.

So, it came that for the first time in many months, Herr Andreas could sing Matins and Laudes alternately and correctly in his church. The bitterness and unease left him. Once again, he heard the tranquil echo from the world above where no complaint or alarm of war would be heard ever again.

When they came back out into the sunlight, he said:

"When was the last time you sang Matins?"

"On Sunday," Herr Peder answered.

The rector could not hide his surprise.

"You pray the hours even though you are Lutheran?"

"Why not? I learned it in Uppsala from Bishop Lars."

"In Latin?"

"We sang the hymns in Swedish; the antiphons and responses were in Latin for the most part. But the Archbishop would like to put them in Swedish too."

"Do you pray the whole Divine Office?"

"Not all of it. I have other things to do in Vi. On weekdays it is at best a few of the smaller hours. I pray most of them on holy days, except for the idolatrous prayers to Mary, you understand."

"That is cheating. All or nothing!"

"I have all! All that benefits salvation. For you, the hours are good works that you do for God. So you need to stack them up so desperately much—and it is never sufficient. For me, the hours and all other prayers are a beggar's path to a gracious God. It is sufficient if I come forward for grace. Then I have the complete fullness of God in faith."

"Snip snap. Faith and faith. It is your old way! Faith without works is dead. Show me your faith without prayer, without fasting, without holy living, so shall I show you my faith in poverty and chastity—and the worship of God with fasting and prayer."

"So now we are there again." Herr Peder laughed. "I have, of course, told you that you will never come to understand this until you first experience the anguish of the soul. But first, God must show you that the sinful worm crawls in your shiny halo, and this is what you most of all do not want to see. But now I am too tired to dispute. If there is peace in our land again and we manage to live, then we shall take up this duel again. But then I will lay the Bible out in front of me."

"The new heretical Bible, I bet—but not Thomas Aquinas for then you will lose."

Herr Andreas spat with conviction before the feet of his guest.

"If I win with just the Bible, then it is enough," he said. He spat just as powerfully back. Then they both laughed.

They had taken the path past the parsonage. Herr Peder wanted to say something to his wife before they continued. The other stood outside the yard. He sat on the edge of an empty water trough, pushed his hood back, and warmed his tonsured head in the sun. When his guest came back over the wet embankment, he said derisively:

"Is my lord brother finished with the vain worries of this world? *'Qui sine uxore est, solicitus est quae Dominei sunt, quomodo placeat Deo,'* says St. Paul. He who does not have a wife concerns himself with the Lord's service. But he who has a wife, he worries for that which belongs to this world, whether he can please his wife."

Suddenly the derisiveness in his face gave way. He asked with a tone of confidential covetousness.

"What is it really like to be married?"

Herr Peder looked him straight in the eye with his sharp look, which was dampened today by vigil and exhaustion.

"It is beneficial," he said, "very beneficial. A veritable school for faith."

"How so?"

"Then one first understands what a great sinner he is, and what Jesus means as a savior."

Herr Andreas looked puzzled.

"This is what I mean. As long as I lived the celibate life, I ruled over myself. Then it was no great skill to pretend to be a sanctified soul. If my temper was poor, I just went home to the parsonage. I slept as long as I wanted in the morning and could write and read when it suited me. And when one does just what one wants, you feel good. At the time, I called it holiness and peace of mind. Now I have a boy who screams all night. When I should be working on the sermon, Margareta comes with a broken shuttle, and when I finally get the train of thought back, the threads in the loom are tangled on her, and before we get them in order, it is a new mess in my poor head. After doing that dance for a year, you are under no delusion of becoming a saint. But a man knows ever more about grace than he did before. A man learns to live from pure mercy. And so he learns to be thankful that he can serve his neighbor amid all this everyday life instead of serving himself with a bunch of spiritual fabrications that God has never asked for, and that don't serve anyone on earth."

Herr Andreas didn't answer, though he should have felt like the winner. He had come to think that he had fled Ravelunda, where the farm laborers needed directions, farm work needed to be kept running, and travelers should be given shelter, and kept himself in Fröjerum, where he could come and go as he wished and was seldom disturbed by anyone. He had always considered this good as a sign that he wanted to live completely for God and, in his way, imitate the holy life of hermits. Perhaps it was because he did not want to have his patience tested when he had to settle disputes concerning mares or conduct an investigation concerning a broken whip?

The two men had made it a good way down to the lake. The cold dew in the grass had long since soaked through their shoes. It didn't matter now because the sun was shining, and the day was warm and clear. The air was not clear like other fall days but glittery and flickering. Steam rose from the marsh.

They finally neared the broad valley floor by the beach where Askanäs lay on an elevated flat between the fields. Today, Herr Andreas noticed that he could see his family farm without his heart hurting as much as in the past. He was letting go of the world. This last year he had so often thought about the possibility of losing both his livelihood and life, and Askanäs had brought him so many worries that the gray square of log cabins no longer stood there as his childhood haven of peace, but instead appeared to him as a gray and ugly collection site for all the injustice and unseemly things that filled these evil years to the brim.

From a long distance off, he could already see that there were fortified camps in the yard. A dozen horses were grazing in the fallow. A soldier with a red sweater and torn gold trousers hanging down over his calves stood at his post by the gate to the estate. They could hear all sorts of noise and racket from the grounds within the estate.

The rector was sick to his stomach when he saw the post. It was the first time he had seen a watch positioned at Askanäs. But he didn't say anything to Herr Peder.

When they reached the entrance, the soldier stepped to the side reverently for the priests. Herr Andreas spoke to him in German and led them. Both Berent Ochse, the First Sergeant, and Herr Tönjes of Sponga were in the yard. Herr Tönjes was the one who held command here because he belonged to the nobility of the realm and was considered to be among the great men from that part of the country. He was still a very young man and a newly commissioned knight. That meant that the German first sergeant was in charge of managing and arranging everything in the camp.

Immediately upon stepping through the gray gate into the yard, they noticed that something particular was in the making. The sun illuminated colorful clothes and newly furbished steel. Grinding stones hissed in front of the livestock sheds, and rusted daggers and swords laid about all around them. Two soldiers scalded a pig outside the brewhouse. Herr Tönjes stood in the middle of the yard, swearing. The sun was warm and shown over the motley spectacle.

When the two priests approached the knight, they felt like a pair of black jackdaws in a cage full of parrots. The work continued all around them with shouting and whistling. No one seemed to be bothered by them.

"God's peace, Herr Tönjes," the rector greeted him. "What is new today?"

The knight stood straight. The young ruddy face with its thin, silky soft beard, gave a broad smile when he answered.

"Humble greetings, now and always for sure, Herr Pastor! Now we scrape the last papistic layer of soot from out of the oven! Herr

Måns is on the march through Kinda and shall let all the forest thieves make a descent that they will not soon forget. They have said long enough that they would slay us men in red. Now it is we who will color their dirty rags as red as kirsch."

Herr Andreas straightened up with alarm. He measured the knight with a fearful look.

"Good luck on the trip, noble sir. For us, it is quite nice for you to find other things to stick rather than Fröjerum swine."

The knight blushed but pretended to miss the point. He turned and gave orders to the soldiers standing by to distribute enough gunpowder to the arquebusiers[1] so they could fill their horns. They were to load the rest on the packhorse that would take the other route. He turned again to the priests and eyed Herr Peder without any visible respect.

"Where are you from, sir?"

"I am the pastor in Vi."

"Peder Knutsson in Vi? Herr Tönjes brightened up. Then you would be a brave man and a friend of the crown. What a pleasant surprise to meet a man like you in this papistic den of thieves, but what are you doing here?"

Herr Peder hesitated a little with the answer. If he could not find someone to escort his Margareta to the plain, it was just as well that word did not spread that she was here in Fröjerum.

"We had some important things to speak about, Herr Andreas and I," is all he said. "Which way are you taking now?"

The knight threw a suspicious look at the Fröjerum priest.

"Such a thing is not revealed in war," he said curtly.

"Do you think I'm going to cut trenches in the road," Herr Andreas smiled mockingly. "In any case, I will gladly leave you alone with Herr Peder. Perhaps he is more trustworthy. I have a particular parishioner up there that I ought to greet," he added and slowly began to go up to the brewhouse where the soldiers were preparing to stick a pig.

Herr Tönjes watched him closely and then turned to Herr Peder. His face had now become timid.

---

[1] A rifleman using an arquebus.

"What do the peasants say over to the east?" he asked so softly that it could not be heard by the attendant soldiers who were shining his hip plates just a few feet away so that the sand shrieked against the rough metal.

"They are not rebelling, but they are close."

"Is it true that the people are arrayed against the judge?"

"Here and there, people find hints that this is true," said Herr Peder evasively. He did not want to bear witness against Joen of Brohult. He continued with even more evasiveness, "I should advise you, young lord, do not try to go south of the Sommen. It is easy to escape in the forest. Instead, take the Hola road east to Linköping and then up the Stångån. It will slow you down a few days, but at least you will get there."

In his heart he thought, unless they have also blocked the Hola road with barricades at Skrukeby—but he barely dared to think the suspicion through to the end. His mind was constantly racing as he tried to reach a decision concerning his wife and boy. Should he entrust them to the soldiers and ask Herr Tönjes to take them with them to Linköping? He looked at his boyish face where inexperience and uncertainty lurked behind the boisterous words. The man was not sure of himself. It was precisely for this reason that he sneered and looked on others with condescension.

In the meantime, Herr Andreas went over to the two soldiers occupied with the slaughter. They didn't even acknowledge him. He went forward and checked the mark in the sow's ear. One clip at the top and two further down—it was the mark of the Seved's farm. He had supposed this. Just yesterday, Elif from Seved's farm was talking to him and the churchwarden and complained about the sow that disappeared from the acorn pasture in the communal forest belonging to the village.

He turned and went back to the middle of the courtyard.

Herr Tönjes suddenly began to give out orders to the pageboys again. They lined up the horses and watered them before getting them saddled. Even Berent Ochse had come forward. He and the knight counseled with Herr Peder.

The first sergeant was a stocky man, with red hair, a bald chin, and a blonde mustache under wide nostrils. His eyes sunk deep within his face and were bloodshot. Perhaps because of a bender. He was very excited.

"The devil's crucified sacrament, I tell you, and when it rains peasants for forty days, we will bury them all. Not a one will survive! I was there when they slaughtered the peasants at Frankenhausen[2] in twenty-five. I know what they are good for. They come together, shoot the bailiffs, murder, scream, and rant—if there was just one of them with a proper weapon, and when they take a few lead bullets in the belly, they turn and disperse—like possessed pigs. These forest thieves!"

Now the priest could not remain silent.

"Forest thieves? There are no thieves living here, but only honorable people in this forest! I have known of nothing amiss in my parish for many years, except when we have had soldiers posted here. A man should not speak of forest thieves when he is scalding a stolen swine!"

Herr Tönjes looked like a blushing schoolboy for a minute. But the embarrassed face squeezed into a harsh grimace, and his eyes narrowed hard on the priest.

"God's death and suffering! What dare you slander us with?"

"I slander no one with anything. I only say what I saw: the sow over there has the mark of the Seved's farm on its earlobe, and the farmer told me just yesterday that she disappeared from the acorn pasture, she and many more."

"Do you then know to whom the acorn pasture belongs?"

"Yes, it is the village commons."

"Precisely! All the oak forests belong to the crown. A priest ought to know that! And the acorns fall from the crown's oaks, so the acorns belong to the crown. Now the peasants of Fröjerum have been cheating the crown of acorn bacon for years, and now we take our share. The peasants have not suffered any injustice."

The priest looked at the nobleman with amazement.

---

[2] The Battle of Frankenhausen, May 14th and 15th, 1525, was the climax of the German Peasants' War, where Philippe of Hesse defeated Thomas Müntzer, a violent Anabaptist preacher.

"When did you become a bailiff, Herr Tönjes? Do you have the right to receive the King's taxes? Without accounting and registration?"

The knight clutched the empty glove in his belt. His lips pursed, and his face became even redder.

"I do not have time to stand here and quarrel," he said. "He who has something to complain about can write to the judge. It will go bad for you. Here there is enough with withheld taxes among the peasants and the damn devil's papistry among the priesthood, so that it would suffice to bring hellfire on all of you. We are Lutherans in this country now."

"I can hear that in your coarse oaths," said the priest with ice in his voice.

Now the empty glove flew out of the belt and straight toward the priest's face. He just barely managed to stop it with his hand. Slowly he bent down and returned the glove with a bow. He was extremely pale and said nothing. There was silence all around.

The knight realized that he had crossed the line. He pursed his lips and stood stiffly, trying to look stern. He looked perplexed.

The sun shed its warm glow over the yard. The horses looked for blades of grass on the uphill slope, and a crow carefully stepped among the scattered leathery peaches. Berent Ochse watched his commander with blinking red eyes. His mouth stood open under his immense mustache, and his bottom lip stuck out as if it was waiting for beer.

Herr Tönjes never needed to speak. A soft whining sound broke the silence, a trembling and gentle tone that arched over their heads. In the next second, it slammed heavily and softly against the knotty wood in the cowshed, and there, a shaft shivered from impact with its iron point buried deep in the wood.

Berent Ochse was the first to realize what was happening. His mouth shut a moment, hard knots formed at the corners and it opened again, square and red, and the firm bass voice echoed out his orders: the arquebusiers would load and get in position along the western courtyard, and he posted four men at the gate with shortened halberds. Now he spoke broad Plattdeutsch.

The men were immediately in position. Three men climbed up on the roofs of the cowshed, brewhouse, and storehouse. From there, they looked to the north, east, and west. The gate to the farm was to the south. He had already posted a man there, but apparently, he had not seen anything. The bolt had come from the east.

Only when everything was clear did the first sergeant make his way to Herr Tönjes, who was quickly putting on his armor. The attendant was getting an earful as he fumbled nervously with the leather straps.

"Calm, calm!" said the German in a fatherly voice. "We shall burn the noses off these snipers."

"Veit," he called to the soldier on the storehouse roof. "Do you see anything?"

"Yeah! The whole meadow is full of peasants."

"How many?"

"More than I can count. Perhaps sixty, maybe a hundred."

Herr Tönjes had become very serious: "This smells of treachery, you lords can leave," he said, addressing the priests. Berent Ochse took him by the arm and went up to the arquebusiers who had crowded together behind the great house, where they were rushing wildly to throw on their greaves and helmets.

Herr Peder looked at his ward suspiciously. His eyes were dark and wearied by the vigil of the night.

"Andreas," he said, "this is crazy. You have to speak to the peasants. The greatest catastrophe that has ever happened in your parish could strike by evening."

Herr Andreas looked up at the sky to the area from where the bolt had come. He was still just as pale but said nothing.

"Andreas," continued the other persuasively, "this will hit your entire parish. It will mean life and death, rack, and wheel. You *must* speak reason to them!"

Herr Tönjes came back. He had regained his confidence, and his upper lip lifted slightly again.

"Herr Andreas, you stay here as a hostage. And perhaps Herr Peder can do us the service of going out and listening to the peasants to find out what the meaning of this spectacle is."

"I will be right back," he said. "Only agree not to shoot."

He disappeared through the gate with a long stride. Herr Andreas followed him with his gaze, which he then allowed to sweep over the vicinity that seemed like the roof of a barn in the way the yard sloped to the south. Down below, the valley was in the deepest peace. The lake was as blue as on any early weekday, here and there were yellow birches, and the red leaves from a pair of maples lit up the bay. Otherwise, everything was still in the green of summer. A mild and affectionate humidity permeated the air, and the blue mountains disappeared in a distant glimmer.

Now Herr Peder's voice was heard outside the southeast corner of the yard.

"Stop! Don't shoot!"

Then there was silence again.

The scout on the storehouse roof reported that the peasants gathered around the priest. They seemed to be speaking past each other.

The arquebusiers had finally gotten all their armor in the right place and began to load. Two of them had heavy double-barreled guns. The others had more common half barrels.

Once again, there was a tense silence. Berent Ochse spoke softly to Herr Tönjes, while their pageboys attended to the saddles. The other noble lords came and greeted the priest without really knowing what tone they should use. It was silent again. There was a constant hum of excitable voices down in the meadow.

"How is it going down there?" Cried Herr Tönjes to the squire who had climbed up on the cottage roof to try and listen.

"I don't see anything . . . The peasants stand and push in a ring just like at a fight."

Another hour passed. Herr Tönjes counseled with the other lords. Then he went to the first sergeant and said something. He nodded. And again, orders whistled like the lashes of a whip through the tense silence.

There was rustling and clang of steel when the Landsknecht laid their heavy arquebuses over their shoulders. The shooters turned left and marched down to the gate with Berent Ochse in the lead. The noblemen and the priest followed after them with the horses and pageboys. Only then did the soldiers come alone with their halberds and battleaxes.

Outside the gate, the troops swung left and marched around the corner up to the forest on the east side of the farm, in the middle of the crowd of peasants. The arquebusiers formed wings; they set their forks in the ground but did not set their arquebuses in them. Between them stood the other soldiers, with their halberds and battle-axes at the ready. Herr Tönjes was the only one of the nobility that remained in his saddle. He waved his hands.

The peasants gathered in great confusion. Some of them raised their crossbows, while others screamed not to shoot. Herr Tönjes waved once more.

"Calm, calm, men—do not shoot at your own priest. Put your crossbows down! If you send one bolt at us, then you will receive twenty bullets in return."

The peasants lowered their crossbows but did not disperse. The crowd cried threatening slogans and insults:

"Swine thieves! Beer bellies!"

"Release Herr Peder, then we can speak rationally," yelled the knight. "Safe passage for the priest! You others stay down there."

Herr Peder came up the slope. The Fröjerum priest watched him walk up the hill with a tired gate. Behind him, he saw many familiar figures in gray homespun woolen skirts, some chainmail here and there, and old rusty helmets that he recognized from the cottage walls of the parish where they would hang above the high seat. But suddenly, his gaze fixed on a figure with colorful pants and a modern helmet with plates for the face. Who in the world was that? And right in front of him stood a man with a long, slender battleax of a type that the people of Fröjerum had never seen before. What was this?

Herr Peder arrived. He was even paler than before. His shoulders hung heavily, and great pearls of sweat glimmered in his dark hairline.

He went right through the formation of soldiers without looking to the right or the left, and straight up to Herr Tönjes.

"God bless us," he said shortly. "Herr Måns has been defeated in Kisa. Jorgen von Ellingen and many other noblemen are dead, and the rest of the soldiers were cut down in the forest."

Berent Ochse looked at the priest sharply. His eyes seemed to have cleared. They were gray as steal and hard.

"That is a lie!" he said. "Old wives' tales! Damn peasant babble!"

"No," said Herr Peder. "It is more likely that it has happened, and all is true. Strangers have come to the village with plundered wares, armor, and darts that have never hung in a peasant's cottage. There is evidence enough."

Herr Tönjes had straightened up in the saddle. His lean, boyish cheeks had become angular and hard.

"Good," he said. "Now we don't have to debate concerning which road. Now it is only a question of whether we shall need to ride over the bodies of this mob or not."

Herr Andreas stood completely motionless among the noble lords. He looked out over the meadow, where a few splendid oaks grew between hazelnuts. He could recognize most of the men down there, though he had never seen them before with this cumbersome entourage. Both churchwardens were there. John was unarmed, but the other carried a crossbow. The crowd kept crying: Swine thieves! Beer Bellies! Intermittently they cried: Release our priest!

Herr Andreas stood and looked up to heaven. He saw a red flickering dance in the sky. It stretched out and flew together to form a fiery a sword blade pointing at the earth. In the distance, he could hear Herr Peder's voice speaking calmly to Herr Tönjes.

"No, lord, this is not a common uprising. Most of the peasants have only come here to demand honorable payment for four pigs and three sheep and a fine for the servant boy that the soldiers struck lame at the Eneberga Mill. It is a reasonable demand and no common uprising."

Herr Tönjes stared at the bold priest. Once again, he was an awkward schoolboy.

"What are they demanding?" he asked.

"Eight marks örtuge for the animals, and five marks Danish for the boy. It is not unreasonable."

Herr Tönjes turned to the other lords. He backed his horse up a few steps, and they withdrew a bit to the side closer to the farm. The peasants began to come closer.

"Swine thieves! Beer Bellies!"

Berent Ochse's commanding voice rose above the chanting of the peasants. The shooters lifted their arquebuses and noisily placed them in the forks. Their fuses billowed with smoke. The peasants remained in the meadow noisily winding up their squeaky crossbows. Herr Andreas stood completely motionless and looked up. The sky was very blue, full of glittering sun rays and fiery red flickering. Before his eyes were blinded, the red sword-shaped flame appeared to fall to the earth again. Did he dare believe that it was an omen? A revelation from God of what was about to happen?

Berent Ochse was speaking from somewhere within the glittering halberds before him:

"They already have us on our heels. We should be shooting, not talking."

Now the noble lords returned from their council.

"One might well make a faithful compromise with them," said Herr Tönjes, half embarrassed. "If we give them the money and shake hands with them for a peaceful retreat, can their word be trusted?"

He looked at Herr Peder.

"Next to the word of God, I know of nothing as trustworthy as a peasant's word in these woods. You know that yourself, Herr Tönjes."

"The knight bowed thankfully and asked the priest to go down to them again and negotiate."

Herr Peder returned after a bit with five peasants, the churchwardens among them. They stood in the middle of the field with the arquebuses aimed at them. Herr Tönjes got out of his saddle and walked over to them with two Swedish noblemen and Berent Ochse.

The pastor remained among the soldiers. Over their heads, he could follow what was happening down in the meadow. His ears caught the disjointed sentences of the negotiations. Payment for the animals and the man's troubles should be made on the spot, the bolt would be considered a warning shot, and the soldiers would have free and safe passage to the district boundaries. Berent Ochse said something to the effect that the peasants should offer hostages. Then Jon of Flodlycke was heard answering with his strong voice:

"Hostages are taken from thieves and mobs. Among honorable people, their given word is enough."

Berent Ochse turned from the peasant with disgust and appealed to his commander: It would be to test God to trust an empty promise. The churchwarden's calm voice was heard again:

"Those without honor do not trust any other good either."

The first sergeant's broad head spun around as he grabbed his sword hilt. The Swedish lords calmed him down. One began to count the money. Herr Tönjes shook hands with John of Flodlycke and then the others. And so they parted ways.

It seemed that Berent Ochse was not satisfied with the outcome. He begrudgingly commanded the arquebusiers to take the forks from the ground and form up for a retreat. The attendants came out with the pack horses. Herr Tönjes addressed the pastor reservedly.

"Now you can go, good sir. Keep the peasants to their agreement."

He shook hands heartily with Herr Peder.

"Many thanks. This will be remembered. One does not serve the kingdom's cause for nothing."

"There is still a little to negotiate. The troop should go south around the lake west to Flodlycke until they reach the main road to Ödesjö and Näs. If you don't reach Näs before evening, you can rest at Ekestad or Bocksholmen. The next day you should cross the district border, and finally on the third day reach the edge of the forest at Skrukeby."

The priests had made their way down to the peasants. Here there was still a division. Some peasants from Brohult, who came from Kisa with blood on their bear spears and daggers plundered from nobility in their belts, thought that they should shoot down the redcoats and drown the soldiers. Herr Peder spoke calmly. They should wait and see. It was always best not to shed blood. They had kept to the law and their rights, and they would have justice, both in the matter of recompense and acorns.

Herr Andreas was quiet. He was very tired and exhausted after the excitement. He did not really know what he wanted. When the settlement came about, he had felt as if the clear sky became overcast, and the glittering sunlight faded away in disappointment. Certainly, he was glad that none of his own were shot among the thieves, but Herr Tönjes, with his smug upper lip and open distaste for the holy church, burned his soul. He would have gladly been left dead in the grass if only these oppressors of peasants and church plunderers laid there also. Would there ever be better times in the land without letting the ax fly?

Then finally, Jon of Flodlycke relayed the word he and six men gave, and all the parish folk nodded in agreement. Those from outside the parish would have to be patient. The peasants dispersed in small groups. A large crowd made its way up to the church-village. They all still wanted to talk a bit and drink a mug of beer before they went their separate ways.

On the other side of the meadow, the soldiers had set themselves in motion. They had a drummer with them who beat rollcalls, a threatening farewell salute. It rumbled badly in the pastor's ears. It was as if he was provocatively pounding the same tune over and over again: We'll be back, back, back . . .

Halfway to the church, the road turned right to Flodlycke. The churchwarden waited there.

"Now, I follow them home and see to it that they do not make any mischief but leave the parish in an orderly fashion," he said.

A couple of peasants from Flodlycke accompanied him, swinging their steel crossbows so that the burdock heads along the ditch swirled. The churchwarden followed slowly. He gradually made his way up the hill, alone and unarmed, and waved to the troop that they should turn here and follow him. The soldiers came along in single file past the hawthorn bushes on their side of the meadow, a long row of variegated color in the flood of sunlight. Halberds glittered, and the drum kept beating.

The two priests walked together. Herr Andreas was very quiet, so Herr Peder began to speak about his wife. Now he turned to the matter that there was still no other way out than to ask to see if she could stay at some safe place in Fröjerum.

Herr Andreas was still quiet. He looked paler and weaker than ever.

"If you want," he said, finally, "then it may as well be so but at your own risk."

He turned around and eyed the long line of peasants who made their way uphill with crossbows and axes. He stood in his black habit tall and straight, while they tramped on past in the warm sun. When Elif, the peasant from Seved's estate, came by, he broke into conversation with him and began a roundabout explanation of the matter. The peasant looked at his pastor, then at Herr Peder. The money he received as recompense for the sow beat against his leather pants.

"I promise," he said finally. "You are an honest priest, Herr Peder, who wants to do right by men, we have taken note of that today. So no injustice will happen to your woman if she wants to stay under my roof."

He left the rest of the arrangement for the two pastors to work out among themselves. He departed alone, walking up the road in deep thought. The grass was almost dry; the bare spots on the ground were firm and hard. The air was very warm, saturated with the rain moisture and the weak scent of wilting leaves.

Herr Andreas walked and grumbled about his fate and that of the church.

That this was the hardest storm of heresy and unbelief as anything that had shaken the church's old tree, that was completely clear to him. But he had no real clarity concerning what the heresy was. He had always imagined that heresy was apostasy from the church. He had thought that heretics met together in small groups that rejected the true church and began to worship by themselves. But here in this land, no one began to worship by themselves. No one had left the church, and no one had turned their back. This new thing came from the church herself, through her bishops and the diocese! Was not this Peder of Vi a full-fledged heretic? And yet he was the church's consecrated servant who managed one of the church's congregations, with great care and with his bishop's approval! Was he not a traitor who took a wife and gave up the narrow path of self-denial and the mortification of the flesh? And yet he had only followed the instructions of the church's own counselors who gathered in an upright manner, and the example of the church's own archbishop who was consecrated in the succession of the apostles by a good catholic bishop, that received his office in Rome! If Herr Peder was a heretic, then no Christian ought to have any dealings with him, and yet they had sung matins together today, kneeling at the same altar and praying the office as brothers; and they had stood as fellowmen against the powers of the world, embodied by Herr Tönjes and his soldiers.

Herr Andreas shook his big head and took a deep breath. Christendom had never before found herself in this position. And here he should find the right way without any help or guidance!

The uncertainty was the worst. Herr Andreas remembered how he wrestled with his fate last spring when the order came that the church's silver should be carried to Skeninge[3] and entrusted to Master Norman? In the cool spring evenings, he had walked back

[3] Modern day Skänninge.

and forth between the church and the parsonage, with neither sleep nor certainty. While the first-morning sun gilded the jagged edges of the freshly budding leaves on the birch trees, and the birds chirped in the willow thickets, he had sung nocturnes alone in the church and cried to God with the utmost anguish. He had no one to ask for advice. The peasants expected that he would give them the redeeming word, the dean was a miserable coward. John Larensson of Brohult whined and protested, but he had no sensible suggestion for action. So the day came once again, and he began the heaviest journey of his life through the forest.

Again, he lifted his hanging head with a jerk. He *would not* dwell on the misery. Perhaps—perhaps a new day yet dawned. The Dalecarlians had driven tyranny out of the country before. Why would not the Smålanders be able to do the same today?

But in such a case? Was it not mindless foolishness to let the soldiers escape? Was it not treachery against the peasants in Kinda and at Kronoberg? Was it not false sentimentality that he was happy they had not shed blood among the buttercups in the pastures of Askenäs?

His thoughts went in circles again, and Herr Andreas tossed his head. He sought out Herr Peder again.

"And you . . . what do you plan to do?"

"As soon as I get Margareta to Elif in the church-village, I ride home—and that as fast as my tired nag can trot."

"And then?"

"I do my service as usual."

"But what if Dacke comes to Vi?"

"Then, I keep the church open for him as I do for others."

"But if he forces you to christen and consecrate in Latin?"

"Then, I will do it. It is better if I can do it in Swedish, but it is not a matter of salvation."

"What if he demands you to do the Latin Mass?"

"I will go along. Nils Dacke is not supposed to be churchly enough to know if I skip over the ungodly yet canonical sacrificial prayers of the Mass. Surely he will be satisfied if I mumble and mutter for myself in the choir, and then I will mumble good evangelical prayers for my own edification. And because he does not understand the mass, so I will preach afterward in Swedish so that he understands it. He cannot forbid that since both the Franciscans and the preaching brothers did that before me."

"What do you plan on preaching for him?"

"That we are all sinners who need to repent."

Herr Andreas was silent again. He was too tired to bicker anymore today. Everything went in circles, with no right side, with no beginning and no end.

They reached the church-village and made their way up the last steep hill after taking a minute to rest just outside the churchyard wall. The day was unusually warm, and the humid air forced a sweat. The men laid down their weapons and adjusted armor. The ill-fitted chain mail and iron helmets chafed under their weight.

Herr Andreas looked out over his parish. Far up in the northwest on the other side of the valley was Flodlycke at the edge of the forest. Something flashed in the trembling air. Was it a damp bucket of water at the fountain, or was it a harness?

Now the crowd parted ways. Herr Peder had already turned off on the path to the parsonage. Some of the peasants continued south, followed by a pair from beyond the parish who wanted to hurry on into the forest with the great news. A pair of peasants from Brohult remained. They had relatives in the church-village. So it happened that the majority stayed in the middle yard.

Herr Andreas waited in the village square for his ministerial brother to come back with his family. They turned into Seved's estate. Herr Andreas spoke good words to the peasant's wife. He was not entirely consistent at this point. At the funeral luncheons and weddings, he had often spoken bitter words against the wives of the clergy. But today, he made an exception. Though he wanted his parishioners to have a righteous abhorrence for married priests and their wives, today, he did not want any ill will toward Mother Margareta. The wife of the Seved's estate also seemed to very quickly get over her astonishment at receiving such an unexpected guest in the house. There was no great difference between them.

Then came the farewell. Herr Peder stood with his foot in the stirrup out among the mud puddles in the pasture where straw floated in dung water, and hens pecked at cow pies. He clumsily swung himself into the saddle, fixed his frock so that it laid well in the saddle, and waved one last time to Herr Andreas.

"See you soon . . . with peace in the land. Be careful of the horde . . . and watch yourself!"

"*Bonus pastor animam suam dat pro ovibus*,"[4] answered the rector with an enigmatic smile.

Herr Peder looked straight ahead for a minute.

"Yeah, that's right," he said. "A good shepherd gives his life for the sheep. *His* life—but not that of others."

He turned halfway in the saddle, bowed down and whispered:

"Whatever you do, Andreas, see to it that your parishioners in Fröjerum do not have to pay blood money. Justice will stand, with God's help, both the church and the kingdom will be saved. Only do not put justice at the end of a pike!"

Herr Andreas was quiet. There he stood in the blazing sun with the course black homespun sticking to his sweaty neck, within him he heard the wild alarm of the storm on the Eve of Epiphany. Herr Peder slept on his pillow that night. But there in the firelight his brother Martin had sat and said the very same thing. Martin thought more about the crown, Herr Peder thought more about the peasants. Did no one think about the church? Was no one concerned about justice?

"*Dominus tecum*,"[5] he said at last. "God's will be done."

Herr Peder grabbed hold of the chapped and knotted reins. The mare stepped slowly out between the gray sheds. It splashed and sloshed around the horse's hooves, and the mud that had already dried into a gray sock up to the hocks received a second coat. Just before the road which led out to the square he turned and yelled:

"Yes, God's will be done! And God's will is peace of mind and not uneasiness, says the prophet. *Pax tecum!*"[6]

Then he was gone.

Herr Andreas pulled the frock off his sweaty neck and walked slowly to the middle yard. Inside the cottage, there was a great gathering. The peasants from Brohults who had been at Kisa had had a great day. One cheerfully drank from the only pewter mug in

---

[4] "The good shepherd lays down his life for the sheep" (John 10:11).

[5] The Lord be with you.

[6] Peace be to you.

the cottage, and the other had found the wooden tankard with the immense bow handle that simulated two merged antlers and slipped over his hand when he drank. They crowed and bragged about the great victory and drank deep draughts for the fallen lords. A toast for Ellingen. One for Glasenap! And one for tall Herr Svana!

They invited the priest to come forward. Only now did he receive more information about what had happened. The Upland military had advanced along the Stång River. They made camp at Kisa. The German soldiers refused to go further if they did not get paid, and most of them were veterans from the German wars, and the top soldiers served for a double salary. They also wanted to count one more mark on each gulden than what the king wanted to concede. So there was an ongoing mess with their pay. Now it had become precarious at Kisa, the peasants had blockaded all the roads in a single night, and when the enemy sought to escape on a secret path, the peasants got to test their crossbows in the forest. The German soldiers did not stand their ground well. Before they were able to set their forks and get ready to shoot, their necks were full of bolts, and their long halberds with the splendid curved grooves just got stuck in the branches. It was a funny dance where the poorest peasant could get a nicer set of armor, and a prettier sword than the stupid keeper of the swanky horse farm in Kleva could ever have dreamed of buying.

A toast to the horse farmer!

Herr Andreas lifted his head and sat motionlessly.

A bell toll broke through the hum and thrum in the cottage's dim light, a hard and clear brassy toll, then another one, and then another. An endless silence followed in the cottage. Herr Andreas watched as mouths opened with shock over the tankard brims, froth clinging to the corners of their lips. Their dark and shiny eyes filled with bewilderment. Another three rings followed, then three more, and again three. Then the priest got up. This was a death knell. A death notification must have come to the village, and it was a man who was dead. It must have been a sudden death because no one had called on the priest.

Herr Andreas left without saying a word, and the men of the village followed just as quietly. Death's majesty immediately sobered their celebratory spirits.

Up in the steeple, the great bell had already begun to swing into the ring that would follow when the toll quit ringing. The ringer pulled with bitter rage, the hairy brown arms formed a single bundle of tendons and flexed muscle, his face had twisted into a distorted knot, and a single, golden brown tooth bit into his bottom lip. The bell kept ringing hard and wild until the priest got there.

"Who is this for?" cried Herr Andreas, as soon as he had passed through the churchyard wall.

The sexton pulled and pulled. Only when the bell was horizontal in the steeple did he release the rope. Panting heavily and with wild eyes he said:

"The bell, she tolls for the churchwarden of Flodlycke. For Jon Ebbeson, she rings. She rings for the revenge of a murdered man."

He caught his breath again, gasped, dried the beads of sweat from his forehead, and began to speak.

"The churchwarden followed the soldiers away from Flodlycke to show them the right way. So he took his leave. But Berent Ochse stayed after the others and said: Today you have maligned an officer of the King! The Devil take you! Then he ran his sword through Jon's bowels and throat and called to the soldiers, who chopped his head off and threw it between his legs. Then they left on their way. Torkel, Jon's second son, came running to Flodlycke with the news."

The priest sank to his knees in the grass while the man was still speaking. The peasants stood, dead quiet and bewildered. Here and there, they crossed themselves slowly.

Herr Andreas did not know what to say. His lips mumbled Latin prayers. He hardly knew himself. His eyes looked down and stubbornly adhered to the same chip on the main span of the bell tower, an old, dried and chapped chip with drips of tar on the edges. The sunshine was unspeakably warm and lovely, and the late summer air was heavy, saturated with rain and dew. The spirit of harvest and excitement permeated everything. But in Flodlycke, the churchwarden Jon Ebbeson lay dead, Jon of Flodlycke, the unarmed, the willing servant, the best of Fröjerum's people, shamefully murdered against faith and law.

Now justice was to be found only at the end of a pike! But it was the king, the unchristian tyrant who had been first to impale on his shiny weapons. There was only one answer to that. Had the bolts been able to try their case in court today at Askanäs, this would never have happened.

The great bell finished ringing. Still, one last toll followed long after the others. The air still reverberated with the after stroke.

Then the priest got up. His eyes looked far off, far out over the gathered parishioners, far out over the church hill, over the village of Flodlycke and the great forest behind it, far into the sunlit blue sky. Bloody flickers danced before his eyes again, the sword blade that fluttered over the village fell again. Now he knew what it meant. His face was pale and angular but shined with a gloss that did not just come from the sunlight and sweat. He lifted his right hand.

"Woe to the tyrant!" he cried. "Woe to the church thieves! Woe to the destroyers of convents, land usurpers, and plunderers of peasants! Woe to the mighty who has thousands upon thousands of sheep but takes the poor man's only lamb! Cursed be the king who dictates violence, who seizes silver from the altar, steers from the barns, and swine from the acorn pastures! Cursed is he who sics foreign bloodhounds on his own people! Now the wrath of God falls on King Gustav. Now the poor hills that have imbibed innocent blood cry. Now it is time to drive the oppressor out of the country as our fathers did before us! Ring, Lasse, ring as long as the bell holds. Call the people to arms! Ring so that it is heard in Årtebol and Spannarp. Ring so that they blockade the roads in Drängsmarken again. Why do you stand here?"

He stared at the peasants.

"Why are you standing here? Berent Ochse still walks free in the woods. Run to Askanäs! Row across the lake! Before morning dawns, all the people to Ödesjö and Näs will know what happened. When Berent Ochse wakes in the morning, he will have a hundred drawn crossbows waiting in the forest. None of us here are worthy of life so long as the oath-breaker goes unpunished."

He was panting when the peasants broke free from their paralysis and bitterness began to find expression. They cried out to each other and began to beat the churchyard with heavy thuds where they stood. And then they stomped off toward their farms with clenched lips. They did not tarry long before they again rushed downhill to the lake with rattling armor and helmets.

Herr Andreas had fallen before the great beam, where the main strut connected with the gigantic center post in the bell tower. His lips murmured over and over again.

Pie Jesu Domine, dona ei requiem, dona ei requiem . . .[7] His thoughts were in Flodlycke.

Both bells had begun to ring again. They would not cease until the last ray of light faded out, and the cool night air of autumn crept out from the marshy meadows.

* * *

A single light breeze fluttered across Lake Mälaren and shattered its mirror image of the Gråmunkelholmen's[8] round defense tower. Otherwise, the wide expanse of water lay completely still, golden and enigmatic under the flaming western sky.

Scrivener Martin enjoyed the tranquility as he sauntered along the southern hills alone. The last week had been nasty and stressful. Every day new stacks of illegible concepts and drafts, urgent letters about inspections and salary, petitions to the general in Östergötland and Upland, letters of admonition and injunction to bailiffs and commanders, to miners at Salberget, to Herr Svante in Stegeborg, Herr Måns in Bro, to Göstav Olson, Lars Siggesson, Söverin Kiil, and a hundred others. The whole of this summer had been a witch's dance. By Trinity Sunday, everyone knew that Dacke had gone to the forest and gathered a host of random people around him. On top of it all, His Grace had been sick, suspicious, and unreasonable. He had finally departed for Söderköping the day before yesterday. Now a person could breathe again.

Scrivener Martin stood high up on the cool stone slabs between the twisted dwarf pine trees and looked out over the city. To the left stood a few windmills like black silhouettes against the gold evening sky, down below him were a pair of low hill cabins made from gray knotted timber and surrounded by cabbage gardens. Even farther down, the evening's golden light fell colorfully and warm upon the battlements of Södre Port and the fortress roundabout. The embrasures

[7] Faithful Lord Jesus, give him peace.

[8] This island is now called Riddarholmen.

and moat were deep in the shade, a strip of water showed clearly and shiny as heaven between the heavy earthen embankments. The city of islets swam in the middle of the motionless water, a conglomeration of redbrick walls that flickered like flames in the evening light and green turf roofs with a glimmer of copper brown at the bottom against which chimneys contrasted like white scores. Amid this clutter of houses and gables rose St. Nikolai, which seemed to spread its immense roof like protecting wings over the city. The tower watched vigilantly over the water, and it lifted his sharp needle-like spire high above the horizon. Just a bit further away was the royal palace, piled up with her impressive round tower. Behind that was the dark forest of the northern lands.

Scrivener Martin loved to drift about up here among the hills. He did not thrive in the hustle and bustle of the city. Up here, he was almost as alone as when he was a boy running barefoot in the hills above Askanäs. The lake there lay just as shiny before his feet. The hills were just as steep so that from up above one could look down on the tops of the tallest pines, and the forests were quiet and dark around the water in the evening.

Today he had sat in the warm scrivener's cottage and yearned. There he heard nothing but the tramp of the newly arrived soldiers through the window, drums beating, and the quartermasters screaming with their sharp voices as they sorted out the rolls. New and great reinforcements would go south tomorrow. Martin had written the report from the castle bailiff concerning the newly arrived grain shipments from Finland. He had almost quarreled with him to get him to stop asking about the dried pike and the remaining hops. People never dared to act on their own! The king would rant and rave and say that the bailiff had lumpy black porridge in his head when he asked him about such things.

Today as he spent the time sitting and writing about the Finnish grain shipments and the bishop's visitation from Delsbo and the missing oxen, his thoughts had flown out through the open blue window and found company with the sparrows that fluttered around the roof. As soon as he finished the work, he hurried down over the drawbridge to Österlånggatan[9] and made his way out of the city. Now he sat here on the slope and exhaled.

---

[9] A main thoroughfare in Gamla Stan, or the old town of Stockholm.

The air was still warm and completely still. The hill under him began to cool, but if the birches down by the shore had not already changed to a golden yellow, he might have believed that it was an August evening. He let his eyes sweep over the landscape to the north, which quickly descended into dusk. It was hard to remain in Stockholm now. Time after time, he heard familiar names mentioned in reports from the south. They were heart-stopping. Orders went out to Herr Måns to take Kinda and quash the rebellion. News came that the priest in Brohult gave a speech inciting insurrection. And a few weeks ago he had picked up in passing that it was now so hostile in Holaveden that a couple of fähnleins consisting of soldiers from Holstein and some Swedish men of arms who were supposed to meet up with the royal commander's force in Jönköping never made it any further than Fröjerum.

This time he felt himself go pale. Since then, his body had been so uneasy that he had trouble managing.

Once again, he let his eyes sweep along the jagged outline of the hills that stood dark and impenetrable against the darkening day. The heights around his home were just as dark, but higher and wilder. The plain next to the lake sat like a bright star weaving its tips into the dark wilderness. Just now, clear cuts must lie as drab as unbleached linen, visible in the dusk like bright blisters on the forest's dark forehead. In the middle of this bright star sat a square gemstone, this was Askanäs. What did it look like at home now? And what was Anders doing? The crazy papist—had he let himself get carried away in the uprising? And what did the neighbors do—his childhood friends who were now farmers on the estates, Sune and Elif and Tall Staffan and Erik of Dikareby?

He had crossed his arms over his knees and put his chin on his wrist. Far off, a single bird flew to the south over Långholmen. He envied it.

There was scraping on the stone behind him. Someone was approaching. He saw the dark contours of a single man between the twisted pines. It was a peasant with loose pants and a large coat. Martin turned again to the city.

The stranger came closer as the scrivener eyed him suspiciously. Now he could see the man's face in the dusk, a large, childlike face with blond eyebrows, watchful gray eyes, and a pair of nervous folds around his nose that sometimes flattened out. The scrivener looked at him with amazement.

"Kort, is that you? What are you doing here?"

"I thought it was you," said the other. "What are you doing here?"

The scrivener did not try to get up. Kort Lange was a scrivener like himself, a native Stockholmer with German ancestry, a calm and honest companion. He had worked in the chancellery until August. Then he had disappeared. Martin had never learned the reason.

"Come and sit . . . Where are you living now? Why did you quit the chancellery?"

The other sat down.

"God commanded me to do it," he said.

Martin looked at him, bewildered. The man just stared straight out over the city with his deep-set eyes peering out from under his bushy blondish white eyebrows. It was hard to say what he thought.

"God? How do you know that?"

"Do you not have a conscience, Martin?"

"That I have."

"Perhaps, but it has been obscured. Is your heart not sickened by your work?"

"Yeah, there have been plenty of travails with it this summer. Writing until you get a cramp in your arm, and then taking abuse on top of it all, until the backbone is twisted."

"You see the fault of others, but not your own."

"What do you mean?"

"You are guilty, yourself. Why do you bear false witness with your pen?"

"What are you babbling about?"

"Every day, you write things that are not true. Satan's black blood flows through your pen. It flows in poisoned streams throughout the land."

He had turned to Scrivener Martin. He spoke slowly and somewhat in monotone. His face was turned from the light and hard to discern. His eyes had flashed white for a second, but now they were shut. His eyes almost seemed disgusted, but he still spoke with intrusive gravity.

"I tried to the very last to be faithful, but God showed me that I should be faithful to him instead. Do you remember the letter concerning the Scotts that I showed you this summer? Do you remember how His Grace commanded the citizens to swindle their gold as an advance while he offered them beautiful speeches and empty smack all the while thinking of how he could get his hands on it? Do you believe I could ever have been saved if I continued to write such letters? Do you remember the grain tax which would have been raised from the Nylanders after the Åbo bushels, but would be sold again after Stockholm's which is less? How many times have you written to bailiffs this summer telling them to promise the peasants whatever they want but calm them down? There is no authority above me, says His Grace, if he only comes to terms with the Smålanders, then the Östgoths will learn to be happy. This treachery is not right. It is in the service to Satan that such things are written . . ."

"Was that *why* you left the chancellery?"

"Yes, that was it. My poor soul was in danger. God spoke to me in a dream. He commanded me to leave the path of Satan."

Scrivener Martin felt a bit awkward and tried to change the subject.

"Why do you dress like a peasant?" he asked.

"Because a Christian must leave the world and swear off all of its vanity. Do you believe heaven's gates would ever open for ruffled collars and harem pants? Do you believe one meets such silver-trimmed doors in the heavens like in a castle courtyard? I went down that path once—just like you do now. But God's spirit commanded me to leave Sodom."

"Sodom? Is that what the royal palace is?"

Kort Lange made a slow hand movement out over the city.

"Sodom is there. Have you heard the coarse oaths of the nobility on the castle steps—that is Sodom! Have you seen the whoredom in the alleys? Have you listened to the racket and brawling in the taverns? Have you seen the women—with hairpieces and silk gloves and lace even on Sunday? The flirtatious playing with the eyes in the middle of the Storkyrkan! That is Sodom!"

Scrivener Martin looked at his former coworker with rising bewilderment. He felt awkward and was quiet. The other continued with a stubbornly persuasive voice:

"You should take God's word more to heart, Martin. You call yourself evangelical, but you know no more about God's true gospel than the clouded papists. See . . . we read the Scripture, the whole great Bible . . ."

"We . . . who is we?"

"Oh, I forgot to say: I work with Gert Hubmaier now, in his scrivener office. He is a truly evangelical man. The light came to him many years ago, when God sent the great Livonian prophet to us . . ."

"What are you prattling about?"

"About Melchior Buntmakare, you know! The most powerful preacher that ever spoke in Stockholm . . ."

"Do you mean Melchior Hoffman, who made all that mischief before the council of the realm in Västerås on New Year's Day?"

"He didn't make any mischief! That was some mob misusing his name. He only wanted to purify worship from the idolatrous graven images, vestments, and altars. He only did what Master Olaus wants to do but does not dare to do. He brought many to their senses here in the city, many who from that day have carried the Spirit's light, both Gorius Holste and Hans Bökman, and Lukas Bårdskäre too."

"Ah, so that is the rabble that you have fallen in with!"

Apparently, the other man had prepared for this objection. He spoke earnestly:

"Yes, they have been accused of a lot of evil, but that is not the truth. They were quiet and serious men who only wanted to follow God's Spirit without pretense and falsehood."

Scrivener Martin felt uncomfortable. He could not quite remember what exactly the case was against Gorius Holste and his entourage, but the main thing was treason. Was it not an actual attempt on the king's life? He stood up.

"I'm going home now," he said shortly. "Do not speak of traitors and assassins if you want my company."

"You judge by the eye," Kort said, "you like all the others. So did I at one time. But the Spirit opened my eyes and gave me the new light. You ought to concern yourself more with the word of God, Martin."

They climbed through the crevices down the mountain. The first stars of the night sky started to shine above them. The water's golden mirror had darkened to silver and then a blackish blue. A few shining lights glimmered down in the city. The scrivener was quiet. Kort Lange kept close to him, and when they reached level ground, he took up the thread again with the same stubborn persistence.

"Martin, you call yourself evangelical, but you do not live according to the gospel. Or is it not right that you have not yet paid the merchant from Lübeck in the Tyska Brinken[10] for the mittens as you promised?"

"Is it true that you spend your money on Spanish wine and prostitutes? Was it right that you cursed the wine merchant's employee when it was actually your fault that you ran into each other on the street?"

"How do you know all that?"

"I only know a tiny bit of that which the entire city knows. But have you never cared about what God knows? You sit and listen to Lasse Helsing's uncouth stories, and you laugh, and you tell a murderously unchaste story yourself. If your mother had been in the room, you would never have spoken of such things. But now it was only Lasse Helsing and the bartender, Gert Lampe and a few rough customers—and the Lord Jesus. He sat in the empty stool just behind you, and he listened and shook his head."

"Martin, you live in darkness—and yet you have God around about you, and over you. You believe that you sin in secret, but when you blow out the light, God's great clear eye burns above you in the dark. You believe that you are alone with your thoughts and rule freely over the pictures in your heart, but you stand before God, who placed you in the sunshine in the middle of the palace yard. There you commit your sin, openly and shamelessly before eternal and incorruptible witnesses!"

They had come down to the flat headland just before Södre Port. They crossed the moat at the roundel and approached the drawbridge outside the external port tower. The scrivener went ahead with a long stride. Kort Lange followed him like a shadow. His voice sounded just as subdued as it was tenacious.

---

[10] *Tyska* is Swedish for "German," and *brinken* means "slope." Tyska brinken was the name of a street in Stockholm named for the German parish church that was the center of a German community in Stockholm.

"Martin, you are fleeing. Just like I did. I fled for weeks and months, saying: I am a Christian. I am a baptized Christian. I believe everything that a Christian shall believe, and it is faith that makes a man righteous before God. I listened to Master Olaus. I went to the scriptures. I was as good a Christian as anyone I knew. And yet there was a fire that burned within me, day and night. It was the Lord's angel that beat me and said: One thing you are still lacking."

They had passed the port vaults and came out into the city. The air which had been harsh and cold out on the headland now stood lame and lukewarm between the walls of houses, filled with the strong smells of wastewater between the cobblestones, and from the innumerable dark alleyways where bright tallow candles burned between stacked sacks, over cards and dice and beer-stained corner tables or through hearth smoke in sooty middle-class kitchens.

Kort Lange took the scrivener by the arm and whispered:

"You ought to concern yourself more with God's word, Martin. Now the plague is near. Perhaps the fourth horseman will ride through the dark even tonight, he who rides the black horse . . ."

"What do you mean?"

"You should concern yourself more with God's word, Martin. Have you not read about the seven seals in Revelation? First comes the rider on the white horse. He is the prophet, he has a bow in his hand with the arrows of God's word, and he rides out to win. He has already visited us, though only the chosen saw it. Then comes the rider on the red horse. And to him was given that he should take peace from the earth and that they should all kill themselves as they do now at Kronoberg and Linköping. And to him was given a huge sword, and that now rages with its bloody edge from Söderköping to Kalmar. But then comes the rider on the black horse, and he has a pair of scales in his hand, for he brings famine and costly times. And of him says a voice among the four creatures: a day's wages for a quart of wheat, and a day's wages for three measures of barley, and don't touch the oil and wine. Do you know what that means? The hard times are already upon us. Money is without value. The king may order all he wants and what the örtuge should buy; he cannot stop Scripture from being fulfilled as it is written. The distress in the land shall be so great that a measure of barley costs three days' wages, and oil and wine and all the foreign goods shall not be had for money. It will not harm the fulfillment of prophecy as it is written. But when the fourth rider comes—and he comes soon!—then a fourth of the kingdom's inhabitants shall perish, for he rides on the pale horse who has the color of a corpse and his name is death, and hell follows after him."

They had come a long way up Västerlånggatan. Above them, the pale twilight still shimmered. Kort Lange had not let go of the scrivener's arm.

"Martin," he said, "come with me up to Gert Hubmaier, then we will read the Bible together . . ."

"No," said the scrivener hard and shook himself loose, "if he has anything to do with Gorius Holste, then I am wary of sticking my neck under the executioner's ax."

"Judge not without a hearing, Martin! A year ago, I would have answered the same as you."

"And after a year and for all eternity, I plan to answer in the same way."

"God does miracles, and he shall open your eyes . . ."

"Good night, Kort. Watch yourself with the *schwarmerei*!"[11]

"You should concern yourself more with God's word, Martin. Good night to you!"

He disappeared down Långgatan. The scrivener fumbled his way through the alley and came up to his room. He could look out over Lake Mälaren and the Södra Bergen through his little roof window. The lake still mirrored the weak light from the west. Gråmunkekyrka on the island stood completely black against the horizon with her ridged turrets sharply contrasted against the fading day.

He felt ill at ease. No man had ever before spoken to him like Kort Lange. He ought to have laughed at him and given him a kick in the ass. And yet . . . Kort Lange was at least right about one thing.

---

[11] *Schwarmerei* is a word Luther used for various fanatical religious movements, perhaps similar to the way people use the term *holy roller* today. It was used for such people who felt led by the Spirit beyond the words of Scripture. The word is actually recognized in English as a German loanword but has fallen out of use. For the purposes of this book though, it cannot be simply replaced with "fanatic," as in other treatises. It is meant to conjure the image of bees swarming around a beehive.

Day after day, he walked with great uncertainty. The great work that should give the kingdom statutes and security, he had never seen so far from completion as now. The whole of Småland was in full rebellion. The Östgötlanders vacillated, and the Upplanders and Dalecarlians were unreliable. In the south, old King Christian and Berent von Melen and all the prelates[12] who had become refugees stuck their fingers in the pie. People said that they exchanged letters with Dacke, yes, that the emperor himself smelled an opportunity to help the papists. The King himself was out of sorts, discouraged, and the whole realm suffered. When he was at his worst, he spoke of buying himself a duchy in Germany and calling it quits with the worries for these Swedes who were as stubborn to drive as untamed oxen.

It was also a fact now that the king had not had any success since the German chancellor had come into his service. He lacked his old touch with the people, he should control everything himself, and because it was impossible for him, he had to rely on subordinates who had power but no discretion. That King Gustavus judged and guided was one thing. He had risked life and limb for the sake of the realm when no one else dared to come forward. But then a foreigner like this Pyhy came along with his stuck-up nose and domineering manner. In turn, the people refused.

Martin looked out the window again, while he chewed on a piece of coarse bread. Off in the west shown a thin slice of moon. It was a particularly bright new moon. This evening, excited eyes would look out over the yard at home, off over the uneven ends of gable beams and roof ridges and up to the darkening night sky. In Askanäs and Flodlycke and Årtebol, young mothers and boys would secretly kneel and bow and wish for something that was their heart's most secret desire.

What was Anders doing this evening? He wondered. What was the upright Jon of Flodlycke doing? What were the millers Karin and Sexton Petrus and the people in Sevedsgården doing? Why did he

---

[12] King Christian thought this might be his chance to retake Sweden. Berent Von Melen was an adventurer who had double-crossed King Gustav. There were bishops and priests who found themselves as refugees both in Denmark and various German trading towns, Danzig being the most prominent, who also plotted to retake land and positions in Sweden.

feel such a strange uneasiness and homesickness? This evening he almost wished that he had never been a scrivener or resident in the mercantile city, but sat as a peasant in Askanäs, a true peasant with black hairy hands and hunched back.

He went to lie down and drew the comforter over himself. As usual, he prayed the evening prayer he had learned from his mother:

God's archangel guards our home,
In his hand, the lamp's flickering flame
And His other holds life's tome,
In his arms, he bears Jesus' frame
And so we sleep in Jesus' name.

"Amen," he added and shut his eyes. But peace did not come. With this exception, the evening prayer had always brought him comfort. It was like a charm against all evil. He had never really thought through who it was that he prayed to in this old childhood prayer.

But this evening, peace never came. At first, Martin blamed it all on Dacke for troubling his home village and the future. But then he admitted the truth to himself: Kort Lange had gotten to his conscience. There was a barb in there and it ached.

He turned heavily toward the wall to sleep. It was now completely dark around him. But above him in the dark burned God's bright eye, an ever-open eye that let his jealous and piercing gaze rest on him, uninvited, unavoidable, and powerful enough to explore all the hidden secrets.

ON THE DAY OF WRATH

February 1543

Herr Johan Turesson, the royal councilor, got up from his chair and paced back and forth while he read. He fidgeted with his closed fist in the air and hissed as he breathed through clenched teeth. His eyes were fixed on the paper the whole time.

Scrivener Martin kept a watchful eye on him from his corner. He knew that the great sheet contained the King's exciting prospective manifesto that he planned to issue to the public in Östergötland and Småland in the new year. He had difficulty controlling his curiosity.

Now Herr Johan sat down again, tossed the paper on the table, and continued reading with his back hunched over, while both fists pounded the tabletop, and the whole of his weather-beaten face was wrinkled together in one broad grin.

"Oh, you precious Jeremiah! This should suit their taste! A royal party for our sour bellied papists from Vadstena. Now they get it, they scream for everything old and ancient. Funny, funny . . ."

He had folded his hands over his stomach and rocked back and forth. At last, he was ready to share.

"You should hear this:

> "We have understood that a public outcry has arisen, that the peasants request that which is old and ancient by which they mean the reduction of taxes . . .
>
> "When the general government's rate of interest is reduced, then it will follow that one receives fewer men of war in the kingdom. Thereby the government's enemies will have prime opportunity to revisit the country—an old and ancient custom! It seems useful to us and to be a good custom that the kingdom should be strengthened

> with numerous good and capable men of war, similarly excellent guns and swords which have not been customary from of old before us. And with such an excellent group of warriors comes a great cost, much greater than what old custom is accustomed to paying. One does not want to consider this but always cries for old custom . . ."

Herr Johan stretched his legs out comfortably so that the spurs cut wood splinters out of the floor, laughed again, and continued to read some examples:

> "What the kingdom benefited from such old customs we give for your consideration. Merchants were robbed of ships and goods. The people were thrown overboard and drowned like dogs. Events such as these were common in both the era of King Hans and in King Christian's era also, along with murder and arson; these are also old customs! From that time, many Swedish men lay like dogs and rams and did not have to enter the churchyard. And so we put it before our understanding, faithful Swedish men, to consider if these old customs of our fatherland are useful . . ."

The royal councilor made another jump and fired the final point:

> "So, dear Danneman,[1] it is our hope that no one with reason or right shall with truth say anything other than that we have taken care of our poor fatherland and the common man with all fidelity. And we will not answer alone in this world before people but also before the highest judgment, which is God's righteous judgment who is righteous and knows all truth . . ."

The royal councilor had pulled his boots under the stool again and sat up in a courtlier fashion that fit the solemn conclusion. He laid the mandate on the table and slapped the palm of his hand on his leather pants.

---

[1] A term used for the representatives of peasants.

"That ought to oil things up—even for our arch papists here in Vadstena and Linköping! As filled and occupied as they are with visions of St. Brita and the Virgin Mary's milk! His Grace knows how to deal with such people."

Scrivener Martin nodded in appreciation. These were the king's ways, his old straightforward thinking concerning his old people, which the common people will understand and like. It was a different tone than all the boisterous "Our Royal Authority," which entered the land with the German Royal Councilors. This would play well in the countryside. He could see Fröjerum's peasants gathered on the church hill with matted beards, dented helmets, and a wise watchful glimmer in their watery blue eyes. A speech like that would make an impression on them—if only his brother Andreas didn't naysay the good impression afterward.

Martin returned to his work with the rolls, clapping his heels against each other under the table. The floor was cold, and it was drafty in this makeshift scrivener cottage housed in a gable room of the parsonage. The whole of Vadstena had been made a fortified camp for the winter housing troops with the priests and monks and even in the convent. He could count himself lucky that at least he was regularly under the roof of a habitable house.

He had now been here for just over a week. When it became apparent that Dacke did not intend to keep "the chicken peace" that began in October after the defeat in Kisa, but that the war would blow up again, he had not been able to control himself and asked to follow the commander into the field. The king granted this request because he was born and raised here and could be useful for his knowledge of northern Småland's forested tracts. Now he sat here as a sort of secretary to the Supreme Quartermaster, Herr Peder Brahe. Before his departure he had received instruction from His Grace himself: he was to keep an eye on the young Herr Per so that he would be sparing on money and preferably also on the expensive Spanish wine that he had sent so that the war commander did not drink it all, but save it for the soldiers who deserved to drink courage for their legs when it came time for a decisive tussle with Dacke.

From Nyköping, he took up company with Måns Bryntesson, chamber scrivener, who now sat in front of him at the oak table and manipulated the goose quill with frozen blue fingers. He had hardly looked up from his paper while the royal councilor read. Måns had had a hard day today. He was to clear up the hopelessly tangled accounts of interest rates from Aska and Dal. Here the bailiffs had now run the whole day, but not one could be the wiser concerning what they had collected, what was rightfully replaced with money, and what they donated on dubious grounds or let disappear into their pockets. And now the king had demanded to receive an orderly report before the Sunday of Oculi and threatened to otherwise pour wax and tar on the heads of both bailiffs and scriveners for burning tapers.[2] It was thus only human if today Måns Bryntesson was not inclined to admire His Grace's gracious eloquence, where he sat and hunched over his neatly lined page and his hopelessly tangled smudging.

Herr Johan had continued to dig in the big bag that came from Gripsholm. He pulled out three more letters, laid aside two, and broke open the third.

Scrivener Martin wrote and listened. He now had an immense desire for all sorts of news. This time he did not have to wait long. Herr Johan looked up from the paper and turned directly to him.

"Martin, do you think we might have a couple of great seals in the camp?"

"The High Steward's is the greatest I have seen. What do you need them for?"

Herr Johan smiled again with his broad smile.

"It shall be set here next to the Dalecarlian seal and make it out to be Helsingland's or Lappland's or Moscovian, or whatever can give the matter a greater reputation among the forest thieves. His Grace wants to prepare a proper bit of roguery for them. Here he has gotten his hands on a letter from the Dalecarlians where it says that common men and mountain men have sent out a large army to punish the traitors because the Dalecarlians are citizens of the realm just like the Smålanders and do not want to suffer the destruction of their fatherland by a dishonorable highwayman, who can apparently keep three wives but has never been able to keep his word. So, they

---

[2] *Tåperier*, an archaic Swedish term used often by Gustav Vasa as a derogatory term for Catholicism. It referenced the ritualistic burning of tapers, or slender candles.

have now sent a fähnlein to Östergötland to help the king, and after that, they shall send ten more so that they will come with as many people as there are junipers between Norra Vedbo and Kinnevald."

He held up the paper and smiled like a bridegroom.

"And now His Grace commands that we immediately within the hour find two of the most wretched souls in little Niels Hansson's Dalecarlian Fähnlein, the two who are the most foul-mouthed of them all, and give them money so that they can swagger like chieftains among the people and send them down to Holaveden to stir Lententide joy among Dacke's collaborators. Haha! Were I not gouty in my old legs, I would run with them just to hear it!"

He rubbed his hands.

"How is it with the seals?" he added.

"We should wait for Herr Lars to come," said the scrivener evasively. He had become serious again. He wished that he could be just as delighted as Herr Johan over the king's plans. But ever since the evening last fall when he met Kort Lange, he had a wound in his soul that bled at the smallest provocation. Was this right? Should one falsify records and send out imposters, even against rebels?

Once again, he saw the peasants of Fröjerum before him, gathered on the church hill where they listened with open mouths to the strangers, and doubtfully thumbed the wax seals under the writing. Was it right of a king to have fun with his own people? And if now his brother, the cunning papist, revealed all the fun?

He sat still and looked straight ahead. His gaze had come to rest on the great sheet of parchment, on which a bailiff recorded his scribbled accounts. It was apparently a fragment from some Latin Mass book. He could just barely see a blood-red flower interlaced in a capital D. He absent-mindedly read on further: *Deus in adiutorium meum*[3] was written across the top. He could finish the rest himself: "Make haste to help me, O Lord."

He suddenly became attentive. He repeated the prayer to himself over and over again. Far away he heard the echo of the schoolboy's song under the vaulted ceiling of the cathedral. The old, monotone melody faded far down in the huge church. At the time, he had hardly

[3] God come to my assistance. (The word that introduces the hourly prayers.)

even thought that this was a real prayer. Now it suddenly took on life and meaning for him, where he sat and mumbled it over and over again: *Domine, ad adiuvandum me festina.*[4] This was just what he needed: that God would now come and help him. But God did nothing, he said nothing, he only watched. Everywhere, night and day, he now felt his burning eye over him. Every time something did not go right, he turned his accusing eye on him. It seemed to suck him into his guilt, put it somewhere in his repository, and turned to him again, just as burning and just as unmistakably clear-sighted.

He was interrupted in his contemplation by the sound of hooves clattering against the frozen ground outside. The body of a horse obscured the small gable end window, and heavy, wooden-soled boots kicked the snow off the stone steps. It was either a courier or a report man. Such came and went day in and day out.

Martin stuck his foot out and pushed the door open to help the rider find his way. He tromped in, white with hoarfrost in his beard, thumbed his hat, and inquired after the supreme quartermaster.

"He is out," said Herr Johan genially. "You can deal with me instead. Where are you coming from?"

"From Herr Måns, who stays with the soldiers at Hof. He has learned from the pastor in Appuna that Dacke's camp is by Skrukeby."

Herr Johan whistled and fiddled with his whiskers.

"Then there will be a fun little dance here. How many forest thieves can there be?"

"Twenty or thirty thousand, they say. They have been swarming out of the forest all day long, and still, it is only thought to be half the party."

Herr Johan became serious.

"Do they plan to go to Vadstena?"

"Lord, they plan to hunt all the officers up in Kolmården and all the soldiers they plan to put under the ice in Bråviken so that the king can save them till summer and ship them frozen to Germany when the waters open up again, now that he is so skilled in trade and business and has so diligently pondered what is best for the nation. That is what Dacke's scouts said in Väderstad yesterday."

---

[4] Lord, hasten to my salvation.

Scrivener Martin could not help but smile. He knew the tone from his childhood drinking beer at the church festivals. It was no good to keep up with the old men when they began to jest. The king's Dalecarlians would have to be pretty forward with their muzzles if they were to have any success in Ydre and Vedbo.

Herr Johan was no longer smiling. He stuck out his bottom lip and sat reclined with his arms resting on the armrests.

"Did you get any more information?"

"Yes, of course, that Herr Måns returns with a fähnlein before the evening because he cannot defend Hovgården if Dacke departs tonight."

Herr Johan nodded hesitantly.

"A nice story, this . . . follow me. We will go right to the commander."

He got up, fastened on his sword, took the leather hood from the hook, and the worn gloves from the table. He did not look happy.

Martin twisted around in the stool, reached his arm out, and pulled the door shut after they departed. Then he got up, rubbed his hands against each other, and went over to open the other door, that which led to the kitchen. The room where they worked had no fireplace, but pinewood crackled in the kitchen hearth. A lone soldier stood and stirred the iron pot of cabbage soup long into the evening. It steamed hot and strong. Scrivener Martin let the damp steam waft into the gable room that had caused Herr Johan to command the men to keep the door shut earlier. Herr Johan did not like cabbage soup.

The chamber scrivener looked up from his paper, grimaced, and asked:

"Do you think that Dacke will come to Vadstena?"

He continued without waiting for an answer:

"I wish he would come here and burn the whole city and these papers too. For all I care, he could burn both Stockholm's Castle and all the nation's accounts and His Grace too so that no one could snoop about and find anything in the ashes."

Martin Ragnvaldsson became angry.

"Whatever are you whining about?! Do you want the kingdom's defeat just so you can escape the inconvenience of writing a decent index?"

The chamber scrivener looked long and hard at his colleague.

"Do you believe that it is only about me?! Take a look at your accounts! Do you not see mania there? Forty thousand marks for the Knutmass and sixty thousand for the Candlemas . . . There's a waterfall of silver running through the camp, and almost all of it goes to foreign soldiers. Everyday costs more than ten great estates. Everything the king collected from the churches in all of Småland and Östergötland has gone just as quickly to soldier's salary."

Martin Ragnvaldsson was quiet. He had gasped when he heard what the salary had climbed to currently. Almost all the Germans were double-wagers, the best and most expensive warriors that ever existed. The chamber scrivener continued:

"Don't you think that this is insanity and mismanagement? First, His Grace plunders the churches for their silver, and the peasants go mad enough to take up arms. Then His Grace recruits expensive foreign mercenaries to force the peasants into keeping the peace. Then all the silver goes to the Landsknechts as payment for chopping the heads off of Swedish men. When the dance is over, the churches are empty and plundered, His Grace's treasury is plundered and empty, the peasants are plundered and decapitated, and the foreign mercenaries travel home to Germany with all the church silver in their pockets. Is there any rhyme or reason to such a story?"

Scrivener Martin wanted to answer, but at that very same moment, he heard hoofbeats in the yard again. He went and looked out through the frozen windows and then hurried back, closed the kitchen door, and sat down again at his workstation. The chamber scrivener looked at him scornfully:

"Shouldn't you find a couple of seals too?"

Out in the yard, he heard the noise of men getting out of their saddles, and the light rattling and crackling of horse tackle being gathered up. The door swung open, and both the scrivener and the chamber scrivener flew up from their chairs. It was Peder Brahe himself, the Supreme Quartermaster, in company with Johan Turesson, Arved Trolle, Lars Siggesson, and even a couple men from the Council of the Realm. Herr Peder was a very young lord, not much over twenty years. The skin of his cheeks, red like apples from the cold, could be seen through his thin beard. A sense of emergency appeared about his mouth. His eyebrows furrowed in deliberation as he fixed his eyes. He spoke heavily.

"This will not do! I try to make a decent impression for the fähnlein: arquebusiers for them, crossbows for them, halberds for them. But immediately, there arises a cursed race for requests. Anders wants to pair up with Oluff, and Oluff wants to pair up with Per, and they all come to me and complain. Per has the butter tub, and Oluff has the tinder box, and Anders has the leg of lamb so that I cannot separate them! God's death and suffering! Can I order my people according to butter boxes, jars of jam, and flour bags? Does not war require guns, swords, and halberds? What is this for war readiness? I would assign the majority of them to the *forlorn hope*[5] and let them run like sheep to their villages. But the light infantry would be diminished, and the fähnlein would be hardly half strength!"

The lords had entered the room, loosened their baldrics, and blew in their cold blue fists. Herr Johan waved calmly with his large worn leather mittens.

"Calm, calm, dear Per, as it has gone before, so it goes now also. The chief thing is that the battle is on open ground and not in the forest. If the men can see the banners, then they hold together. But we must buy some time for us to practice a little with them."

"And that is why I want for us to retreat from Vadstena,"

Herr Peder interrupted, "I have heard enough now. And I know my reasons. If the whole force runs with the council of the realm and the commander at the head to Linköping, then it will be said that no one dares to oppose Dacke in all of Östergötland. Then there will be rebellion even up in Helsingland and before the Day of Our Lady! Either we take Dacke by the beard while he is here in open land, or we don't take him at all."

He threw his gloves on the table so that the finger plates rattled. He blew into his great coarse fists again. Herr Johan mumbled

---

[5] The forlorn hope was a specific military regiment often tasked with first assaults and the toughest fighting. Different countries and militaries at different times had various ways of defining the forlorn hope. Often it was made up from the ranks of diminished squadrons, conscripts from prison and irregularly trained men.

something about being cautious and at least sending out scouts, but the colonel disrespectfully cut him off.

"We pull Dacke out of bed tomorrow. It starts tonight. An hour after Midnight."

He turned to the scriveners who still sat at the table.

"Done for today and out with you. Martin, you will follow me tonight. Be at hand to write orders. An hour after midnight outside the city hall. Go get some sleep! Now, war command, gather around me."

He had turned to the young lords. The scriveners gathered together their implements and tumbled out clumsily because they had been sitting so long in the cold.

A wet, cold wind tore in from the lake where the heavy, low gray-blue sky looked threatening. A snowflake danced here and there between the houses.

Scrivener Martin went down to the square to find the inn where he normally ate with some of the command. A few sleds squealed on by in the snow loaded down with sacks and barrels. They were on their way east. The drivers sat together like ruffled birds, powdered with snow.

Just as the last sled slid by one of the occupants looked up. A pair of bushy eyebrows looked out from under a leather hood and fixed a watery blue gaze on Martin Ragnvaldsson. Suddenly, the traveler hopped out the sled and hurried over to him.

"Kort!" cried the scrivener with amazement. "What are you doing in Vadstena? You always show up where one least expects it!"

"Business trip," answered the other matter of factly. "Now, I am on my way to Skeninge."

He had kept the scrivener's outstretched hand in his. His voice was quietly appealing.

"I'm staying there a few days with Gregor the barber-surgeon, just behind Our Lady's church. Could you not visit?"

"Impossible. I have no time. It begins here tomorrow."

"One has time for everything important. You ought to consider the state of your soul more, Martin. Right now, there are many of us evangelical brothers in Skeninge. We usually gather at Gregor's. You should come along sometime."

Martin was quiet. Kort heard the sled whistle around the corner further on and looked Martin over, pressed the scrivener's hand and said once more:

"Come before it is too late."

Then he ran off after the sled.

* * *

Dazed and frozen, Martin went out into the winter night. He had slept in the priest's kitchen, on the on top of the stove that had retained the warmth from the oven. Now he was shivering as he walked down to the place where Herr Peder's adjutants had already saddled.

There had been a change in the weather. The wind had abated, and it was snowing. Large soft flakes landed like a sheer blanket over the frozen crust.

Scrivener Martin sat down heavily in the saddle and looked up at the night sky. He felt the flakes tickle as they fell on his face. Around him, he saw only a soft grayish haze that faded into the black night, wherever one tried to penetrate it.

He rode slowly through the gate. He would have rather trotted in order to stay warm, but he was afraid of running someone down in the street. He could hear the soft tramping of feet in the snow everywhere. A stallion neighed, and his own answered. Far off, someone carried a torch that shined red and fluttered between the dancing snowflakes.

Everything was chaos down in the square. The soldiers shoved and shouted without finding their banners—sleds and oxcarts with their high-pitched squeaks parked in the streets all around. Little Niels Hansson, chief of the Dalecarlian Fähnlein, could be heard through all the noise, swearing in the singsong Dalecarlian dialect.

Martin rode up to the city hall and kept some distance from the fray. A fähnlein of Landsknechts marched by rhythmically, and in proper order. A drumroll echoed between the houses lining the streets, but no one sang. They covered their mouths with snowy scarves, and helmets nodded to their sleepy pace.

The Dalecarlians gathered with arquebuses and crossbows behind the Germans. They mumbled and murmured and made rhymes about

Dacke. For many of them, this would be the first time they fired at anything other than a lynx or a hare, and one could feel the tension in the air.

Now the commander came riding up. The firelight flickered on his young and dogged face. He went right up to the steps of the city hall, and little Niels Hansson went straight to him with a snow-white ermine scarf hanging off the shoulders of his shiny armor.

"Now we are going to catch Dacke in bed and so prove him to be foolish," said the commander. "So this means that no one is to try their matchlocks or fire any test shots on the road."

"Trust us," said the captain as he stood up straight. "When the Dalecarlian Fähnlein comes along, Dacke's thieves are worth no more than blueberries."

"That is good." The commander laughed. "Now show what you are capable of. Sit up and let the people get started. The fähnlein will go over Orlunda and Bjälbo. The guides are waiting at the customs booths."

He rode out into the open again. The captain mounted his horse and gave the command to depart.

"Move out! Dalecarlians move out!" The cry could be heard all over the square, and the noise proliferated in the alleys. Dalecarlians passed by silently in small clusters, with the practiced gate of hunters. Now, others belonging to the forlorn hope began to gather. Some did not know where they belonged, and there was endless quarreling among the drivers.

The commander rode back out into the square and waved the scrivener over to him. Martin put life into his half-sleeping knackered out horse and steered between the sleds and wagons.

"Now I am leaving you this fun market," said the commander. "The cavalry waits at Strå, and Herr Måns is already leaving for Hovgården. I have to catch them. You stay here, Martin, and tell the lieutenant to get himself on the way with the forlorn hope within a quarter-hour. Those who are not yet ready can come after with their butter churns and pork bellies best they can. We cannot wait until they pluck every chicken in Östergötland. Farewell, we will meet in Appuna or Hogstad."

He spun around and trotted away. The squires followed.

Martin found Hindrik von Segen, the lieutenant, who was to lead the forlorn hope today. He, too, was a very young man, a tall, coarse giant with a wide, good-natured childlike face. His eyes were light blue. He squinted a bit and moved a little leisurely. He had just straightened out a traffic jam of sleds and half-drunk drivers who slammed into each other in the street and now made their way through the soldiers who searched for their bundles tested their daggers and stomped in the snow.

The scrivener accomplished his errand, and Hindrik von Segen found a drummer in the crowd. He ordered him to beat a drumroll. A minute later, the call went out over the square and in the alleys: "Move out! Move out! Forlorn hope, move out!"

The lieutenant had stood in the saddle and taken the drummer next to him. Slowly he rode along the road to Strå and turned in the saddle to make sure that the crowd followed him. When he saw that the whole street was full of halberds and steel points that flickered on the silhouettes from the fires down in the square, he increased his pace.

Out in the field, it was hard to see the winter road under the new soft snow. The train soon lengthened into a thin line of sleds and people. Scrivener Martin rode behind the sled with wine barrels so he could keep an eye on them. It snowed very slowly like large white down feathers that seemed to hover freely in the air before laying themselves to rest on his sweater sleeve. A person could just barely see the figure in front of him as a formless black clump. Otherwise, everything was snow and night, white ground, white flakes, black space, white and black merged into a blurred mass without boundaries or end.

As Martin sat in the saddle, he felt a strange sensation. Was he saved? At dawn, the lead bullets and bolts would whine in bloody earnest. Somewhere before them in the dark lay the great forest where Dacke had his camps and his thirty thousand men. Perhaps today, the Swedish chronicle would be written, and her course would be determined for a long time to come. How often had he not heard stories of such battles with the Jutes? Today, another bloody foundation stone would be set for the building of Sweden. He was not afraid, yet there was a tremendous uneasiness, and it gnawed at his heart.

Was he perhaps still afraid? The spasmodic tension had knotted up in his chest at the same moment he had heard that he would follow Herr Peder. He had never really dealt with it. To see gunsmoke from a distance, to hear the reports of gunshots, to keep track of the commander's field box and cash during the fight and perhaps help the field surgeon to stop the bleeding on the surgery bench, that he had considered. But to ride with the commander between the banners, that was another thing. The thieves would shoot at the commander with everything they had, bolts and bullets, but the commander had his splendid armor, he sat as if in a little house. It was another thing to ride in his red sweater and fur-lined leathers amid the hailstorm of bolts. Perhaps, he would be on the barber-surgeon's bench today.

How would it feel to have a bolt hit him? If he took it in the underbelly, he was almost certainly lost, or if he took it in the breast, it could stop between the rib bones. Only if it went through the calf or arm, did one go to the surgeon's bench.

It was perhaps the most frightful thought to be strapped down by the leather straps on the bloody oak table. Martin could feel the field surgeon's frozen fingers fumble in the edge of a wound. Now he stroked the knife against his leather pants, tested the edge against his thumb, and pressed it steadily into the flesh . . .

The horse stumbled into the frozen rut, and he tumbled forward in the saddle. He sat up and tightened his knees. It did not do to sit here and sleep. And it served nothing to torment himself ahead of time with thoughts of bolts in his body.

The train came to a halt, and the sled in front of Martin stopped. Martin did not stop. He continued to ride past the crowds to look for the lieutenant upfront. But the lieutenant had gone on ahead to catch up with the cavalry because the commander had summoned him. The forlorn hope would have to wait until they returned.

The whinnying and rustling of armor that rattled when the horses threw their heads back could be heard clearly up ahead. The cavalry did not seem to be too far ahead of them. The scrivener felt calm again. As soon as he spoke with the sober common men that sniffed their noses and brushed the snow from their crossbows, the picture of horror left. Everything was back to normal. And so long as they had the cavalry ahead of them, they were protected from any surprise in the dark.

He could hear quick hoof beats on the frozen ground again. The lieutenant appeared out of the darkness, polished steel covered in snow, giving orders to march. Scrivener Martin returned to his wine sled.

It had quit snowing and blowing slowly from the west. Perhaps the storms collided. The night was very dark, the sky was a solid wall of clouds, and no one could see anything but snow and more snow that disappeared into the dark wherever they looked. Some sleeping villages covered in a soft blanket of snow appeared in passing. Not once did a dog bark. They had to have been on the road for two hours now.

They passed by another sleeping village under the long low roofs. To the right of the road, a white mass appeared from the dark. It was a heavy fortress-like tower, nestled among the snow-covered forest, silently, and frozen with a single little black eye looking down at the endless column that passed by. He heard voices in the sled before him:

"Now, we are in Hof."

"This is halfway to Skrukeby."

Martin rode on quietly. Tall trees lined the road showing the black outline of the branches under the burden of the heavy snow. Up above the night was pitch black and impenetrable. The small eye high above, up there in the menacing church tower, hung on the back of his neck. Tensely and suspiciously, it followed him in the dark. He could not escape. Something was bothering him.

How would it go if he took a bolt to the belly today? If he now ended up in a frozen knechts'[6] grave with a broken bolt in his ribs, what would happen then?

For twenty years, he had never doubted the answer. At that time, his childhood faith was still pure and white as yesterday's snow here in the field. Mother Bothild's faith-wise hand still laid blessing over his boyish head. Then he would have prayed to the Virgin Mary and died calmly, certain that Mother Bothild would have mass read and burn a candle before the image of Saint Anne until she was certain she had

[6] A *knecht* could refer to soldiers in general but more often meant a member of the *Landsknecht*, a term for mercenary forces from Germany.

redeemed him from the fires of purgatory. But he had since lost faith in both Saint Anne and the Holy Mother of God. Now he only wanted to believe in Christ. He had learned this from Master Olaus. He had even said this and confessed it before his brother. But was this what it meant to believe in Christ: *only* to believe?

Certainly, he believed! Since childhood, he had bowed every time he heard the Savior's holy name mentioned. That Jesus was God's Son and the world's Savior that his name was above all names in heaven, and on earth, he knew that. Thus, he believed.

He felt the eye again, staring at the back of his neck—a light, a still, burning, unbearable light glowing with a silent accusation. The eye Kort Lange had spoken of was there.

Do you believe? The eye's glowing ember asked. Do you believe? Why then do you live as a whoremonger and blasphemer right before God's All-Seeing Eye? How can you write those lies, speak that which is false, laugh at that which is shameful?

"You are not truly evangelical!"

Now it was Kort Lange's voice that spoke through the wind.

"You do not know the gospel! You listen to a sermon on Sunday, on Monday you drink yourself drunk together with Jörgen Organista and Hoparegränd, on Tuesday you tell the landlady that you don't have any money, but on Wednesday you still have money enough to buy a silk scarf, and on Thursday you go to the furrier's little maid telling lies and making pillow talk."

Scrivener Martin hopped out of the saddle. His frozen feet ached when he put them on the ground. He had to walk to get rid of the thoughts.

They marched now on the poor streets over the endlessly flat fields. A hundred hooves had kicked the snow. No one could see if this was the way the original road went, and the sled runners often scraped against the frozen furrows. The wind had turned to the northwest, or they had turned to the east.

Did he really believe in Christ?

That Christ died in our place. This he had learned under Master Olaus's pulpit. That we are all sinners, this he had also understood. But just as fully that God would punish sinners. These didn't quite go together, but he more likely belonged to those who would be punished both for his oaths and for the debts he never considered paying, and for that which he did to the furrier's little girl.

He climbed in the saddle again and gave the horse the spurs. He ignored Kort Lange, Master Olaus, and the eye and all together—at least for now. At Skrukeby, where Dacke had made camp in the snow-covered fields, that was where the fate of the kingdom would soon be decided. Behind Dacke stood powerful actors. Rumor had it that he dealt with both the pope and the emperor. If he kept the field today, King Gösta could lose his crown in the bloody snow before the evening.

But he wouldn't keep the field! As usual, the king had not slept the time away. At least seven or eight regular fähnleins were at this hour on the march over Appuna, Bjälbo, Skeninge, and Högby. More than half were the finest Landsknecht available for enlistment in Germany. Things had changed since twenty-one.

They had entered a belt of forest. The visibility had cleared so the troop train could see the treetops against the night sky and a church tower to the right up in the heights. They soon saw another one above the forest, but this one was straight in front of them.

The scrivener suddenly noticed that the line of sight in the east became a shade lighter. The church off in the distance had to be Hogstad. He could see it now, and the roofs in the church-village no longer appeared like white streaks of snow but silhouetted against the light wall of clouds. Dawn was breaking. Both animals and men seemed to notice it and increased pace. The company turned to travel, slowly and noisily, over the fields straight for the daybreak.

The lieutenant came riding up and ordered the greatest possible silence. Martin could see that all the sleds and wagons stopped in front of the church-village while the soldiers continued after receiving their quarter-pint of wine.

The front of the church gradually became black with sleds. The soldiers gathered around the wine barrels and quickly emptied their mugs. The scrivener never needed to silence them. They were tired from the march and understood from the extra food rations that the enemy was not far off. So they dried their mouths with their hands, made sure the powder was dry, or the bolts were where they should be and disappeared eastward between the gray houses.

Martin passed the church on the plateau and took in an overview of the terrain. The gently sloping field of snow on the other side was strewn with infantry, who made their way east in loose formations. To the south, groves of trees melted together into a belt of forest. They occupied the front of the south edge of the slope. Holaveden[7] began here.

He spied eastward to see if there was any life in the early dawn. Some farms were visible between snowdrifts, but nothing moved.

But just then there was a flash in the blue darkness off in the distance. A couple of moments passed and then came the bang, the rolling thunder of guns spread like waves over the fields in the still of the morning. Another two cracks followed. The echo rolled between the black ridges, but he didn't see any flashes.

The soldiers down in the pastures had stopped. He heard the lieutenant's voice yelling something, and the whole crowd began to pick up their pace. In the farms down to the east, there was life and unrest. He heard loud cries and watched as black dots moved about in the snow. No one was shooting now. He couldn't see even a trace of the cavalry.

Soldiers could be seen quickly moving through the snow in groups. Their panting breath smelled of Spanish wine from afar. The scrivener went back to the supplies. He didn't feel afraid anymore, just curious. He would rather shirk his responsibility for the sleds and hurry eastward toward Skrukeby to see how the battle developed.

There was a long wait again. Martin arranged the dispensation to soldiers that were still coming in and sent them further. He let the transport personnel arrange their sleds so they could continue in any direction they desired. Meanwhile, he walked along the churchyard wall and looked eastward. The cavalry broke out from the groves in the north and occupied Skrukeby. The snowfields were spotted black with people, but he didn't hear any gunfire.

Luckily, Ture Bodvidsson now came with the reserve troop and put an old first sergeant in charge of the sleds. Martin took this

---

[7] A belt of forest between lake Sommen and the southern shoreline of Lake Vättern. In the middle ages, it was considered the border between Småland and Östergötland.

occasion to look for the commander. He climbed back into the saddle and trotted over the field to Skrukeby. He heard a single shot at the forest's edge far out ahead of him. The dispersed troops began to gather in formation around their banners in the various pastures outside of Skrukeby. A couple of fähnleins went eastward to the woods where a high and foreboding ridge blocked the view.

He immediately entered a depression that blocked his view. When he reached the crest, he saw the whole royal cavalry come toward him from the left. They rode in wide formation, at a leisurely pace, and the lances pointed in every direction. He recognized one of the lords who he just helped with a letter in Vadstena. He rode up to him and received information: The Dalecarlian fähnlein had come to the village first. Little Niels Hansson wanted to show his bravery and rode straight out to meet the forest thieves, almost alone. His shiny armor shimmered far off in the half-dark. Someone fired and then the whole game was destroyed. The forest thieves had escaped to the ridge toward Mölleby without leaving so much as a hen behind them. Now the commander made up a plan to pinch them. He would hunt them himself with the infantry through the forest. The cavalry could not be used effectively in the trees, so they would follow the meadow side to the east and descend to the Svartån.[8] They would wait in the valley until the forest thieves were chased out of their hiding places.

Martin thanked them and rode on whistling. It was still a great day. If the commander could carry out his plan, the war would be over before this evening.

Shooting increased steadily up on the ridge. The first fähnlein had already entered the forest, and it was apparent that they met with resistance. The gunshots got louder the closer he came to Skrukeby.

The forlorn hope came to the rescue crossing the field diagonally. He galloped to catch up with them and trotted right through the crowd. He waved cheerfully to the lieutenant as he passed. They were now just south of Skrukeby, and he could see the black gunsmoke

---

[8] The Svartån is a river in Östergötland (Svartån, Sommen-Roxen to distinguish it from another river by the same name the Svartån, Öjebro-Vågforsen which is to the north).

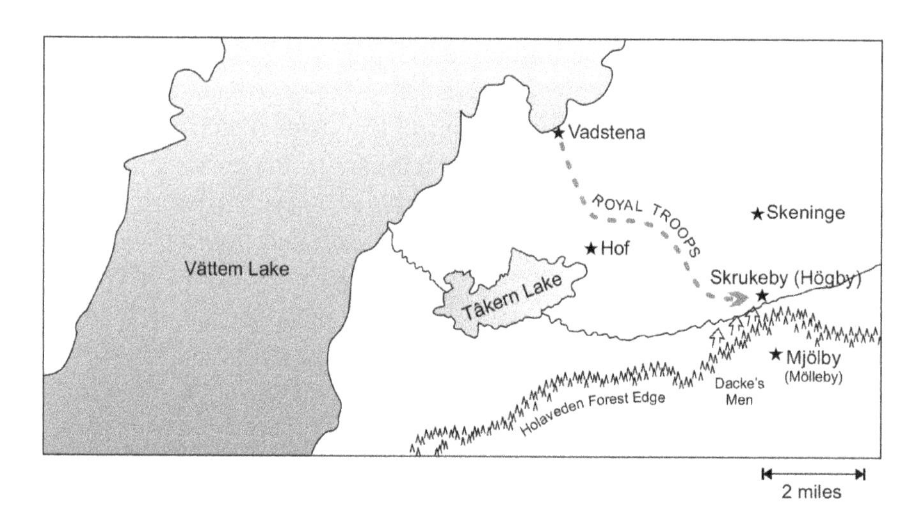

billow between the white branches up on the ridge straight ahead of them. No one could tell him where the commander was.

Strangely enough, many of the fähnleins had stopped on the slopes east of the village and seemed not to be leaving that area. The closest two were enlisted fähnleins, then a Swedish and then one or two comprised of the Landsknecht. In front of the nearest fähnlein stood the royal councilor, Johan Turesson, and some other lords deliberating with the war council. Martin turned his horse in their direction to find out where the commander was. He could hear one of the Germans, Berent Ochse, he was called, quarreling with the Swedish nobility a long way off. Berent stood bowlegged in the snow with both hands in his belt. His bottom lip pushed forward, glossy and red while he spoke. He was quite vexed.

"It doesn't fall to us to go into the forest with these soldiers," he said. "If the Swedish King wants to have respectable warriors, he can offer a respectable war. Running in the forest and being shot in the back by forest thieves, my men are too good for that! I lost two and twenty men in one day when we were leaving from Fröjerum through the forest there. If they send the men out to us, the pig dogs, then we will put them down! But we fight *here*, nicht drüben!"[9]

He pointed to the forest, and his comrades concurred. They were respectable warriors, and they would do their service respectably, if

[9] Not over there.

only they found a nice place to fight. But they would not send their halberds in among the Swedish branches ever again!

The Swedish lords shrugged their shoulders. The Germans were afraid of the forest. They had taken note of that already last year in Växjö. They wanted to have open fields around them, no trees. Some of the younger lords tried to say that they were still under the commander's orders to drive Dacke's men through the forest into the arms of the cavalry. They were obligated to obey without question. Then Johan Turesson, the royal councilman, laughed his broad laugh and said:

"Obey, little Per Brahe? Ha, ha, I have been like a father to that boy and let him ride on my back before he could reach my elbow. I can still chastise him if he becomes too defiant. He should have better manners and not give himself to the melee in the forest. He is too good for that."

"Is the commander in the forest?" the scrivener asked, disturbed. This whole time he had thought that he was further on among the fähnleins.

"He went in with the Dalecarlians over there by the barn at the edge of the meadow a little over a half an hour ago," said Herr Ture. "But leave your horse here if you plan to follow him."

The scrivener did not hear him but trotted up to the edge of the forest. He had to notify the commander that the fähnleins had abandoned him. Otherwise, a tragedy could occur here today.

The shooting, which had been intense all along the ridge, had now died down to the north. A fähnlein had fallen back from the edge of the forest there in disarray. The men carried some wounded with them.

Martin cut across the fields to reach the hollow on the right where the forlorn hope had entered the forest. There was a good and well-worn path the last groups used before disappearing in the woods. They kept course straight for the sounds of battle, which were loudest just here on the southern edge of the ridge. Further up to the left was another path through the trees; it had become restless again. Martin heard the sound of yelling, screaming, and the clash of weapons as men fought in the melee. Gun salvos would crash through the forest intermittently, followed by the clear and hard whine of crossbow bolts. Great clumps of snow kept falling from the branches. A wayward bullet whined out into the pasture and thudded against the frozen ground.

Suddenly he caught sight of some figures between the snow-covered trees, then another pair, and after a minute, another crowd swarmed out onto the pasture in disarray. The scrivener turned his horse and began to ride toward them. They yelled that he should keep away and save himself: Dacke's men were after them. He rode straight into the middle of the group. They were in complete disarray. Details of their story were a confusing mess, but they managed to clarify that they took a different route than the commander. They met up again in the forest, but they did not dare shoot for fear of hitting the commander's men. The forest thieves took advantage of the opportunity and showered them with bolts until no one could endure it any longer. Their leader took a bolt through the throat that nailed him straight to a tree. He hung there like a grouse left to cure on a wall. Innumerable men had fallen this way. The battle was hopeless from the beginning because the thieves had the higher ground in the forest and could shoot farther and more accurately.

They made their way through the pasture as they tried to catch their breath. The whole field was littered again with stumbling figures.

Martin let his thoughts run. If Dacke's men broke through here, then the fähnleins would still catch him. It was more important that the commander got the message before the forest thieves overran all his men. So, he turned again and rode along the forest as fast as the horse could trot. He reached the hollow and took the path into the forest. Shooting continued with no sign of letting up on the slope. The intensity seemed to even increase up on the ridge. It was not long before he saw dark bloodstains on the path. The snowdrifts were all trampled by hundreds of feet, junipers, severed moss, and broken twigs littered the ground. His horse struggled with the steep climb and stumbled between the stones. Martin climbed out of the saddle and took the reins in his hands before continuing. The snow was deep and began to get slippery as it started to thaw. The road continued to ascend incessantly.

He stopped, dried the sweat from his forehead, and took a minute to look for the sun. The day was completely gray and without shade. It must have been between nine and ten. The shooting continued relentlessly up ahead. He trampled on.

* * *

One of the peasants left the cottage as the pale dawn broke. Cold air blew in and woke Herr Andreas, who was sleeping in his coat on the bench by the wall. He sat up shivering and looked around in the dark. A sour humidity permeated the air that still managed to feel raw and chilly. Everywhere he looked, he saw clumsy gray figures rolled up together: to his right and left, on the bench, on the floor, by the fireplace, and on the table. Heavy respiration filled the dark, and men occasionally flailed or groaned in their sleep.

They had come to the farm yesterday evening. None of them even knew the name of this estate. The abandoned cottage had black wool noil[10] on the floor among abandoned wool hand carders left by the owners. These were bad signs. This family was on the side of the king and had fled the peasant army.

Herr Andreas rose and carefully stepped over the sleeping bodies on the floor. He pushed the door open and went out into the yard. It had snowed again, a soft, down-like blanket of snow, but now the wind was mild, and the day promised to be fair. Long dark clouds streaked across the gray sky, against which the snow-covered birches showed their white patterns. Here and there, a long white band of snow freed itself from a treetop and fell to the ground lightly.

Herr Andreas slowly walked across the yard and looked around. The countryside opened up to the north. He left the courtyard by the stock shed gable and stopped in amazement. Looking out over the bare hill in the pale light of the morning, he saw what he could not have comprehended yesterday evening. The whole hillside lay open before his feet in the breaking of the blue winter day, an endless expanse of white fields between dark bands of wood. A veil of dark still shadowed everything, but he could make out both Tåkern and Omberg and the open water of Vättern behind them.

Herr Andreas took the picture in with thanks. Vadstena was over there in the distance on the furthest bay of Tåkern. Did the men of the monastery there sing the *Te Deum* just now while the candles

[10] Short strands and knots that have been combed out of wool using stiff brushes called handcarders before spinning.

flickered and the bell rang? He longed to escape to the peace of the Blåkyrkan. He had now been in the war train with his parishioners for a week. He ate and slept with them. He drank their beer and shared their coarse bread. For him, this was pure joy. But he had also shared in their spiritual poverty, and this pleased him less. Over these last nine days, he had not been able to pray the hours, hardly even a single psalm. He had to steal away to pray while he walked in the forest.

It was not as uplifting as he thought it would be to be out in the field where men fought for the holy church. God sometimes chose strange men to be his instruments. The previous fall when Dacke came to Fröjerum for the first time, Herr Andreas had held solemn mass with joy and gladness. But Dacke just sat in the choir yawning, and at communion, as usual, only a couple parishioners from Fröjerum had come forward. Afterward, he asked why those who fought for the holy church did not want to embrace her most holy sacrament. Dacke answered that it was a good and salutary old custom that a person should only go to communion at Easter. He said that as he understood it, it was the Lutheran heretics who wanted to bring the Lord's Supper to the people more often.

Dacke's manner of life was even worse. He had come the first time with a brunette who was said to be his wife. This time he had a blond with him. It probably had not been right last time either. Herr Andreas shook his rugged head woefully. There would be a lot that would still need to be done even if Dacke was victorious. But Dacke's victory was the necessary condition for anything to be done concerning the sanctification of these crude people.

That morning Herr Andreas finally stole away to make a proper morning sacrifice, as good a one as he could make in these woods. He had noticed with horror how quickly the whole of his spiritual life languished amidst these hard living conditions, and how they had exposed another side of his nature, which rarely if ever found expression while at home in the peace of Fröjerum's parsonage. Now he didn't dare let it go on this way any longer. Today he would try to live as a priest again and pray his offices. Matins ought to be the greatest part. He could not do the long readings by heart, but at least he could pray Laudes and Primam. He would dedicate the day to God, this great day that might wash away the church's disgrace and reestablish her cause.

He looked over the hills again. There lay Skeninge. He could see the massive dark Church of Our Lady rising from the snow. An old wound opened in his heart again. It was there that against all righteousness, against all piety, and every law of the church, he was forced to hand over the church silver from Ravelunda and Fröjerum. In the great hall of the Dominican Monastery, he had counted it all up before the German Göran Norman, the royal ecclesiastical bailiff, who put it all in large sacks as if it were nothing but a common business transaction. When he could not help but kiss the golden monstrance goodbye, Master Norman arrogantly smiled with infinite condescension. When it was all over, the chalice was returned, and so too Ravelunda's bridal crown. "To be graciously left to the peasants," wrote Master Norman in the protocol. "Graciously left to the peasants!" His cheeks reddened with blood. Graciously left?! Graciously granted by his royal grace to the peasants in Ravelunda, a bridal crown that they had purchased to be used forever in their parish church? And they did not even receive it back as their property but as a royal loan. He had to go to the fortress along with two of the six men who swore to the crown as *fide jussoreres*[11] that nothing would be missing. Missing! He laughed bitterly. Had anything gone missing from his church, but what the King had stolen?

This Göran Norman who sat there and made an account for the monstrances and chalices as if they were a cattle tithe had done more than anyone to confirm the diabolic nature of the new teaching for Herr Andreas. Was it not clear that it also made the best of its followers into cowardly slaves of the world and princes? This learned German still had the air of being an honorable man and a truly evangelical soul. Nevertheless, he was nothing but a plaything in the hands of an anti-Christian monarch. First, His Grace had made him the highest head of the church and gave him the task of reforming her from the ground up. Yet just a few months later, he sent him as an envoy to Latvia—and the new leader of the church immediately betrayed his flock. Now he sat and watched. What would become of the church if her highest authority took his duties so casually? For them, the church had actually ceased to exist. The only things that remained were the king, politics, and the affairs of the realm!

[11] Surety.

The pastor breathed deeply and looked out again over the hills. Perhaps today, freedom dawned. Down there in Vadstena or Skeninge, were the executioners the king had rented. Now the peasant hordes had come to sweep them out of the land as Engelbrekt had done a century ago. If the King dared to fight, then it might even happen today.

He bowed his knees in the snow, and prayed for victory, prayed for the redemption of God's church from all evil, for her renewal and glory. Then he began to pray Lauds. The humid and heavy wind blew, he shivered and his teeth chattered so that the Latin was beaten and frozen. But his soul was warm. He prayed passionately for mercy and help from the heavens. The old words of the psalter that were born of such joy and agony in millennia past were once again filled with a soul's despairing cries and burning faith, a lonely, freezing, and struggling soul's hunger and longing for salvation.

Just as he came to the hymn's Gloria verse, he startled at a shot somewhere in the villages far down to the northeast. He looked up, frozen to the spot, and barked a laugh at the interruption. Two more shots followed. Then there was silence. He listened, still on his knees, his hands folded in prayer. Through the heavy morning air full of snow, he thought he could hear screaming. It was apparent that something was in progress down there on the hillsides. He mumbled: Holy Mother of God, pray for us! And then, he rushed into the yard. The peasants were up. They tumbled out, stiff and awkward.

"Gather your things!" he cried. "They are shooting down at Skrukeby. We need to get on our way!"

The peasants had come to life in the neighboring homes also. They did not need much time to get ready. One road led down to Skrukeby through the meadows. They waded through the light snow with long strides. The dawn became ever clearer and they could see down over the slopes through the treetops.

Suddenly Elif of Sevedsgården stopped and pointed with his spear. The others turned to the north, where the forest opened into a small glade. They saw a little church-village down on the flat ground from behind the trees. The black weatherproofing of the church gables contrasted starkly with the snow. But what first caught their attention was a stream of people, an ant trail of small black bodies swarmed east across the snow-covered fields. Horses could be seen in the pasture behind the church, a larger mass of horses and sleds than they had ever seen at any market.

"That is Hogstad," whispered Herr Andreas. They had all become cautious and quiet.

"That means something is happening at Skrukeby," he added. "Nils Dacke made camp there yesterday. Now we commend our souls to the Lord and do our best. Have courage, men!"

The crowd began to move again. Like gray wolves, they slid down through the winter landscape. The only sound was the dull thuds from the steel of their battleaxes slapping loosely on their wooden shafts. Once they came right up to the forest edge. Between the trees, they glimpsed a long train of black figures moving eastward like themselves.

"Watch out for the open country!" they said. "Keep to the woods."

A couple of shots were heard ahead of them to the east. They increased their pace. Some nibbled on a crust of bread or gnawed on mutton. One ought not go to battle on an empty stomach.

They could not say if they had been on the move for one hour or two. The shooting up ahead picked up pace again. It came quite a bit closer too.

"Lock and load!" cried the deacon. "There are soldiers beyond the glade!"

He had stopped between two snow-covered trees that looked like white spines with their heavy branches. Crossbow cranks squeaked. He notched a bolt. At that same moment, a gunshot rang out close by. The bullet slammed into a tree trunk and snow fell like white glitter. The deacon darted away, dropped to the ground, and shot.

"Watch out!" he yelled. "Get around the glade! Be careful of open ground!"

In the blink of an eye, the host had disappeared into the forest again. Panting with exertion, they made it back up the hill and around the main corner of the meadow in the cover of branches. They all locked and loaded as they spread themselves out in the woods. Then they made their way north. They could hear screaming and occasional shooting all along the ridge ahead of them.

Herr Andreas felt how his heartbeat in a manner that was not caused by the stiff march alone. As a boy, he had hunted both lynx and wolf in the heavy snow of the woods. But this was something different.

It broke out again below them in the forest. This time he saw the flash. The bullet whined as it flew by, clipped a branch, and shook the snow loose. The peasants of Fröjerum disappeared behind trees in a flash. Now the bolts whistled down between the branches. They made less of a fuss but were almost scarier than the bullets. They stole their way forward with a quiet hiss and silently penetrated anything soft, whether snow or living flesh.

The arquebuses below them barked, and black gunsmoke belched between the snow-covered bark and twigs of the bushes. Snow fell from the sky. The men of Fröjerum shot like hares from their hiding places to find better aim. Quietly and accurately, the bolts made rain.

Now they were drowning. For a second, they watched as a lone man ran. His steps were heavy as he struggled to stay upright with his heavy weapon. Then he fell face forward in the snow and never got back up. Others yelled to each other between the trees. It hit the priest hard. Was this not the Dalecarlian dialect?

The peasants of Fröjerum rushed down the icy stone slopes, stole through thick stands of spruce, and darted through some clearings. They had the enemy on their heels. An owl screeched to the right of him. The peasants advanced. That was comforting to know.

The enemy had come to a halt again. Screaming and cussing filled the forest. It was no longer just the Dalecarlian dialect, but also the voices of high nobility. Then a volley of bullets broke out louder than any others that day. This time there were at least twenty arquebuses at once. The echo bounced off the cliff faces, bullets whistled and slammed all over the place.

The priest saw Elif of Sevedsgården falter and fall face forward. He rushed to him. The warm blood had splattered the snow and flowed out of his nose and mouth. Laboriously, the priest rolled the heavy body. Lars and Gisle from the church-village came to help him.

"Let it be!" he cried. "Shoot while the others are loading. I will take care of Elif."

In actuality, there wasn't much to take care of anymore. The bullet had gone right through Elif's breast just below the neck. His life drained out into the snow, a warm red river. His hands dug in the drift, he seemed to grasp for air but could not get it down his mangled throat. Another flash broke out down there among the trees, and the bullets howled through the trees. Clean white flecks fell in the bloody snow around Elif. The white glitter instantly turned to a purplish red.

Herr Andreas searched in his leather bag and pulled out the chrismatory. He cautiously took the three small bronze flasks that had been forged together out of the sheath. The last, marked with a large clumsy I, contained the holy oil for extreme unction. He knelt in the snow and supported the bloody head while he made the threefold sign of the cross and prayed that the devil's power would be eliminated in the name of the Triune God and through the imposition of his hands and those of the holy church. He thumbed the oil and anointed Elif's eyes, praying that all sins he had committed through these eyes would be forgiven him. He anointed his ears, his nose, and his mouth so that the holy oil mixed with the blood and read the same prayer for forgiveness *per istam sanctam unctionem.*[12] A bullet whistled over his head. The whole forest was full of death, screams, and smashing. He was not concerned with it. He anointed Elif's hands and feet, praying for forgiveness for all the sins he had committed with those feet and hands his entire life. He thought about the apples they had stolen together as boys, he thought about the blows he gave fighting on wild Saturday nights, he thought about blue spring nights in Fröjerum when the thickets were white with blooms and the shining silver moon hung over the marshes and it was so easy for a twenty-year-old boy to take the wrong paths. Blood ran out of Elif's nose. He prayed for forgiveness for all he had done and left undone with body and soul, on a holy day or workday. Then he wiped the oil off in the snow and prayed: *Kyrie eleison,*[13] *Christie eleison* . . . a bullet slammed into the rocky path behind him and ricocheted into the snow with a whistle. Another howled into a tree trunk. It was as if giants were fighting each other in the wood. He continued steadily: *Kyrie eleison. Pater noster qui es in coelis . . .*[14]

[12] Through this holy anointing.

[13] Lord have mercy.

[14] Our Father who art in heaven.

Elif opened his eyes. He stared helplessly out into space. His course hands dug in the snow. Then his gaze caught the priest's face just as he finished the Lord's Prayer. Elif's face seemed to catch a glimpse of something safe and confident. In the next second, it was distorted again. He struggled to breathe and writhed in the snow. His chest tensed in a powerful arch. Yet another bullet came screaming and hit the dying man in the thigh.

Only now did the priest realize that this whole time he had been sitting like a target for the king's soldiers. He stood up completely, turned defiantly against the enemy, slowly made the sign of the cross, picked the chrismatory up from the snow, and walked away. Someone in the pine thicket over by a rocky outcrop yelled his name. It was Gisle from Östergård. He had drug himself there, leaving a red trail in the snow.

Herr Andreas looked around a moment in the woods. Fröjerum's men had advanced a bit, but it was apparent that they feared the force majeure against them. They did not dare enter into hand-to-hand combat but made use of bow and crossbows alone. Yet the partisans and the redcoats were at a standstill. They just stood there and made one salvo after another, so that the whole forest shook amidst clatter. The few men from Fröjerum had formed a thin chain, they crawled behind pine trees and shot their bolts with cold hands.

The priest looked anxiously at the red splatter on the hill. He saw at least three areas with large blotches of blood in the snow. It may have been the royal soldiers who spilled their blood in retreat, but he feared that it came from his own.

Gisle yelled from the brushwood again. Andreas rushed over, but Gisle was shot through. His life was waning, and there was absolutely no hope for him. He lay on his back and held his hands on his blood-soaked sweater. Herr Andreas sat next to him. He had trouble holding his tears back.

Gisle knew what to expect and had called for the priest to give him last rites. He made his confession and received absolution. Then he too was anointed with the holy oil. The noise of battle intensified below. Herr Andreas hurried on.

The next man who lay in the snow was Måns of Långstena. He was shot through the chest and almost cold. The priest anointed him.

Now he cried. Never before had he anointed three parishioners in the same day.

The next man was one of the peasants from Flodlycke. Herr Andreas found him in a pile of stones with a shattered femur. The man was still conscious but bleeding out fast. So Herr Andreas anointed the man. The man was in tears as he spoke of his home and wife, and Herr Andreas promised to do what he could do for her. In quiet despair, he calculated that this unfortunate day had already left Fröjerum with four widows and fourteen fatherless children. It was far more than he could comprehend; he could not undertake the care of so many. He did not want to see any more death.

While the peasant from Flodlycke slumped between the stones, the priest sat and listened to the shooting. He was stunned. As if in a dream, he saw the deacon from Årtebol pass by with his left-hand shot through. Then he sat up and helped him put a dressing on the wound.

"We have to get reinforcements so we can go at them with the spear," said the deacon. "It can't go like this any longer. For every one of them we knock off, five new ones come. Erik of Kvisslehult is shot, and so also Sverker of Dikareby. They are stone dead, so you don't need to go there. But Tall Staffan from Helgetorp still lives and would be glad to see the pastor come."

The deacon continued up the hill. Herr Andreas got up and went closer to the battlefield. He met Jon of Flodlycke's oldest boy. He had come running to get more bolts off the dead. They had begun to run out of them up ahead.

Staffan of Helgetorp sat leaning against a coarse pine tree that covered him from the fire. A bullet had shattered his shin. The ground was nothing but a pool of blood around him, and his foot lay unnaturally twisted inward. His face was a pale yellow under the soot and dirt. When he saw the priest, he bowed sadly. Herr Andreas wanted to try and stop the flow of blood. Tall Staffan only waved.

"Let it be, pastor. It is useless. I cannot even get my boot off; it is so mangled."

The priest stood before the sundered man and felt bitter. Was he not the one who gave the battle call? Did he not advise them at New Years to join Dacke in the field? Could he ever again look the women folk back home in the eye? Six widows and over twenty left fatherless . . .

Now it was time to give Staffan the last rites. Staffan was a very young man. He had neglected both confession and the Lord's Supper for the last few years. It was best to start at the beginning.

"Staffan," he said, "when you set out with this train, you gathered all that you needed: crossbow and bolts, bread and vittles. Now you will go no further. The bullet in your leg came as a bidding stick. Now it has departed, and now you go to heaven. Now see to it that you prepare yourself so that you make it there."

"I won't make it there," Staffan said with remarkable flatness.

"With the help of Jesus, every man can make it," said the priest.

"It serves nothing, pastor. Let me be. Go to the others! There is still *some* hope for them!"

"No more or less than for you!"

"The pastor doesn't know that."

"Of course, I know that. The thief on the cross was saved because, in his hour of death, he repented and praised and glorified Jesus. You shall be saved today, Staffan."

"The young peasant from Helgetorp waved again with his hands, just as flatly and convinced as when he declined help for his mangled leg."

"The Pastor doesn't know . . . It is just as well that I just say it: I set it up so mother would burn to death in the sauna."

Herr Andreas felt himself become pale. The whole county knew that the old mother in Helgetorp burned in the sauna. But that the accidental fire could have been planned, no one had thought of that possibility even if the fact that the old woman didn't get out successfully aroused suspicion.

The peasant gave the priest a watchful look and noticed that he was pale. He bowed calmly to confirm.

"Now, the pastor knows that," he said. "And now the pastor will leave me . . ."

There was whistling and shrieking above their heads. The forest was filled with screaming and yelling. Strange figures hurried past, gray highwaymen and ragged beards and long bear spears.

Herr Andreas bent over the wounded man.

"I am *not* going, Staffan. Not before your soul is saved. Can you not repent?"

"If I were healthy, pastor, then it would go well. Then I would travel to Rome or Compostella. If only I live, I would fast and give to charity."

"You can do that now too, Staffan. You can give your animals and silver spoons to Fröjerum's church."

The peasant looked at the priest inquiringly and then shook his head.

"That repentance does nothing. Then Malin and the children would be impoverished. It is I who should atone for my transgressions and not them. I burned my mother in the sauna, and now I may burn in hell. That is just. But that the innocent should suffer for their father's transgression that is not just."

Herr Andreas gave up and tried a different tack.

"Have you prayed to the Holy Virgin? Prayed to the saints, prayed for their intercession, prayed for their mercy . . ."

"I have not prayed, pastor. I have wanted to, but I am ashamed to come empty-handed. A man shall atone for his transgressions. For manslaughter, one is fined, and that is fitting. For deadly sin, one gives money to the church and fasts and does pious works. But I have failed at all that, and now I am empty-handed. If I came now and prayed, the saints would have to laugh at me."

He attempted to lift the mangled leg, and his face twisted. He swallowed hard and continued.

"Heding, who struck the Western Goth at the market in Skeninge during my dad's day, he was able to travel to Linköping and seek grace from the bishop. After seven years, he did penance. Every year he fasted for seven weeks on bread and water. Every Sunday, he stood barefoot in the entrance to the church and sat on the porch during the mass. He was not able to look upon the body of the Lord that whole time. He sat on the earthen floor and ate, he was not to go to a christening, and every morning he said ten Our Fathers and ten Ave Marias. He did the harsh penance, and so he was free. But for the murder of a mother, only the pope can absolve, they say."

"There are exceptions, Staffan. In the urgency of death, there are many exceptions. Then even a common priest like me can absolve from hard sins—if anyone is truly repentant."

"Yes," said Staffan. "Gudmund of Bredaryd, he had an indulgence like that. He had bought it in Linköping. He could receive absolution for everything on his deathbed. But I must do penance first . . ."

The priest sat and stared down at the ground. Blood oozed out of his clothes, where it was soaked up by the snow or ran down onto the exposed lichens. He had often encountered this way of thinking. The peasants had an unwavering confidence in an honest penance. If one did wrong by people, he repented of it. If one sinned against God, he gave money to the bishop and fasted for God. One of the punishments could be absolved with gifts, just as manslaughter was absolved with weregild.[15] But everything should be reasonable in one way or another. Then one was free. There was logic to this, logic and justice. It was hard to say anything against this. Right must be right, both in heaven and on earth. This is why he was so perplexed. He dared not use the power of the keys before Staffan did penance in some form anyway. Neither would he try to convince him to give away any of his poor possessions—the widow and children need them before anyone else. If he could just persuade him to do something else for penance, then he would not hesitate to say the absolving words that his heart longed to say to the man as he bled out: *Ego te absolvo*—I absolve you.

The shooting kept escalating the whole time. There were no longer any salvos, only an unceasing popping and occasional cheers of joy or cries of disappointment and pain. The fighting came closer. Some stranger ran past panting under his heavy arquebus.

"Retreat, Herr, he yelled when he saw the priest. Now they are coming! We must get up the mountain if we are to get help."

Then a pair of peasants from Fröjerum appeared. He waved to them.

"Help me with Staffan so we can take him with us."

"Let me be," the peasant said. He was almost in despair. "You don't know what evil it will cause. I can't drag this shattered leg in the snow."

---

[15] Blood money paid to compensate a family for damage when a person has been killed.

"But the redshirts will take you," said one of the peasants. "They will torture you to death."

"They will not have time," Staffan said tiredly. "And it makes no difference. To move with this leg is just as good as driving in a bone screw."

The others stood undecided, leaning on their crossbows. They dried off their faces. The priest could not tell if it was sweat or tears; they wiped away.

"Promise that you will be willing neighbors to Malin," said the wounded man.

"We promise."

So they nodded, wiped off their faces and spat. Another bullet whistled past. They lifted their crossbows, grabbed Staffan's bolts, and ran off.

The priest rose. He looked at the wounded man perplexed. Then he gathered himself and said almost harshly:

"When the need is great, the penance is short. Now say ten Our Father's and ten Hail Marys. Then beg St. Anne and the holy mother of God to pray for you. Hurry, and I will be right back. I only want to see if there are many lying in the snow."

There were many lying in the snow. Herr Andreas was horrified to see one gray bundle of rags after another as he ran down the slope. He reached the first—stone dead. The other lay face forward. He lifted his face looked and looked again. Was this not Erik of Dikareby? He saw the helmet that had fallen off of him in the snow. It was Erik's helmet with the curved cock comb. Shaken, he laid the massacred face back in the bloody snow and staggered on. The next man was lying over a great flat stone slab. Even from a long way off, he could see that it was a parishioner. The broad, green bandages that wrapped around the gray homespun belonged to Linnart, the oldest son of Flodlycke. The churchwarden's wife had cut the green bindings from an old coat that Jon had worn many years ago. The tracks in the snowdrift showed that someone else tried to drag Linnart with him. The body had carved out a broad groove in the slushy snow, and the heels had made two crooked tracks. Along the right side, there was a red trail.

He came up to the boy who lay with half-open eyes and looked straight upward. His hands were a waxy yellow—the red trail in the snow lead right up to his side. Herr Andreas bent over and listened with his ear to the boy's open mouth. He was still breathing, though weakly. In the flick of a hand, the priest took the chrismatory that he placed on the stone. He loosened one of the shoes to be able to anoint the dying man's feet. Gray figures stumbled by with heavy steps. They yelled something. He only heard it as a distant and surreal echo. Everything was drowned out by the din of his own blood thundering in his head. He felt a mask of red heat and sweat over his face. Was he dreaming? Was this a nightmare? No, the snow water dripped coldly between his fingers, and the boy's wet shoes smelled sour and nauseating. This was reality, clear as day. Seconds were precious. He began to pray as fast as he could, stopped only by his own heavy breathing.

"*In nomine Patris et Filii et Spiri . . .*"

A bullet smashed into the stone. The clang of metal and moss whirled in his ears. He hurried faster with his prayers and stretched out his hand to rub his thumb in the chrismatory. Only then did he discover that the little bronze container was gone, swept away from the stone by the bullets. He jumped up and searched on the other side in the snow. It was splattered with anointing oil. The chrismatory was mangled, and the ointment lost.

Wild wrath gripped him. Would these church plunderers and peasant murderers also keep him from giving the last rites to the dying? With his thumb he rubbed the last of the oil in the vat. He reached for Linnart. He solemnly anointed the churchwarden's boy. It was the last parishioner he would be able to anoint today.

He straightened himself. The whole time it had crept up on him, but he had not turned around. It had felt just like it did when he walked along the walls of the churchyard on autumn evenings: a nasty feeling of a secret danger, a dark power, that floated out of the dark of night between the graves and touched between his shoulder blades with a giant distended finger—and then a desperate determination: don't look behind you, don't look behind you.

Now he looked behind him. He looked down over the forest. A hurricane had gone through and shook all the snow down and broke the roughest branches that now hung shattered in the crowns. In the churned up and dirty snow lay weapons, garments, helmets, and contorted bodies. He swept it all up in his gaze and then stared down the slope. He caught a dark shadow between two pine trees that quickly disappeared again. Another figure took three long steps in the opening between two spruce trees. There they came.

What should he do? Here he stood with his smashed chrismatory. As a priest, he had nothing more to do today. His eyes flickered, and it thundered in his head. He began to half run up the ridge and kept himself hidden behind fir trees. The fight had let up for a moment. The soldiers farther down threw their arquebuses over their shoulders and worked their way closer.

He stepped over a fallen man who still held his cocked crossbow in his stiff hands. The bolt was in the groove and set lightly in the dark knock. He bent over . . . Larsbo-Sven! Another parishioner. He could not remember in which order.

He stopped again and panted. This was more than he could handle. This one day alone had cost his father's parish more young men than otherwise died of old age in a year. Was this the blood tax King Gustavus took out on his people?

The wrath came back to him in a hurry. This was a craziness surpassing all reason . . . It was like the Black Death. The only difference was that it was a single godless man who was guilty of this lamentation.

Some branches cracked just below him in the forest. He sprang up and turned around completely. There stood a Knecht just fifty ells from him with an arquebus over his shoulders and the fork in his left hand. Flabbergasted, he stared at the priest. In a second, he slammed the fork into the ground, jumped behind a tree, threw up the gun and aimed.

Herr Andreas looked at the dark mouth of the arquebus like the eye of a dead man starring at him. He saw a pair of white smoke clouds that freed themselves of the muzzle and floated apart between the trees. Now the fuse met the lock.

He threw himself down, carelessly hitting the ground. There was a flash, crashing and howling in the air above him. He thought he felt the wind of the bullet crack like a whip through the air. Within a minute, he had pulled the fallen man's crossbow to him. He weighed it with pleasure in his hands, remembering boyhood hunts for fox and roebuck in the woods around Askanäs. Now he lifted it to his eye. His forefinger caressed the trigger. In the middle of the knock, he saw the arquebusier's blue armor. He pulled the trigger and lowered the crossbow as he watched the bolt make its arch.

He cheered loudly. The man grabbed his left arm, and the arquebus fell in the snow. The priest bent down and whisked up the bolts the peasant from Larsbo had left. He stuck them in his belt and rushed up the hill. He stopped in the thickets between a pair of branches and wound up the crossbow. His hands trembled with an all-consuming wild and voluptuous excitement. His eyes searched the forest from behind pine needles. He hooked the string and loaded the bolt in the groove. If he no longer needed to serve with the christening oil, he would serve with steel points.

He waited. He had no idea how many hours had passed since the fighting began. It was broad daylight now, the skies were gray, but there was a weak reflection of sunlight on the snow. Once again, he spotted a dark shadow down in the forest. He aimed, but he never got a clear shot. The knechts kept coming closer.

Suddenly it hit him that it was foolish to stay here and wait for the force majeure. He quickly slipped away between the branches and trampled further in the snow, constantly uphill. He heard owls screeching and the drums beating far ahead in the forest. His own held the line there. The fight was in full swing further north.

Suddenly a bolt whistled right at him. It hit the slope right in front of his feet. Yet another came floating down. It barely reached there and fell with a dull thump in the snow. The priest's legs picked up momentum again. He struggled up the steep slopes, stopped a bit to lean against a tree trunk, and catch his breath. Then he continued. He had thrown his hood back. His whole face burned with dry sweat curing his skin.

These bolts were far more dangerous than the bullets. An arquebus was heavy and clumsy, but a man with a crossbow could run just as fast as he could without it—or faster. He strained with the last of his strength and stumbled through the snow, which was now wet and heavy. He faded off for a minute. Half asleep, he remembered Staffan. He ought to have sought him out. But he did not believe he could successfully find the place now. The knechts had to be there already. He consoled himself thinking they would soon fall back again.

Now he saw the first men in the chain of peasants. He waved and yelled at them, not to shoot by mistake. They recognized him and called back.

Panting, he threw himself down in the snow as soon as he was safely among his own. He laid on his back and watched the crowns of the pine trees dance against a blood-red sky. Behind his closed eyelids, a heavy drumbeat played relentlessly, but it no longer bothered him. He lay still and felt the pulse beat in his throbbing throat. Finally, the cool crept in under his coat and chilled the drops of sweat like ice. Then he sat up and looked around.

The peasants began to advance again. Reinforcements came constantly. Soon they would be able to go to spears. There was another flash down below, and the black smoke hung between the branches. But Dacke's men also had arquebuses, and they stood on higher ground and could shoot further. He watched the knechts fall back again. Gray bundles could be seen here and there in the snow.

He grabbed hold of a tree branch and swung himself up with effort. Then he turned looking for the drummer who continued to pound the drumhead, relentlessly and with little skill. The drummer stood in an open place with some other peasants around him. He was well dressed. Andreas turned his face down to the valley. His eyes were slits against the snow, and his red beard flailed in the wind. The drummer was barking orders loudly to the men who ran by.

Andreas was amazed and took a few steps closer to see. It was Nils Dacke himself! Dacke stood here beating on his drum while the men fought down in the woods? Was he trying to drown out the loud reports and screams below for fear?

The priest despised him completely. Shuddering, he went back down the slope with a determined grip on the shaft of his crossbow. His legs were not very steady. He was weak from running.

He reached the frontline, rested his crossbow on a large stone, laid flat on his stomach, and took distant aim. The shot went, but he did not notice anything. He looked up and aimed even more carefully. This time he saw the man down there fall. He pressed his lips together. He had two bolts left. He fell behind the stone and began to wind the crossbow up again.

He let another bolt fly and then sat down behind the rock motionless with the weapon on his knee, realizing what he had done. He stared straight forward without looking at anything. It was as if the daylight failed. It was as if the priest's frock was stripped away from his body and fell off in sooty flakes. The only thing that remained was a freezing naked man, for whom suddenly a fearful truth had been revealed.

He had forfeited his office!

How could he forget himself like that? He had not even thought about it. A man had pointed his gun at him within thirty yards, and he had shot back. It was so natural: my life or your life. Then he just continued. And then he remembered that every cleric that shed the blood of man suffered at that very moment from incapacity to perform any priestly function whatsoever. He was prohibited by canonical law from doing anything before he obtained the Holy Father's dispensation and forgiveness.

He sat completely paralyzed. Then he threw the crossbow from him. It was as if at the same time he threw everything away in the snow, everything he had loved more than anything in the world up till now: the right to be a Christian child, the right to celebrate the mass, the right to forgive sins and anoint the dying. Only the Holy Father in Rome could return the right to him. Now he was just as hopelessly lost as the matricidal Staffan. He would not be able to travel to Rome during this confusing time, and then be able to return to Fröjerum. That was precluded. He bowed his head in his hands and cried. The whole violent tension and fatigue, the whole grief over the fallen, and the fierceness of this horrible slaughter of men flowed together with the shame and despair that came when he realized he was unfit for the priesthood. He cried like a helpless and abandoned child. He cried as he had never cried since he laid and sobbed in Master Gottschalk's deacon stables as a schoolboy.

* * *

Martin Ragnvaldsson stopped a couple of times and looked between the trees. He saw something lying in the drift, a formless and snowy bundle of homespun, in a ring of red poppies. In one place, something stuck up out of the bundle: a gray shirtsleeve and a bloody fist with two fingers hanging loosely by a bit of skin. Scrivener Martin shut his eyes and looked the other way.

The snow began to fall, and it was hard work to move forward. The horse reared up at the racket from the arquebuses that were even closer now. He would rather have tied the old mare to a tree, but he did not know if he would be able to come back the same way.

The tracks after the battle were all a tight mess. Two lightly wounded men came limping down the path. The one had his forearm raised. The other had a flesh wound in his calf. He limped along with the fork from an arquebus like a crutch under his arm. They laughed and said that the commander was going to clear up the forest. At first, they had had a hard fight but now the forest thieves fled up to the ridge in earnest. There had been a proper struggle in the woods, and they had suffered major losses.

The scrivener felt comfortable again and continued up the hill. The shooting seemed to be slowing again. A whole pile of arquebuses with their forks lay nicely stacked on a coat by the side of the road. He stared at them in wonder. They must have been left here during the advance. The men who handled them were either badly wounded or dead. He looked between the trees to investigate. War was a bloody business.

He continued straight forward. It was apparent that the worst of the battle happened here. Everywhere lay fallen branches. There were royal knechts lying dead in harnesses and helmets. It was these same men who had kept him company in Vadstena last night.

Suddenly he stopped. He had lost the path and ended up in a small clearing. On the one side grew a thicket of spruce, on the other side some bare bushes. Many tracks ran straight over the glade. The snow had been swept off a couple of firs by some invisible hand, and inside the bushes, sat balls of soft snow at the bottom of the boughs; otherwise, the twigs were bare.

There was something between the firs and the willow thicket that caught his attention. It was similar to the tracks of a large deer that had dragged itself through the snow. There was a river of red in the left corner. He followed the track past the grove of trees just behind him. A little higher up on the slope lay a great flat stone. A dead man lay stretched out across the stone. It was no knecht. He did not have a harness, and the hat that lay in the snow was a common felt hat. It was one of the rebels.

Scrivener Martin went to him out of curiosity. It was a very young man. Strangely enough, he lay there with bare feet. The pant legs that covered the ankle were wrapped in green strips of wool. His face was not full. It was the open face of a boy, light, and beardless. It could have been any of his childhood friends back in Fröjerum. The boy looked remarkably like the churchwarden in Flodlycke. It was strange that such a man would join with Dacke.

Suddenly, the scrivener bent over and looked at the dead man's knife and went completely pale. The long dagger had a house mark on the bracket, a crescent moon with three notches. He had seen this mark before—as a boy in Flodlycke, and most recently in the silver inventory from Fröjerum.

He let the horse go where it wanted and hurried on. He searched through the trees and set his course for the next corpse. He examined it and breathed easier. It was an unknown man. The next man lay face down in a pool of blood. He grabbed him by the hair and lifted his head, but he let it down immediately. The man was unrecognizable.

He happened to see the glint of a helmet in the snow and stopped again. Then he lifted the helmet with trembling hands. There was no mistaking it. He had worn this helmet himself when they played war as boys in Dikareby. This had belonged to the peasant Sigge. Erik Siggesson and Martin were almost the same age; they had worn the helmet alternately and fought with toy arrows so that the splinters flew. He could still hear the boyish laugh through the still evenings of July.

He bent over again. He gently laid his hands on the dead man's ears and lifted his head. He looked for a long time and then laid it back down silently. It was Erik of Dikareby, his childhood play buddy.

Half stupefied, he got up and moved on. He did not want to see any more dead men today, but he was driven to them by an irresistible force. He looked for one after the other. There was Måns of Långstena, who he used to help fish. There was Erik of Kvisslehult, just as freckled as before. There lay Sverker, who had also played in the meadows of Dikareby.

Finally, the scrivener stopped before a tall man who lay all rolled up behind a spruce tree. He had escaped to this place like a wounded animal. He had tried to stop the bleeding from his shot-up leg with snow. His dead hand still held a bloody snowball against the wound. His face with the weeklong stubble was turned upward. A huge birthmark sat like a brown lichen on one temple. Two gold teeth had bit into his bottom lip.

When Scrivener Martin saw the face, he began to cry, hard, as one cries for a brother that has been accidentally shot. This man had served as a laborer for mother Bothild. He had carved wooden swords and whittled bark boats for the boys. He had taught them to hold the reins and ride bareback. One Easter morning, he had carried Martin up the endless steps to the church because he could not miss Easter Matins. A more honorable laborer had never served at Askanäs.

He heard a cry of pain within the forest and the noise of crossed spears and tips off in the distance with the heated cries from men in hand to hand combat. Scrivener Martin sat beside the hired man from Askanäs and cried. He laid Erik Siggesson's head down, folded his hands, shut his eyes, and placed the folded hat under his neck. Then he felt like a traitor, a fratricide, among all these dead men. In the face of this excess of misery and suffering, the great idea of nationhood fell to tatters. He no longer thought. He only felt strongly and intensely. Something that caused so much unreasonable suffering for people could not be right. He remembered the chamber scrivener's words from yesterday with appalling clarity: First, His Grace plunders the churches and taunts the peasants into rebellion, then he hires knechts with the church's silver and sics them on the peasants. Then the churches are empty, and the coffers are empty, the peasants all shot, the farms deserted, and the knechts leave with the silver.

Yes, this was insane. It was a crime. This devilish authority, this unmerciful regime that sacrificed the people for the state; it was the creation of an evil spirit! And he had served this satanic power! Had he not written payrolls, and orders and mandates for the knechts who would shoot all his childhood friends?

He got up and stumbled on through the snow. His horse followed him slowly as the shooting came closer. Some wounded men passed by at a distance; two men carried a third. Someone screamed over by a large fir. It sounded like he was trying to shout at someone. Scrivener Martin had enough of this. He wanted to turn around, but he could not abandon the man over there. He went closer.

It was a tall man who sat leaning against a pine tree. He had slipped down so that only his shoulders leaned against a root where it joined the tree. His head leaned forward, and he was unnaturally pale. A lower leg bent inward at a right angle where it was shot through. The man still had his wits about him and looked at the scrivener with large eyes.

"Is the pastor coming now?"

He rubbed over his eyes as if he did not see clearly. Then he directed his inquiring eyes back at the scrivener. He spoke very weakly.

"Herr Anders . . . It should have been Anders . . . but this is Martin of Askanäs."

The scrivener winced. Now it was his turn to take a close look at the man. Really . . . this waxy pale man was Tall Staffan from Helgetorp.

"Staffan!" he said. "You actually recognize me?"

Staffan seemed to be laboriously searching his thoughts to straighten them out.

"Martin," he said. "Martin . . . it should have been Anders . . . or can *you* absolve me?"

"Absolve?"

"Yes . . . for matricide. I burned my mother in the sauna. Now I shall burn in hell for it . . . I want to do penance so badly . . . But I cannot."

"You want to be forgiven?"

"Yes, forgiveness . . . But only the pope can give it to me . . . and perhaps a priest."

"Only God can give forgiveness," Martin said flatly. He understood this well from the preaching of Master Olaus. "And you receive God's forgiveness for Christ's sake if you believe."

"But what should I pay for penance money then?"

"Penance money, Christ has paid that for you! He paid it with His suffering and death on the cross. That is why you receive forgiveness if you believe in Jesus."

Staffan looked at the scrivener inquisitively.

"How do you know that?"

"It is written in the Bible."

"So then, it is true?"

"It is God's own clear word!"

Then the wounded man looked at Martin suspiciously.

"Do you promise?"

"Yes, I will do that, with an oath if you want."

Scrivener Martin was stunned by his boldness. Perhaps it was Tall Staffan's pale yellow face, where soot and sweat made dark squiggles over the white complexion that caused him to throw all caution to the wind.

Staffan still looked doubtful.

"Do you believe there is forgiveness for once such as me? Who murdered his mother?"

Martin began to understand the context. He would rather have fled. He had no right to speak here. He stood under the wrath of God himself. But he answered firmly:

"Yes, there is—if you regret your misdeeds."

"Should I not have regret? Three nights mother has stood by my bed in burning clothes . . . Twice I have wanted to walk into the sea, but I dared not. I have lived as a villain, without communion, without blessing, without peace in my own home . . . and I have not deserved better."

Martin did not know what he should say. He tried to think of what Master Olaus would have said. Perhaps he could sing a hymn for Staffan? Slowly he said: "There is *one* peace for all—through Jesus Christ, our Lord. May I sing a song for you?"

For my lost cause, Christ shed his blood
And for my guilt did penance
When on the holy cross of wood
He suffered all my sentence
And bid me peace and welcome
He now my Savior has become
Who makes my home His kingdom.[16]

---

[16] The tune is "Nun Freut Euch," or "Now we all rejoice." It is a Luther hymn that can be found in the Lutheran Service Book, #556. The translation used in this story was the translation of Olaus Petri. His translation has this line about Christ doing penance for us that is not translated this way in any English translations I have found, but it is obviously important to this conversation.

Martin was no singer. His voice struggled and sounded a bit flat in the forest. But he sang powerfully. Within him, he heard the hymn singing in the Storkyrkan.

The dying man had listened with half-shut eyes. Now he looked up again.

"Was it for my guilt he did penance?"

"Yes."

"For me too?"

"For you and the whole world."

"Even for a matricide?"

"Yes, and for all robbers, murderers and prostitutes . . . as long as they want to believe and receive it."

"May I believe it?"

"Yes, you may!"

The doubt in the dying man's eyes began to change into something that looked like expectant joy.

"Can you promise it?"

"Yes, Staffan, with an oath."

"Do you dare stake your salvation on it?"

"Yes, a thousand times over."

Staffan was quiet for a moment.

"Would you sing that verse for me again?"

The scrivener sang again, still struggling and a little flat. Staffan lay completely still with closed eyes. Then he mumbled.

"For my lost cause, Christ shed his blood/And for my guilt did penance/When on the holy cross of wood/ He suffered all my sentence/ And bid me peace and welcome/He now my Savior has become/ Who makes my home His kingdom."

The remainder disappeared in an unintelligible garble. The shooting picked up again in the vicinity, branches broke, and snow fell in heavy landslides. Caught by an impulse, the scrivener bent over and yelled in the dying man's ears:

"Listen, Staffan! Jesus said to the thief: today, you shall be with me in paradise. To—day—you—shall—be with me—in paradise!"

Perhaps something brightened up in Tall Staffan's face. Or did he just become a shade paler?

Scrivener Martin wasn't sure how long he had sat next to the dying man in the snow. Finally, the fight came so close to him that occasional bullets whistled past or slammed into the ground in the very close vicinity. Some knechts were visible between the trees. They came running with arquebuses over their shoulders, stopped to catch their breath and load. So they set up their forks and aimed. Many others appeared. They also turned around and loaded.

Suddenly, Peder Brahe's voice bellowed between the branches.

"Don't run, men! Stay calm, load, and aim . . . share the powder so that there is enough for everyone. Wait until we form up, then we will shoot a salvo and shave the forest clean. After that, we can go home and rest for the day."

He caught sight of the scrivener and came over to him. He flipped his visor up. Sweat ran in streams over his red face, and his eyes shined.

"Where are the Landsknechts keeping house? And the Upplanders? And all the fähnleins of this immense host?"

"They are standing in the field by Skrukeby, waiting for Dacke's men," Martin said. His voice had a scornful and hostile ring in it.

"Can you believe it?" The commander laughed. "There they stand and rest while I do all the work with the forlorn hope and a few Dalecarlians. But we have shot well and hacked the forest thieves like aspen leaves. They litter the entire forest now, several hundred I'm guessing. The worst is that they shot my ensign—a shame for such a promising man."

He had loosened the plate on the left underarm and carefully lifted the sweater. There were a few blue bruises, dark and bloodshot against the white skin.

"The pack of devils," he said. "They can't even secure the tips on their bolts. They hit like rocks. Here it looks as if you were beaten by apprentices in the back yard. But those taken by snipers have no honest wounds to show."

The scrivener had risen when the commander came forward and stood like a statue. His face was pale and completely motionless. He looked down at the ground. Herr Peder didn't notice anything but continued just as boisterously:

"We don't need to spare the powder now, boys. Give them the parting blow so that they neither see nor hear. Then we gather up our things and go home. You, with the crossbows, make sure we don't have forest thieves directly on our heels. Take the wounded to the field surgeon. There is one there, by the way" he pointed at Tall Staffan with his sword.

"He looks like a forest thief," Peder added the next minute adjusting his helmet.

"No, lord," said the scrivener quickly. "He is no forest thief. I know him well."

The Commander stared at his scrivener in amazement, looked at Tall Staffan, and said:

"You're in danger of becoming nearsighted, you ink-spiller. That man doesn't belong to us. The scabbard gives it away. Kill him, men, and let's go."

He waved to a pair of knechts who were leaning on their long-shafted halberds looking on. The one swung his ax and took a firmer grip on the shaft. The scrivener felt the blood rise to his head. With two long steps, he was in front of the dying man and stood straddled across his chest, which heaved with death rattles.

"Then you will have to kill me first," he said.

The knecht stared at him, confused, and let the ax down. The commander who already turned to go to the line of fire made an about-face. He released the strap to his arm plate, which he held between his teeth while he tried to make a knot. His eyes were no longer boyish, but steel gray and hard.

"What sort of treachery is this? Do you keep company with forest thieves?"

He took a step closer.

"Out with it now! Who is that man?"

"An old neighbor of mine."

"That doesn't concern me! Did he fight for the King or Dacke today?"

"He has fought for the faith of his fathers and his native home."

The scrivener was amazed at the calm in his voice. His low-key tranquility seemed almost straightforward. He was so tired from the night-watch and fasting that he had not thought through the consequences of his words.

Now the commander's patience was coming to an end. Martin noticed that his nerves were already taxed beyond the breaking point. He clenched his fist at the scrivener.

"Now you be quiet, traitor! Or do you want me to open your belly and gag your mouth with your intestines? Do you know who you serve? Whose payment do you have in your purse? Whose horse are you riding? Whose seal do you wear on that coat?"

The scrivener felt the ground give way under him. He still stood straddled over Staffan's dying body. Without answering, he pulled off his coat, undid the buttons on his red sweater sown from the fabric he received in payment for being a scrivener. He pulled it over his head, put it all together, stepped cautiously over the fallen man, and went over to the commander. With a deep bow, he laid the sweater in the snow before his feet. He loosened the purse from his belt and let it fall in the bundle. With his sweaty shirt stuck to his chest, he stood before Herr Peder and looked him straight in the eye.

"Noble Herr, with God as my witness, I have never had a treacherous thought in my mind but have only served His Majesty with life and limb. But if I have to watch my best friends from childhood be slaughtered like unruly animals, then my service has become too much for me. There lies my sweater and money, and there is my horse, and now I ask permission to . . ."

He couldn't say anymore before a crashing salvo from the arquebuses drowned everything out. Wild screams followed, from pain and the whining of bolts. The commander turned in a flash and rushed to the line of fire. The knechts grabbed their axes and hurried after. There was already hand to hand fighting among the branches over to the right. Arquebusiers withdrew in disarray, and the commander ran around and tried to find men with crossbows to make a stand.

Scrivener Martin thought for a moment. Among the screams in the forest, he distinctly heard his hometown's dialect. It burned him. He felt like a caged animal who hears the call of the wild. For a second, he wanted to run into the forest. But then he thought. The murder of nobles, arson, papistry—that way was closed to him. Now, he would withdraw to other areas. He stayed with Staffan for a minute, thinking it all over in his head. Staffan's fluttering chest had ceased to move. Martin stroked his cheeks almost affectionately. Staffan was still warmer than the snow.

So, then he slipped his coat over his ice-cold shirt. He turned and looked hesitantly at the sweater lying red in the snow for a moment. Just a moment—then he pulled his coat tight and walked down the hill without looking back.

* * *

The forlorn hope gathered out in the field where the fähnleins stood in black cadres. With quiet exhaustion, the knechts cleaned half-melted snow clumps from their armor and thumbed their bruises with frozen red hands. Now and then, an extended cry alerted the camp to the field surgeons' tables or to the nobility who argued excitedly. The commander went right to the council of the realm, and they, in turn, berated him for having risked his life in a way that did not become a field officer.

The early winter dusk already fell upon the snow-covered fields. A few gray shadows could be caught in the forest edge, quick and shy like wolves. Between the junipers, they showed their helmets and fiery red faces. Only to immediately pull them in again and hide further back in the brushwood. They looked shyly to the right and the left. Small clusters of gray figures had grouped behind stands of spruce and boulders. Further out, some came down the ridge with stiff and tired steps.

Out in the fields, the royal forces still stood in closed formations. One of the German fähnleins had begun to move. A whole forest of swaying lances moved a few steps down toward the ridge and then turned to the south. It was enough to make the few gray figures to disappear in the forest as quietly as they came. What could they do here, a handful of peasants with old-fashioned armor and used bolts?

The fallen men lay like black stones in the dim light. Some of the peasants went to work plundering and searching for a helmet or a good sword; others looked for their neighbors or a brother among the bloody heaps. There were not many words. The day had been too demanding. The sacrifice of blood too great. Only Dacke went around and sought to create a mood of victory. There were not many who listened to him.

In Mölleby, on the other side of the ridge, the peasants began to flood together, seeking quarters for the night. Those shot and stabbed were already in rows on the hay, and the cottages were stripped of what meat and beer there was to be found. After a short while, the alarm and bustle rose again. A few salvos of laughter rumbled through the dusk, but there was no real feasting. Everything sunk beneath the heavy, joyless exhaustion. Only the wounded continued to wail, and a few evening wayfarers came limping along in the dirty snow with their rattling booty.

Herr Andreas had found a lone estate down by the river. He left to go seek out his parishioners. He had difficulty looking them in the eye. And he wanted to avoid hearing how many of them remained lying in the forest. He sat on the floor in the dirty straw that was damp with snowmelt. The fire crackled in the fireplace. A few men sought to bind up another's shot-up arm in the firelight. Pale white skin exposed itself between bloody bandages. Other men lay stretched out all around, on their backs, or in balls like injured animals, without being bothered when men stepped over them or were laid at their side.

Herr Andreas tried to think. Dimly he thought that the peasant army had been defeated even if they held their ground. Dacke would be compelled to retreat to the woods. Östergötland would not fall into his hands like ripe fruit. It did not need to mean the cause was lost, but the victory they hoped for was no longer within reach.

He tried to figure out what would happen now. In the morning, they would gather their dead. In long rows of toboggans, they would carry them home through the woods. The parishioners would meet at the district centers. They would mourn as they had never done before, and then there would be a funeral the likes of which Fröjerum had never seen. They would at least bury the men with honor. The survivors would drink to their dead ashes, men would swear to avenge them, and women would promise to remember them as long as they could braid their hair or loosen a shoe strap.

Some strangers had come in and stood in the door hesitantly. Then one of them walked right over the sleeping bodies. He had a message for the priest. One of their neighbors had just died from his wounds. Because they were from Vissefjärda, there was no way to carry him home. Would the priest be so good as to bury him early in the morning, then they would open a grave at dawn here in the churchyard so that he would at least rest in consecrated ground.

They pressured the priest, but he only had one answer to give.

"I can't," he said. "I am not worthy. I shot a knecht today and spilled blood, and no priest that has spilled blood can ever minister again before he is redeemed."

"If the pastor was with us on the ridge today, then the pastor has the right to bury our dead," said the Smålander.

"It's not that way, men, I may not. No one but the pope can reinstate a priest who has shed blood."

The men looked disappointed. But they conceded to this point about the pope. They left discouraged.

No one but the Pope—Herr Andreas let his head sink to his knees. He froze. His shirt was soaked through with sweat and felt as if it was soaked in ice-cold water. He felt the cold rising from the floor through the soaked straw.

No one but the pope—This was his desperate emergency. Obedience to the church now prevented him from serving the church! He had to suffer it out of love for his church, as the love for the church had hitherto irresistibly forced him to be a priest. He felt that he could not return to Fröjerum again, so long as he was unqualified for ministry. In the morning, he ought to disappear in the crowd. Perhaps he could still serve God's cause with a crossbow. Or perhaps he could be of use as a scrivener for Dacke. But to keep the Lord's laymen in his hand, absolve men of their sins and make the children of Christians into heirs of heaven, that was forbidden for him. Would he ever do it again?

He dropped the helmet that he turned in his hands and wiped his eyes. Then he rolled up in a ball, shivering with aching joints. He pulled his hat down over him so that no one would see that he cried.

* * *

The plains around Skeninge were lifeless and deserted in the twilight. The snowdrifts were not blue like other winter evenings. It was just a heavy and joyless dark falling from the bluish-gray clouds. The snow had been packed together in the thaw. It was all a lackluster gray.

Scrivener Martin came with heavy steps walking on the great road from the south into the city. Before him, the Church of Our Lady raised her snow-covered roof ever higher against the sky, and the dark shadows of the tower walls grew in the dusk. His legs were stiff, and his groin ached from all the exertion and riding. He made his way through the wet snow with great effort.

The city was silent and motionless. Sheds and warehouses blocked the view of the merchant city houses, and not a single light was visible out on the plain. The immense church lay as if on watch with a half-open eye looking over all fields and roads around her, visible to every eye that happened to glance across the plain, he felt naked and exposed before the invisible eye that burned up there in the heavens somewhere behind the clouds. But this evening, he entertained no fear. He was on his way home.

Within the city, he asked for directions to Gregor the barber-surgeon's house. He received directions to a little stone house just behind the church. The whole ground floor was a warehouse with small windows behind fixed shutters. Up above, there was a weak ray of light shining through a small window.

He hesitated for a moment in the gateway. Then he conquered his insecurity and fumbled up the steps between the cold stone balustrades leading to the door. His hand rested on the doorknocker.

Again, he hesitated.

He heard a shrill and monotone voice inside that seemed to be reading something, but not like a calm and stayed canticle. It was an eager, pleading voice that sometimes climbed up to a loud shouting. Then it fell back again to its old domain, and some other voices murmured ascent.

Martin knocked.

The voices inside abruptly abated. He heard steps coming, and the door opened. A little black-haired man with a broad face and dark goatee stood in the cool and half dark interior hallway. His eyes were sharp and questioning in the dim light.

Martin asked for Kort Lange.

The lively little man instantly brightened up and invited the scrivener inside. The door to the interior room opened up, and Kort Lange stood in the light and with an inquisitive face at first and then with amazement.

"Martin! What a happy surprise . . . Welcome!"

He took his friend by the hand and brought him into the warm chamber.

"Now you stay here this evening and the rest of the night. When do you have to return to Vadstena?"

"I should hope never," said the scrivener. Then he saw the amazement of the others and added:

"I have come here to begin a new life. I thought I might ask for your help."

He was not bothered that the others stared at him. Kort Lange said with his soft voice very solemnly:

"Welcome then, Brother Saul—today you shall be called Paul."

He turned to the others.

This is Martin Ragnvaldsson, whom we just prayed for . . . so the Lord hears the prayers of his people.

Only now did Martin look around. A pair of candles lit up the little room that was shaded blue with dark hangings. There was a fire glowing in the fireplace over in a corner. Strangers sat along the wall, apparently people of the merchant city, though their clothes looked like that of peasants. They greeted him heartily.

"Take your coat off and sit down," Kort Lange said.

The scrivener was a little embarrassed, but he unbuttoned his coat and took it off. The others stared in amazement at his bare shirt.

"Yeah," he said, bemused, "my red sweater is lying in the snow. There was a curse with it . . . it held me close to the devil. So I tossed it . . ."

The others exchanged a long look and nodded.

"Tell us," said Kort Lange and pushed a chair forward. Martin sank heavily and wiped his brow.

"What shall I say?" he said. "Blood and misery, cursing and crying . . . Where should I begin? Today, King Gösta has fed the ravens for decades to come. The whole forest is full of bodies. They lie in heaps. The blood has made red streams in the snow. The stench of manslaughter reaches all the way to Mölleby . . ."

He snorted as if he tried to get the smell of blood out of his nostrils. Then he put his hands up to his face and leaned forward, with his elbows on his knees. Then he moaned.

"Jesus, Jesus, Jesus, . . . they were all slaughtered. Ground flesh and bloody chunks . . . Erik of Dikareby, Staffan of Helgetorp, Gisle, Torkel, and Elif and Larsbo-Sven, all of them are dead . . . Lord have mercy upon us."

His broad shoulders began to shake from grief. Kort Lange laid his hand on him slowly.

"We knew that it would go that way," he said slowly and searchingly. "We knew it in advance. He who grabs the sword perishes by the sword."

After a moment, he continued.

"But you shall live, Martin. Today God has subdued the old in order to give you something new and better."

There was silence again.

"May I show you something, Martin."

The scrivener looked up.

"What?"

"Your debt of blood."

"What do you mean?"

"Brother Martin," said Kort Lange with the same quiet authority. "Today, you have been able to see the worldly life of perversion. Be glad that you have been able to see it while there is still time for repentance. For in the midst of this worldly life, you have stood up until this day. The blood that cries up to heaven in Mölleby forest, you have been present to shed yourself. The royal knechts have murdered with led and swords today. You have long murdered with your tongue and eyes and the heart. Anyone who hates his brother, he is a murderer, the apostle John says. You have hated the wine merchant's servant that you beat in Helga Lekamens Gränd. You have shot sharp arrows with your tongue against Mattias Ålänning in the chancellery. You mocked him for his speech and his skewed mouth and made life bitter for him. When one hates there will be fights and quarrels, when twenty hate, there are disruptions and feuds, when thousands hate, there is rebellion and war and misery without end. But all that begins with a single man who hates. And you have done this. Because you have been like the many and the many like you: half-Christians, quarter-Christians, tenth-Christians, Evangelicals by name and heathen in fact, that is why it looks as it now does in Mölleby forest."

Scrivener Martin still sat hunched over. If Kort Lange had said any such thing a half a year ago, he would have hit him on the ear and kicked him out. Now he thought of the blood puddles in the forest, homeland, limitless doom climbed and accused him and overwhelmed him with his bloodguilt from which he must be cleansed.

"What shall I do?" he said.

"Hear what God says," Kort Lange said. He went to the table and paged through a heavy Bible. Then he began to read:

> Behold, the LORD's hand is not shortened, that it cannot save,
> or his ear dull, that it cannot hear;
> but your iniquities have made a separation
> between you and your God,
> and your sins have hidden his face from you
> so that he does not hear.

Scrivener Martin sat still with his face in his hands. His body was dead tired, and his thoughts stopped. There was a dark void in his head, that was filled with the heavy and authoritative word of the Bible. Kort Lange continued to read:

> For your hands are defiled with blood
> and your fingers with iniquity . . .

Scrivener Martin lifted his heavy head from his hands and stared at them. No, the blood wasn't visible. He had almost sensed the smell of it—the blood from the murdered men of Fröjerum, who died at the hands of the church plunderers that he kept accounts for, and a tax screw that he had been tightening. And this was perhaps just one of the sins. "And your fingers defiled with iniquity." He felt a need to wipe his hands off on his trousers. It was as if something was stuck fast on them: long, sticky threads of impurity and guilt. What had these hands not done? Money stolen in childhood, mice tortured to death, and improper behavior, fighting as a young man, and bloody wounds, drunkenness, fornication and whoring, promissory notes never redeemed, jealousy letters, and improper letters . . .

He noticed that he had not listened to a thing Kort Lange had read in a long while. He was attentive again.

> Their feet run to evil,
> And they are swift to shed innocent blood . . .

This again was a description of himself? He heard the tramp of his horse on the road to Hof. Yes-it had cheered him up to be at the fight. He had seen with the expectation to this bloody day, but another thought plagued him, the thought that perhaps he too would get a bolt in the belly.

> The way of peace they do not know,
> and there is no justice in their paths;
> they have made their roads crooked;
> he who treads on them knows no peace.

"It is true," the scrivener mumbled. He sat with his face hidden in his hands again. "He never knows peace . . ." no, he had not had peace because he had not wanted to know the way of peace. Perhaps, he had gone the right way for a long time. He had wanted to be a righteous Swede, an honorable man, an irreproachable officer. But he had constantly made small steps toward the wrong paths. He had not made a violent break with the good and true God, but he kept himself content with the miserable idols. He had worshiped mammon in his careless business deals. He had one temple in intoxication, and another in lust. He had constantly crept there on crooked roads to sin secret sins, full of shameful pleasure and bitter enjoyment. Yes, it was true: he who wanders, he has no peace.

Kort Lange continued reading:

> Therefore justice is far from us,
> and righteousness does not overtake us;
> we hope for light, and behold, darkness,
> and for brightness, but we walk in gloom.
> For our transgressions are multiplied before you,
> and our sins testify against us;
> for our transgressions are with us,
> and we know our iniquities.

Scrivener Martin crouched down under the light as if someone hit him. Again, he thought: it is true, every word is true.

Kort Lange finished reading.

"Martin, Brother Saul," he said slowly, "do you acknowledge your sins?"

"Yes," the scrivener said with unclear voice. He still held his face in his hands.

"Do you want to be absolved of them?"

"Yes."

"Are you prepared to forsake the world and all its vanity."

"Yes!"

The scrivener's voice had become firmer and more distinct. But he still kept his face nestled in his hands.

Kort Lange closed the Bible and bowed to the others. They slowly rose and came up to the scrivener. He felt their hands on his head, a bundle of warm hands, heavy and light, trembling and fixed on each other. They touched his hair, his neck, and his shoulders.

Kort Lange spoke, authoritatively and ceremoniously:

"So, we absolve you, our brother Saul, in the name of our Lord God. Your sins are forgiven, your misdeeds redeemed. They will never again be remembered because you have repented. And now we prepare you to walk among the Lord of Sabaoth's chosen—from now until eternity."

"Amen," said the others and lifted their hands from the scrivener's head.

"Beloved brothers and sisters in the Lord," said the little dark man, now we kneel and pray for this our newborn brother Paul, that he may grow up and be strong in the Lord.

They knelt on the floor. Martin himself lifted his head from his hands and fell on his knees. The others in the room began to pray, all at once, some loudly and shouting, others mumbling whisper. He didn't bother himself to hear what they said. He prayed silently. He had not prayed like this since he was a child on his knees at home in Askanäs at his mother's side before the crucifix and the candlelight in a niche in the wall. He felt that he returned to his childhood peace. Amid this strange and weird environment, he felt as if he came back home. And at the same time, something new had begun, something unknown and captivating. He had exchanged kings today. Now he belonged to the Lord Sabaoth's elect. Kort Lange had called him "Paul." He understood that these friends expected something great from him. Yes, Lord, he prayed, let me do something for you, something great and completely for your glory.

Some rattling on the door knocker interrupted the prayers. Everyone went quiet, and some stayed on their knees. Scrivener Martin caught himself stumbling as he got up. Was he still afraid to serve his new king? He shamefully went to his knees again. The little man with the goatee took a lamp and went to answer the door again. Martin could hear the exchange of words in the hall. A knecht's loud voice requested that the barber-surgeon come with him immediately. The wounded from Skrukeby had come, and the whole cloister of the black brothers was full. The barber-surgeon excused himself, saying he was busy. The other became abusive and began to swear. The barber-surgeon finally promised to come as soon as he could. The other took his leave, and the little man shut the door.

"The curses of the world and the devil's invocations follow us even here," said the barber-surgeon when he came back in again. "But let them not disturb our devotion. It is not every day a Christian can enjoy fellowship in the brotherhood of the faith."

The prayers began again. They invited the scrivener to pray out loud. He did it awkwardly, stuttering. Then a man sang while still kneeling. The minutes passed. The scrivener felt a sting in his conscience. Ought not the barber-surgeon go to the wounded? But he shoved the thought away. If one dedicated himself to God completely, then he had to put all worldly things on the back burner. Nothing could be more important than worship.

Another song followed. This time it was a soft and lively melody in German. The scrivener hid his tired head in his hands again. He could not think anymore. He let the strong wave of song and warm fellowship carry his will.

The barber-surgeon took his leave and promised to return soon. Kort Lange read again from the large Bible. Martin was infinitely tired, but at the same time, buoyant. He leaned against the wall, pulled his coat over his shoulders, and let everything pass as if in a dream.

It was late, but they kept praying and singing more songs. The barber-surgeon still dallied, they determined to part ways.

Only when they were alone did Kort Lange begin to talk about Martin's future. He had a suggestion that he had kept for a long time in case his friend would want to leave the world. Gert Hubmaier, his housemaster, had been saying for half a year that he would have work for a scrivener if he could find anyone who was truly evangelical. It was a good occupation, in particular for one who wanted to stay unstained by the world. And so they could work together. If he needed to escape the king, Martin could disappear and leave the country for half a year.

Scrivener Martin sat silently by the wall. He only smiled. So, God arranged everything for his children. Before one could cry, he had heard. Before one knew enough to worry seriously, they were relieved. He felt happily confident. He was finally home. The eye that had watched over him for half a year accusingly and without compromise shined anew with pure, fatherly mercy.

He laid his head back against the wall and shut his eyes. He felt quite comfortable and calm in the heated room. It had even dried his sweat-soaked shirt. Somewhere far away, he could hear Kort Lange's voice ever firmer. Bloody pictures passed by again, the gun smoke billowing between the branches, the trees swaying and the knechts, the whole forest danced around, as the wounded were lifted and drug around in circular tracks of blood over the clouds. Tall Staffan's sunder shot leg stretched out like a bloody wire and whirled around. Amid this witch's dance, the Church of Our Lady's towers rose with her strict and watchful eye. Then everything was extinguished in empty darkness where only a single light shined, a single candle before the picture of the Savior on the wall in Askanäs. He was home.

Kort Lange suddenly fell silent and looked at his friend, who had not answered in a long time. Then he made a little grimace. He had spoken of the Spirit's sealing of the elect, the most important and holiest thing he knew to speak of, and during that time, his friend had sat and slept. But then he remembered that the scrivener had been on the battlefield earlier today, and he forgave him. He let him sit and went to the bench on the wall, where he began to prepare for bed.

SO THAT EVERY MOUTH MAY BE STOPPED

June 1543

The sun was finally bright and warm. Herr Andreas stretched out, trying to make himself comfortable as he lay face down in the blueberry bush. It smelled of pine needles and juniper. Now and then, a gust wafted up from the newly leafed birches further down at the edge of the forest with the smell of sap and flowers.

The priest pulled the red flowers from the blueberry bush and chewed on them. When he had eaten all he could reach from where he lay, he crawled forward a bit without getting up. For a moment, he thought about rolling on to his back and sleeping in the sunshine. But he knew that he would feel the hunger even more if he rolled over. It was best if he stayed as he was.

The sun warmed his gray peasant frock and threadbare green trousers that had a pair of wide holes torn in the knees. He had tossed his conical hat in the moss, and the sun could burn him all it wanted. His sinewy neck was red as copper. Thick hair covered his tonsure—it had been three months since he had last shaved it. He looked as if he had spent all spring waiting in ambush.

The old priest cautiously lifted his head and looked down at the village between the junipers. He could see the long gray houses in the church-village between the spring green meadows. Above them, the church's black gable shot up out of the oak's bright foliage. He looked at it with longing. Were he not so spent, he would not have cried.

During the four months that had passed since that bloody day in Skrukeby, his old world had fallen apart bit by bit. For a couple of weeks, he had been Dacke's chancellor. He had both authored and printed his letters, pre-read the few letters that came by letter carriers, translated them into peasant speak, and suggested the answer. In these short few weeks, he had received an unsuspected insight into the whole old, tangled rattail of complex interests behind the rebellion. With horror, he had seen how Nils Dacke used his power to beat old antagonists and promote his own family.

When there was finally a lot less to do with the pen, and the whole chancellery had been reduced to four sheets of unused paper along with his worn writing cloth, he excused himself and disappeared with a free company out on the plain. The parts around Skeninge were once again inundated with royal troops because the Upland forces had penetrated Kinda. For a few days, the forest men had hunted bailiffs between Åby and Normlösa while burning estates that belonged to the nobility. Laden with booty, they returned to the forests. But Herr Andreas somehow felt worse off than before, as he walked between the sleds. He could not get rid of the smell of freshly burnt flesh, and the cutting cries of distress within the cottages echoed in his ear.

They were chased far down into the forests of Småland. Dacke had called all the people he could down to Asboland. At Hagelsrum, they waited in the forest and looked out over the lake when the royal troops formed endless columns over the ice. He had felt silent despair when he saw them approach in unfathomable masses; heavy cavalry on steamy horses, colorful soldiers with pennants and plumes, Swedish knechts wearing dented helmets, wagons, sleds and field cannon as far as the eye could see. But the peasants had nerves of steel. They let the main force pass and then broke out of the forest, subdued the reserve forces, and plundered the supply train.

The day before Palm Sunday, they shivered with cold as they crowded behind the massive rubble outside Högsby. As far as the eye could see, the forest road was an endless clutter of uprooted trees, tangled together and covered in snow. But here the royal army turned around and went back, before moving east in a large arch. They broke through it with forced marches. By Good Friday, while a pale and weak sun illuminated the endless snowdrifts without being able to melt a single patch of ice that crusted the snowdrifts on their peaks, they had stopped together on the edge of a forested ridge between two lakes. This time the peasants were caught between the Dalecarlians and the Germans. The whole atmosphere was a howling roar. No one could even say where it came from anymore. It just roared, thundered, and raged all around them. It was as if the men were being flogged by whining whips. As if in a dream, he had seen Dacke carried away with blood cascading from where a bullet had penetrated his thigh. Then they had all dispersed in the forest. As evening approached, he had stood in abandoned livestock shed high up on the ridge and looked out over the cold blue landscape. Under a lifeless sky lay the endless forests, heavy with snow and dead, as if it had long since given up hope for spring. Only down on the ice did black points swarm like ants: the royal army made its way west. His last hope was snuffed out with the sunset.

Then the road steadily descended into the darkest depths of degradation. The rebels formed small bands and settled in the forests. All those who had farms or wives returned. Only those who had received a reputation for the murder of bailiffs or plundering forays kept themselves hidden. People came to heel at churches from Ydre to Tunalän. The king was gentle with his conditions. Offered the prospect of keeping their life and farms, the peasants who had been so thoroughly intimidated were driven into his camp in droves. Then there was famine. The fields had stood dry the previous summer. Now everything had been completely consumed: seeds, chaff, and bran. There was grain to the north, but the king had blocked the roads. It was not worth showing up there without a bailiff's pass. This softened the peasants, and their backbones became like toast soaked in milk. More than one went to the church hill and swore fealty to the king only because he had tired of hearing the hunger pains of his children in the evening.

Dacke suddenly appeared again in May when ice still covered the forest paths, and the frost was just as reluctant to let go in the birch groves. Like fire in fresh-cut straw, the rebellion flared up again and billowed for a moment with pale flames. But it was only the loose people, the landless, lousy men and discredited people that followed him now. For a few short weeks, the hunt was on again in the forests. The king's knechts even made pursuit up toward Rumskulla in the most God-forsaken wilderness where the primeval forest was made impervious by intertwined branches. Now they could go hand to hand. They went forth quietly and steadily, and they had help among the people of the district. More than one estate had begun to ban the rebels and shame them for having brought fire and sudden death to the district.

The bullets and bolts still whined here and there in the branches. Now and then, a knecht fell in an ambush. More often, a rebel was taken when he appeared at a farm to beg for milk or steal a hen. Then his friends could hear the cries far off in the woods as they tied the man to the breaking wheel: wild cries of despair that made his friends stuff their ears with moss and retreat further into the pathless wilderness.

Herr Andreas had suddenly pulled his head down and pressed it into the blueberry bush. Far off in the countryside, someone was walking along the grain fields. The priest followed him with the watchful eye of a highwayman. Then the muscles of his neck relaxed, and he laid his head comfortably on his crossed arms. The man down there had turned toward the church-village. He would not take this road. There was no risk to him lying here in the sun.

The priest knew how the resentment had set itself like bitter dregs in his dry mouth. Here he was lying within spitting distance of his church, like an animal in the dirt. As long as the sun was up, he dared not show himself, for no one could know who had become a traitor. He knew that he would be met with open hostility on more than one farm. Others might smile mockingly at his worn peasant clothes and pretend they did not know him. There were only two places where he hoped to be met with the same esteem as before. But he did not want to go there for fear of bringing them misfortune if he was caught.

Had he not forfeited their respect? Was he not a highwayman and a thief, a robber, and a man of violence? He had broken all God's commandments since he left Fröjerum and sullied all holiness and purity that had once been his crowning glory.

It was quite inconceivable that it could have gone the way it did. He had lived a holy life for years, consecrated to serve God. He thought he could almost feel how the divine grace permeated him, how the power of the sacrament and the purity of the devotional life filled his being down to its most essential fibers and re-created him into a man of God. But all that was needed was for him to come out of his familiar clothes for a couple of short days to expose the sinful nature that lived just as healthily and irrepressible as ever behind the polished exterior.

The catastrophe had come after the unfortunate day at Skrukeby when he lost hope of ever again returning as a priest to Fröjerum. From that day on, everything changed. All that he gradually built up over many long years had been destroyed within two weeks. Before he became a rebel, he had erected an ever-higher tower of spiritual exercises and they had lifted him above the everyday, profane world. He had lived high up there in the clear light and solitude before God. The whole of this proud edifice that he had built with so much effort by prayer and fasting, privations and solitude, had now been crushed with a single blow. When he crawled out of the rubble, he encountered a completely different world. Bearded faces grinned at him without respect, as raw words and course shame rained upon him from all sides. He had more than enough to deal with just trying to get a daily ration of food and fending off fatigue without having to defend himself against his tormentors.

As long as he continued to keep company with his parishioners, he had at least been able to maintain the shine. They revered him and showed respect. They left him in peace if he tried to do his devotions. But from the day he forfeited his office and became a common man stripped of his priestly attire, the last remnant of his old life was scrapped. His days before had been filled with pious exercises. Everything had been directed upward. All that he occupied himself with had one goal, to glorify God and sanctify himself. When he was at times forced to have something to do with men, he had met them in his attire as an officiating priest, a father confessor, or a baptismal officiant. This had preserved his wall against the world and kept it undisturbed. Now, that wall had been breached, and he stood among other sinners like a destitute and helpless man. Now his days were filled with profane chores and the thousand difficulties and stressors that belonged with a field campaign among a band of peasants gone feral in the countryside that had already begun to suffer a lack when it came to the most basic necessities.

These rough-hewn strangers, who had now become his peers and comrades, did not show a trace of reverence for him. When they came to realize that he was not qualified to carry out his office as a priest any longer, they called him Sin-priest or freemartin and showered him with shame. He did not care and answered them with their coarse language. That won him respect. He quickly became as rough mannered in the mouth as any of the others. He even began to swear foul oaths that had never before crossed his lips. He did not quite understand how it came about. It only required a few hard nights in the snow, an exhausted body, the anticipation of a stressful encounter with the enemy and an old leather strap that broke just when it was time to get away, and then oath after oath sprang from his lips—coarse, terrible oaths that profaned both the mother of God and the Lord's Holy Body, and which gave him incredible delight when he uttered them. Afterward, he could be quite ashamed of himself, but when another critical moment came, and his excited fingers fumbled with the crossbow so that it fired early, it broke loose again, even wilder and more hateful than before.

Of course, he found that the coarse language helped him assert himself. In this new world, everyone looked down on him and had their fun with him. He did all he could to rise and be welcomed by his new comrades. He hit like a devil. What was lacking in power, he replaced with daring. He was the first when it came to sneaking up to the knecht's camps in the forest and the last to turn from a lost abatis.[1] At the fire in the evening, when the volleys of laughter echoed and the uncouth speech was given its promised time, he quickly became better than the others. He taught himself all that could be learned in this way, and because he was more quick-minded and skilled at communicating than the forest people, he soon became well known and received everywhere.

Then he received a highwayman's respect and was taken in as a comrade and peer. No one called him Sin-priest anymore. If they called him anything now, it was the Wild Priest. He was proud of this, though he knew that there was a lot of sin attached to this proud title.

It was hardest for him to break with fasting. In the beginning, he had at least tried to keep up with it. But it was quite pitiable. It was right in the middle of Lent when there was hardly any flour to be

[1] A crude field fortification.

found, and the fish were scarce in the frozen brooks that ran through the hilly forest. They had resorted to whatever game they could shoot, and to the booty from the livestock sheds of nobility. The others mocked him for his qualms. He was just as much a sinner as they were, so he could eat meat too when God sent a roebuck straight into their path. One evening when they were on the long march to Dacke in Asboland, he had been left in the snow, hungry and shivering. His comrades had slaughtered a pig and cooked it over the fire. Then he yielded to the temptation and ate big juicy slices of the fragrant meat. He got his strength back and felt an animalistic contentment. He continued living this way, never with a good conscience, but always with great enjoyment.

Naturally, he had also gotten drunk, first in pure despair, and then, again and again, to get a respite of loose-lipped joy in this inhospitably hard existence of blood, starvation, and dread of the breaking wheel. Though he was always ashamed by the hangover, he had never felt so humiliated by his drunkenness as by this, that he had broken the holy fast.

He had now lived as a highwayman for three months. There were few deaths of the highwaymen that he had not been present for and none that he could commit to the earth as a priest.

He finally came to his senses one evening. He was lying in an abandoned lean-to a charcoal burner had made in the forest and chewing on the lichens that covered it. Peder Skägge, Jöns Verkemästare and Birger in Skulebäck had just compromised, Klement in Broddebo was dead and buried. They had just buried with honor and respect in consecrated earth in the cemetery at Vi before public opinion changed. Peder Djup and Frodde Skräddare had fled south to the forests of Blekinge. Those who were left did not resemble honorable rebels in any way. They were simple thieves and forest rabble.

That evening Herr Andreas laid awake for a long time and thought about everything, while thrushes played outside and the summer night's golden sky shown through the collapsed roof. Everything passed by in unmerciful clarity: the helpless defeat of the church, the meaningless sacrifice of blood, his fallen parishioners, his own misspent life, and the holy office that he had once received but forfeited and sullied.

By morning he had reached a determination in his frozen and starved body. In the evening, he had only wanted to stay and wait for death. But despite everything, when he woke wet with dew and shivering the next morning, he had half a determination with which to get to work: He would do penance.

Really, it was all foolishness. But once it had come, it fastened to him hard. Fragmentary parts of the office clung to his hunger-pained head, melancholy melodies, inexorably distant in their delicate purity. Somewhere far down there in the south, in happier lands, they still sang the holy songs. There were still cloisters where a sullied sinner could still go to confession and do penance. If he could only get there, he might be able to do penance for his sin-stained life and find sanctuary behind the wall of some monastery. Yet again, he would be able to live in the beauty of the daily offices and perhaps—perhaps he would one day be able to celebrate mass once again. If God granted him to live long enough, he would do a true penance for everything and win back God's favor, His Grace.

The only question was if he could somehow reach this fortunate land. That all Swedish ports were closed to him was abundantly clear. But over in Ronneby, there was still a small and uncertain path out into the great world. Ronneby merchants held with Dacke because King Gustavus did his best to destroy their business and drag it up to Kalmar. Thus, it was not out of the question that he could find a ship to the Netherlands or perhaps straight to France if he could just get the money.

There was one place on earth where he might be able to find money, the money that would set him up to flee the land and perhaps do penance for his aching heart somewhere behind a monastery wall.

He departed the next morning. He pilfered milk and half-finished cheese in the livestock sheds. So he kept his spirits up. And now he had the goal within sight.

Herr Andreas looked out between the willows on the hill again. His eyes tentatively followed the gray roofs in the church-village, where they laid like long glittering silver bands in the sunlight. Far in the east, the village ended in a large grove of hazelnut trees, where the farms had their milk pens under the tight canopy of leaves. Below the grove, streams glittered in the meadow between high tufts of grass and black puddles trampled by the animals. On the other side of the hill was a pile of stones with a single pole. That was the place.

Almost three and a half years had passed. On a windy winter night just before Christmas, he and the churchwardens had stood there in the pale moonlight that filtered down between snowflakes. The churchwardens had shoveled up the shallow frozen earth. The black earth and muddy water resembled a bloody wound under the snow. Then they buried the old bronze box with the church's coin in the dark hole. Jon of Flodlycke had laid four stones in a cross for a marker, and soon the white snow-covered it completely. No royal bailiff would ever be able to find the place. Only he and the church-wardens knew about it, and they had sworn silence until the last of them had seen the approach of death. Jon of Flodlycke had been murdered by the knechts the following autumn. Lasse of Årtebol had died from the wounds he received at Skrukeby in February. Of the three, he was the only one left.

What if Lasse had told the secret to someone? It would have been strange for him. But he might have believed that his pastor was also dead.

The pastor bowed his head and bit into a dry tree branch. It was more bitter than he could stand that his parishioners would not know if he lived. But he was so ashamed of his lost office and over his human degradation that he did not want to let anyone know. He did not know any more about Ravelunda and Fröjerum than rumor allowed for a highwayman's campfire.

Once again, the tendons in the thin neck tensed, and he lifted his head. His bronzed skin wrinkled between his sunken eyes, and his gaze hung uncertain and hungry at the single stick behind the pile of stone. Then he leaned forward again and began to rip blueberry blossoms and dig grass. It was far into the evening.

* * *

The summer night's light dusk took forever to fall over the countryside. He could see a golden streak in the sky above the village of Flodlycke. A lone night owl fluttered its silent wings between the pines, for a moment it seemed to stand still in the air, and then it disappeared. He saw gold petals of buttercups on the hill in the dark grass.

Like a great black stroke, the pole stood over the gray heap of stones. Far up in the meadow, a single cow made its way to the hazel grove. Her heavy tramp in the mud was the only sound that broke the windless silence.

Herr Andreas stood among the black junipers on the edge of the forest on the other side, black, upright, and as motionless as the trees. He held a staff made of juniper with a broad hook that he had carved into a spade. He looked over each of the black gates suspiciously in the dark under the hazel trees.

Finally, he silently moved the few steps toward the pile of stone. He looked around one last time. Then he was at the pole and looked at the ground with bated breath. Here . . . two steps to the north. Grass and cow parsley had woven themselves over the stones, but they were still there. Palpitating, he moved them aside and began to dig up the damp earth. White roots came up. The rich earth squeaked between the soaked stones. He burrowed down deeper, scraped, and pried. Many times, he hit something hard until he finally felt the corner of the bronze shrine with his wet and dirty fingers.

He rested a moment, listened, dug again, kneeling with earth under his nails and his worn pants soaked with dirty water. Then the shrine released, and he held it between his trembling hands. A minute later, and he was already on his way to the forest.

In among the branches, he threw himself down on his knees, pried the shrine open with the point of his knife. Then he emptied the coins into his worn-out purse. Only when he had closed it and put the loop over his head again so that it hung heavy and large against his bare skin inside his shirt, did it hit him that he had stolen this. The money did not belong to him, but the Fröjerum Church. Certainly, they were lost to the church. Here in the swamp, they were worthless. If he put them back in the sacristy, the king would probably take them. He would rather keep them himself. The church's cause was just as lost as ever now. Could the church, then, use her money for a better purpose than to help her last faithful servant flee this heretical land? Had not Bishop Johannes himself taken the church's silver with him when he sailed for Danzig?

He stood hesitantly with the shrine in his hand. Should he throw it among the trees? It was a beautiful shrine, shaped like a church, with columns and arches engraved on the long sides. It had sat in the coffer of Fröjerum's sacristy since time immemorial.

He had begun to walk toward the dawn that was breaking between the trunks. He still held the shrine indeterminately between his hands while the heavy purse beat against his chest. He dripped with sweat. Was this not still parish property he had around his neck?

All talk . . . What did they lose that wasn't already lost? And because they had spared all their tithes, they were certainly left without harm.

But still, the peasants had stopped tithing, was not the church harmed by that? Had he not robbed his church?

He didn't sort it out. He would confess it when he could finally go to confession again, somewhere far away in a strange land. There was a lot that he would have to confess to then.

He had found the trail through the alcove along the hill that made a large arch south of the church-village. On top of the hillcrest in the north, the silent longings intertwined. Here and there, a black window gaped in the gray timber. The roof ridges were unevenly split and pointed jaggedly against the bright summer sky. A weak wind carried the smell of the pig huts and stables and from the long-swept slopes that drew bright stripes in the steep slopes down to the brook at the bottom of the valley.

The priest stopped and drank in the familiar smell that reminded him of the late evenings of childhood at Askanäs. He continued walking, stopped again under a heavily blooming rowan, and looked up at the village. The last time . . . He would never again see the dawn from the northeast light up the gray timber on the gable of the Elif estate cottage. Never again would he hear the rustle in the aspens at the churchyard wall and see the steeple's powerful profile point to the night sky.

His gaze stopped at the church. He could see the cross high up on the gabled roof. There on the roof, the point of the carved wind vain stretched high above the treetops, like a hand that pointed to the sky.

He had gotten to the point where the great path led up to the church, how he would turn off to the south—forever.

He couldn't do it. He stood still for a long time, still holding the bronze shrine between his hands. Then he went straight down the path in the direction of the church-village.

On the other side of the hill, he entered the willow thicket and began to work his way up to the church slowly. He avoided the open places down by the church hill that had been trodden and stripped of vegetation for centuries and kept himself in the thickets on the outskirts. Then he reached the churchyard wall along the west, and there he stood directly against the steep crest.

Silently he shuffled over the wall and picked up the shrine that he had placed on the wall in front of him. Now he stood in the tall grass in the village of Dikare's graveyard. In three places, the ground was bare. He saw freshly turned turf, and freshly made crosses hammered into the ground. He observed them silently. This is where they had laid Sverker and Erik, who he had seen fall in the forest at Skrukeby. That day must have cost the village of Dikare a third life.

Shyly he looked around. The dim light illuminated newly dug graves everywhere, which had not yet grown gray from age and weather. It was a memorial to the meaningless fight he had drawn his home village into.

He walked on through the grass. Here was the Helgetorp section, there was a single new grave between the tufts. He stopped. Then that is where Tall Staffan was laid to rest. Lingering, he walked over to it and took off his hat. He gave a silent promise that if he were ever again worthy of stepping before the altar, he would say a mass for Staffan's soul every month. If he could have, he would have bent his knee and prayed for him, but he was not able. It had been many weeks since a single prayer had passed over his unclean lips.

He walked through the long grass again and felt the purse heavy against his chest. He stopped and slowly pulled it out, untied the knot, and took out two big silver coins. He laid them under the dense leaves of the dewlap at the foot of Staffan's cross. Perhaps his widow, Malin, would find them there when the grass withered in the fall.

He looked around once more before he stole up to the church door. With the shrine under his left arm, he opened the creaky door, threw a quick look behind him, and stepped in with a thudding heartbeat.

In the dark, the eternal lamp's golden star glittered in front of the altar. Through the smell of mold and old wood, he could still smell the incense that permeated the benches and vaults. He stretched out two shaking fingers to the basin of holy water. Yes—there was still water. It must be the old Sexton Petrus who still kept watch for the sanctuary of his fathers.

He crossed himself for the first time in weeks. He sank to his knees before the shining star for the first time in months. Still, he could not pray. But his soul was a single great longing for purification and forgiveness, a single great prayer to turn back again to the life from which he now was excluded for the sake of his sin. He had put the shrine in front of him and made a deep bow, as deep as on Ash Wednesday so that his forehead touched the floor.

He still felt unworthy to pray. But he felt enveloped by the intercession of the saints. Motionless, he lay prostrate and felt how the mysterious powers flowed over him. The air that he breathed, the darkness in which the star shined, the great stillness filled with voices from the past and the world beyond, everything breathed peace and tranquility, sanctifying power. Here his heart was at home, even if he was shut out.

Slowly and with trembling, he began to stutter prayers to St. Anne, St. Barbara, and St. Martin. They were the first he dared to turn to. They had been people like himself. Perhaps they would understand him. Then he dared to pray a short prayer to God's Mother, without yet lifting his head from the floor. He prayed for grace to be able to do penance, to live long enough that he could atone for his misdeeds.

Then he took a deep breath and began to silently recite the fiftieth psalm: *Miserere mei, Deus, secundum magnum misericordiam tuam . . .*[2]

Never before had these words been so brimming with meaning. He slowly recited the whole psalm to the end and then continued with the sixth, the thirty first, the thirty-seventh, and all the other psalms of repentance. Only when he had recited all seven to the end

[2] "Have mercy on me, O God, according to your steadfast love; according to your abundant mercy" (Psalm 51:1).

did he lift his head and look at the eternal lamp that indicated the altar still preserved sacrament since the last mass he had celebrated here in the winter. Christ was still bodily present in his sanctuary.

His eyes that now accustomed themselves to the dim light could make out the golden form on the altar behind the choir screen's black trellis. Hesitantly he rose and went up to the choir screen gate. Here he had to stop. Perhaps it was bad enough that he, a dirty and unclean penitent dared to go so far. Silently he set the shrine before the choir door. Then his longing eyes observed the altar that he would never again kiss, and the barely visible figures of St. Anne, God's Mother, and the little singing angel that he would never again be able to see in the radiant light. Then he cast a shy look at the Jesus Child, the unfathomable ruler with the iron scepter, that would come again to rule and judge the sinners of the earth.

He made his way to the door stopping at the side altar with the offering chest where they kept the picture of St. Stephan and the processional banners. He knelt there for a moment, quietly. When he got up again, he looked around one last time before stepping out into the churchyard.

It had brightened up a little. Herr Andreas moved silently back the same way he had come over the stone wall, hurried carefully back down the hill, and crossed the footbridge to find himself standing in the grove. Now, he actually felt changed and happy. Stinging hunger no longer pained him. He was filled with the same sense of peace and clearness of thought that he always used to feel on the evening of Good Friday when he had fasted the longest. Now he was on the way again. He was a penitent, the poorest in Christendom, and yet a member of the church. He had been able to rejoice. Once again, he had a path before him and a goal. Now he could pray again, and he could do penance, he could fast to the glory of God, and suffer for the sake of his salvation.

He began to enter the forest. Before the sun was up, he would be out of the district and engulfed by the great forest. And then he would continue without rest or break until he reached the harbor in Ronneby.

Here was the fork in the path where the path went up to the parsonage. Herr Andreas stood right at the foot of the parsonage hill. Up there lay the low familiar house in the wonderful dawn, that came straight from the north, dreamy silver-gray, completely calm and still filled from end to end with life and familiar memories. The fresh green turf spread out before them, behind them stood the dark wall of the spruce forest. Only the cabin's gray roof lifted itself above the treetops behind.

Herr Andreas observed the gable for a long time. The bookshelf was just on the other side, high up under the roof. There he had his three books.

He wondered if they were still there. The smallest and most beloved was a little handwritten volume with the hourly prayers of Our Virgin, with initials in red, gold, and light blue, an exquisite work that Mother Bothild once bought at the estate sale of Herr Bertillus in Ödesjö. It was no larger than he could hide within his coat. And it contained a variety of lovely prayers.

He stood a moment hesitantly at the branch of the path. Then he turned with determination up toward the parsonage. With long stealthy steps, he crossed the open field and came in among the junipers and the stand of hazelnut trees on the other side. With a wide berth, he came around the corner of the estate where all the outbuildings and sheds were. From there, he approached the backside of the cottage. The last bit, he crept on his knees. From the furthest pile of stone and juniper, he watched his old parsonage suspiciously.

The lower door to the little cottage's backside stood half-open. In the grass were some discarded chicken feathers and fish bones. So, the house was inhabited.

Herr Andreas felt for his dagger, loosened it in its scabbard, and stole toward the door. Just as he was about to look in, he came to a dead stop and pressed himself against the timber wall. There was a noise from the stall on the other side of the estate. It must have been a horse that beat against the loose floorboards.

A horse? That must mean that there was a soldier's camp in Fröjerum's parsonage.

He stood pressed against the timber wall and listened. He didn't hear anything with the possible exception of heavy breathing from within the cottage.

Now he shuffled close to the half-open door and cautiously looked in. In the dark, he saw some dirty bolsters in a corner. On the floor lay a shattered cask, some garments, and a helmet. It smelled of sour beer and vomit. Without a doubt, there was a soldier camp on the estate.

He hesitated a minute, but they were sleeping it off. It would not be too dangerous to look in. Quietly he stepped up to the door jam. His worn shoes stepped softly on paver after paver and came to the door of the cottage. It too was open.

He stood a long time in the doorway, motionless. So, this was Fröjerum's parsonage! In the corner by the bed where he had his place of prayer, his best down pillows lie heaped together, completely soaked and stained by vomit. Freshly forged and beaten bullets littered the table along with crumbled cheese, leftover meat, and a wooden plate. The carved handle of a knife rose above the devastation on the table in which it buried its point. The beer had run over the floor in dark torrents, where bread crusts swam. In between were shards of crushed clay jars, scrunched pages of paper, and heaps of clothes—even women's clothing.

A half-naked man lay prostrate with his head hidden in his crossed arms on the bench along the wall. In the corner bed, he saw at least two figures behind the broken curtains. He could smell beer, sweat, and vomit as well as the estrus that permeated the room. Herr Andreas recognized the aroma well from his life as a highwayman. It had once tickled his nostrils with wild and raw lust. Now it tormented him.

His eyes had searched up to the gable. He tried to peer into the darkness. But then his eyes turned to the half-dark—or was it the dawn that began to sift in through the ceiling window? He saw the bright shelf edge clearly against the wall blackened with soot. But there above, the wall was just as dark. The shelf was empty.

He almost felt relieved. Had the prayer book been there, he would not have felt at peace until he had retrieved it. He always felt strange coercion to do what he didn't dare to do. It had often got him respect for courage among the raw forest men. But he knew himself best how he always trembled inside with fear.

Even now, he felt how his knees began to give. It was high time that he left. Quietly he crept back through the little cottage, put his feet on the threshold again, and took a long step out into freedom.

At the same moment, he had the feeling that someone came to tackle him. A bar stuck between his legs, and he felt a powerful blow to his shins, stumbled, and fell face forward. Before he hit the ground, the stranger was on him. He threw himself with violent power on the back of Andreas, emitting the triumphant roar of a wild animal. He twisted Andreas's arms behind his back so that they seemed to be wrenched out of his shoulders, and pressed a broad knee in his upper back so that he lost his breath. Now Andreas heard a huffing and coarse voice, like a shriek and another shriek. Within the yard answered a rough human echo, heavy steps trampled in the grass, and before he could lift his head from the ground, the man fastened his arms behind his back with sturdy leather straps.

Finally, he stood on his feet again. His whole body trembled as he stared at the bearded faces with bloodshot eyes. They ripped the words out of each other's mouths.

"Satan's vagabond, I saw you when you snuck across the meadow. Then I watched you up at the chicken hole . . ."

"And the chicken thief fell for the trap! What did you plan to steal?"

"Are you on your nightly sauna course, you womanizer? You could have at least taken your best pants . . ."

One of them stuck the lance shaft in the hole in the knee of his pantleg and leveraged it against the back of the knee so that he tumbled backward. Coarse fists caught him and shoved him forward. The whole entourage surrounded the edge of the yard.

Some other half-dressed men tumbled out from the stock sheds and feed barns. Someone went into the cottage to wake the chief, he said.

The hustle calmed down some when the chief finally came out. He was a young man, pale with a thin beard, slight limp, and bloodshot eyes with blue bags.

Herr Andreas stared at him. He had seen this face before—only somewhat younger and softer. He remembered an oddly warm fall day with clouds on the lake. He heard the noise of rattling armor on the yard in Askanäs. This was Herr Tönjes of Sponga. He had developed into a man during the past year. His face was confident and worldly. Now he wanted to hear these men who had become bloated with beer and the good life earlier that evening.

Herr Tönjes received the report and looked indifferently at the prisoner.

"Search the thief," he said briskly.

A coarse hand ran up the peasant coat and groped under the shirt. With a meaningful grunt, the man pulled the heavy purse, cut off the neck rope, and handed the purse over to Herr Tönjes. Herr Tönjes loosened the knot, dug in it, and stared at the prisoner in amazement.

"Where did you steal this?"

The priest was silent. Herr Tönjes looked at him again with a bored expression.

"Will you make it necessary to torment you before we hang you?"

The priest was silent.

There was a glint in Herr Tönjes's tired gaze.

"Twist his legs," he said briskly.

The men slapped the prisoner around with habituated hands and found a pair of wide boards. They began to loosen his shoes.

"Now. Will you confess, you thieving bum!"

The prisoner seemed almost stupefied. He mumbled a barely intelligible:

"I am no thief."

Herr Tönjes glowered at him. But suddenly, he bent forward, tugged hard on his beard, and lifted his face so that he could get a better look in the graying summer night dusk. Slowly he turned his face sideways while keeping a hard grip on his chin and looked over the trace of the tonsure on his head. Then he let go of the beard and got up.

"Put him on his feet again, men. This is the finest capture you have ever made."

He bowed in jest to the prisoner.

"Welcome, welcome, worthy Herr. But how has it happened that the desire of my soul would come to me so quickly? It was you we sought in the deep forest, from Näs to Brohult and the end of the world. No visitor could be dearer to us!"

And again, he became tight and short.

"And now the truth shall come out. To whom does this money belong?"

He held the purse up. The prisoner's eyes shown with defiance.

"Fröjerum's church and never any to you!"

Herr Tönjes whistled a long and meaningful whistle. Then he turned to the knechts.

"Put him in irons and keep him in the cellar. Set four men to keep watch, and they shall swear with their life that he will not escape and then set double posts around the yard. Saddle Bjälbo-Sven's horse. He shall ride in half an hour as a messenger to Herr Måns in Bro."

The awkward locks rattled when they brought the chains out. They shackled him, ankle to ankle and wrist to wrist. He walked haltingly and hunched over as they led him away. The short iron chains hindered him from taking full steps, and he constantly tripped. Dawn was in full swing and flooded everything with warm golden light from the northeast.

The cellar was at the upper end of the yard, where its roof decayed. The knechts opened the loosely hanging door and threw the prisoner to the back of the dark hole. He tripped and fell on his face before they shut the door and locked it with a padlock.

Herr Andreas laid on the floor inside the cellar motionless. He had scraped himself in the fall, and the blood ran from the fetters that chained his hands together. Dark drops of blood fell onto the earthen floor, among the half-boiled cabbage leaves, eggshells, and herring heads. He did not notice. He lay face forward with his head buried under his fettered arms. As if in a trance, he heard the knechts hammer on the lock that had malfunctioned.

It took a while before he had a proper thought. It was as if everything froze for him in spasmodic anxiety. An overwhelming malicious power of misfortune had entered his existence and driven everything else out. Reason, faith, and will had all ceased to exist. There was something new that had come, a black horror, that filled his soul, a great fearful darkness that forced him to the ground kept his thoughts bolted down and filled everything with a single annihilating thought: he would die.

Die . . . shoved by rough fists, reviled, treated like an animal, hung by a rope or executed by the sword. He would be left like a truncated corpse with his head between his legs or hung in the forest as food for the birds. This darkness consumed him, overshadowed him, enveloped him. There was only one little point of light left where he could still breathe, there the flames of thought still flickered—but at any moment could annihilate him and fill the empty room where he remained with this impenetrable black night.

He could not think of anything else. This darkness dominated him completely. He felt it come over him. It exuded anxiety and triumphant evil. A hard and sticky hand reached into his head, grabbed hold of his brain and squeezed so that every reasonable thought disappeared, and nothing remained but insane anxiety.

He did not know how long he had lain there like that. The sun filtered in through cracks in the roof. The horror of death still paralyzed his thoughts. But other sensations also began to force their way into his consciousness with the power of their pain. He shivered in the cold. His shoulder joints ached, his pant legs stuck to his shins, and they burned as if they were on fire. His shackled hands had swollen, and hunger tore into his intestines.

The black cramps that slashed the back of his head with their claws still kept him pressed to the ground. He was prostrate and lifeless with his face in filth. Though the frost would shake him from time to time, he had a definite fever. The great darkness still paralyzed his understanding, but in his feverish delirium, this darkness began to take shape. It towered up like a mountain, a trembling mountain of black masses that twisted like giant tangled earthworms. The mountain's peak lifted itself like a black skull. Suddenly it was filled with hangmen, dead bodies swinging in the wind, blackbirds flew past and fought in the air for pecked out eyes and loose finger bones. The head lifted itself higher, two empty eyeholes separated in the darkness, they grew and expanded, snakes and lizards slithered out of their dark centers. Then they spread apart, the whole skull fell, and the parts danced in wide arcs. Purgatory rose up between the cleft. Red, billowing smoke whirled in the dark, long rows of small flames danced under the distorted bodies, the gleaming wild staring eyes and hard clenched teeth behind grinning lips. All danced around in the red firelight that finally joined together in a crackling whirlwind of smoke and sparks, filled with long piercing screams.

The sparks spread again like the stars extinguished in the boundless dark that once again rose and twisted like the rattling body of a reptile. One at its foot had a red, bloody and vicious eye. The red eye expanded and sputtered tongues of fire that were thrown forward like hissing snakes that snapped and bit at the air. The eye grew to a giant sun of blood and fire in the dark. Something completely evil and deceptive glowed in the center. It sank ever deeper. The sun became a glowing pit, a deep abyss in the dark, a smoking hole sucking in, and exhaling the stench of its hot breath.

The gap widened. Within its depths opened a limitless expanse of black and red, of darkness and fire, of night and embers, of cold and fire. The demons ran forward like a leash of howling dogs with wild eyes and tongues hanging out of their jaws with melting black wings and shiny claws. Now everything was thrown together, bloody pictures blended together: fire and night, light and darkness. Human bodies laid about frozen stiff in the dark moor between shiny mirrors of ice. Grinning faces shot up out of the ice, pale hands groping toward the dark sky. The ice thundered. A black body ran forward at a gallop, the roaring faces were massacred, and bones were crushed and cracked by groping hands. The darkness devoured the body, a roar of horror chased over the ice and went in a wide arch over the frozen expanses. The death carriage appeared again and came forward, followed by new crazy cries of pain and resentment.

Everything was dark; slowly, a weak firelight glimmered up from the night and fell in rows of figures crumbled together. They squatted with smashed faces and chewed on their cut tongues. Then they vomited rivers of black livers and bile. Disgust distorted their faces. Then they began to chew on their flesh and vomit again.

When they sank into the darkness, green flames fluttered and danced over a bush of intertwined thorns. Naked figures sat there like plucked birds, glancing at each other with hate-filled, watchful eyes. Between them lay black snakes coiled together with vigilantly lifted heads. Again and again, the naked figures hissed. They reviled and cursed each other with a passionate hate. Every time, the snakes struck quick as lightning with their heads and bit hard into wrists, jaws, and lips. The men tore loose from the snakes and twisted in ineffable torment, blue and bloated, but they could not leave it be and continued to reproach and mock each other. The red day was snuffed, only their eyes glimmered with hate in the dark, a hate that was just as bottomless and eternal as their despair.

Everything danced around again. The abyss widened into an infinite grotto between immeasurable cliffs oozing with moisture that enveloped the deepest and lowest of all darkness. This darkness was living. It heaved and moved, glittering with slimy skin and rattled with scaly armor. It radiated a mysterious power that petrified everything and permeated the night with the unfathomable mystery of the Evil One. Then the mysterious evil would rush out of the night again, as soon as the black, mountainous mass turned itself down there in the deep.

Everything began to dance again. The black darkness and the red flames made huge arches and seemed to say: forever without end, eternal and everlasting . . .

The cellar door opened. Someone was on the steps. It was quiet for a moment. Then a coarse voice said:

"Are you dead, or are you just pretending you false Satan?"

Someone came up and kicked him in the side. He lifted his head. The knecht grinned wide with mockery.

"Eat your cabbage soup and be glad, you papist devil. In the morning, we hang you. If the king doesn't take you to Stockholm, of course, to cut you and put you on the wheel."

The man left and closed the door behind him. As he passed, he spat in the clay bowl with the cold cabbage soup that he put in front of him on the steps.

The priest slowly sat up and stared in front of him for a moment. Then his thirst took its toll. He removed the knecht's slimy loogie from the bowl with a splinter of wood. Then he put the bowl up to his mouth and drank. Then he eased across the step to the wall where a small ray of sunlight fell through the weathered cellar door and warmed his frozen shoulders. His mind slowly began to work again.

"Purgatory or hell?"

Some of his sins were venial, but he also had more than enough deadly sins. He would hardly have any opportunity for confession before the execution. He would have to drag the whole of this dirty mess across the threshold to the other side. No one would say a prayer or read a mass for his soul. The best he could hope for was an infinitely long pain in purgatory if hell did not open its maw and devour him for all eternity.

He contemplated the unfathomable face of the Jesus Child above the altar in Fröjerum's church. A pair of great round eyes stared absently into space as if at some distant target and looked as if they had long since reached a decision, a decision no amount prayer could change. Had Christ determined to destroy him? Was he rejected and condemned? Was this why he suffered ruin, just now when salvation had just winked at him?

He slid his quivering body a few inches along the stone wall so that the ray of light should fall on is naked chest through the gap in the flared shirt. The paralyzing seizures that kept him prisoner began to leave slowly. Death's dire reality remained, but amid this hostile darkness, his will began to move again.

On the one hand, it was a will to doom and annihilation. He felt a desire to sink into despair and bitterness, to freely let himself be devoured by the great darkness, to scream, to curse and blaspheme God. But against this despondence rose another will, one that caused him to resist, one that did not want to be devoured by the darkness but to seek an opportunity to continue the fight for life.

Naturally, the situation was desperate. With only a few days or even hours left to live, he had an abundance of iniquity and penance that had barely begun. And yet: as desperate as his position might be, if he was shut off from God, God could not hinder him from continuing his prayers outside the closed gates of heaven. He could use the hours he had left to live to pray and repent. Then God could do what he, in his unfathomable majesty, was pleased to do.

He rose laboriously. The fabric tore loose from his wounded shin, and a fresh rivulet of blood flowed between the scabs. He knelt with great effort and turned to the stone wall, put his shackled hands together, and began to recite the psalms of repentance. In between them, he would say ten Our Fathers and ten Ave Marias. Then he recited *Dies irae* and Birgitta's fifteen Wound Prayers with fifteen Our Fathers and fifteen Ave Marias. Then he started all over again with the penitential psalms, still on bended knee with his head against the stone wall.

* * *

The warm June sun had lured the first children down to the swimming hole on the Stångån. Carefully, they stuck their white feet into the cold water, splashed a few drops on each other, and fled up among the reeds with screams.

The smith's two ragged cows grazed in the marshy meadow, still emaciated after the long winter famine. The smith had his shop further down, sitting between a few gray farmsteads and two blooming rowans. The high chimneys rose from the sea of flowers, black and cracked. There behind them was a stone bridge and a glimpse of the great road to Norrköping.

The children suddenly became quiet and looked down at the bridge. Two riders came off the plain at a sharp trot. The hooves clattered against the stone, and small white dust clouds faded in the sunshine. On the other side of the bridge, the riders stopped for a second. They wore peasant's clothing, but their effortless manner showed that they had not subjected themselves to long years of hard work, just as their straight hands and thin fingers betrayed that they were not common peasants.

The man who rode first was taller. He had an open and smiling face. It seemed that the sharp trot brought him joy. He could just as well have been a nobleman in disguise. The other sat stooped in the saddle and dried the sweat from his forehead. Then he said:

"You should make it quick, Martin. You know that Master is impatient. I will ride to him with the money now, and then you come as soon as you finish talking with the old woman. Don't forget: this evening at seven o'clock, at the skinner's in Tannefors. The Lord's Spirit be with you!"

"And the blood of Jesus with you, also!" Martin answered loud and joyously so that the half-grown children who stopped and waited in the sunshine at the closest barn gable also heard it. They looked up in wonder at the strange greetings.

The scrivener set his spurs into the horse again and took the path up to St. Lars, without noticing the boys with their wide eyes watching the back of his neck. He was in a radiant mood. He and Kort Lange had just been to Söderköping and sold hides and iron ore on behalf of Gert Hubmaier. There they had very unexpectedly met new evangelical brothers. They had had some wonderful evenings with endless prayers and songs. They had even been able to see a pair of friends shed their harem pants, colorful sweaters, and all the remaining satanic pomp never again to wear them.

Now he would take a minute to swing over to Mother Drude, Master Gottschalk's widow, who now lived in the old house behind the castle. He had visited there at the beginning of the year when he was on the way to the camp in Vadstena. She had been exceptionally kind to him though she had a house full of soldiers. She had been the same pious and God-fearing woman as before. The only difference was that now she had sympathies for the evangelical faith.

It was this that gave Martin the idea to seek her out now before he returned to Gert Hubmaier, He knew he would be doing scrivener's work for the rest of the day once he talked to Gert, and he badly wanted to try to get Mother Drude to the meeting tonight.

Midday approached, and the sun was shining between the house walls. The city began to get its characteristic summer smell of dust, sewer, and fermenting garbage. The flies already swarmed in the blue around the sewage in the streets. The gray gable of Master Gottschalk's house rose high above the alley like it always had. And as always, visitors were met at the gate by the light smell of honeysuckle, which clung in heavy bundles all along the garden walls. Inside stood the dilapidated log house wall on one side, gray like before and greenish-black roots in the board liner. Straight ahead, the old stalls leaned on each other with the turf roofs and even higher stood the stone house, a wealthy merchant's home with proper windows and steep exterior steps that led up between the clinging bunches of honeysuckle.

He tied the horse up at the iron ring in the stall and went up the familiar steps. The door was open, and he stepped in. He could see through the gap in the door to the left into the kitchen where he had sat many times as a boy. The roof was just as high and just as sooty, borne by the same worm-eaten beams. The heavy cupboard over by the wall stood open, and the earthenware bowls glowed in red rows. Over at the table by the window, the sunshine radiated its warmth. Old linen was there shining snow-white in the sunlight. Mother Drude had just sat down and started mending the spring wash.

The door to the inner room opened, and a little old lady with sparse gray hair stood at the threshold with surprise.

"Martin! What in all the world . . ."

He hugged and kissed her on the cheek. As an answer to her surprise question, he began to tell her about his new work and his plans. The old woman smiled happily. They sat down at the table.

"And I thought that you had become insolvent! Or that you fell into misfortune and were looking for refuge! Why have you dressed yourself up like a peasant?"

Martin became a little tight in the face. He glanced at Mother Drude and answered:

"I have become a Christian!"

The old woman threw her hands together.

"A Christian? You have been a Christian since you were a child!"

"No, no mother, perhaps a sham-Christian! But I had never been a true Christian before February of this year."

The old woman sat sewing in her lap and staring at him.

"Were you not baptized as a child?"

"Ach, baptized, . . . but that was all. I mean the true faith and the gifts of the Holy Spirit and true Christian life, that I did have before this winter, in Skeninge, the evening after the great skirmish in Skrukeby."

Mother Drude's lips pursed together. She looked down at the worn towel and began to sew again.

"You have to excuse me, my dear Martin, but I can't comprehend a word of what you are saying."

Martin began to tell about his encounter with Kort Lange and all that happened up until the evening with the barber-surgeon. He had told it many times before; the words and pictures came with calculated power. He noticed that the story made an impression on the old lady.

"God bless you, my boy," she said. "I see that you want to be a faithful Christian. But what does that have to do with your clothes?"

She could tell that Martin had heard that question before. He describes the life of the world disparagingly with all its vanity and all its ability to snare souls. He talked about the peace he felt when he found the courage to clean house of all the misery. He didn't say anything that could directly hurt the old woman, but he chose his words so that they were a calm critique of one aspect or another of her own life. She must have sensed it because she said:

"And I had believed I was a true evangelical already . . ."

Then she added with a questioning look:

"You don't mean that Martin Luther and Master Olaus are wrong?"

Martin had also heard that question before and recognized the suspicious glint in the eye that always accompanied it.

"Martin Luther has the Spirit of God, and Master Olaus, too," he hastened to say. "But they have only done the beginning. They have given us God's word, and they have put an end to the pope's tyranny. Now we have only gone further along down the path."

"What do you mean?"

"I mean that we must take God's word seriously and begin to preach about true salvation and the Spirit's light. Luther has taught us that we are not saved through pilgrimages and candles and clerical clothing but through faith in Jesus. And he is right. But he has not put forth how that faith must be. Neither has he said how we receive it."

The old lady looked puzzled again. Martin anticipated her question.

"I mean, people need to hear that we must enter through the narrow gate, through the dark night of the soul and the struggle with repentance. And so we must forsake the world. Otherwise, we do not believe rightly. It is this that the evangelicals are now beginning to get the world to realize. Now the reformation will be completed. It is high time. The worldly ways of heathendom still remain even within the church. Everywhere we still have painted statues, papist robes, and altars—just like in a house of idols."

Now the old lady let the hand towel fall on her knee and looked at the scrivener sharply.

"You do not mean, Martin, that you want to remove the altar from the cathedral? And Christ on the cross?"

"You shall not make unto yourself any graven image! So it is written in Scripture, dear mother, the sooner our churches are purified from forms, we can never worship in spirit and truth."

He noticed that Mother Drude looked upset and took up another topic.

"Mother, do you know Bernt Skinnare of Tannefors?"

"I certainly do . . . but God forgive me, I have never been able to like him. He is always talking about himself so much."

The scrivener swallowed.

"It may well be that he has his faults."

He bowed and took the old lady's hand.

"Mother?"

"Yes, what then?"

"If Mother would do me the great pleasure, she would come with me this evening to Bernt's place. Not for his sake but for mine. There shall be Scripture reading and song, and many true evangelicals will be there. I cannot explain everything for mother now, but if mother comes herself, mother will hear."

"It is so far," said the old lady evasively. "And I do not like going out in the evening in those corners."

Martin brightened up.

"Excellent, then Mother will have company. Elin ought to come with, and some other God-fearing people that mother believes will receive God's word . . . Say, would you come, Mother, for my sake?"

The old woman withdrew her hand. Now she leaned forward to look down in the garden through the little open box in the lead window. She looked at the front gate, where she heard someone walking.

The old lady squinted to see better. Then she bowed.

"Now, you will receive a better answer than I can give. That is Peder Knutsson."

"Who?"

"Peder Knutsson of Vi. He also belongs to my boys and always stops in when he comes to the city. Now he has been here for three days to account for the collection and make arrangements for some church land."

She could not say anything more before the priest stepped over the threshold. The scrivener recognized him immediately. Twice before, he had seen this stocky figure: one summer day in the Stockholm Castle and a stormy night in Fröjerum's parsonage. He was just the same with his round head, the low, black hairline, the red face, and dark, playful eyes.

The priest went forward and greeted the old lady. Then he turned to the scrivener with a puzzled look.

"Good day, Herr Peder," Martin said joyfully, "we have met before . . ."

The priest wrinkled his forehead.

"That's right," he said. "But truly, I forget where. You are not from Vi and not from Brohult . . ."

"Well, actually from Fröjerum—and the Stockholm Castle, if that matters! Martinus Ragvaldi, *quondam scriba regius, nunc autem mercat Holmiensis.*[3] At your service, worthy Herr."

He made a deep bow.

The priest was a shade redder in the face.

"You must excuse me, Martin Ragnvaldsson. It was your own fault I took you for a peasant. Why do you dress yourself in this way?"

"Because I have become a Christian since we last met."

There was a hint of admonishment in his voice. The priest stared at him, but the scrivener did not let him speak.

"May I ask you a counter-question, worthy Herr? A question that also deals with clothing? Where in Holy Scripture is it written that priests shall dress in a frock and collar, in robes and copes? And where in the Holy Scriptures does it speak about organs and stain glass windows and all of your idolatrous temple trinkets? The only thing in all of the Bible I have found concerning idols is that it says they are forbidden! A priest ought to think on that seriously, rather than be surprised that a Christian man departs from the world and leaves behind sinful trappings to live in purity and save his soul . . ."

A slight smile crossed the priest's face.

"Yes, yes, young friend, I hear that you are one of the new monks. It brings me joy to see a holy man. And this then is the new order's uniform?"

He pinched the gray material.

"It is easy to stand and jest," said the scrivener sorely. "Especially when one can't answer in kind."

The priest laughed again.

"There is probably a lot to say in kind here also—though I would rather laugh than quarrel. Do you not see how absurd it is with you, *schwarmerei*?[4] Here we throw the doctrine of works righteousness off the front steps, and you yell 'bravo,' like all the others when cowls and pilgrimages and fasting and monkish vows end up in the gutter.

---

[3] Martin Ragnvaldsson, formerly the royal scrivener but presently a merchant in Stockholm.

[4] Again, this is a word Luther used for various fanatical religious movements.

But then you run straight over there and pick up the false holiness again and carry it in through the backdoor. And then you say: If you want to be a Christian, you must have a gray frock and indistinct hair and coarse wool socks. But if you have a crucifix and altar and a chasuble, then you are no Christian. When will we learn that holiness does not rest in homespun clothing or silk fabric, but comes with faith in the Lord Jesus Christ?"

"What of your own ceremonies then? Is not your church so full of paintings and crosses and trinkets that common people can hardly find a place to sit?"

"Calm, calm, here. We have enough ceremonies, but we do not believe that they are necessary for salvation. Certainly, we have our old customs if they are not in conflict with God's word. One has to have some type of custom! In such things, God has left us free. But we never say that any works of any type are conditions for salvation. It is the pope and you *schwarmerei* that say so. In essence, you are of the same mettle. The Pope says: shave your head and fast on Wednesday and Friday and pray the whole psalter every week, and then you will be holy and pious. And you say: comb your hair flat and wear gray clothing and pray with your own words, and you will be holy and pleasing to God. But we say with the gospel: Believe in the Lord Jesus, and you will be saved. It is the difference between faith in grace and faith in works righteousness."

"Of course, and so you are so justified by faith that you can do contrary to God's command! Who has given you permission to make your images of God?"

"God himself has done that when he let his Son become a man. No one shall try to make an image of the invisible God, but the Son became man so that our eyes would be able to see God and his salvation. By the way, Christ is the end of the law, both in questions of idolatry and Sabbaths and all the rest. And by the way, how are you, holy lord? Do you keep all the statutes of the elders? Do you live according to the law? Do you keep the Sabbath on Saturday?"

"No," answered the scrivener astonished.

"I can believe that. You still retain some Christian freedom! But it is so similar with all slaves of the law and works righteous Christians: one picks a commandment here and there, and then finds a few extra contortions, and then one puffs himself up with them and wants that to qualify for righteousness. But he who wants to be justified by the power of the law, he has fallen away from Christ, Paul says so clearly."

The scrivener could hardly hear anymore.

"We have had enough of this dead doctrine of faith," he said. "Just believe and believe! As if that would create any true Christianity! Show me your faith *without* mortification of the flesh, *without* the struggle of repentance, *without* ignominy, then I shall show you priests the evangelical faith—*with* sacrifice, *with* struggle, *with* mortification of the flesh and deprivation of all that is vanity right up to the next collection of trinkets."

Now the priest put his knuckles in his side and looked at the scrivener a long time, up and down and up again.

"Do you know that your brother the papist said the very same thing, to a tee, one year ago in Fröjerum! Show me your faith, he said, without fasting, without celibacy, without obedience, then you shall see mine: with pure living, with poverty, with mortification. You can take each other by the hand, you and Andreas. It is the same leaven: the proud old Adam, who can't possibly keep his wits about him when it is revealed that Christ's righteousness is really enough for a sinner and that one has *everything* when one believes in Christ. If we shall be saved by poverty, or obedience, or repentance or anything else, then Christ is nothing. One must choose here. The pure gospel tolerates nothing at its side."

"But, that's enough now," he continued. "God give that you find your brother and try to make him an evangelical rather than prowl around here in the flock and distort the thinking of simple Christians. But so it is with you, *schwarmerei*. You never plow up new fields. You leave the papists in peace, but where the gospel finds a soul with better thoughts, then you nestle in."

"Where is my brother?" the scrivener asked without concerning himself with the rebuke. He realized that he had found other things to think about.

"He learns to wander in the wild forest. He was last seen in the area of Rumskulla. He was in the company of Per Skägge. The man who shot the bailiff in Fagerhult. He was gaunt and wild-eyed. Otherwise, he was healthy."

The scrivener had become rather contemplative. He went over to the old lady who had long since sat down at the table and pensively observed the bickering men, while she mended her linen.

"Farewell, dear mother, and God's peace," he said. "Now I must go to my work. Try to come this evening."

Mother Drude gave a hearty farewell but gave no promise. The scrivener bowed stiffly to the priest.

That wasn't very successful, he thought as he walked down the steps. Now, Peder Knutsson is undoing everything for her.

He led the horse out through the gate, swung himself up in the saddle, and rode straight down through the city. The air was now very warm. Not even where the cellar doors stood open was there any longer the feel of the damp and raw winter chill. He enjoyed the warmth and the uninhibited folklife that now spread out from open shutters with swarms of half-naked children, rooting swine, and whistling journeymen.

Gert Hubmaier owned a huge warehouse, and a loft shed down by the river. The scrivener urged the horse as soon as he came through the worst crowd in the square. He was a little uneasy for having tarried so long. Master Gert was moody and unpredictable, and there was a lot to do today. Now during the campaign, lots of money had gone into circulation, and there was a shortage of almost everything else. They had done resplendent business all spring, and just yesterday had a new order for fabric, salt, and spices come from Söderköping. Fantastic sums were paid for such things now in the land, and it paid to sell away before the prices sank.

Martin leaned forward in the saddle as the horse trotted in through the low gate. He sprang out of the saddle, handed the reins to the stall boy, and went up the steps to the loft. From the gallery, he heard vehement voices. It did not bode well.

The voices came from within the great room. The scrivener knocked cautiously on the little door knocker, but the knocking was obviously drowned out by the noise inside, so he slowly opened the door and entered.

The room was full of people. In the half-dark stood Gert Hubmaier at the bedpost between the two bunks and spoke heatedly right in the face of the barber-surgeon from Skeninge, who was very pale and kept his hands stretched out, half-open and spasmodically trembling as if he wanted to grab the words. On the beds sat many figures crammed together, Kort Lange, Bernt Skinnare, a pale woman with an excited expression on her face and many others that the scrivener recognized well from the evangelical gathering in the city. On a stool by the wall sat a stranger with a blond patriarchal beard and searching eyes, a low table sat before him with beer tankards and mugs as well as two goblets of wine. Many of those sitting held their tankards in hand.

Gert Hubmaier did not let the surgeon get a word in edgewise. He spoke quite heatedly.

"And what have you come with? Do you know how long I have had the Spirit? For sixteen years, mind you! Since the eighteenth of November, the year 1526! For six weeks, I struggled with the dark night of the soul. I tasted the very pain of hell. In the evening, the Spirit came, I sat and listened to the prophet. Then there was such a pain in my side that I need to go out into Västerlång street, even down to the roundel and back again. Then the new man was born. Then I went in and threw myself down, and the prophet laid his hands on me, and I was possessed by the Spirit. And now the same Spirit says: drive out from you those who are evil! Sweep out the old leaven! That which is unclean or blasphemous shall not enter the city. If you want to sleep in linen sheets and have sensual shirts to tickle your flesh, if you want to twist your mustache in the wind and have fur collars and hoods and enter the heathen temple in Skeninge, then you go do it. He, who is unclean, continues to defile himself. But he who will be in the Israel of God, he will subdue his flesh. Here you see . . ."

He tore the gray frock at his neck.

"From this day forth, I wear my wool shirt. And I will never again set foot in any church so long as the idols remain. And he who receives communion at the idolatrous altars, he is to be considered a heathen and a publican and does not remain with God's people."

The barber-surgeon finally had an opportunity to say something. His small eyes flashed.

"Who has made you pope, Gert? You loose and you bind, and you anathematize as if you had the keys of heaven! *This* is sin, and *that* is sin and *this* is sin! Is it you, or is it God's congregation that should decide this matter? I shall pray to be able to know the other's reasoning here: is it sin to have sheets and robes of linen? Is it a sin to go to church? Is it a sin to make the sign of the cross? Is it a sin to have fur trim on your coat? What do you say, Martin?"

He turned to the scrivener who had barely been able to adjust his sunblind eyes to the dim light of the loft.

"What in the world are you arguing about?" he asked.

There was a burst of answers all at once. Gert Hubmaier and the barber-surgeon put words in each other's mouths. The more impartial listeners over on the bed tried to make their way in to sort it all out, but they only added to the confusion. The scrivener understood this much, Master Gert and the blond stranger, who had come from Lübeck, had agreed that one had to take mortification of the flesh more seriously in order to work against the incipient relaxation that had become common among the evangelicals. The stranger had brought this finished program, and it had immediately pleased Gert Hubmaier and Bernt of Tannefors. But today, when the friends from Skeninge had come to participate in the meeting with the scrivener, they had not wanted to submit to it but reproached the brothers of Linköping for highhandedness and tyranny. So this was the reason for the racket. Perhaps some of the loudness was because of all the deep droughts of beer they had drunk on this hot day.

Scrivener Martin was happy to avoid answering to this common commotion. He did not like his master's measures of reform. Master Gert was stubborn. If he got something in his head, he would trudge through it without delay. The worst was that one never knew what he got in his head. That this last was overexcited and unreasonable was clear to Martin. After all, there had to be a limit to the measure of self-deprivation that true Christianity required.

Now the barber-surgeon had found words again.

"If we are going to speak about sin in God's Israel, then I only want to say that I believe that there is more sin in taking advantage of the distress of the people by jacking up prices in times of dire need than to have a fur-trimmed frock in the summer . . ."

"Is that directed at me?" asked Gert Hubmaier sharply.

"You can learn that down on the square," said the barber-surgeon. "Ask who is the most expensive for salt. Ask who sells old spices for the same price as fresh. Ask who is the hardest when it comes to claiming old debts . . ."

Master Gert squinted and smiled disparagingly.

"You run in the streets, all you want, and hear what the people are whispering. I have never had a weakness for the praise of men."

"Neither will you receive any praise," said the surgeon dryly. "Not even on judgment day when it shall be asked if you fed the hungry."

Now Gert Hubmaier lifted his hand and pointed at the doorway where the dust danced in the sunlight.

"Out, you blasphemer! Out of my house!"

"With pleasure," said the surgeon. "Out of here! That is right! Whoever wants to hold fast to the gospel, he follows me! Out of here!"

"And he who wants to enter through the narrow path, he stays," yelled Gert Hubmaier. "Whoever wants to forsake the world and himself, he stays!"

There was general confusion. Most walked toward the door and crouched one after the other to make it through the low door jam. The barber-surgeon stood outside, urging them all to come. Bernt Skinnare and a couple of other inhabitants of Linköping gathered around Master Gert. Kort Lange stood a little off to the side of them, looking disturbed. Scrivener Martin had not left his place by the door. The whole performance had disgusted him. He knew well that his friends had their individual faults. But up till now they had kept quiet and showed each other a friendly appreciation. Unity in faith had overshadowed everything else. Was that perhaps the problem?

He crossed the floor over to Kort Lange.

"What do you plan to do," he whispered.

Kort looked helpless.

"We should wait a bit. He doesn't mean bad. It is the heat and the beer that is making him irritable."

"And where would we go?" he added.

The whole time, Gert Hubmaier was speaking sharply and rebuking those who were leaving. They were equivocators and false, he had known that for a long time, he said.

"If we left the king, we can very well leave Gert Hubmaier," Martin said quietly.

Kort Lange looked at him shyly.

"But then we had somewhere to go . . ."

"Should a Christian not dare to leave empty-handed if his Lord commands it? Where did Abraham have to go when he left Chaldea?"

"Yes, if only we had a clear command . . ."

Martin looked out in front of himself for a while. The last of the barber-surgeon's entourage just went out through the door.

"In any case, Gert Hubmaier shall not be able to rule over me," he said. "I have not rejected the pope in Rome to live under a new pope in Linköping."

He went for the door. Gert Hubmaier yelled after him.

"Martin! What are you planning to do?"

"Go back to work," Martin answered calmly.

"Stop a minute! You have to answer first: are you with us or against us?"

"I don't want to be with anyone but God."

"Don't dodge the question! Do you want to live a holy life or not? Do you want to obey what the Spirit has proclaimed to us?"

"Concerning tow linen shirts?"

There was a hint of mockery in Martin's voice. Gert Hubmaier became red, and his tone was sharp:

"Clearly now—are you with us or not?"

"I follow Jesus, and no one else," said Martin who went for the door.

"Go then and follow Satan; it's your suicide. I had almost expected it of you. You have always had more of the world's joy than the grief of God's children on your face. Even in your easy gate, I have noticed that you do not carry the cross. Here the word is true: the dog returns to its vomit, and the washed sow wallows in the mire . . ."

When Martin had reached the bottom of the steep stairs to the loft, he straightened up and breathed in the fresh summer air. The others had already left the yard: their loud voices could be heard outside in the street.

He stood a moment and thought to himself. This meant that he had been dismissed. Then he could just as well go his own way. He had received his salary fourteen days ago, and he was just as happy not to meet Gert Hubmaier right now. The saddle, the coat, and the other personal articles he would just as well pick up some other time.

But where would he go now? He slowly walked out to the street. The others had already disappeared up into the city. So here he stood all alone in the dusty street without a clue concerning what should happen to him. He hesitated a minute. Then he went aside between a couple of sheds and knelt. He prayed long and committed his cause into God's hands. During the prayer, his brother and Fröjerum suddenly came to mind. He began to pray for his brother Anders, as he had so many times before. And all at once was filled with a great certainty: God had freed him so that he would find his brother. He would save his soul before it was too late. This was the path that the Spirit showed him.

"Thank you, Lord Almighty," he mumbled. And then he added: "Because it is your will, dear Lord, then you can also find me a horse and the other things that I need. Thank you, God Almighty."

While he was still kneeling, he did an inventory. He already had a saddle, and fifteen marks in savings. For twenty, he could perhaps get a decent horse. So he lacked five.

"You can get me the five marks, good God," he mumbled. Then he got up, smiled a bright smile to the two laundresses that stood surprised and stared at him with laundry baskets between them, and went up to the city to find his five marks.

The road was long. First, he made a detour to the horse trader and immediately found a horse that wasn't in its best years but looked decent enough. He haggled the price down to 19 marks. Now he had to find where he could borrow four marks. He tried first with the friends from Skeninge. They balked. None of them had the cash just now. So he overcame himself and went to Mother Drude. He had hardly laid the matter out before he regretted it. She looked very sad, and he could tell how much it hurt her to have to say that she only had this old house left after Master Gottschalk. It was Martin who had to try and comfort her with good words before he left.

Depressed, he walked into the city again. He passed by the old gray schoolhouse with an uneasy feeling. Even now in the summer heat, it seemed to be filled with the damp cold of long winter days, with coughs, with hoarse voices that rattled in the chorus, and of screams from punished children.

He meandered over to the churchyard behind the cathedral and entered the alley between the low wooden houses on the other side. Suddenly he heard someone calling his name.

He turned on his heels. It was Peder of Vi.

"I only want to ask forgiveness," the priest said and walked right up to him. "I was quite heated up at Mother Drude's. And so I lost care. It is so with my poor heart. The true faith I want to confess, but I have a long way to go toward love. I could at least have said that I am glad that you take God's word seriously. If you continue with that, God shall soon enough shed light for you and give you a right belief, if time allows. Don't be sour on me . . ."

At first, Martin looked nonplussed. Then he was a little red, and finally, he smiled a bright, broad smile.

"Not at all, not at all," he said. "I am used to abuse. And there was a good purpose to what you said, though I did not quite comprehend your meaning."

A mischievous glint returned to the priest's playful eyes.

"No, the Spirit's light is needed for that. But it comes with time if one holds to God's word."

"Where are you going now?" he asked.

"To my brother."

The priest's eyes stopped and got big.

"What? Have you heard something from Andreas?"

"Not at all. That is why I have to find him. God has told me to go and save his soul."

The priest smiled again and took him by the arm.

"That matter, you can leave to God's holy gospel. You are too short in the coat for it. But God bless you if you can get your brother to hear the gospel . . . Though first, you ought to have a little better understanding of it yourself."

The scrivener no longer looked proud but interested.

"Say," he said, "what is it that Anders needs to hear?"

"First and foremost, he needs to learn what sin is. No one can understand the gospel before he recognizes sin properly. And among the papists, they do not properly comprehend what sin is. They add up sins at confession: lies, fornication, intoxication, and anger, all neatly sorted, counted, and stored away like wares on a trade counter."

"*Is* that not then sin?"

They had begun to walk up the alley.

"Thank you very much if that is not sin! But *this* sort of accounting for sin is not enough. When all that we can find is set upon the table, and we believe that the Lord can now come and see my sins, then we still have a bottomless stock in front of the table, under the floor and deep within the heart."

They came around a corner, dodged a team of oxen, and continued.

"And the sin deep within the heart, it is much worse than all the others together. Martin Luther calls it the sinful person because it sits in the actual person. Man is born with it. One sleeps with it. We carry it with us here, straight through Linköping, and it will be with us when we lie down on our death beds."

"But one has to pick that layer of sin up also and put it with those on the table?" Martin interrupted.

"If that were possible, yes. But you see, it is not a stock of solid garments that one can pick up, but it is only a black hole. And the black hole begets and births sins without end that pour out onto the ground in a steady stream. A person has enough to do just to pick them up and give them to the Lord so that they don't pile up too high. But to go to the hole itself does not do."

"But it has to do!" said the scrivener. Then he squeezed his lips together.

"Have you tried? I tried for three years before I finally gave up. I crawled on my knees in the middle of the cold floor in the morning while it was still pitch black in the dark and prayed for a pure heart. I lay behind the high altar at the cathedral church and prayed until my legs went numb with exhaustion and cold. But when I came out, I immediately thought that I was better than Lasse Västgöte, who hardly prayed his little morning prayer."

The scrivener looked even more seriously.

"Is it a sin to think that?"

"Son, how can you ask that? You shall love your neighbor as yourself! You shall be holy, for the Lord your God is holy!"

"Yes, but such things as that can't count, can they? They are just temptations! And if one doesn't fall for them . . ."

"Then it is bad enough that you have the desire to do evil. Is it not written in Scripture, 'You shall not lust'? Does Jesus not say that he who looks upon a woman with lust has already committed adultery with her in his heart? It does not help you a bit that you did not act on it . . ."

They had come out to the north corner of the city and caught a glimpse of lake Roxen like a blue streak over the cabbage gardens. With small steps, they continued over the field.

"You must understand this," said Herr Peder. "Search your own heart! Here you have lived like a true Christian for many months, you think, and so you worship, and you pray, and you sing, and it is all lovely and wonderful. But then another steps up and speaks and immediately you sit there and make remarks in your heart and think that you could do better. And then you look at the girls for a minute and are terrified because now you have improper thoughts. So you pray for forgiveness for it, and then you tell yourself, and then you sit and think that it was good and spiritually rich that you said . . ."

"How can you know all that?" the scrivener asked in amazement.

"I have always been conscious of it myself. One time up in Uppsala, we had an impulse of the new papistry and wanted to be holy in ourselves. And incidentally, I had the same evil heart that remains to this day. It was that which crawled out today at Mother Drude's and gave birth to some black voles. I am glad that I met you so that we could clear it up."

The scrivener gave the priest a long look.

"You still have the Spirit, brother."

Now the priest laughed.

"Yes, you say that only because I preached the law for a bit. It is always the same with you, *schwarmerei.* If one is just sufficiently sharp with the law, then you hear God's voice speak. God grant, that you also hear God in his gospel."

"What then, is the gospel?"

"It is that for the sake of Christ, God should have delight in such condemned sinners like you and me when we believe in Christ."

The scrivener looked puzzled again and asked:

"Can one then sin as much as he wants?"

"He who believes does not want to sin at all," said the priest. "Therefore, he watches and prays and passes up as much of the black misery as he can. But he never becomes pure. Except in Christ, you understand. But now we should speak about your brother Andreas. He is a man of glory, but he does not know what sin is. He has lived such a decent life ever since he was a boy and did all that the papists can call good deeds. And deep within, he is a little too proud of his holiness. It is the most precious thing he has on earth. And I would sincerely like to help him become a saint if he would only not lose Christ . . ."

"What should one then say to such a man?"

"The same as you need to hear yourself, dear brother: that we may count all our own for sin and dreck, so that we may win Christ."

"But in fact, it hardly helps just to *say* the thing," he added. "Neither Andreas nor you will learn to believe it before God's law crushes all your virtues. What the law says it says so that every mouth shall be stopped, says St. Paul. It usually goes so that one is fundamentally unfortunate and may see how miserable it is with himself and the others amid all their piety. Then one has his mouth stopped with shame and lacks all desire to talk about their love for God and their great sacrifices."

They were now on their way back toward the city that was flooded with midday sunlight. The sunlight was dense across the plain, and the mountains by Stjärnor disappeared in a blueish gray haze. The scrivener was quiet for a long time. He went and thought about the words concerning misery amidst all piety. With this in mind, he thought through all the miserable events of the day. Suddenly he said:

"Tell me something: what should one think about the internecine conflict that is found among serious Christians?"

"That it is because of trusting in works, of course, and works of holiness," the priest answered without blinking. He gave the scrivener another of his glances, glittering with a restrained smile.

"I understand there has been a fight among the saints," he said. "I could have said so beforehand. It went the same for us up in Uppsala. Some drank wine and beer and the others only water. Some fasted before the Lord's Supper, and the others did not, and the third did not want any communion at all so long as the Archbishop bore a miter and staff. And so there was a break without end. It has to be so, once you have landed in works righteousness. If a man lives in justification by faith, then he knows that he is a sinner who can only be saved for Christ's sake. Then he is happy if only the gospel is freely proclaimed and there is access to the sacraments. Then he can leave all ceremonies and leave off judging the lives of others. There is no good deed that can be prescribed beforehand. When a sinner believes in Christ and is pardoned, then Jesus and the Spirit take their abode in the heart, and it is a joyful and willing spirit that sincerely wants to serve his neighbor and do all good wherever it presents itself. But these good works cannot be prescribed beforehand. They come of themselves, and so they are done well, as God would have them done, and it is always something good for the neighbor. Then he does not wear his horsehair shirt, but day after day, he goes and is decent toward his sour neighbor . . . But if we want to become holy through our works, then the deeds must be prescribed. And because there is no such description in the Bible, one has to try to knit them together himself. One person finds one thing and the other another, and there is quarreling without end because work-saints are jealous self-promoters. Because they have become so exhausted and sour by their holiness, they will not let anyone else's holiness come into fashion. Among the papists, it went well because the only holiness that meant anything was the holiness that the pope required, and there everyone has to follow the same path. But we who have separated ourselves from the pope come to have as many sects as there are crazy slaves of the law who happily find some new sort of works-holiness. This is the punishment for that we do not hold fast to the precious gospel of justification through faith."

They had entered the city again. The road was empty and dusty between the gray planks.

"And when do you get on your way?" asked the priest.

"As soon as I can."

The priest looked up again with a quick glance.

"Can we not keep each other company? I am riding home in the morning at sunup."

The scrivener blushed.

"I have not been able to arrange for a horse just yet," he said.

Herr Peder nodded when he saw the other's embarrassment.

"You lack money, I understand," he said. "How much?"

Now the scrivener recounted the whole vexing story about what had happened today. The priest nodded as if it was the most natural thing in the world.

"Come with me, we will see," he said.

They continued to the hostel in front of the city hall. The priest went in and came out again with four silver coins.

"You can borrow them if you like," he said. "But it is better for me if I do not have too much ready cash. It is too easily spent."

Martin thanked him exuberantly. To himself, he thanked God for his mysterious ways.

They decided to meet the next morning just before sunup. It was best to ride before it became too warm.

Within less than half an hour, Martin had finished horse shopping. He contentedly led the animal out of the gate and went to get his saddle.

Down by Gert Hubmaier between the merchants' sheds, it had become quiet. Martin went in and found Kort Lange in the shade under the gallery where he stood and measured fabric.

"Where is Master?" he asked.

Kort nodded in the direction of the stalls.

The merchant came out at the same time. He was calm and sober and perhaps a bit ashamed.

"Have you come back, Martin?" he asked. "That is good. I had thought to send for you and say that you may happily continue to work for me as long as you conduct yourself as you have so far. The rest I don't care about."

"Thanks, master," said the scrivener, "but now God has led me on another path. Now I want to thank you for good employment before I gather my things and take my leave."

Gert Hubmaier shook his hand without saying anything. Martin went into the stall and fetched his saddle with the coat and the unpacked leather bags. He began to saddle the horse. Kort Lange came up to him.

"Where are you going?"

The scrivener pursed his lips and tugged on the saddle a bit.

"Home to Fröjerum," he said, "to save my brother."

The other looked at him wide-eyed.

"Is your brother home again?"

"No, he wanders about the forest free as a bird. All the more why he needs me."

The other was quiet for a moment.

"Beware of the world and your own flesh."

"Yes, brother . . . you do the same. I am almost beginning to believe that this gray shirt has been an ornament for our proud flesh."

Kort Lange looked even more puzzled. But he didn't say anything.

Only when the scrivener set foot in the stirrup did he say:

"Martin, promise to never be unfaithful to the true gospel!"

"That I promise," said Martin as he swung into the saddle. "The *true* gospel . . . Are you really sure that we have found it already?"

"Yes," said the other quickly. "Of course, we have the Bible."

"Correct . . . There we have the gospel. But do we have it *here*, that is the question."

He beat his chest. Then spurred the horse, waved his hand, bent deeply forward in the saddle, and disappeared through the gate.

WHAT THE LAW COULD NOT DO

Midsummer 1543

Domine, ne in furore tur arguas me,
Neque in ira tur corripias me.
Miserere mei, Domine, quoniam infirmus sum . . .[1]

As he started the psalms of repentance again without really knowing how many times he had done so or in what order, he had come to think about Herr Tönjes's lighthearted and bloated face with the blue bags under his eyes. He imagined the moist skin wrinkle and age, the mockingly deep mouth flatten out, the limp chin fall, and the lips tensed and twisted in a fight with death. That is how he would look in death. And then his naked soul would begin the gruesome journey, where the hounds of hell and all the devils waited in the dark . . .

He jerked and froze in fear. And again, he had thought vindictive thoughts while his mouth rambled unintelligible words of prayer. He went back to the last verse that he was sure he had recited in devotion and began again:

Et anima mea conturbata est valde:
sed tu, Domine, usquequo?[2]

It was not the first time this had happened. While he recited *Dies irae*, he thought about the maiden they had with them at the

---

[1] "O Lord, rebuke me not in your anger, nor discipline me in your wrath. Be gracious to me, O Lord, for I am languishing" (Psalm 6:1–2).

[2] "My soul also is greatly troubled. But you, O Lord—how long?" (Psalm 6:3).

camp in Visseboda. He recited *Jesus dulcis memoria* and remembered the great battle at Skinnarbacken, and it still heated his cheeks with wrath for the shame that the servant from Bodakara added to him. He wanted to search his soul and began with the five sensual sins—but he had hardly asked himself how he had sinned with the tongue before he remembered all the unchaste speech and all the wild quarrels streamed over him and filled him with impure or resentful thoughts.

He had stopped reciting the penitential psalms. What did this serve? Was this contrition? Was this contrition of the heart? Without which penance was worthless?

He did not rightly know himself if today was the fourth or the fifth day he had been locked in this hole. The time was infinitely long with the smell of mold and dark down there. Nothing happened here, but that the door opened in the morning and evening, then someone set a crust of bread and a bowl of cabbage soup or watery broth down on the step. During the day, a small ray of light traveled across the floor from the left stone wall to the other side. But today, not even that much happened. It had begun to rain outside. Heavy drops slipped through the dilapidated roof and made small puddles in the rubbish on the dirt floor. Now he could not even stretch himself out. Because he could not stand upright here inside, he had to lie straight down on the dirty floor whenever he wanted to straighten out his back. Now the water formed into dark puddles. He crouched together on the stairs. The fetters chaffed his persistent wounds, and it smelled bad in the corner where he made his latrine.

But all this paled in comparison to the pain that his sins gave him. Was he forsaken by God? Had God fixed an irrevocable judgment of wrath that was now being brought to completion? Was he a church thief who stole his own church's money? Had God left him in the enemies' hands because of this? Was that why he would dangle in the wind and spoil the air on gallows hill? Was this why his bones would be pecked apart by the birds one after another and dragged away by the hangman's scabby hounds rather than being buried in consecrated earth?

And this was the least of the misfortunes! That he even thought of the shame that would be attached to his name in the countryside, it was just one more proof of his impiety. It was then a thousand times worse than that he lost the crown of salvation, that he had been found lacking in the test, that he was eternally shut out from the saints in heaven and would find his lot in the burning sea of fire. For that was really his lot, of that he felt more and more certain. He had prayed to God to find life until he had been able to do penance. That same night God had handed him over to the executioners. He had prayed for grace to die after he had received absolution and the sacrament. God had answered by closing the last path to a true seelsorger.[3] He knew well what St. Thomas taught concerning confession, that the desire to confess could replace the actual confession if only true contrition were found in the heart along with true faith that sprang from a love for God. But now God had denied him just this contrition and this faith. In the beginning, he had thought he possessed it. He had never before prayed as earnestly and humbly as he prayed the first few hours of his imprisonment. He poured his wounded soul out in a stream of prayers. He laid everything out in dust before God. He bowed to his counsel and praised his name. He was willing to take everything from his hands.

But then it all began again. The longer he prayed, the more sin stepped forward. Hateful, impure, defiant, and blasphemous thoughts crept up within him. He found to his horror that he was still full of obstinance toward God. He was not humble, for he got caught up thinking that he had still been the most zealous servant that God had in Fröjerum for many long years. He was not repentant, for he could feel more contentment than horror when he remembered his deadly sins. Neither was his faith characterized by love, for he could be bitter against both God and man. He felt a wild lust to make fists and curse God and call him an oath-breaker and liar who forgot his promise and let his church be trampled by the unfaithful and handed over his most faithful servants to be ruled over by the devil.

It was worse in the loneliness of night. When the last bit of sunlight falling through the holes in the ceiling was extinguished, the cool dampness crept out of the cold ground, and his swollen body trembled

---

[3] *Seelsorger* is a German term for a pastor who is known to take special care of his flock and truly tend to souls. It is a term that is still used in English-speaking Lutheran circles today. There really is no English equivalent.

with chills. Then the horror crept in, a wild and frenzied horror, that he felt as a boy when he would travel home by himself in the stormy fall evenings and hear Odin's Wild Hunt[4] run right through the forest on the other side of the lake and come ever closer. The same horror now laid upon him like a panting predator as he lay face down in the dirt. Then it drove its claws into him, tickled the back of his neck with its heated breath, and whispered: "There is no God! It is we who have the power. *The powers* have the power. We have lied to you for a long time. You have annoyed us. You have refused to sacrifice the silver to the source. You have refused to pour lead or smoke a horn or cross yourself backward.[5] We have tiptoed after you in the forest. We followed you to the cairn and pole. We ran before you to the parsonage and woke the knechts in the yard. We set the trap for you outside the backdoor. Now we put the brand into your wounded flesh. Then we take you by the wounds and hair. Now we have our revenge!"

The priest made his way higher up the stairway to keep himself from a dirty rivulet that worked its way closer through the rubbish on the floor. He coughed violently, a high-pitched cough like a tear in a broken air pipe. His teeth ached. Was it scurvy? Now it made no difference if all his teeth fell out. Then his dead man's skull would at least not grin so badly when it was pecked clean by crows . . .

He slowly straightened his stiff back. No—this was like sinking in a quagmire. He would not allow despair to have power over him. He knew well that he still had a few short hours or days left that could possibly change his eternal fate. If he could bring forth a true contrition, then he could at least pray with half a heart. He still *wanted* to atone for what he had broken. Perhaps it would still count . . .

He knelt again. He had to put one knee in a puddle now. Then he began again:

Domine, ne in furore tuo . . .

---

[4] Odin's Wild Hunt is an element of Scandinavian folklore and fantasy. On stormy nights, people would believe they saw or heard Odin and his entourage riding in pursuit of prey, and this was often thought to be an omen of tragedy to come.

[5] These reference various forms of black or folk magic common to the area: for instance, "to pour lead" references Molybdomancy, an art of divination which begins by pouring molten metal into water.

* * *

The sun-drenched fields steamed, and the vaulted sky was high and clear. Only in the south could one catch a glimpse of a long row of high stacked clouds that stood in a straight line above the horizon and stuck their heads out of the haze. Bright and clear sunshine saturated the open country of Kinda. The wide water glittered, and the forested headlands were like longships on the sea.

Herr Peder glanced at his travel companion. He began to think all the better concerning this openhearted *schwarmerei*. It was now the second day of travel. With an easy gait, they traveled along the great road to Vimmeby. Here in the open fields, they could ride side by side. In the forest, they had to ride single file through the trees.

They just crossed an open field where a few solitary ears of grain waved between the midsummer flowers. The priest turned in his saddle and pointed to a group of scrubby trees that stuck up over hazel shrubs with their blackened branches.

"The first deserted farm," he said.

The path passed right by it. They stopped between the broken-down fences and turned into the yard that was flanked by a pair of half charred linden trees. There was a blackened square of ashes and charred remains where the home had stood. Fresh green grass had already sprouted up out of the earth, and white chervil covered the charred logs. In one place there were great white bones strewn about in the ashes. They were the remains of some burnt animal that was dug up by the dogs. A long white skull with a staring eye and exposed teeth had been pressed into the soot.

"There will be many more," said the priest. "Here the king's knechts began to pillage as if they were in the land of an enemy, and it continues all the way down to Horn. It was revenge for their defeat at Kisa."

They continued quietly over the meadows. The lake spread out in a blue expanse, the sky burned with sunlight, the rowans scented the air, and the hills were full of strawberry blossoms. But in the villages, the apple trees had been singed with fire, and between the weeds, one could see the black bottom of soot and cinders. Here and there, silent men went and hewed logs that looked bone-white among the black dirt heaps.

Martin Ragnvaldsson sat and thought about a letter that he had been present to write up some time that last winter. His Grace had given the war command a sharp admonition to finally give their men freedom to pillage and plunder so that they could freely gather and take from the townspeople, farmers, and others whom His Majesty had in mind. His Grace had let it be understood that so long as the royal forces advanced so mercifully and spared both friends and enemy, it would never go well. So, the war command should think differently, and that would have a greater impact.

In print, things had gone well with the boastful words. But here was how the gruesome reality behind them played out.

"Peder," he asked unexpectedly, "what do you think of the king?"

The answer came without hesitation.

"He is sent from God."

"You don't mean that . . . rather from Satan? Is he not a coarse sinner? A slave of mammon and a bloodhound?"

"For sure, he is a sinner. Have you never heard that God rules the world through sinners?"

The scrivener looked puzzled.

"Don't sinners do the devil's work?"

"Of course—and still God forces them to take part in his government. There is nothing so strange as God's rule."

He pointed out over the countryside.

"Look here, how God rules. While we ride here over the meadow, God is ceaselessly active all around us. He commands, and everything sprouts up and grows. He clothes the ground in the grass. He causes the oak trees over there to leaf. He gives birth to starlings, and none of them shall fall to the ground apart from his will. Within ourselves, God creates anew at this moment. He orders our hearts to beat and our lungs to breathe. He gives our hands the power to hold the reins. This and everything else that happens in nature is God's first mode of governance in the world and keeping his creation with power."

He pointed again to the lake where a single cloud of smoke billowed out of the forest.

"Look now. People live down there. In that village and every other village, there are parents and house servants, the village assembly, and elders. Children are born and fostered there. They are governed and ruled in a thousand ways. And wherever you come upon people in this world, God has always created a certain order—even among the Turks. That is also a way God rules. He drives people to build families and establish kingdoms, and he gives us parents and judges and authorities. In all of these offices and callings, God is active. Just as the grass grows here and blooms according to God's will without having any idea about God, so one can do God's work as fathers or judges or king without asking even a tiny bit after God. Without knowing himself that he is a little servant who helps with God's great work."

"But God's work is to save the world? And King Gustavus does not give even two straws to save his people!"

"Stop a minute. Do not just jump immediately over into the second article. God is, first and foremost, the creator, and it is that we are talking about now. The creator holds his creation together with power. He does it by giving life and breath to all. He does it by giving us birth and daily bread. He also does it by giving all people their office and authority. The authority has nothing to do with salvation. It is established to keep order on earth. Just as parents can give their children food and clothe them without fearing God, so can authorities keep order in the land without being in the least a Christian. Thereby God does his will. God wants to create a dam for raw wickedness. He wants to hinder bold and obstinate people from having a free course to evil. So he has set authority to rule with the sword and avenge and punish those who do evil. This has nothing to do with the gospel. It does not lead souls into God's kingdom, but it keeps external discipline and order on the earth, and it is not to be despised. It is a part of God's providence."

They rode through the oak forest. The loose canopy of leaves was like a green sky in the sun around the black trunks. The scrivener had an objection to counter Peder's point.

"But if the authority himself acts badly and uses the sword to suppress justice for the innocent rather than punishing the evildoers. If, for example, the king takes away the acorns from the peasants and wants to extort an unfair tax because their pigs eat the acorns?"

The priest nodded.

"Yes, yes, so it almost has to happen. The authorities abuse the power they receive from God. Nevertheless, it is better in the world despite that than if there was no authority at all. You may remember that we are all complete sinners, most of us remain quite coarse, who must be disciplined with blows. A hard authority can be a well-deserved punishment for our hard hearts. And if a prince is overly harsh, then there is enough iron, wood, and hemp in this world for God to remove him one way or another. But so long as God allows the authority to govern, you can find yourself in that regiment."

"So do you really think that King Gustavus is a king after God's heart."

"That is another question. The king can answer that himself in his prayer chamber and before his court preacher—and on judgment day. It does not concern us. For us, it is enough to know that God still allows King Gustavus to rule and that it pleases God to govern his sinful Swedish people through a great sinner."

The scrivener looked contemplative.

"Do you really dare to say that all authority is from God?"

"Yes, I dare . . . because it is written in the word of God."

"Do you then think that one should sit with his arms crossed and resign himself to all the evil that happens in the world?"

"Not at all! For the first, you shall instruct authority if you happen to hold the preaching office: both King and bailiff should know their Christian duty. For the other, you shall keep justice with power in everything that comes your way, if you have any office yourself. And if you are not placed to either punish or preach, or even govern, then you shall not sit with your arms crossed, but you should clasp them hard and regularly pray to God for your prince, that God gives him a new heart or removes him. There are fearful powers that put the point of the sword to an unfaithful prince when faithful people pray for him."

"Do you then mean that a man should never try to push a tyrant out of the way?"

Martin had a very particular reason for his question. Among the evangelical brothers, one and another had whispered that God's hourglass was to soon run out for the antichristian king and that abomination of desolation ought to now be removed from the throne . . . They did not say anything more, but all knew the conspiracy from the year 1536 for which Hans Bökman and Kort Druvenagel and many other evangelicals were tortured and murdered.

"You ask more than any man can answer," said the priest. "A Christian never rebels. He knows that he is worthy of eternal condemnation for the sake of his sin. Consequently, he can never have a worse authority than he deserves. To suffer injustice is hard but salutary. One should not try to escape the cross with violence. Then one leaves the gospel and places himself under the law again. So long as one lives under the gospel, one may forgive without limit and forgive himself without end. But to try to take revenge in one's own hands, that is to leave the kingdom of forgiveness and subject oneself again to God's immutable law. And it is a shame if one falls under the retribution. He who takes up the sword shall die by the sword. The Master said that just when Peter wanted to take justice into his own hands. God still allows the sword to go where it is needed. He can set one authority against the other. He can set the council against the king and the king against the Kaiser. And finally, he can use the sin of one to punish the other. It is essentially the most wonderful aspect of God's reign that he links Satan's deeds so that they serve divine justice and retribution. I believe that God can allow a rebellion or a murder that in itself is clearly sin, to be a part of his good reign."

"Just look at what happened here among us this last year," he continued. "The peasants ran off and rebelled. They sinned with all their plundering and murder. So they have received a terrible and wrathful judgment upon themselves. But at the same time, the King received a flogging across his hardback, which looks as if it softened him up. It is said that all of his new-fangled government arrangements are now finished. King Gustavus has learned that he cannot deal with his people like serfs on a large German estate. Pyhy is said to be out of favor, have you heard that?"

"Has the chancellor fallen out of favor? Isn't he on a mission to France?"

"He is on the way home to answer for his gross extravagance. The bishop told us in Linköping that His Grace now goes around and thunders against Pyhy and says that just now when he is needed most here at home, he has stayed away in France and is now already on the second half of the year's pension and good day dances with Madam de Tampas, Madam de Säll, and Madam de Massa, while His Grace dances here at home with Gudmund Fässing, Per Skägge, and Nils Dacke—with very different benefits! As His Grace says. True as my word: When sometime in the future we can look back on this unfortunate and bloody year, then we shall see how God governed in the midst of all the sin and made use of our missteps and misdeeds to the benefit of our poor people."

The scrivener had become quite thoughtful. Among the evangelical brothers, there had always been an inexorable either/or. Either one belonged to God's people and lived holy and pure, or he belonged to the world, and then one had nothing to do with God at all. And that the government, military, the council, the judges and all the others belonged to the kingdom of the devil and the world, that was self-evident to them. That God could do something good even through sinners, that was a new thought for him.

"But," he said contemplatively, "that would mean that sinners serve God without knowing it, and have the right . . ."

The priest slapped his knees with his rider's crop so that the horse jumped.

"Oh, you arch papist! There you betray yourself. So you take it for granted that salvation comes through works? And yet you call yourself evangelical! If justification could be won through the power of the law, then even the Sultan could enter heaven if he was fair and gentle. But now justification comes through faith in Jesus. Even the fairest judge and the holiest prince and the best mother sin more than enough to deserve eternal hellfire. All the good we do as God's instruments in our earthly callings and office, this has not even the least meaning for salvation. It is God's way of holding his creation together with power. But to save his human children, God has established a completely different order in the world. Martin Luther calls it the spiritual realm. This realm does not rule by the sword, but by the word which does not operate by force and threat of punishment, but by the gospel and forgiveness and purely good gifts. Just as God governs his sinful world with princes and armies, with judges and the rod, so he has also put a church in the midst of this sinful world and governs over our souls with priests and preaching, with baptism and communion and absolution. And here he asks all sinners to believe in Jesus and he who believes, God has forgiven everything and has made him right from pure grace and dwells in his heart and drives him to willingly suffer all and serve all. The man no longer needs to be threatened with the sword or coerced with the law. He only does all the good that he comes to do because faith cannot be anything but active in love. The man is thus faithful to his authority and gladly helps with the governance of the kingdom."

The scrivener who sat with his eyes fixed on his saddle pommel looked up.

"Do you mean that I could return to the service of King Gustavus?"

"Yes . . . as soon as you have your sins forgiven and begin to live by grace."

"Never," yelled the scrivener almost with a shriek. "If one has once worked his way out of the snare of sin, he should never stick his head in it again!"

Now it was Herr Peder who looked up at his travel companion and said:

"Tell me, St. Martin, was it a holy and pure service that you did with Gert Hubmaier? Were you completely loose from the snare of sin? In business dealings and all?"

The scrivener blushed.

"No, not always," he said.

"I tell you calmly, *never*," said the priest. "Nothing is holy and pure in this world. We may do what good we can and keep ourselves humble and daily return to the seat of mercy to receive a share in Christ's merits, who alone can make us with all our deeds pleasing before God. When a man begins in the school of God, one believes that one shall be able to run away from sin, as one runs away from a troublesome master. This is why young people so happily enter monasteries or become *schwarmerei*. I found myself on the same path once. But now I have learned that I live closer to God as a housefather with two children—and a farmer with sixteen head of cattle, and a royal bailiff with a steady fraction of the crown's steady tithe. I live by the mercy of my Savior, where I am placed . . . and now I think that you could live closer to God in all humility in the king's chancellery than in the fine cloister that Gert Hubmaier keeps for you."

The scrivener was quiet. It seemed that he wanted to say something to the contrary. The priest saw it and laughed.

"I know what you are thinking: This is a comforting doctrine for slaves of the world. I will only say: It is moderately comfortable if you live before God's all-seeing eye. Then there is judgment every day—but grace too with every new day. It is much more comfortable to do as your gray brothers. Then one has God in one of his saddlebags and the world in the other. Before God, one prays and sings, mortifies his flesh, saves souls, and becomes holy. He keeps his affairs on the other side as a completely different thing that doesn't really have anything to do with piety. It is to distort the whole of Christendom. God does not want to have my good works. My neighbor shall have them. God wants to have my faith. So I shall trust him, pray to him at every turn and receive the Word that works faith within me. Before God, I shall not try to be pious. There I shall recognize that I am a great sinner. I shall not come jingling my good works. That is only to tease and challenge God. They are still like worm-heavy apples. There is always something wrong about them, and before God, they do not do. But to the neighbor, they can be good. You can very well foster your children, be decent toward your wife, serve your king, and help the poor, though there is much pride and smugness remaining in your poor heart. So God will use you to serve your neighbor even though you are a great sinner. He will not make you into some saint that he can put up among his pure angels, but he will let you live by grace and all the more grace you receive from heaven the more shall you serve here on earth—without demanding to be rewarded or asking to get a halo for it. His true saints, God places them to feed children or to sweep the barns or write in the king's chancellery—and they are glad that great sinners such as themselves can be able to do some little service here in the world for the sake of Jesus Christ."

The scrivener was not willing to agree. He laughed and said:

"Next, you will say straight up that it was a *sin* to leave the king's ungodly chancellery?"

"Yes . . . almost! There, you had your calling. There, you were placed by God to serve your poor people. Now you have run to Gert Hubmaier instead. There you serve only yourself. For you did not take that place to get cheap spices and good clothes for your poor neighbor? No, you took it to live your own fine little sanctified life for yourself. Just like a monk! But how do you think it goes for your poor neighbor and with the whole of your poor people if all the Christians fold their hands and will not have anything to do with common people and common work?"

The scrivener smiled again and shook his head.

"I understand that you want to have me back in the castle," he said. "I will never go there again! One cannot! If one wants to be pious . . ."

The priest stood up in the stirrups so that he was just as tall as the scrivener and looked him straight in the eye.

"Want to be pious! I will tell you one thing, Martin: it is the greatest sin there is to want to be pious! So long as a man wants to be pious and holy, he thinks only about himself. He is captivated by his own notability. He wants to be someone—even before God! If he does something good for his neighbor, he does it only for his own sake because he heard that that is what a saint should look like. The whole time he looks out for himself and the good he does, he gathers it all up together and amasses it like the dragon with his worthless gold in order to have something to praise himself for before the throne of God. This is why God has to make every self-sanctified fool into a truly great sinner in order to overcome them. Sometimes he lets them fall into coarse sin, others he plagues with their sinful depravity until they despair and recognize that they really deserve eternal condemnation. So long as we watch ourselves and want to be holy, we are nothing but coarse sinners, even if we see a halo in the mirror. The worst is that people have such an unbelievable desire to look at themselves. They are normally not cracked before they see that the mask of sin creeps in everywhere and that they are more loathsome to watch than a decaying dog's corpse on the side of the road. Then they might finally desire to see something different. And then the Holy Spirit will be able to turn their eyes to Christ in earnest. Then they notice that the Savior alone in all the earth can atone for such abominable sinners. Then they think that Christ is the loveliest person there is to look upon. And he who sees him and believes him, he at that moment receives the wonderful gift that only God can give: to be able to see his neighbor and discover him just when he needs help. He no longer thinks about doing good deeds, but he does good. He no longer wants to be holy, but he has the Holy Spirit, and therefore he serves. He does not see the holy saint before him as a model for how he ought to be, but he only sees the neighbor who suffers need, and he goes to him to serve him."

The scrivener became quite closed and looked in away from the priest. Finally, he said:

"Have you ever had a real struggle with your conscience when it came to your work?"

The priest's dark eyes brightened.

"Have I! Do you remember that night in the parsonage at Fröjerum when you saved my life? At that time, I was as despondent as a man can be. At that time, I believed that King Gustavus was the Antichrist's instrument and that he would persecute and root out all true Christendom in the land. In the following few weeks, I would have followed anyone who wanted to rebel. I spoke with a couple of priests about the matter. But then a message came from Archbishop Lars. It went silently from man to man as it has so many times these past years. He asked us to be calm and pray. We should preach God's word with all earnestness, discipline sinners, offer forgiveness to all, hold the mass with all reverence and christen children as before. So we should all stay where we were as long as we could freely preach God's word and administer the holy sacraments. We should calmly let mockery and humiliation pass over us, in worldly things we should not trespass the law, but when it came to God's Word, we would rather suffer death than fold an inch."

"And to this end God has helped us," continued the priest. "It is better by far for the church now than a few years ago. The Norman madness with its superintendents and seniors is not spoken about anymore. We have retained our bishops, and you shall see that God saves as much freedom for our church as she needs to save souls. It had to have been God's special providence that we received Archbishop Lars precisely during these terrible times. He is a model for us all. He never quarrels about his power or his honor, as the chancellor always did to his shame. But he fosters his priests, he creates an evangelical order for us in the church, though it seems the King does not want to have it published. It doesn't mean anything, because we still follow Archbishop Lars. Deep within, the king is in his own way happy with his Archbishop because he knows that Archbishop Lars is one of the few here in the land who simply wishes him well even when he contradicts him, and he is faithful to him even in his prayer chamber. The Archbishop really wants to serve and does not think of himself. So the King does not want to be rid of him, even if he dares to have his own thoughts."

"But now if the king will finally dismiss him? Is not then everything jeopardized? What do you say then?"

Finally, for once, the priest answered with a single word:

"God."

"What do you mean?"

"I mean that you should consider God. This is not the wisdom of a statesman. It is not just the work of man and human wisdom. If God has called Archbishop Lars to save the church for us, then he lets him live until he has done his work. Look over there, at those oak trees that stand there . . ."

He stopped abruptly. Both of them turned. It was the clank of steel like when a shield scrapes against hip plates. A little further up in the meadow, they could see a knecht come riding at a sharp trot. The horse was warm and foamy.

They pulled up on the reins and waited for the rider, but he just greeted them and continued down the road. The priest, however, caught up alongside him.

"Where are you coming from?"

"From home," said the knecht and smiled with his few brown and broken teeth. "Who is it that asks?"

"Peder Knutsson, the priest in Vi and appointed collector for His Grace—so you do not need to sneer so broadly."

The knecht shut his mouth.

"Don't be mad, Herr," he said. "A letter carrier learns to keep his mouth shut these days."

The Priest took the opportunity.

"Perhaps you have learned something new that I may need to know?"

"I should believe so," said the knecht. "We have caught the priest in Ravelunda, the traitor. I have just been to Herr Måns in Bro . . ."

The priest's dark eyes got big, then were riveted on the rider.

"You can't be serious! Where have you taken him?"

"He is in Fröjerum, at the priest's quarters. He had stolen the church's silver and wanted to flee the country. Now he lies in irons in his own cellar, and I have been to the judge and received orders."

The priest hardly dared to breathe.

"And what has the judge ordered?"

The knecht grinned again.

"As if the left hand knew what the right was doing!"

He tapped his saddlebag.

"I have it here, behind two seals. If I break them, I break my own thumbs. But this much I understand, that Herr Måns plans to ask the king because he sent word to Vreta at the same time as he gave me leave."

The knecht saw what an impression the news made and willingly explained further: they had quartered in Fröjerum under Herr Tönjes, three whole fähnleins sent specifically to take the wild priest dead or alive. Then he had run straight into their arms, and Herr Tönjes needed no more than threaten him with torture before he had confessed that the money belonged to the church. So now he will probably be hung as a church thief . . .

The priest let his horse slow a little so that he came even with the scrivener. Martin had heard everything and had turned white as a sheet. They rode along quietly. The knecht had now gone a good piece ahead of them. Finally, the scrivener said:

"Do you still believe that all authority is from God?"

The answer came harsh and short as if the priest had a hard time speaking.

"Yes, because it is still written in the word of God."

The scrivener swallowed.

"But if the king now allows Anders to be hung?"

It was hard to read the priest's face because of the sharp trot. His lips were pressed together hard, and the broad chin had a couple of folds. Suddenly, something glittery fell on the leather reins. Was it a drop of sweat?

The scrivener never received an answer to his question. The road narrowed, and the priest forced himself a horse length ahead. But the scrivener could see that he had wrapped his hands in the reins and bowed his head forward almost imperceivably.

* * *

Three and a half years . . .

The scrivener counted on his fingers. Yes, it had truly been almost three and a half years to the day since he had last seen his home country. He had come on the same road that time, but then all was swept over in windblown snow and rapidly falling winter twilight. Now the evening sun flooded over the fresh greenery, the lake reflected the evening clouds and a warm breeze blew from the forests in the distance saturated with the smell of the mire.

The path slowly descended through the country, and the horse trotted along briskly. The scrivener immediately took the path to the church-village and the parsonage. For four days, he had endured since they came to Vi, but the fifth day he could no longer control himself. They had not been successful learning anything other than that Fröjerum's parsonage was so well guarded that spears and halberds stick out from every window in all the cowsheds. He had determined to travel there himself and try to get some information. Perhaps the priest was right when he said that it was a fool's errand. They had, in any case, prayed together on the stone floor in the church in Vi, and then Martin had taken his leave.

The traces of unrest could be seen everywhere in the country. The judge in Bro now made vigorous efforts to stamp out the last traces of rebellion, and Martin noticed the results. The knechts occupied the villages and the roads were blocked. Twice, the scrivener skirted their posts, and twice he was checked. The pass that Gert Hubmaier of Stockholm had obtained for him to use for his mercantile business had cleared him. Now there still remained the hardest thing: To learn something about Anders.

He hesitated a minute in the foliage just outside the church-village. To the left, he caught sight of the parsonage, and his heart pounded hard. He had to force himself to be reasonable. Overcoming himself, he turned the horse to the right and rode through the birch forest in a wide arch around the church-village. Only on the other side did he turn up to the village and cross the marshy meadow with the stone cairn around the old pole. He jumped off his horse and led it under the huge hazel bushes up to the village street. There he disappeared right in through the first gate to the right and stepped into Sexton Petrus's yard.

The low gray house looked older than anything. A few ruffled hens burst into the dirty yard where the rainwater remained in the deep ravines and reflected the gold evening sky between the black edges. A goat bleated on the cottage roof.

Scrivener Martin stepped over the cobblestones that almost disappeared in the mud and knocked on the weathered door. He called into the dark. Finally, a faint voice answered from the hearth.

At the same time, something moved on the other side of the yard by the door to the swine shed. A muddy wooden clog was lifted over the high threshold, followed by a gangly figure hunched over deeply in the low doorway. There stood old Petrus peering into the evening light with a cracked bucket in his hand and coat soiled with swill.

The shriveled gray face lit up when he recognized the scrivener. He clumsily set aside the bucket and attempted to dry his hands on the front of his pants, but that just made them dirtier. He tried again on his shirt and succeeded a bit more. Then he greeted leisurely.

The conversation started as cumbersome and carefully as always. They sat down by the cottage wall. The goat hopped down from the roof, stared curiously at the stranger, and leaped in through the open shed door. Slowly, the sexton began to tell what he knew.

It was the night before the St. Botolph's mass when it happened. In the morning, when he came to ring the first chime, he had found the church's old cash box standing before the choir screen. First, he had thought that it was goblins playing tricks because the church-warden in Årtebol had said on his deathbed that the money was buried in a place that only the priest knew about. There they had put the body of Christ above the shrine and stones in a cross, and afterward, Lasse in Årtebol went there and recited a coarse curse over anyone who touched the treasure.

So, when Sexton Petrus found the shrine in front of the choir gate, he splashed it with holy water before he touched it. Then he knew that it was empty. He had been even more certain that the powers were in play and had carried it in and placed it down before the tabernacle[6] without opening it. But then it had been said that the knechts up in the parsonage had taken a prisoner who

[6] A vessel set on the altar where the remainder of the host for the Lord's Supper is kept in Roman Catholic churches after the congregation has communed. It is believed to remain the body of Christ until such time as it is consumed, and therefore becomes an object of veneration.

they kept detained in the greatest secrecy without even saying who it was. Sexton Petrus felt his poor back had been sufficiently abused enough already, and so he wisely avoided going there to ask. Instead, he spoke friendly with the girl in Spjutängen, who used to get visits from one of the knechts, and before the next morning, she came to him trembling. She told him it was the priest they had detained at the parsonage and that he would be hanged because he had stolen the church's silver.

Sexton Petrus then understood what had happened with the theft. The priest had planned to flee from the area and thought it was best to take the church's money with him. There were greater and more dangerous church thieves in the land than Herr Anders.

The old man glanced at the scrivener a little suspiciously, while he said the last bit. Martin remembered the conversation on the Eve of Epiphany almost three years before. He hurried to say.

"Don't worry, dear old man, I am not coming on behalf of the king this time. I left the king's service long ago. Now I am out looking for my brother . . . Do you think it is worth my time to go up to the parsonage?"

"You could well do that," the sexton said slowly. "It is empty and deserted up there now. Yesterday Herr Tönjes and his whole company left. They did not feel safe here because it still may be that there are those who want to set the priest free."

He gave the scrivener another shy and suspicious look. Then he continued:

"They departed in the morning, first the transport and then the shooters. Herr Andreas sat on a horse with a sack over his head, and he traveled with a double guard of soldiers on either side. They traveled down through the region of Ravelunda and went to Sponga, I think. Herr Tönjes has a stone house there, and he is safer there . . ."

The scrivener bowed forward and hid his face in his hands. The sexton was quiet. After an hour, the scrivener straightened up again and dried the tears from under his eyes with the backside of his hands.

The old man patted Martin on the shoulder. "I have enough heartache myself, but I feel for you," he said slowly. "I have served four priests at the Lord's altar here in this church, but none have been like your brother. If they take his life now, God will be merciful to his soul. I will burn whatever candles I can scrape together before the Mother of God for his sake. But I do not believe he needs much of that sort. Your brother has helped so many souls to paradise, so he has enough of them who pray for him up there."

The old man pointed up to the light evening sky that shined a warm golden yellow.

The scrivener had wanted to note his reservation with Petrus for the bad theology but could not find the right words. The old man continued.

"Your brother was a remarkable man in his ability to prepare people for death. I have been the sexton here for nearly fifty years, but never have I seen such a preparation for death like his. First, he kept a long period of confession. I sat outside during that, but sometimes still heard parts. He could draw out a man's sins, one after another. When he finished, there could not have been many left. Then he forgave the sins, and then I carried in the Lord's body. Then he gave the holy anointing, and finally, he prayed. First to the Holy Trinity and then to the Savior himself. Then he prayed to Mary and all God's angels, to all the patriarchs, prophets, apostles, martyrs, virgins and saints. And finally, he admonished the sick man not to trust in what he had now done and not in any prayers or works, but to set all his comfort and all his hope in the inconceivable mercy and grace of God . . ."

The scrivener sat quietly. He did not quite know if he should try to disabuse the sexton of his delusions. He was uncertain but could not help but feel that even amid all this papist rubble, there was a bit of true faith.

The sexton got up.

"Now I have to ring the Ave bell," he said to excuse himself.

The scrivener got up too.

"May I go with you?"

The old man nodded a little puzzled. They walked along the village street. While Martin gazed on the old homes that he had not seen for so long, he took the opportunity to hear what had happened during those three years. Sexton Petrus talked in a tranquil manner, and told everything in colorful pictures: the warm fall day when the knechts murdered John of Flodlycke and the consecrated bell rang for revenge until the forests on the other side of the lake disappeared in the darkness of night; then the wild hunt through the forests days thereafter when the peasants successfully defeated half a squadron of German knechts and came home with glittering harnesses and unblemished halberds—though the one who was really guilty, the one with the cleft chin and the big lips, had escaped. Then Dacke came and met with the peasants. He had offered to get them good weapons and promised help from Hertig Albrekt and Bishop Hans and even the Emperor. Then everything was rather calm all the way up until it was almost Candlemas Day when peasants from Värend and the people from Kinnevald passed through for two whole days, and everyone who could carry a crossbow followed them on the eastern Hola road. But this trip smelled bad. On the fifteenth day, they had come back with their dead, and if the peasants from Värend hadn't helped, they would have never made it home—there were so many. For three days, they worked to dig graves, even with six men toiling at the frozen ground. There had not been so many graves opened in the Fröjerum's churchyard since the Black Death. And they had stayed open for a long time because it was almost three weeks before Herr Peder of Vi could come to bury the fallen. Herr Peder spoke comfortingly of Christ and about the Savior's wounds and blood and then held the mass with all reverence, though he was said to be a heretic. They had heard nothing from their own priest, but that he had spilled blood in Skrukeby and wanted to make a pilgrimage to Rome to receive forgiveness. So they had become like sheep without a shepherd. Sexton Petrus had read a few Hours of the Holy Cross[7] in the church and sang Matins and Vespers on Sundays. They had celebrated the days of Rogation as usual, though no one could properly bless the seeds because the priest was gone. The sexton read the same Swedish prayers for the dying that the priest had used, but for the Lord's body, they had only been able to get a very little piece which he fetched from the tabernacle with shaking hands.

They had come up to the churchyard wall. The old man climbed over the old wall with stiff legs on the worn steppingstones that marked the old shortcut. Then he went up to the steeple, took off his

---

[7] Horae Sanctae Crucis, prayers focusing on the cross of Christ.

weathered hat, crossed himself, folded his hands, and mumbled a prayer. Then he spat in his hands and pulled on the rope.

The scrivener removed his hat too. It was actually contrary to his convictions, for all this with the sexton was all papist pomp with no basis in the Bible, and just like the sign of the cross ought to be done away with, but he did not have the heart to upset old Peter. So he stood there with his bare head, and when the first heavy bell toll rolled out through the countryside, he bowed his head and folded his hands. All around the countryside, it was just as tranquil an evening as he ever remembered from childhood. The bell tolls seemed to roll over the gray roofs of the village and out over the small fields like a wave. It had certainly reached Askanäs. Was there anyone there who bent their knee this evening like his mother always did behind the high-backed bench when the bell rang for Ave?

His mother had lived so completely before God's face. From his earliest years as a child, he remembered her kneeling at the corner of the bed, or before a crucifix on the wall, with her hands folded together, eyes shut, and the small face stamped by the deepest of devotion. He was accustomed to thinking of all such things as meaningless postures. But he still wanted to make an exception for his mother.

Only when Sexton Peter let go of the rope and picked up his hat did Martin wake up from his daydream. He was a little ashamed. He had stood with his head uncovered and not prayed a word. Was he in actual fact, more worldly than his mom had been with all her papistry?

The sexton stood and thumbed his hat a little perplexed. The tall bent figure seemed to grow smaller under the pressure of his uncertainty.

"See, it's just that I usually go into the church and pray for the dead at this time," he said.

The scrivener gave a friendly bow.

"Then I will go with you."

They crossed side by side over the turf, where bronze blades of grass waved in the wind. The sexton pointed out over the churchyard where the newly cut wood crosses stood out amidst the greenery.

"There are so many from this last winter," he said. "They had all received the body of the Lord before they went. Your brother anointed many of them during the battle. But many fell without absolution or anointing. So I pray for them. Herr Joen of Brohult taught me a powerful prayer of indulgence. It gives indulgences for as many days as Christ had wounds in his holy body. This was five thousand four hundred seventy-five. I recite it every day for some of the dead. And then I also recite some prayers for my own poor soul."

When they entered the church, Sexton Peter reverently took the holy water and bowed his knee, but Martin stayed standing. This was too much for him.

Without noticing anything, the sexton took a few steps forward, kneeled on the oak floorboards, and began to pray. He prayed for a long time and mumbled to himself. After a little while, the scrivener began to make out the words.

"Lord Jesus, place your bitter death and pain, your worthy dignity and innocence between your righteous judgment and my hard sins. I do not ask for what I deserve, but I hope and ask on behalf of your holy and very blessed death and the full power and strength of your suffering and merit. I pray you that you atone for me with the same love with which you have redeemed from all distress and sorrow . . ."

Now the scrivener sank to his knees. The whole of his heart was in prayer. None of the evangelical brothers could pray better than this. Old Peter's shaking voice was once again inaudible, but the scrivener continued to pray for himself. He suddenly felt at home in the sanctuary of his fathers. He began to realize that not everything had been darkness and vain faith in the past. Since he had received the Spirit in Skeninge, he had considered everything in the past as aberration and dead pomp. He had condemned all his beautiful childhood memories from trips up to the black wooden church as the devil's illusions. Now he began to realize that God was at work then too. Perhaps the old church here on the hill in its decay has still been a church of God? Perhaps both his mother and the old Peter and many others still had a true faith in the Savior?

That reformation was necessary was obvious. But was it necessary to sweep away all the old? Would it not mean that one denied God's own work in the past? Was it not more reasonable to take away the abuse but let the church itself remain? Yes, could one not let bells ring and bare one's head in prayer under their heavy tolls?

He prayed again—for his brother Anders, for the old sexton, for the whole district. The whole of his old love for the home country had been awakened. He felt that he had never quite been in agreement with the evangelical brothers. Even if he could, he would at this moment not have been able to break apart the altar there in front, before which his fathers prayed for so many generations. He was glad that the altar remained and that the candles stayed straight in their slender and ornate candlestick holders. If only God's word was preached purely and clearly, then everything else could well be left alone. It was then his fathers who, with humble hands, put it here to God's glory. He did not want to trample on their work. He would rather thank God for it.

Then he began to pray again and give thanks. Before him, the old Sexton Peter knelt on trembling knees. Above him, the last of the daylight fell through the opening in the west gable, and a mild and melancholy expression illuminated Christ's thorn-crowned face. Scrivener Martin looked up at them, looked into the suffering expression that was still filled with an elevated peace and a secure joy of victory, and prayed again for his imprisoned brother, for his pardon and salvation.

* * *

The manor estate in Sponga resembled a farmer's oversized home. The hallmark was a stone house that rose high above the wooden barracks with its gray walls. A row of small apertures under the eaves betrayed that there had been a stronghold built here to dominate the isthmus that went out between the lakes. Now it had been overgrown by immense trees, and the kitchen building and stock houses leaned against its thick walls.

Scrivener Martin uneasily observed the gray outbuildings under the low shingled roofs. He had been riding all day, and the horse was sweaty and exhausted. He had finally reached the destination, but now he hesitated. He had no idea whatsoever how he would be able to meet his brother.

Tired, he got out of his saddle. With stiff legs, he walked a few steps in among the aspens. Taking the reins again, he made a lap and got the horse into a beautiful trot before riding into the yard. He made straight for the stone steps that lead up to a small door. There he swung out of the saddle as lightly as he could and looked around.

Some servant boys were greasing a wagon's axles a bit further down in the yard.

"Hello," he called to them, "is Herr Tönjes home?"

A knecht that was sunning himself by the granaries came up and bellowed:

"What are you screaming about, yokel?"

The scrivener cursed his peasant's shirt. Then he straightened up and walked with the easy gait of a nobleman straight up to the soldier. He looked at him sharply, straight in the.

"Watch yourself, and answer properly. I am Scrivener Martin Ragnvaldsson, and I have drawn up letters of complaint before against oafish knechts. At the time, I was scrivener to Peder Brahe himself."

The knecht looked unsure of himself. The scrivener immediately took advantage of the situation and asked curtly:

"Where is Herr Tönjes?" I have an urgent errand.

"He just went down to the smith."

"Good, run to him immediately and notify him that he has a visitor. March away!—and you, boy, water this mare for me and dry her off under the saddle."

The knecht went away. The servants immediately took over the horse. Quietly to himself, the scrivener thanked God for the time he had been in the godforsaken war camp at Vadstena. He had at least learned how to give orders.

He crossed his arms and pretended to look around imperiously while he waited. In actual fact, he felt as if the ground faltered beneath him.

Tönjes was seen on the path down by the lake. The scrivener went straight over to him, greeted him courteously with his hand on the grip of his dagger as if it were a sword. He did not give the knight time to say anything but presented himself.

"Martin Ragnvaldsson, at your service, Herr. I come from Stockholm—well, most recently Herr Peder of Vi. For ten years, I served His Majesty's chancellery, and now I have been a scrivener for Commander, Colonel Herr Peder Brahe, and an envoy and merchant for Gert Hubmaier, the one with the great mercantile in the German District and the three ships, if he is familiar."

The knight looked at him suspiciously.

"You have rather lousy clothing for such fine work," he said.

Scrivener Martin again cursed the fiction with the peasant's clothing. He tried to look unbothered and said:

"It is not always fun to ride alone in the forests at this time. Then one might have a reason not to poke the forest thieves in the eye . . ."

"Here is my pass," he hurried to add. "From the royal bailiff in the Stockholm Castle."

The knight looked over the pass. While he read, Martin thought as so many times before that it was lucky that the good Botved Larsson had no idea that this, "honorable, good man, Martin Ragnvaldsson from Småland" for whom Gert Hubmaier requested the pass along with many others was the same Scrivener Martin who left the chancellery so suddenly and of whom it was said left with a quarrel and ill talk against His Grace.

The knight handed the pass back to him, visibly calmed.

"And what is your errand?" he asked.

The scrivener looked him right in the eye and tried to make his voice firm.

"It's about my brother, the miserable papist. I have heard that he has been imprisoned for rebellion and that he is to be executed. We have not seen each other for many long years. I became an evangelical 20 years ago, and after that, we hardly saw each other. And now I must try to reach him before he dies. I have ridden here for all I could to ask you, Herr Tönjes, for this favor."

The knight's face became tight, and he looked at the scrivener suspiciously again. He was slow to answer.

The scrivener continued doing all he could to hide his anxiety.

"In over ten years, we have only met once. It was almost three years ago when I traveled on behalf of the king through the whole county here to assess the church's silver. At that time, we had a heated argument, brother Anders and I. Had he heeded my counsel at that time, then this would never have happened."

The knight's face softened a bit. The scrivener quickly continued.

"We thought differently already as young boys. We both went to the Latin school in Linköping, but I fled and went into the service of the King. He held fast to papism, and so it went as it did. Now I have only one desire. I want to be able to see him before he dies. We are the last two of the family on our father's side."

Herr Tönjes became calm again, and his face loosened up. He lifted his eyebrow and nodded graciously.

"That will be granted to you," he said. "You are an honorable Swede. I see that. For the sake of order, I will put a knecht at the door, who will hear the conversation. And then you will have no more than half an hour. You can go in up there to the right. Then I will have the prisoner brought up. I have a weapons inspection over at the smithy. You are dismissed."

The scrivener bowed. Quietly he thanked God and prayed: "Lord bless these thirty minutes."

Herr Tönjes gave his orders and disappeared again. The scrivener went up the steep stairway and entered into the cool below the high arched ceiling. To the right, the open door gave way to a spacious hall with whitewashed walls, a high ceiling, and a heavy dark brown wooden table in the middle of the floor, flanked by four high backed chairs and turned legs.

The scrivener sank into one of the chairs. He was completely overwhelmed by the stress. He buried his hot forehead in his hands and prayed, with his head resting on the table.

A long-time passed. Finally, the scrivener heard heavy steps and the jangling of iron fetters against the stone steps. Someone set a halberd to the stone floor.

The scrivener had gotten halfway up and was stunned with his hands hard pressed against the edge of the table. In through the door shuffled a tall, emaciated figure. The clothes had long tears, and the frayed edges were caked with clumps of mud, the whole ensemble was covered in filth and dirt. Traces of blood could be seen on one shin, and an ulcerous sore could be seen through the holes in the dry mud.

The prisoner slowly shuffled across the floor. Every step hurt him visibly. He sank heavily into the chair right in front of the scrivener and set his fettered hands on the tabletop with a shriek. His face looked straight into the scriveners' with wide, dead eyes.

Martin also sank in his chair and stared with wide-open eyes at his brother. He couldn't quite comprehend anything. He first and foremost remembered Anders with the high shiny tonsure and the little dark crown of short straight hair just above his powerful forehead, the wise eyes, and the small chin. This man had messy and stubby hair. It was short and dirty and messy, sticking up into the air. His eyes were feverish and expressionless, his mouth was half-open, his breath smelled disgusting and his face was covered with a half-grown beard, rough and bristly. Thick layers of soot and mud covered his pale-yellow complexion. It looked as if he laid with his face in road dirt.

One of the knechts put a thin hourglass on the table. They stomped out. One of them stood in the door opening, indifferently leaning on the halberd. The sand in the hourglass began to run.

Finally, the scrivener came to his senses. He put both hands forward, gripped the priest's right hand hard and said:

"Brother, Anders, poor brother. God bless you!"

The other looked at him with his feverish red eyes and answered:

"No, Martin, that is done now. He doesn't bless me anymore. He only curses me."

Suddenly his big head fell forward. He hid it in his hands and sobbed.

"And I believe that I curse him too . . ."

The scrivener swallowed, trembling he said:

"Anders, brother, God curses no one who repents and flees to his mercy."

The other shook his head that he still held in his hands.

"But I have no true contrition in my heart . . ."

"You may if you pray to God for it,"

Now the prisoner looked up.

"I have prayed, Martin. Oh, if you knew how I prayed. Time after time, day after day, till the moon was shining through the cellar roof, and I was lying helpless in the filth. When I was first captured, I had contrition. But it was only the fear of death. It hardly lasted a day. Then came the despair and the tedium with prayer and evil thoughts. Now I know that I am reprobate."

The scrivener let go of his hand to grab his brother's arm and shake it.

"No, Anders, you are not reprobate. This is only the dark night of the soul. You must stay faithful through it. It is the agony of repentance. I have been tested by it myself, and all the evangelical brothers have felt it. You shall only bear the cross and pray to God so that you are born again, and then the peace comes, the heavenly peace that surpasses all understanding. It comes as soon as you have forsaken the world and yourself."

Martin saw that his brother's face was twisted with pain. He only just realized that his fetters scraped huge wounds in the skin and that the exposed flesh was red. He immediately let go of the priest's arm. He made a grimace, coughed, and said.

"The struggle and peace I have experienced long ago, Martin. Peace came when I sacrificed Askanäs and myself, my money, and my right to a wife and children. It came when I prayed to God to take everything if I could just have him. It came every time I consecrated myself to his service and said no to the world once again. But now it no longer comes. I have sinned. I have lived a wild, bloody, and evil life this winter. And now I repent and want to be pure again. But I *cannot* purify myself. I do not rule over my heart. My repentance is not right. My love is not true. My contrition is not true. God no longer watches over me."

The scrivener sat quietly, with his hands folded and looked at his brother expressionless. He had not expected this. He had prepared himself to disabuse his brother of all his false assurances and all his papism, his trust in the saints, his faith in pilgrimages, and fasting and relics. But *this* distress was the last thing he expected to find. What should he say now?

"Tell me a little about what happened," he said.

Gasping with feverish chapped lips, the priest began to speak about the murder of John of Flodlycke, about the rebellion, about his life as a highwayman and his misfortune. He didn't leave anything out. His facial expression was a single great gasping thirst for help.

The scrivener sat quietly. This did not fit with his experience. Even among evangelical friends, one felt the struggle of repentance and the distress of sin. But it was usually short. Had one confessed his sins well, the peace came and the power of victory and joy. This with Anders was something new. He racked his brain, trying to figure out what it was that was now left for him to do. He had repentance. He had confessed his sins. He *wanted* to do better. Still, he did not. Something was lacking in his repentance. But what?

"Anders," he said. "Do you read God's word?"

"It is hard for me now," said the priest. "I have not seen a book for almost half a year. But most of it I can recite from heart. I used to read the psalms every week and three or nine lessons in the morning—that is a couple of chapters a day—and then the texts for mass every day. Now I recite the penitential psalms six or eight times a day, as much as I can remember of the hours and from the Holy Passion of Christ. I have enough of God's Holy Word, you see. There is no excuse for me. It is only my evil heart, and my lazy will . . ."

The scrivener sat stunned. He had never thought that a papist priest read the word of God so diligently. He had always thought that it was his evangelical friends that really read the Bible. But he wondered if any of them read it as diligently as his brother. The psalms every week . . . He was silent.

The hourglass had half run out. The scrivener folded his hands and prayed in quiet despair. Everything that he had prepared to say was worthless here. He had meant to speak intrusively to his brother and admonish him that he must repent in the right way and receive God into his heart. But that someone would *want* to, and yet still *not be able to* come to God, that he had never thought to be possible before. What was it that he lacked?

"Anders, brother," he said, "I too have had my spiritual destiny since we last saw each other. God has brought me together with many true Christians, and I have been able to see so much that I never thought possible. That God was so powerful and gracious, this I had never thought before . . . But of all that I have seen, I have noticed that there is one thing that is indispensably necessary if one wants to find peace with God . . ."

The priest looked up with a searching look.

"And it is that he surrenders his very soul and gives his whole heart to God."

The priests head sunk forward again.

"That is what I cannot do," he said. "Don't you see—my very soul is somehow poisoned. I think I pray to God so sincerely that he shall forgive me for the sake of Jesus and his most bitter pain. But just then, I come to think about the knecht who spit in my cabbage, and I am filled with loathing for his wickedness. I pray for true contrition, but I feel Herr Tönjes take me by the chin and twist my face around as if I were a horse or a calf, and the wrath wells up again like a black wave within me. I want to sleep in the name of Jesus in the evening, but I lie there and think about the men from Skulebäck who were the first to ridicule me for wearing peasant clothing . . ."

Now it was the scrivener who looked down. He was very red.

"That could just as well be said of me," he thought.

"And so it is that I do not love God either," the priest continued. "Otherwise, it would be a joy to pray. It was a joy to pray the first day, but after I had prayed for a few hours, I felt a great aversion and disgust. While I pray, I wonder how long the prayer has left. When I make it to the seventh penitential psalm, I almost feel relieved because it is the shortest . . . And if I pray with my own words, the thoughts leave me, and I think about what I should desire if I, for once got to eat real food again. Or I wonder if they will torture me before I die, and I think about how devilish that red-bearded knecht looks as if he wants to twist my legs. I can't even pray an *Our Father* attentively and devotionally from beginning to end. So little do I love God . . . What one truly loves is easy for one to think about, right?"

The scrivener continued to look down and did not answer. Within himself, he thought: All this could just as well be said of me. Except that I have never prayed for hours like him . . .

He glanced at the hourglass. Now there was not much time left. The sand was almost ready to run out. He folded his hands so that his knuckles went white. Then he looked up to the ceiling—My God, My God, why have you forsaken me?—he cried within himself. He did not receive an answer. He was just overburdened with a great powerlessness. The priest began to speak again.

"Where have you come from, Martin?"

"From Peder of Vi."

"Greet him and tell him that if there is any possibility to collect what is remaining of my tithe, then I ask him to take it from the landowners and wealthy and give it to the poor widows and the fatherless. And if the king leaves anything of my possessions in Ravelunda, then I ask him to divvy it up among those who lost their fathers this last winter. You can attest that it was my last will. And if there is yet anyone who wants to think good of me, then commend them to God's mercy that they pray for my sinful soul."

There was a silence again. The sand continued to run. For the scrivener, it felt as if life ran out of his own perforated heart. He felt deathly tired. In vain, he tried to remember what it was that Peder of Vi had said that his brother needed to hear. He could only remember that he said that the papists did not know what sin was. But in any case, it didn't fit the question concerning his brother. Hardly anyone could feel and repent of their sins more fundamentally. And then Peder of Vi had said something about Christ's atonement. But this he had hardly bothered to listen to. Completely puzzled and with deep sorrow stuck in his throat, he said:

"Anders . . . The blood of Jesus, God's Son, washes away all sin."

The prisoner nodded his dirty head.

"Yes, Martin . . . when one repents and believes with a true faith that contains love, but it is just that which I do not have. What does it help me that I believe when sin has such power within me? Can faith alone save me? Faith without works is dead . . ."

The scrivener sat stupefied. His brother had said precisely what he and the evangelical brothers always said. That faith without works is dead, this was the Bible verse that was most often cited in the house of Gert Hubmaiers, and in his fight against the priests of the church, they had always maintained that Master Olaus and the priests taught people that they *only* had to believe, and forgot to mention works were also necessary: that love was also required, and repentance and complete denial of the self before there could be any talk about a true Christian faith.

"What should he then say?"

"You have enough true repentance, Anders," he said uncertainly. "Otherwise, you would not mourn so despairingly over the hardness of your heart."

The priest smiled bitterly.

"The cursed flesh can mourn enough, but it cannot *love*. When a man is so close to hell as I am, he does not need much piety to mourn. But when he cannot even at that time love his enemy, then it is hopeless? Is it not?"

The scrivener sat quietly. The priest's words singed him like a branding iron. Did he love Gert Hubmaier? And Herr Tönjes? And His Grace?

Now there was just a little gold tip left of the sand, as big as the top of a pinky finger. Martin pressed his forehead hard against his folded hands.

"Lord Jesus," he prayed out loud, "can you not do a miracle of pure grace? We have nothing to give you, nothing to come with, only you must do a miracle of grace, or we are lost."

The priest looked at him with his swollen red eyes.

"A miracle of grace? Such a great miracle of grace? Then the heavens must first be rent. Then must all justice be set aside. Then black must be white, and sin is righteousness. It can never happen, Martin, it can never happen. God's holiness and glory forbid that it should ever happen. He must curse me. And when he has done it, I ought to say: *Deo gratias.*[8] Praise the name of the Lord!"

His bloodshot eyes widened and stared at the scrivener penetratingly.

"But now I believe that I will say instead: Curse you, God. Cursed be you who allowed me to be born. Cursed are you who let me be tempted and let me fall but forbade me to do penance!"

He swallowed. He hid his face in his hands again.

The knecht at the door moved to him.

"The time is up, worthy Herr. Now we had to take him back to his cell."

The priest lifted his face from his hands and stared at his brother, expressionless. Then he got up slowly and began to slap the iron fetters against the table. The scrivener hurried after him and grabbed hold of his arm.

"Anders! You cannot. You must take heart. Pray, cry, beg, and scream . . . until God hears you! I shall pray for you all that I can and am able. Only promise that you hold out. You *may* not despair. You must hold out."

The prisoner turned his hanging head shyly and gave the scrivener a long look.

"Martin," he said. "Have you seen a horse tied up because of overexertion? There was one at Skulebäck. It lay on its side. Its tongue hung out of its jaw where foam ran out into the grass. Its legs were dead and stiff as tines, and its stomach was swollen like a carcass. Only the eye lived, wide open and excruciating. Do you think

[8] God be praised!

it helps to spur such an animal? Do you believe it helps to ask it to hold out?"

Anders crossed over the threshold and down the stone stairway. The iron chains clattered after him.

In the yard, he turned around between the knechts and stretched out both hands.

"God reward you for coming, brother. God bless you. If you can, pray for both of us, I can't do it anymore. Pray that I at least don't curse God."

The scrivener took his hands and didn't care that the knechts saw his tears.

"Yes, Anders, I promise to pray for you. Don't forget that there is still one who prays: Jesus."

The prisoner shook his head slowly.

"He prays for the faithful. But . . ."

The scrivener became eager.

"Yes, Anders. Jesus prays for you. I *know* that he prays for you. And perhaps he does other miracles. A miracle of pure grace. Of pure inconceivable grace."

The priest looked up, half in disbelief, half touched.

"Do you really believe that he would want that? *Rex tremendae majestatis . . .*"[9]

"Yes," said the scrivener. "Do you not remember what it says after that: *Qui salvandos salvas gratis . . .*"[10]

"Do you begin to quack in Latin, you monks?" bellowed one of the knechts. "Are you trying to fool us?"

He brought the halberd down between them.

"Now it is over. The priest is going to the cell, and you may not follow. There are strict orders about it. March away, old man. In the other direction!"

They took the priest between them, and the clinking walk began again. The scrivener stood and watched them.

"God's peace, Anders!" he cried. "Jesus prays for you!"

---

[9] Oh King of dreadful majesty (from the famous gradual, *Dies irae*).

[10] Grace and mercy you grant free.

The other didn't answer anything. The scrivener folded his hands and looked up to the sky.

"Lord," he prayed, "do a miracle! If you care about us, Lord, then do a miracle. If you have power, Lord, if you live, then show it now . . ."

He stood motionless with his hands pressed hard together. Nothing happened. The knechts and the prisoner disappeared behind the granaries. The air trembled in the sun, and a swine rolled leisurely in the muddy ground under the beech trees. The scrivener's head sank to his chest. He slowly walked down to the well where his horse grazed. He dried his eyes and began to fumble with the saddle. One of the servant boys looked out from behind the hay cart ready to run and help, but when he saw the stranger's distressed appearance, he sat down and watched. All the certainty and command had left the scrivener. Like an exposed child, he fumbled with the buckles on the saddle. It was as if he was lost. When the horse expanded his abdomen, Martin couldn't bring himself to tighten the strap, but let it stay three holes outside the usual. The servant saw it and grinned with disdain. Only then did the scrivener wake up from his daze. He turned his back to the hay cart, squeezed his lips together, set his knee to the horse, and drew the straps so that it cracked. Then he swung into the saddle and trotted away.

The servant boy's mocking eyes burned him on the back of his neck. They added to the despair and bitterness that filled him. He slowly tried to sort out what had happened, and the more he thought about it, the more bitter he felt. It seemed to him almost meaningless to try to be a Christian. Here he had first made commands like a knecht, ignored humility, was quiet about the reason for his peasant clothing, conjured up a whole story about his leaving the king's service and chose his words carefully so that Herr Tönjes would get the false impression that he was a good servant of the king and an up-and-coming man among the city's merchant class in Stockholm. So he had tricked himself into this dangerous conversation. Here he had come to save his brother. Instead, he had received such a coarse insight into his own heart that he wondered if he had ever been a Christian. Now it was clear to him that, in actual fact, his papist brother sacrificed and denied himself, prayed and read far more than Martin did himself. And yet now he was in a state of despair! How would it then go with himself? All that Anders accused himself of was in his own heart too. Did he really love God properly? Had he forsaken himself? Did he love his enemies? No and again no! But then he could, in fact, not believe properly!

Suddenly he noticed that the horse was already shiny with sweat. Without thinking about it, he had pushed the animal to the extreme. In shame, he quit using his spurs and let it trot with long reins. It was not his intention to ruin it.

Ruin it? He remembered his brother's picture of the fallen horse. Could a Christian finally fall that way? What then became of God's power? Was it all just imagination?

He straightened up in the saddle. Imagination or not, he had still promised to pray for his brother. Anders did not yet have the noose around his neck. For this, he would pray for him. Then it would go as it would with Gert Hubmaier and his evangelical brothers, with Herr Peder and the Lutherans and Master Olaus and the Pope and all of that misery!

What was the truth? Even a couple of weeks ago, when he came to Linköping, he had felt completely certain that he possessed the light of truth and knew more about salvation than most other Swedes. Now he began to doubt that the papists were so blind as he believed. His brother Anders was perhaps even better than himself. Yes, was he really a Christian?

He had come to the fork and hesitated a moment. Then he let the horse turn to the south and took the trail through the woods to Vi.

GOD HAS DONE

1 July 1543

A wide river of golden sunlight reached down to the churchyard gate. It had been a tranquil summer night when its descent began early in the morning. It had started high up in the gable, washing the smooth limestone behind the chipped lime plaster trim in a brilliant red. Then it made its way down the roughhewn stone wall of the church, highlighting the coarseness with long sharp shadows before it finally lighted upon the grassy meadow by the church gable where the flowers stretched themselves east in long expectation. It then continued along the well-trodden path across the churchyard. When it reached the corner of the Torkelsfalla vegetable garden, the sexton went up to the steeple and rang matins. A few old men and a couple of children walked by. They could hear the priest chanting within the church where his echo hung long and reflectively under the stone vaults. He was practicing some part of the new mass in Swedish. The clear voices of children sang over and over again, "Lo-o-o-o-ord, have mercy upon us . . ." and then it was quiet. The light step of children danced away along the paths between the gravestones.

The sun was now high enough to look down over the ancient ash trees just to the east of the path gate. It would soon be time for the old sexton to go to the steeple and ring the first bell for mass. He sat on the threshold and warmed his gouty legs in the sun. Down on the well-used square in front of the churchyard wall, the priest anxiously paced back and forth, periodically looking down the street.

The torturous morning capped off the excruciating and long week that had followed for the priest after his return home to Vi in the company of the scrivener. For four days, they waited for news from Fröjerum. Rumor said that Herr Anders still sat in the parsonage cellar locked in chains. But on the fifth day, the scrivener could no longer hold out. He saddled up and rode off to Fröjerum determined to have a conversation with his brother. Herr Peder tried to dissuade him. Martin's own position and understanding were so weak that he ought to have avoided the wasp's nest.

Nevertheless, Martin left, and, strangely enough, he was successful in meeting Andreas. God had mercy, and so he had taken the opportunity he received through the incomprehensible grace of God! It went as one could expect. From Martin's disorderly account, Herr Peder had come to understand that Andreas writhed under the curse with which the scriptures put everyone who let it all depend on works of the law. As the honorable man he was, he had sunk to the bottom. Once God started to poke holes in his tiny soap bubble of holiness and clean living, Herr Andreas began to see how weak his contrition, repentance, and love had been. And naturally, Martin, the lamentable *schwarmerei*, had no idea what to say to him. Thanks to the fact that he sat fast and hard in the same works righteousness himself and believed in all seriousness that a person should earn his sanctification through contrition, self-denial, prayers, and love! Herr Peder had scolded him for being an arch-papist and said that he and all his evangelical brothers in Stockholm knew less about the gospel than the pope in Rome.

Herr Peder regretted that now because Martin had taken it to heart pretty hard. He returned from Fröjerum sufficiently broken before Peder had said anything. Martin lost his fresh and open manner and kept to himself in the back yard and suffered from rather serious angst and anfechtung. His dark night of the soul was so bad that if anyone came to speak with him, he would just look off to the side and rarely answered with even a yes or no.

None of this even compared at all to the bad news that came yesterday evening just as the evening bell began to ring. Herr Peder sat in his room praying that the good God would have mercy upon Andreas and Martin and his own perverse and loveless heart when a knecht with a waving pennant and a plum in his hat ran into the yard with a letter. Herr Peder received the note with a sense of unease and reluctantly broke the seal. It contained a short order from the circuit judge: "In the morning following matins, the priest in Wij, vördig

Herr Peder,[1] should be ready to prepare a one Andreas Ragvaldi, a former priest in Ravelunda and Fröjerum and condemned traitor, for death. That same day, at noon Andreas Ragvaldi would receive his punishment and, by the extraordinary mercy of His Royal Grace, be executed by the sword, though as an obvious church thief and brigand, he should very well be obliged to hang from the gallows. Herr Tönjes of Sponga would escort the condemned man to the thingstead[2] in Vi, where the prisoner was to be prepared for death as a Christian."

The priest did not sleep much that night. He had been on his knees in the hollowed-out cabin floor, crying to God. He had walked over the yard and listened up in the loft where Martin sometimes prayed, sometimes cried, and sometimes collapsed. He had never felt so miserable. This is all because of my arrogance, he thought. I have cursed Martin for his foolishness as if it were the easiest thing in the world to bring a slave of works to faith in Jesus. *Hic Rhodus, hic salta!*[3] Now I have to try and show how it is done myself.

He wrung his hands.

"Lord," he mumbled, "for the sake of Andreas! You have laid one last opportunity in my hands, so give me strength from on high to use it! If this is your hour, then rend the heavens and let your grace flood his soul! Let not those who hope in you be brought to shame through me!"

The great bell began to ring, and the priest went back to the altar. He lingered there a while as the bell toll faded. The first of those who rode on horse to the church were already on the hill, and small groups of people on foot followed. They came early today. The rumor of the execution had already spread.

---

[1] Here the text begins to use German spellings to indicate the nationality of the judge and the knechts giving the order. It says the priest in Vi, worthy Herr Peder.

[2] A place for communal gatherings and legal assemblies, usually a meadow where executions would also typically take place.

[3] From the Latin version of Aesop's Fables. In this particular fable, an athlete boast that he achieved a stupendous long jump in Rhodes. A bystander challenges his claim and asks him to repeat the achievement right there.

When a bit later, the sexton walked up to the steeple for the third time that morning, the church hill was already full of people. When the first bell toll resonated over the wooded meadows and rolled away to the dark edge of the forest in the north, a trumpet answered from the woods. A glittering entourage broke out from among the pines, and the warm air flashed with the polished iron and the dark dents of the shiny helmets. They came ever closer, right up to the church hill.

The entourage was large. Herr Tönjes himself rode with thirty cavalrymen, and the footmen were about double that. He was like a bishop before the world. The knechts slowly made their way up the hill. It seemed that they were tired from the long march. Herr Tönjes rode out front. He held his head high and looked down on the crowds from under his sleepy half-closed eyelids.

The peasants slowly made way for Tönjes without fuss or rush, they had seen him before in a patched leather sweater and apron in the yard outside the smithy in Sponga, but their necks strained to catch a glimpse of the imprisoned priest. He rode in the middle of all the cavalry, bareback on a lean mare with his feet tied together under the horse.

The whole entourage stopped at the churchyard wall. The knechts marched in closed ranks south of the church. A pair of them hurried to find the stocks that were placed in front of the southern church doors today. The imprisoned priest was brought forth and firmly secured. He was wearing a black cassock that reached his feet. It had been fetched from the Ravelunda parsonage the day before. Otherwise, he was unshaven and unrecognizably dirty. He looked straight in front of himself, and he didn't seem to notice when the knechts fastened his feet in the stocks. Herr Tönjes posted six knechts behind him and three to his side, all with glimmering spears. The remaining knechts ordered themselves into two rows, perpendicular to the church's whitewall so that they enveloped a large bit of the churchyard with a barrier of armor and blue steel.

Only then did the priest come out.

He looked around for a minute, hesitantly as if the sun blinded him. Then he walked up to the stocks, uncovered his head, bowed, and took the prisoner's hand. No one could hear what he said. Only then did he go to Herr Tönjes and make a formal greeting. He took out a letter, showed it to the knight and said with a clear voice:

"Herr, as a seelsorger, I request to speak to the condemned man alone. The sacristy is the best place, could you have him escorted there?"

The knight waved his hand.

"There will be time, there will be time, worthy Herr, but the pastoral work will have to wait until we are finished with His Royal Majesty's errand. I ask that you stand here—as a witness."

He whistled.

The servant boy led his horse over and sat back down. The horse danced and trampled deep tracks in the gravel, before backing into the church wall. Herr Tönjes let a signal blow and straightened up. He looked stately where he sat in his red attire in front of the white church. His voice sounded strong and authoritative.

"On behalf of His Majesty, our most gracious Lord, King Gustavus, today and for the last time, I offer grace and mercy to those who sided with Dacke's party and his entourage of traitors . . . are the peasants from Skulebo here."

There was a hesitantly raised hand in the crowd. One man took a frightened step forward from the crowd, then another and then another. In the end, there were four.

"And the villagers of Ersmarken and Torkelsfalla?"

Another five came forward. Now it continued.

"And men from Franebo? And who else?"

There were still some more. The latter said their names and the parish people attested that they spoke right and true. The names were noted.

Herr Peder stood and looked at the helpless crowd of gray men. They were from Brohultshållet, and they had all gone to the forest at the time the rebellion flared up highest. Now they stood weaponless and bewildered. Some grinned to show their self-confidence. Most looked at the ground.

Herr Tönjes now reached for a thick letter roll with a heavy seal. The trumpet sounded three times again. Herr Tönjes commanded the people to take their hats off, and then he read His Grace's open letter to the peasantry in the district. The wrathful words reverberated powerfully off the church wall and rolled like distant thunderstorms far down over the thingstead. His Grace reproached his subjects for their terrible sins, first against God and his holy ordinances and then against his true, established Lord and King, though His Royal Majesty never gave the peasants in the country reason for such rumbling and treachery, shame and perdition, such as has now, God better it, occurred. His Majesty had reason to hope for other rewards for all the effort and inconveniences he suffered for them and the poor Swedish Kingdom for almost 24 years, in which he brought them good peace and harmony so that the kingdom's enemies didn't take a hen from them, even less than the robbers and murderers that infested them in the time of Christian the Tyrant. And even though they had so sorely broken out with such accursed rebellion and insolvency, he wanted to give them grace and kindliness again. So he would, for such reason, and with the conditions that they would place 24 settled men from the hordes as hostages and promise His Majesty and his heirs faithfulness and homage, and that they show themselves faithful subjects by helping capture and punish the rogues who still ran in the forest and not giving those men either peace or compromise.

Herr Tönjes finished reading. There was dead silence over the whole churchyard.

"Then we start with the hostages," said Herr Tönjes. "Because the people here have been, for the most part, faithful to His Majesty, one resident of the parish will be sufficient. Now hurry. There will be no expiation before he is chosen."

Whispers from the crowd of peasants broke the silence, climbing to a purling murmur. Then there were shouted threats and protests in broken confusion.

Herr Peder walked over to his people. The peasants enveloped him, and they talked for a long time. The priest returned to announce that they had chosen Folke of Skulebo. Folke had been among those who went to the forest. He had grown sons that could take over the farm, and he was well-heeled enough that those he left at home would not suffer want.

"Good," said Herr Tönjes. "So, you will come to Sponga within two days at the risk of becoming a conspicuous outlaw."

"And now," he continued with a loud voice, "will you all now pledge yourselves to His Royal Majesty, His Royal Majesty's heirs and all of Sweden's civil nobility and the kingdom of Sweden to be faithful and give service?"

"Yes!" they yelled. "Not the nobility," a voice was heard in the distance. Herr Tönjes didn't take notice but continued:

"Will you point out and punish the traitor Nils Dacke and the whole of his army of thieves, wherever they may be found, who still run to the forest and will have neither peace nor compromise."

"Yes!" they yelled again this time even louder.

"Will you pay the taxes, rents, and tithes that you owe His Majesty and the crown?"

". . . Yes." This time the answer was more measured and came with hesitation. Herr Tönjes let his sharp gaze sweep the crowd.

"So I offer you grace, pardon, and expiation on behalf of His Majesty, so long as you abide by these conditions and promises."

He was quiet for a moment. Despite the peaceful conclusion, the atmosphere in the churchyard was not good. There were whispers here and there among the gray peasants. Yet they had not been completely quelled, these self-indulgent peasants, thought Herr Tönjes.

He moved his horse forward a couple of steps.

"And now begins a new era of faithfulness and obedience to his Royal Majesty. It will start today, here in this place. It shall begin with act and deed and not just prattle."

A dead silence returned. All eyes focused on the knight's lips.

"Where did you bury Klement of Broddetorp?"

No one answered.

Herr Tönjes waved to two knechts and pointed out a man to the right among the newly reconciled.

"Now you may answer," he said. "And if you do not answer, then you can occupy the place in the dungeon that will be empty after the priest today. Where have you buried Klement of Broddetorp."

Without saying a word, the man pointed to a large wooden cross.

The knight looked around.

"Is that right?"

A few silent nods were the answer. Herr Tönjes turned his horse.

"Bring the gravedigger's spades here—and as many picks and shovels as there can be found."

The tools came out. People began to understand where this was going, and some even helped. Klement had belonged to Dacke's worst partisans who carried himself arrogantly and made many enemies in the district, though in the end, he was buried with honor and with a great entourage because he had fought like a man both at Kisa and Skrukeby.

Herr Tönjes pointed to five of them who had been in the fight.

"Now dig him up," he said.

The men put spades in the ground. It went quickly in the recently backfilled dirt. Herr Tönjes looked down at them from the back of his horse with bemusement and did not let them rest. The spades grated, and the sweat ran. The peasants came closer. Herr Tönjes called the knechts over and let them form a chain so that the place was open.

Herr Andreas began to watch from over at the stocks. Up till now, he had kept his face hidden from the people by bowing his head. It was as if he neither saw nor heard anything. Now He slowly raised his neck. A pair of fever glazed eyes shined from within his dirty, sunken face. He said nothing, he just watched and watched, first at the working men and then at Herr Peder.

The priest in Vi was very pale. The veins at his temples had become black knots. He held his hands folded.

The sweaty grave diggers had reached the coffin. The spades scraped the lid bare in a matter of minutes. Herr Peder turned away and slowly walked back to the church.

Here Tönjes waved to some of the knechts and said something to them. They sank their halberds into the open grave and hammered at it. One could hear the sound of wood splintering. The knechts worked hunched forward a minute and stabbed and pried with their spear points. Then they carefully lifted. Then they readjusted themselves to get a better hold, lifted again, and pulled the dead body up over the edge of the grave, sandy, covered in splinters of wood and only half-veiled by the tattered shroud.

Herr Tönjes backed his horse up a few steps, and someone brought forward an old bell chord.

"Tie it around his body and pull—together!"

He held his nose and let the horse take a few steps backward. Even the peasants stepped away. The knechts only had to check a few insurgents.

"Put him in there!" cried Herr Tönjes to the hesitant men. He pointed to the old sexton's shed, which leaned dilapidated against the churchyard wall. "You buried the traitor with honor and glory. You buried him in consecrated earth like an honorable man. Now he shall receive his reward for treachery. Grab hold and pull!"

The men put the rope over their shoulders and pulled. The dead body doubled over, knitwear and pieces of fabric remained in the grass. The parish people turned away. All were silent. The men slowly pulled the body toward the sexton's shed.

"In with him," commanded Herr Tönjes. Close it up and set fire to the heap.

A smiling knecht stabbed his lance shaft into the body. A roll of birch bark burned pale in the sunlight. The black smoke billowed into dark clouds. All eyes witnessed the macabre spectacle.

Then a loud voice cut through the silence.

"Corpse abusers, corpse abusers!"

A hundred heads turned as if wrenched by an invisible hand. Herr Tönjes's eyebrows drew together as he looked over to the church. It was from there that the cry had come.

Herr Tönjes heard it again. Now it was firm and full.

"God curse you who violate the grave's peace! God's wrath be on him who abuses the rest of the dead. Eternal restlessness over him who breaks the peace our mother church gives to the bones of those who are faithful to Christ."

Herr Tönjes came to his wits.

"Shut that papist's trap!" he cried. "Punch him in the face until his teeth fall out if he doesn't shut up!"

One of the knechts by the stock pulled his huge riding glove out of his belt and slapped the priest over the mouth, a little lame and insecure as if he didn't know how much of the command was meant literally. At the same time, as the glove struck the prisoner's face, Herr Peder stood in the church door.

"Hold on," he cried, "and you watch yourself, men! Anyone who stands convicted of a crime against the church is under the jurisdiction of the church. Here no one commands but me."

He ran up to Herr Tönjes. The unruly, rough figure of the priest straightened up, and his voice took on a tone of authority.

"Herr," he said. "I am lawfully called upon to prepare this man for death. With the authority of my office, I now demand to talk with this man in private. If I am denied, I will report it to the diocese, that this man, contrary to all Christian order, had to die without absolution through your fault."

Herr Tönjes looked at the upset priest with an air of superiority.

"It's fine by me if you take the loudmouth aside for a bit. It suits us well to be rid of him while we deal with this traitor."

"Take the prisoner to the sacristy. Set six men on guard at the door!" he yelled at the knechts.

The knechts lifted the top half of the stocks. For the first time in a week, the prisoner could move about without foot irons. It was as if he got some of his strength back when he could once again take a step. He carried his head high and looked around suspiciously when he came into the church. The choir screen was gone, a newly painted pulpit shown in bright colors on the north wall, and the nave had been equipped with pews. Otherwise, everything was the same. The picture of Christ remained under the vault. John the Baptist stood to the right, and the altar was dressed as before.

Herr Peder went up the aisle on the prisoner's left as if he accompanied an honored guest through the church. The two priests both bowed deeply before the altar. Then they turned to the left through the low door into the sacristy. Peder shut the iron door behind them and turned the heavy lock.

With a motion of the hand, he offered his guest to sit in the high armchairs by the sacristy table. Herr Andreas remained standing, straight, and thin. His neglected face with the half-inch long beard stubble was flaming red under the splashes of dirt.

"Peder," he said, "you are a coward! You fail the church of God in everything you do. Why did you run away when they began to abuse the corpse?"

Herr Peder looked very still before him. He answered slowly without his normal heat.

"I needed to talk with God."

The other looked at him suspiciously.

"And what did your God say?"

"*Desine ab ira, et derelinque furorem, quoniam qui malignantur exterminabuntur. Sustinentes autem Dominum, ipsi hereditabunt terram.*"[4]

Herr Andreas was silent.

"God said: be still and wait for help from above. You are placed here in Vi to proclaim the Word and administer the holy sacraments. But you are not put here to crush all evil in a day."

Sunlight fell through the small window in the wall, darkened by black clouds of smoke. Fire rustled and crackled outside. Herr Andreas watched flames light maple leaves on fire between the rolled iron rods in the opening in the wall. Then he looked at his brother in the office.

"What help does he who is burning out there have from you proclaiming the word of God and administering the sacraments?"

Now Herr Peder gave a calm smile.

"He is in no danger. In the morning, I will scrape together the ashes and cinders and put it all back in the grave. And the good God knows enough to recognize the dust that was once called Klement of Broddetorp on the day of the resurrection, whether they lie here in the churchyard, or are scattered to winds of heaven. Then it is all the more a pity for Herr Tönjes."

Herr Andreas lifted his eyebrow a moment as if he marveled.

"What do you mean?"

"Is there no pity for sinners? Herr Tönjes is placed here by God to carry the sword and keep justice with power. And so he emerges as the roughest worker of violence. What do you believe is the end of such a man?"

"That I have already told him," said Herr Andreas. "He is cursed by God. But you were quiet and ran into the church. Should you not tell sinners what God thinks of them?"

Herr Peder bowed calmly.

"Yes, it is precisely the task of the Holy Church to tell sinners what God thinks of them. To go to them with the message that God

[4] "Refrain from anger, and forsake wrath! Fret not yourself; it tends only to evil. For the evildoers shall be cut off, but those who wait for the LORD shall inherit the land" (Psalm 37:8–9).

is angry for all their sins and yet still loves them without limit and does not want a single one of them to perish. This message is the only one that can save Herr Tönjes and his knechts. Therefore, there is such great power in that I preach the gospel in the hour when they have some ability to receive it. One should not make God's word into a cudgel and use it against sinners just when they are in the midst of their worldly strife. Then they only believe that one only wants to interfere in their miserable quarrel and are led by their opponents—Just as Herr Tönjes now thought that you cursed him only because you side with Dacke's men."

Herr Andreas looked long and searching at his brother in the office again.

"Yes," he said, "if you could convert Herr Tönjes, then I would believe in your heresy."

"You should believe that because it is grounded in God's word. If Herr Tönjes is converted, then it is neither your work nor mine but God's. We have only to proclaim God's word—and then pray for him."

Now Herr Andreas looked almost a little scornful.

"Do you mean that you have prayed for Herr Tönjes and his conversion?"

"I prayed for him while the men dug."

There came a contemplative, almost embarrassed look on the face of the priest from Fröjerum. He thought about the fact that he forgot to pray for his tormentors. He had certainly reproached himself for not loving Herr Tönjes. But this he had only done because he thought of himself and his own salvation. He had never thought about the salvation of Herr Tönjes. He said uncertainly:

"But does it serve anything?"

"God's church doesn't ask that. She is put here in the world to proclaim the Word. In between, she may pray and suffer."

"But you don't mean that we should leave ourselves defenseless to all evil?"

"The church shall not fight with the sword. The authorities are to do that."

"But if the authorities turn toward the church?"

"Then the church may pray and suffer and forgive until God places another authority there."

"But look now at the king!"

"Yeah, what about him?"

"He is a bloodhound and an evil-doer and a church scavenger!"

"Perhaps. And what should you do to those who persecute you and do all sorts of evil against you?"

Andreas was quiet.

"You shall pray for him and bless him—have you done that?"

Now the prisoner threw his eyes down. He said with a little uncertainly:

"But then is a Christian defenseless?"

"Not at all! Do you not have God? He helps us far more than we have deserved. First, he more often than not keeps good authority with power, disciplining workers of violence so that you can live securely. And if it should please God to discipline us through the hand of those who do violence? Do you have anything to say about it? And what exactly are you?"

"A sinner," said Herr Andreas very quietly.

"Can a sinner receive a worse authority than he deserves?"

The prisoner slowly lifted his dirty face. Now it was calm, and the wrinkles had smoothed out.

"No," he said. "I have never thought about it that way."

Herr Peder nodded slowly.

"It takes a while before a man thinks that way. It is the great mystery of God's kingdom, you see. To receive forgiveness without limit every day, and to forgive without limit. To have a God who does not count sin, whether great or small—and then to not consider yourself whether you are big or small, but for Christ's sake be glad to serve, help, forgive, and bless—yes glad even to be able to suffer for his name's sake. For the flesh, it feels like a pure defenselessness. But you see—we have a power behind us that the world does not see. When we walk in the ways of God and do that which is within the power of man, and all resources are emptied—then we still have hardly touched our assets. Then God's power remains. And when we pray, then we may and shall believe that the victory is won.

"Anders," he continued, "at one time this last fall, I stood here in almost the very same place where I now stand. Outside the church, Dacke's people made a ruckus and howled that they would hang me from the oak in the town square upside down with a bonfire below my head. They, of course, knew that I dissuaded the parish people from getting involved in the rebellion. Here I stood—and there stood the churchwardens. The mass was about to begin, and I was dressed for it. The cup was on the altar. Then we all fell together on our knees. I could only pray: Lord, now it is in your hands. If you want to save us as you saved the three men from the burning oven, then you can do it. And if you want to let us die for your name's sake, then it is a greater grace than we have deserved . . . Then we pulled the iron bar and went in before the altar with the cup in hand. Then God did a wonder. How it happened, I cannot comprehend. But there was someone who screamed that they should leave the church in peace and let the priest be. Then they sat down, and I received grace to preach concerning our Savior on the cross and our Savior in the hour of death so that they became long and smooth in the face and afterward gave thanks for a comforting word that a sinner needed to hear in this evil time."

Herr Andreas had sunk into the high-backed chair. He set his fettered hands on the table. Outside, the fire thundered, and the sparks whirled against the sky in crackling swarms.

Herr Peder breathed deeply.

"Forgive me, brother, here I stand and prattle about myself again. I ought to speak about the Savior in the hour of death. Now it comes to you. Can I do something for you?"

The other looked up. A little scornful spark glimmered in his eye.

"Yes, Peder, if you could get me a truly catholic confessor before I die."

"I would gladly get you whatever papist you wanted if there was anyone to bring. But Joen is imprisoned, the dean is deathly ill, and Bengt in Ödesjö has married his *forsia*[5] and now lives in honorable marriage, so he will no longer do for you. I alone am left—and that I consider myself to be a better catholic than you and thank God that we continue to rediscover the true old catholic church here in the land with God's pure and beautiful gospel. But naturally, that won't make you bite."

---

[5] Housekeeper.

He sat in the chair across from Herr Andreas. This had all sunk in. Herr Peder noticed that the vexation brought strength back to Herr Andreas for a minute. Then the anger was snuffed from his gaze. He was listless and appeared more tired and weak than before.

"Andreas, brother," said the priest, "forgive me that I bicker with you even in this hour. Let's forget all this. Now it is just us two sinners, and above us is God, the only God that exists. There on the wall, we have a picture of his Son, our Savior, the only one that exists. In front of us, we have death and accounting, the same for both of us, though it seems you will go first. Now I ask you as a friend and brother: Do you want to confess and be absolved of your sin?"

"Yes, I would infinitely like that, but not before you. I have been faithful to my church up till now, and so I will be until death."

Herr Peder looked up with his surprised, dark scrutiny, which was now like a drawn blade.

"Have you been faithful to your church? Have you served her without sin and betrayal?"

Anders was silent for a moment and then spoke.

"No . . . no, not in everything. I don't mean that. But you understand: in all my misery, I have still always loved our Holy Catholic Church. And then neither do I want to do anything before death that would mean I had extended even a little finger to the heretics."

The priest answered:

"I too love our holy catholic church! And so, I rejoice that I can serve her at this time. Amid all our affliction, it is still better for the church now than it had been for many centuries. Now we have God's gospel and God's sacraments in their purity and power again. And it is in the power of God's word and in our holy catholic church's name that I now ask you if you want to confess and receive the forgiveness of sins."

Herr Andreas raised his sunken head a minute.

"It doesn't serve anything, *Domine Petre*, he said. If you knew how ill it is with me, you would understand better. I have way too many sins—even in my heart. But at least I will not let anyone take my last crown of glory, this: that I have remained in the old faith right up to the end."

"It is precisely our crowns of glory that Jesus Christ must take from all of us before he can be our Savior. Paul says that all which

I considered gain—all—you hear, even our innocence! That have I counted for shame so that I may gain Christ."

"But innocence cannot be sin?"

"Yes, this is precisely what it can be! When one recognizes it as gain or when one makes it into a crown of glory and steps before God and thinks that this shall apply for something before him—then one libels Christ. Then one takes the Savior's glory from him. Do you remember what St. Paul says: if righteousness could have been won by the power of the law, then Christ did not need to die on the cross. If *you* could compensate for your sins, why then would God have sent his Son to die?"

"Shall we then sin in order to remain Christian?"

"No . . . but we shall recognize our sins. We shall let God's Spirit expose the whole misery, such as it is. Then the whole of our guiltlessness goes down into the sin basket. What are your prayers? Full of conceit and evil thoughts! One-part uneasiness, one-part distraction, and one-part complacency! What are your poverty and self-denial? Full of sin, idle thoughts of yourself, and your own glory! It is pride that secretly creeps in with humility, like a worm crawling in old flour."

Herr Andreas slowly lifted his head. Herr Peder noticed that he listened.

"How can you know that?" he said.

"Because it is written in the Bible. For I know that in myself, that is in my flesh, dwells nothing good."

"But then the saints?"

"It is the same for them! It was St. Paul, the holy apostle who did not find any good in his flesh. And all the holy have proved enough the same. For here there is no distinction, the scriptures say."

"Surely, there must be a difference between sinners and saints?"

"Not before God. It is written in scriptures: For all have sinned and fall short of the glory of God. For God, all the good works of the saints are full of worms like spoiled apples. Here every mouth is stopped, and the whole world stands guilty. Behind the glory of the saints sits the same desire to be considered or to measure up to something, at least before their consciences. There is a sort of pride with it."

"But then ought not all go to hell?"

"Certainly, they ought to! If Christ hadn't died for everyone. If his righteousness is not sufficient to cover all the world's sins, it is just as great a miracle that St. Paul entered heaven as it is for the thief on the cross."

He leaned forward, pressed his folded hands against the table, and spoke earnestly.

"Anders, it is not your sins that separate you from God, but your virtues. Or more properly: it is that you need to have something to bring before you step before God. This is why God has allowed you to be stripped of the shroud of holiness that you wore in Fröjerum. Not because you were zealous and pious. God grant that all priests would be as zealous as you! But because you made it into an article of faith and into your righteousness and put it between you and Christ. Now you are poor, destitute, and naked—like the prodigal son. Now the heavenly Father stands and waits for you. Now he wants to fold you in his arms and clothe you with the most precious garment, which is called Christ's righteousness, in which not a single thread is spun by your hands, but for just that reason it lasts forever."

There was pounding on the door.

The priest jumped and asked hastily:

"Andreas, do you believe in the Lord Jesus?"

"The other looked up with huge eyes."

"Yes, I do."

Herr Peder rose.

"Then your sins are forgiven for his sake . . . Do you want me to absolve you?"

The prisoner looked up again, longingly.

There was pounding on the door, harder.

"But if I can't believe it?"

The priest folded his hands. His eyes shut, and sharp folds furrowed across his forehead. Then he looked up again and said with shaking lips.

"Then you should give God the glory and believe it anyway."

Now there was a whole ruckus of pounding on the door. It echoed through the cool sacristy.

"Open!"

It was the voice of Herr Tönjes.

"Wait a minute, lord!" cried the parson. "I am not yet finished!"

"That doesn't matter. The prisoner shall be executed before noon, and the mass has to be finished before that. That is the judge's order."

Herr Peder remained standing with his hands folded and looked steadily at the prisoner with burning eyes. "*Domine Andreas, omnis, qui credit in eum, non pereat, sed habeat vitam aeternam. Confide, fili, remittuntur tibi peccata tua.*"[6]

Then the prisoner bowed his head to the table and broke into tears.

"It cannot be so simple," he said.

The priest had become pale as a corpse. A violent pounding struck the door. Someone must have slammed the bottom end of a halberd into it with full force.

"If you do not finish now, we will break down the door," cried Herr Tönjes.

The priest braced himself against the edge of the table. It looked as if everything collapsed around him.

"Yes," he said. "It is perhaps best that we finish. I can't form my words anymore. You can take over, great God. Andreas, brother, now God's Spirit comes to persuade your hard, arrogant heart to believe. Only believe so that you will be saved, God bless you!"

He walked over and opened the door. Herr Tönjes stepped in with heavy feet. The tranquility that struck him in the sacristy rendered him speechless. He didn't say anything. He had the prisoner escorted out, and then he too disappeared as if he wanted to avoid being questioned for something. The sexton looked in.

"Should we ring the bell?"

"Yes," said the priest absently. "It is time enough for that."

The sexton disappeared. The priest sank to his knees right where he stood.

"Lord," he prayed, "mysterious are your ways, and your counsel is inscrutable. But you have carried this soul so close to the gates of salvation, so now stretch out your hand, and carry him into your kingdom. Send your Spirit, Lord, force yourself into his heart,

---

[6] Whoever believes in him shall not perish but have eternal life. Be of good cheer, my son, your sins are forgiven you.

destroy the last hindrances, make him believe. In your name, Lord Jesus. Amen. Amen."

The sexton began to ring the bell, and people streamed into the church. The priest slowly got up while he was still praying and began to vest himself for the mass.

* * *

Just as the ringing bell swept over the thingstead with its trembling waves and the still warm air between the oaks seemed to sway to tolls of the great bell, Scrivener Martin began walking up to the church. He looked exhausted and disheveled. He had wanted to stay home today. He did not think he could endure seeing his brother die in this way. But when the sexton began to ring the bell, he was not able to stay up in the loft of the parsonage with his face down in the bed covering his ears when the sound of the trumpet reverberated off the church. Then he pulled on his hat and hurried across the meadow.

A thin black trail of smoke rose from the corner of the churchyard, white ash followed the hot air up to the sky and then rained down like glittering snow. There was a large cluster of horses on the church hill, watched by a knecht dressed in red. A few individual peasants drifted about the church stalls. Clusters of people stood by the church doors pushing their way inside.

The bell finished just as the scrivener passed the horses. As he came closer, he saw that a detachment of knechts stood guard outside the south door to the church. Their armor glittered in the sun, which was blinding as it reflected off the white walls of the church.

At the awning over the path, the scrivener sat a moment on the small wooden bench. He was uncertain of whether he should go inside the church or not. Over the last half-year, he had hardly been to church. The evangelical friends kept worship completely to themselves and regarded the whole sanctification of Sunday as a papist innovation. Some of them thought that true Christians should not observe any special days or seasons, but that all days were the same. Others said that it was Saturday that God appointed as the Sabbath.

Ever since the evening when he kneeled beside Sexton Peter in the Fröjerum church, Martin had had a strange longing to return to church. It was so quiet and solemn in there. It had a tranquility and peace that he never knew among the brothers at their gatherings. At those, the only thing a person could look at was knife cuts in the table or Gert Hubmaier's face. In the church, there was the altar, the cross, and pictures of Jesus.

The scrivener rose and walked over the trampled churchyard. Suddenly he came to a dead stop. Just outside the south door were the stocks, in the stocks was a black figure in a priest's frock. It was his brother.

That was why the knechts stood on watch there!

The scrivener fought with himself. He knew that it was unwise to go there now. Still, he could not let it be. Step by step he was drawn closer. His brother sat face forward with his hat drawn over his head. His knees were firmly secured; his fettered hands were tightly folded.

The scrivener came up close and stood off a bit, observing his brother. His hat covered his entire face except for his small chin with its long beard stubble. There were sores on his wrists along the edges of the fetters. Some flies sat in the exposed flesh. He did not seem to notice it. Across from him, a few small boys stood looking on curiously. Some people from the parish sat on the ground next to the stocks. From here, they could look in through the open doors of the overcrowded church. The knechts stood behind them, motionless and tired. The sun had made them drowsy.

The scrivener approached calmly, and quietly; Andreas did not lift his hunched-over head a hair. He seemed to keep his eyes shut. The scrivener understood that he had kept himself this way the whole time as people passed. The shame was too much for him.

At that moment, Martin felt great solidarity with his brother. Though he thought very differently concerning almost everything, he knew they still belonged together.

Had Andreas fallen asleep? One could almost believe it. His head fell further down and nodded a moment. He sat to the right in the stocks, closest to the church door. The place next to him was empty.

Suddenly the scrivener had an impulse. He walked over to the stocks and sat in the empty place next to his brother. He put his feet against the stocks. He kept his knees halfway up. The knechts stared at him in amazement. He just smiled at them and pointed to the church in explanation. The knechts understood and smiled back.

If he wanted to sit in the most despised place of the parish, all the better for them . . .

Some teenage boys passed. They stopped with their hands in their belts and spat at Herr Andreas. The first missed, and they grinned. The other hit the priest on the shoulder. Then they stopped and leered at the scrivener who stared back strangely at them, wide-eyed.

"Do unto others as you would have them do unto you," Martin said in almost a whisper as if he was entrusting them with a great mystery. They blushed and disappeared.

When the Anders heard the voice, he suddenly looked up, not only with amazement but also with a hint of joy in his tired eyes. He stretched out his fettered hands so that he managed to press the scrivener's hand.

"So I get to see you one last time, Martin, he whispered weakly. This is the third time you have brought me great joy. First on the Eve of Epiphany, then a week ago in Sponga . . ."

"I could not have brought you any great joy then . . ."

"Quiet," said the priest. "Do you hear how they sing?"

He lifted his head and shut his eyes. He had already long sat with his ears turned to hear. First, he had not wanted to hear anything at all. If he had been able, he would have shut his ears the same way he shut his eyes. What did their heretical mass matter to him? But then the words suddenly caught hold of him: "And I know that I am worthy of nothing but hell and everlasting condemnation if you were to judge me as your strict law and my sins deserve to be judged." From that moment, he was wide awake. The prayers had continued with something about God's wanting to show mercy to all poor sinners, who with steady faith fled to God and his inconceivable grace.

Faith—there was that word again. Did he believe it? Was faith alone sufficient? In such a case, he could still be saved . . .

What then reached his ears was like a greeting from earlier and happier days. Clearly and innocently, the children inside sang the old familiar Kyrie. The melody arched over the heads of the crowd like an airy rainbow. It was only that the words were in Swedish. Lord, have mercy upon us, they sang. The children did not sing the remainder alone. There were clear altos and striving manly basses that joined in. This had never happened in Fröjerum or Ravelunda.

Then he heard Herr Peder chant "Glory be to God in the highest," and the voices of children supported by their elders fell in, "and peace on earth and goodwill toward men. We praise thee, we bless thee . . ."

With rising astonishment, Herr Andreas listened. This was completely and wholly the old mass. He had never heard it sung by so many men before. At home in Fröjerum it was, for the most part, only Sexton Petrus, who responded to the Laudamus. It was almost impossible to teach the Latin text to the peasants. He remembered how he had struggled with the foreign words as a boy.

It was during the song of praise that Martin had come and sat by his side. When it faded away, the priest whispered:

"Do you remember when we sat on the stool in the church at Fröjerum and sang . . . Now we sit here again. This may well be our last Laudamus—if God in his inscrutable mercy doesn't let us sing it together in the heavenly choir."

The scrivener looked at his brother, shyly. A new expression had drawn across his face, something weak and dreamy that could be interpreted as thankfulness or peace. He didn't quite know what he should believe. Could some old melody achieve such a change—then it was, in any case, something of the Spirit's work.

Inside, Herr Peder chanted the collect prayer. Herr Andreas bowed his head reverently and prayed along with the prayer. When the epistle followed, he already felt at home with this new thing that was still so old and familiar that he stopped all criticism.

Now the gradual and the tractus followed if it went according to the old order. Herr Andreas listened with excitement. How would they do this thing?

It was a Swedish hymn. The priest was a little disappointed at first, but the longer the song was heard, and the voices inside fill the vaults with the sound of song, the better he understood the meaning of this. Such a song had never been possible in Fröjerum. Maybe it will be now . . .

Suddenly the scrivener began singing where he sat. This time it was he who was captured by memories. The hymn they were singing inside was one of Master Olaus's Swedish hymns,[7] which began,

[7] A Luther hymn Olaus translated into Swedish.

"Wherever you may now rejoice." He had sung it in the Storkyrkan innumerable times. In the confident melody lay all the rapture he felt at the time. Perhaps there was more to the words than he had first understood.

. . . He is my brother worthy,
His love he wants to lure me,
He took from me the wrath of hell,
That I was bound to suffer.

The Scrivener noticed that his brother lifted his head at the last words. Could this help him? He fell in with his struggling voice.

For my lost cause, Christ shed his blood
And for my guilt did penance
When on the holy cross of wood
He suffered all my sentence
And bid me peace and welcome
He now my Savior has become
Who makes my home His kingdom.

Now it was the scrivener who felt something damp in his eye.

"This was the song I sang for Tall Staffan in the forest at Skrukeby," he whispered.

"What?!" the priest turned sharply. "Were you at Skrukeby?"

"Yes. Did I not tell you that? I was the scrivener for Per Brahe. I still went a long way into the forest and was able to see all the misery. There lay Tall Staffan in the throes of death. He was worried about his sins and that he could not do penance. I didn't know anything better than to sing this song. He asked me to sing it again. And then said over and over again: and for my guilt did penance."

"And then?"

"Then I believe he parted from here in peace. At least it looked that way."

The priest slumped forward and hid his face. The scrivener noticed that he cried. Inaudibly he mumbled: "thank you, thank you, thank you . . ."

After a bit, he looked up.

"How did that song go?"

The scrivener recited it again. The priest repeated it thoughtfully.

"'He suffered all my sentence, *and bid me peace and welcome*'—is that what is written? Should I be able to be at peace on this basis?"

"Yes, on what other ground would you ever be able to know peace?" said the scrivener. "If God's Son has died in your place, then you are purchased, and the payment has been made, and it is sufficient and can never be made greater."

He noticed that he spoke like one of the Lutherans. It made no difference to him. If he could help his brother, Anders, he wanted to be as Lutheran as he had to be.

Herr Peder had begun to sing the gospel lesson inside. It was the old gospel for the sixth Sunday after Trinity Sunday, that Herr Andreas knew so well, though it was the first time he had heard it in Swedish.

"Jesus said to his disciples: For I tell you unless your righteousness exceeds that of the scribes and Pharisees, you will never enter the kingdom of heaven. You have heard that it was said to those of old, 'You shall not murder; and whoever murders will be liable to judgment.' But I say to you that everyone who is angry with his brother will be liable to judgment; whoever insults his brother will be liable . . ."

The people inside had risen and listened attentively. Herr Andreas made a calm comparison with Fröjerum, where the most pious bent the knee and prayed prayers during the mass, while the others stood and listened, but without understanding a word. Naturally, it was more proper that the gospel should be read in the language of the people. It had been that way once in the old church when all the people spoke Latin. So Herr Peder was in a certain manner right when he said that it was the old Christian church that was now resurrected to new life.

When the gospel was sung and the people all sat again with tramping and crash, there was a break for a minute. Then Herr Peder's voice was heard again, closer and clearer than before. Andreas of Fröjerum bowed forward against the stock and saw that the priest now stood in the pulpit. This too was something new. Should there be preaching during the mass?

Herr Peder began with a long prayer. He thanked God for all his blessings. He thanked him in particular for showing us when things had gotten so bad for the sake of our sins that we all stood before an eternal death, God in his inconceivable mercy laid all our sin on his Son so that we should be free.

Then he began to explain the gospel.

"The righteousness of the Pharisees was the strictest and most spotless there had ever been found on our good green earth. And then Jesus says here that if our righteousness does not exceed theirs, then none of us will ever enter the kingdom of heaven. Then he explains this righteousness so that no one would dare call himself innocent, good, or holy. For it is murder to hate, it is murder to curse, it is worthy of hell to snub your neighbor. And where is he who has always been friendly to everyone, and has always spoken good words in return for evil? One might very well think about what he has just heard or said these last couple hours right outside the church in Vi so that he could cast a righteous judgment on that event."

It was completely dead silent in the church. Even the knechts outside the door piqued their ears. Herr Peder continued with his rich, passionate voice.

"Therefore, we will neither hide ourselves in God's presence nor deceive ourselves, but everyone without exception recognizes not only that we sin but also that we have sinned, that the poisonous root to all evil sits within our own heart. We should recognize that we are not able to do anything that is veritably good, or pure, or perfect. For our depraved nature comes out everywhere, and nothing else, we look for praise or our own well-being or observe our own righteousness with secret pleasure. When a man ought to forget himself and serve his neighbors from unfeigned love, instead he—in the best case—does good for his own sake, in order to be pleased with himself or to be seen by his fellow men or to receive a richer reward in heaven. Upon all such things rests the wrath of God, for it is nothing more than narcissism and self-indulgence, and it is true and right when we all with one mouth confess ourselves to be worthy of eternal damnation."

Herr Peder stopped for a minute. Both men in the stocks leaned forward and listened just as excitedly. They could see the priest in the pulpit inside and comprehended every word. The sermon continued.

"Therefore, there is no work of man on this earth that will do as payment at the gates of heaven. Therefore, everything is completely and hopelessly lost if our salvation would depend upon the righteousness of works that we have accomplished. Therefore, salvation is lost as soon as a man teaches or believes that there is something good on earth that we must first accomplish before we can be saved. Then a man sets works between him and God. But every work, even the best, is tainted with sin. To push a work in between oneself and God is to place a sin there. If a person believes that deeds should be a bridge upon which they can ascend into heaven. But God's law points at the heavenly sin in the holy works and says, 'See! This you have done for your own sake: You love yourself and not your neighbor! See! This you have stained with happiness for being nobler than the others. This you have sullied with the secret vexation that no one thanked you for your great sacrifice. This you had destroyed when you in your heart looked down upon the wretched sinners who did not want to forsake as much as you! See! Deeds that you dare offer your God as payment for the blessedness of heaven is itself sin. It builds no bridge to heaven. Instead, it crashes into the abyss where all sin and guilt belong. And you shall be destroyed yourselves, you who do this sin!' So says the law, so it goes when a man pushes deeds in between himself and God. Then a man only opens an even deeper abyss between him and the Holy One. Then he puts a rule before Heaven's gate. Not even our love or our prayers, yes, not even our crushed hearts are anything so perfect, so free from laziness, reluctance, pride and complacency that they form a bridge between God and us."

Martin glanced at his brother. He saw that he drank up every word. So far, Herr Peder had really hit the mark, but what would follow now?

The preacher inside took another little break. One could hear people adjusting themselves on the benches. Herr Peder took the thread up again.

"What then would carry us to God? What would be able to make a bridge over the bottomless abyss? Nothing in either heaven or earth except for the Mediator that God himself put between him and us. Nothing other than Christ, God's own Son, who became our brother to build a bridge across the abyss. He has built it with his perfect obedience. All that God asked, he fulfilled perfectly. He humbled himself and became obedient unto death on the cross. He did it in perfect love and with a pure heart. He is the one who on our earth, and with his good deeds, built a solid and high bridge up to the gates of heaven.

"But he does not want to walk into God's heaven on this radiant heavenly bridge alone. In his inconceivable mercy, he has also opened a way for his lost brothers. Before he went to heaven, he gathered up all sin that was in our works, all the shame, guilt, misdeeds, and lust that barred the way to God and laid it upon himself. Then he bore it upon the cross. There he atoned for all when he in our stead suffered a horrible death.

"Then on that day, he opened a path to God for sinners. He atoned for the thief's sins, and he took him by the hand as a brother, he carried him in across the high arch of the bridge of his righteousness and said: 'fear not.' What you have broken shall never be counted. You can walk over the depths borne by my righteousness alone. Only believe. Your sins are forgiven you. The righteousness that you do not possess yourself, you may take from me. You can now walk in peace on the path I have built even into my Father's heaven. Today you shall be with me in paradise. Then he carried the thief in, so he has power and authority to carry every sinner into paradise. And until the end of time, he shall wander, tirelessly and mercifully to seek out sinners and—perhaps in the eleventh hour, when the abyss and death open their mouths wide—to save them in his Father's house."

It was as if Herr Peder's passionate voice took on a softer tone when he came to describe the Savior's mercy. He painted him as a man who has hardened criminals as brothers, but who goes out to seek them in the cold of night and willingly gives his life for their sake. He said that all this the Savior did only and alone out of the inconceivable reason that he who has seen the whole infinite measure of our sins—even the most hidden sins that were committed in the deepest darkness, even the most obscure that were buried down in the depths of the earth, even the finest and most incredible that sits furthest down in the heart—he has loved us without limit, without reservation, and without reason, loved us so that he willingly let himself suffer and die so that we would go free.

The scrivener observed his brother from the side. He had lifted his head to the heavens, which arched over them, an endless, clear, and summer blue. Sunlight flooded his face and, even though it was filthy, it shined.

Inside, Herr Peder continued. Now he described how Christ places himself between God and man, how he took all human guilt upon himself so that it can never again be counted or mentioned. He covers over the whole of this corruption with his righteousness so that God neither sees nor counts anything other than his beloved Son when he looks upon man.

Now the priest turned to his brother and looked at him with a look that shined with boyish gladness. Then he carried both hands with the chain in his direction once again, far enough that the right hand managed to give him a regular nudge in the side.

"You!" he said, as if he had some incredible news. "This is a miracle of grace! Do you understand that? This is the miracle of grace that we needed!"

The scrivener bowed and smiled a happy smile. But he did not say a word.

"To whom does this apply?" Was the next question heard from inside the church. And the answer was: "for all those who believe. Here God's word speaks clearly and powerfully. Because God knows so well that not even our best works are without stain if he were to try and test them. So in his love, he has prepared us a salvation that depends on faith alone. He has let Christ prepare a perfect redemption so that nothing more is proven than that we in faith, receive this work that is already completed. And this faith is not a work that we do. That which we achieve with our own faith that which is strong and perfect, or a faith that we embellish with love or good resolve, with that we immediately make it into a wretched visible work of man, and then we have shoved a new work and a new sin between God and us. Now, this true faith is nothing other than this, that the soul that is poor, destitute, and naked receives the Savior who is rich, righteous, and holy. He who has nothing may receive Him who possesses everything. He who is not able and who has nothing to come with is visited by him who is Lord over heaven and earth and who carries the forgiveness of sins, heaven's blessedness, and eternal life with him. And all this one receives through faith alone, the naked, poor faith that possesses nothing in itself."

Herr Andreas bowed again, nudged the scrivener in the side and whispered:

"You, this is the miracle of grace!"

Now Herr Peder asked his last question.

"And then? When we have been justified by pure grace through faith alone—then works come. Between God and us, as reasons for salvation, there is nothing to place. Faith alone stands there. Works do not have their place between God and us but between our neighbor and us. When grace and forgiveness pour down upon us from above, then the stream floods further. We become endearing and cordial, we help, pray, and forgive. Yes, the more we receive of undeserved forgiveness, the more we have to give of the love that serves our neighbor without asking for reward. But these deeds that in truth could be called good deeds, they have nothing to do with the righteousness that applies before God."

Herr Andreas sat and thought to himself. Had this not been the problem with all his piety: that he shoved his works between him and God? Was this not why he attached the most importance to that which only served to gild himself—celibacy, solitude in Fröjerum, vigils, and the nightly prayers? Was this perhaps why, as he so often wondered, that there was something completely different something that gave a cleaner air when he walked out on the paths to visit the sick and perhaps neglected numerous hours in a row to bring the sacrament to some old wretch in the forest? Was it not conceivable, what Herr Peder had said about himself, that he lived closer to God in marriage than in his solitude? Was it not sin already that he never asked how he knew this and had this, how he sanctified himself and was spiritualized, instead of asking how he could best serve his neighbor?

The scrivener sat next to him and had his own thoughts. He remembered the barber-surgeon who did not want to leave the songs and prayers for the wounded. He remembered the strife concerning the fur trim and linen shirts. Was it not all because they had placed works between them and God? In his blindness, he had believed that prayer, songs of praise, and self-denial were the way to God. Now he saw that instead, the path went from up top to down here. Here came Christ with hands full of heavenly treasure. It was only to take for nothing—and then to go out and serve his neighbor. Where? With

Gert Hubmaier? Had he ever taken the trouble to serve his neighbor? Or perhaps rather of concern for himself and his own good deeds? Would he then go back to the king's chancellery?

Herr Peder was about to finish his sermon. He said that no one could describe beforehand how a man came to act and live when he received grace and was driven by it. But God's Spirit comes to drive him to his place where he is placed to do the good that God wants to accomplish through him in the world. Certainly, the love of God never completely rules over a person. He needs the daily discipline of the law. He needs forgiveness every day anew. But when he constantly receives grace, he is constantly driven anew to act in love. So he finds the right path in just that call where God places here. There he lives in love, reconciliation, and service.

However, this love of God does not set aside the office of the authorities or their power. Because there are so few who allow themselves to be governed by the Word, so God has placed authorities to rule with the sword over all the others, the obstinate and unrepentant, and worldly-minded. Even Christians are obligated to bear the sword when God places them in an office of authority. God can make him a knecht or a leader when he is placed by God to keep justice and peace with power. On judgment day, he may step forward, and God will ask him: How did you use the sword I put in your hand? It will then not condemn him that he punished and executed with it if he did it according to the law and equity. But if he has used the sword arbitrarily and in wrath, with cruelty or falsehood for his own gain or perhaps purely for revenge, then God takes the good sword of the authority and says: This sword that I sent down to my earth that it would be the defender of the fatherless and widows, this good sword that would punish thieves and highwaymen and protect the life and goods of my many poor and helpless—behold! It is stained with the tears of widows and cries of hungry children. Wrong judgments have taken their toll, wrongly demanded taxes and illegally acquired donations here with a rusty blade, and the bracket is still hot with anger, that does not even let the dead enemy rest in his grave. When such a sword has come forward for judgment, then it happens that the evil spirits light a flickering bonfire and dance dances of joy around it, and then they find a rope to tie around the body of the poor soul and throw them in the fire.

Now it was completely silent in the church—the knechts who were half-asleep a minute before stood up straight and glanced at each other. Herr Andreas finally dared to breathe. Should his brother in the office perish there in the pulpit?

Now Herr Peder's heavy voice had lightened, and he began to speak in a fatherly tone again. He turned to everyone who received power from God to govern over others: fathers and mothers over children, masters over manservants and maidservants, authorities over subjects, and asked them to consider that every determination and command that leaves their lips here will be followed by judgment and resolution and action before God's high court. He described how much good God wants to do on earth through the offices he instituted and how much evil comes from their abuse. He took examples from manor houses and courts that everyone could understand. Then he admonished them to sincerely seek forgiveness for their sins, to reconcile themselves with God and to reconcile with each other, so that God's good peace, which has been lacking in the land for so long, would now for everyone's benefit be able to reign in heart and deed. But above all, he admonished all of them to hold to the great article concerning justification by faith, unharmed and rejoice and be thankful in their hearts that a whole and complete salvation has been prepared for us in the Lord Jesus Christ, who for us was made sin so that we in him would become righteous before God.

When Herr Peder came down from the pulpit, and the liturgy of the sacrament began, the priest in the stocks sat for a long time with his face hidden in his hands. He thanked God without any words. He felt how it was suddenly wiped clean between him and his Lord. Just as he sat there under the clear blue sky, flooded by the warm summer sun, so was his soul flooded by the sunlight of God's grace. All terms and conditions had fallen. Today he knew that it was true: my righteousness shall live in faith and by faith alone. Now everything else was so marvelously small and insignificant. Just as his sore legs sat fastened in the stocks and just as his sore wrists were heavy with fetters so was he still trapped by his flesh. And still, it was true: "It is no longer I who live, but Christ lives in me." All his own was absorbed by Christ's life, Christ's death, Christ's righteousness. He knew that when God's fatherly eyes now observed his dirty body and his even dirtier soul, they saw his Son in him. He heard singing somewhere up in the sunny atmosphere: This is my beloved Son, in whom I am well pleased.

What then did it mean if he was still fettered and fastened to sin? It would only be a few hours before he would be free! He lifted his face to the sky and mumbled: "Thank you, Father, inconceivably great, good, God and Father."

Familiar tunes rang out from within the church. It was Sursum corda and the preface; it was the Sanctus and the Agnus Dei.[8] Now they went forward to the altar up front. Did they really go? He leaned forward to see. The people who just knelt during the words of institution were moving. Men and women rose from the pews and pushed forward through the mass of people. He had always wished for this and so seldom saw it realized. It was an old bad practice and rooted in so many centuries, to let the priest receive the sacrament alone. Here the old church rose again to new life.

Again, he lifted his face to the heavens.

"God, you are very good," he thought. "Even when upon the threshold of being with you in glory up there, you let me see a glimpse of the dream for glory on earth: your holy church which will be renewed and reestablished from her impotence and decay. So I thank you, Lord, and thank you a thousand-fold and again."

It had become still in there. Herr Peder sang the Benedicamus. "Thank and Praise the Lord," as it was called in the Swedish mass.

Herr Andreas suddenly woke from his thought and quickly turned to his brother.

"Martin, will you go in and ask Herr Peder if he might bring the sacrament to us?"

The scrivener rose quickly. He had seen and desired to be in there but had not wanted to leave his brother.

Herr Peder had just entered the sacristy and wiped the sweat from his brow when the scrivener came in with his errand. Martin looked like a schoolboy on holiday. The priest's eyes bulged.

"Andreas wants the sacrament? From me? In both kinds?"

---

[8] "Lift up your hearts," the preparatory prayer; "Yes, it is truly good, right, and salutary"; "Holy, Holy, Holy"; and "Lamb of God"—parts of the early church's liturgy of the mass that are still used.

"Yes, most certainly," said the scrivener and smiled. "It is like the Mount of Transfiguration out there."

The priest crossed himself reverently, folded his hands, and bowed deeply before the crucifix on the wall.

"Lord, now you let your servant depart in peace, for my eyes have seen your salvation," he said very quietly.

Then he took the cup and the paten and went out through the church where the congregation just finished the hymn they always sang before exiting: Grant us God Your Grace and Peace All Our Days.

Many people were gathered out in the churchyard. While the Divine Service continued, they had gathered from every direction to see the execution. Herr Peder looked around in amazement at the gray ring of people. They were the faces of complete strangers.

When the people now began to push through from inside the church, Pastor Peder hurried to the stocks. He saw the priest. Without any words, he saw that God had performed a miracle. He prayed.

"*Domine Petre*," said the fettered man, "I ask you for the sake of God's mercy to absolve me of my sins."

Herr Peder ordered a knecht with a movement of his hand to keep the people at a distance. Andreas of Fröjerum bowed forward deeply and prayed where he sat in the stocks.

"Holy, triune God, I confess that I have sinned against all your commandments in thought, word, and deed and with the very desire of my heart. I confess that I have sinned when I wanted to be pious for my own sake and considered my holiness to be a crown of glory. I beg you from my heart to forgive the whole of my sinful life and all my sinful ways, for the sake of my Savior Jesus Christ's death and atonement. And I ask you, *Domine Petre*, that you for the sake of God's mercy would declare me free from all my sin."

Herr Peder lifted his hand. He shook so that it could be seen in the distance even by the packed crowd, and perhaps even his voice wavered when he said:

"Let it be as you believe. Your sins are forgiven you. *Ego te absalvo ab omnibus peccatis tuis, in nomine Patris, et Filii, et Spiritus Sancti.*"[9]

---

[9] I absolve you from all your sins, in the name of the Father and of the Son and of the Holy Spirit.

He made a large sign of the cross. He looked around at the crowd that was in dead silence. Among the knechts who came out of the church he was able to see Herr Tönjes, who stood there a little nonplussed, with a countenance that drifted between insecurity and spite.

"Dear Herr," said the priest. "Free the prisoner from the stocks so that he may receive the Lord's body in the position that is behooved."

A nod from the commander was sufficient. The knechts lifted the stocks, and Herr Andreas fell to his knees in the grass. Martin kneeled next to him. The priest gave them the sacrament, first the bread and then the cup according to evangelical custom. Martin kept his hands folded tight. Andreas had put his hands together. Though the iron chain hung loosely between the fetters and though his head was disfigured by dirt and beard stubble, he radiated with joy like a newly consecrated priest who read the holy mass with the devotion of early youth.

Herr Tönjes had had his horse fetched and stepped into the saddle, hooves clapped down on the church hill where the riders formed a hedge before the covered path. The horses who were delirious from the rustling of the people danced and sniffed the air. The people began to run over the churchyard to be the first to the town square.

The knechts had fetched their weapons and surrounded the prisoner. They ordered themselves with Herr Tönjes riding point, the knechts two by two led by both the priest and the scrivener between them. Here Peder was still wearing his alb and stole. The sexton had taken the cup and paten. All around innumerable soft feet trampled over the churchyard grass.

Herr Tönjes turned in the saddle. He watched the priest and the scrivener who stood there solemnly as if this was the great procession of a church festival. A little suspiciously, he let his gaze glance over their faces. Were they laughing at him? Had they prepared some trick? He observed the peasant crowd suspiciously as it made its way down to the place of execution but didn't see anything suspicious. Calmly he turned again to the prisoner.

"Forget any memories of the wedding feast, worthy lord," he said. "Let your head hang a little, for now. It is lost. In less than ten minutes and there will be nothing left of your life."

The prisoner lifted his head and looked up, first straight into the knight's face, then past him up into the radiant summer sky.

"That's precisely why I am so happy," he said.

The knight looked even more uncertain.

"Am I to understand you think you will be a great martyr?"

"No," said the prisoner convincingly. "I only suffer what my deeds are worthy of."

Herr Tönjes's face tried to express a gracious smile, but surprise took the upper hand again. The prisoner looked first to his brother and then to Herr Peder.

"Say," he said, "can a man ever suffer so much as he deserves here on earth?"

"No," they both said at once.

The knight turned a bit. He felt certain that something amiss was going on here. Then he found himself and said mockingly.

"Lords, have you considered that I can just as well execute all three of you at the same time?"

"Not you, noble Herr," said Herr Peder calmly. "You have only to judge according to the laws of Sweden, and then we will perhaps go free. But God has very good reason to condemn all four of us to death."

Herr Tönjes pursed his mouth. He noticed that the knechts listened, and it irritated him.

"I object," he said. "I do not feel deserving of execution today. My sins are not yet *that* great."

Herr Peder did not let the knight escape his wide burning eyes.

"The wages of sin is death, Herr Tönjes. God has already told you this today, and in his name, I tell it to you again: Anyone who is angry with his brother, he will be liable to judgment, but anyone who says: you fool, he is guilty to the hell of fire. This word also applies to Herr Tönjes Månson of Sponga and Vibynäs."

The knight became very red.

"We do not have time to discuss theology," he said. "I have nothing to do with your judgment. Now the king's sentence shall be realized. Then we may see how it goes with the priests. In the end, it is we who have the power in any case."

Now Herr Andreas smiled and looked the knight right in the eye. He said half confidentially as if he spoke to an old friend:

"You would have no power over me if it were not given to you from above."

Herr Peder bowed in assent. The knight who thought that he had some secret band of brothers against him, turned to the knechts.

"Now we go," he commented. "Watch and keep the crowd at bay. If anyone comes near, then poke him with the shaft of the lance. March . . ."

His broad back hopped when the horse that had been scraping at the turf for a while and tugged at the reigns was finally able to dance away. The knechts followed after.

Martin and Herr Peder kept close to the prisoner. They could still exchange a few words. It was Herr Andreas who spoke first.

"Thanks for everything, Peder. Try to get them a good priest up there in Ravelunda and Fröjerum. One who is faithful to our old church."

Herr Peder looked a bit puzzled. The other noticed it and added.

"I mean the church that we received from God when St. Ansgar and Saint Sigfrid came here. She whom God now keeps and renews before our eyes, the one that is both truly catholic and truly evangelical. The one that both you and I have always served, though we did not always understand it, at least not me."

Herr Peder nodded. The other continued.

"Peder, promise one thing."

"What then?"

"That you will go up and see to it that it does not go badly for all my widows and fatherless children at home. And that the soul care is done properly."

Herr Peder nodded.

"And then one more thing, that you keep after the young priests so that they sing the hours and celebrate the mass with all dignity."

"That matter is for the archbishop. You don't need to be concerned about that."

"I hope. We have so many old treasures that we should not do away with because the new is so wonderful."

Suddenly Herr Andreas smiled a great broad smile. The other looked at him questioningly, and he broke out!

"God is so good!"

Martin nodded wide-eyed, and Andreas continued:

"Think if God had not in his mercy let my sins be so revealed. Then even today I would feel as if I was some holy martyr. I would have thought that I suffered wrong and was someone great and noteworthy. But today it is only the Savior that is great . . . *Deo gratias*!"[10]

There was a moment of silence as the crowd pushed through the gate. On the other side, the riders waited. They formed a protective ring around the pedestrians and kept the peasants at a distance. The whole church hill was filled with the trampling of horse hooves, heavy steps of the knechts, the rustling of weapons, and the dampened noise of the spectators who streamed down to the thingstead.

Now it was Martin who broke the silence. He had been thinking about something for a long time.

"Anders," he said, "if you were to live, what would you do then?"

"Return to Fröjerum and Ravelunda and serve God."

"How?"

"As a priest, I guess."

"Like before then?"

"Yes, though, I would preach more. And try to live less for myself and more for others."

"And then how would you do the mass?"

"I would do that according to the order of the church. We have now as before an Archbishop in Uppsala and a bishop in Linköping. We have the synod and the diocese. What they would ask of me is what I would do. They are my spiritual authorities."

Martin nodded.

And King Gustavus?

"I would pray for him with all my heart."

"And also obey?"

"Yes, in the worldly things. So long as he let us preach the gospel freely. He is lord over our bodies but not over our souls."

Martin was contemplative.

"That would be a narrow path," he said.

Andreas smiled.

"Brother Martin, the *path* is narrow."

They were at the thingstead.

The knechts had formed a square around the little earthen hill that lifted its flathead in the middle of the thingstead. They stood

[10] God be praised.

astride each other and heavy in their gray line, poor Swedish knechts from the king's muster without the foreign plumes and colorful uniforms. Only a dark red sweater here and there broke up the blue-gray row of iron and homespun. With strong fists, they held up their halberds like bars against the people.

Outside the black straight line of knechts, the gray crowd of peasants could be seen with elements of matt green and brown. In the sun, their weather-beaten faces were bright red, and with their view blocked, they strained to see over the barrier of halberds. On the hill stood two trumpeters with golden shirts and a man dressed in black and bare arms: the executioner.

In a cloud of dust, the riders turned and distributed themselves around the hill. After much rustling and swearing, their nervous horses were brought into a passable line. During this time, Herr Tönjes rode up on the crown of the hill. He struggled with his horse that danced back and forth and was already shining with sweat. When he got it to trample in place, he waved to the four knechts who stood closest to the prisoner. They paraded up and positioned themselves at each corner of the flat bare spot on top of the hill. Herr Tönjes, who finally got his horse to stand with all four hooves on the ground, looked at the prisoner a bit puzzled.

Herr Peder and the scrivener had followed. As the lawfully appointed seelsorger, the priest accompanied the man to be executed to give him the last rites. Their eyes met. The knight's suspicious look noticed again that their faces shone with a mysterious common understanding. It was as if two schoolboys shared a great and funny secret.

"Do you want to sing something?" asked the priest.

"Yes," said the prisoner. "Sing for me once again that song that you sang in the church: He for my guilt did penance."

Herr Peder looked at him a bit amazed.

"I know of nothing better than to die having heard what was written there," said the prisoner. "And for my guilt did penance. Then the heavens are opened. Then all my own, my sins and my good deeds are thrown in the same pile and say: I want to know nothing other than the Savior who died for me and atoned for all. I want nothing else to support me but his cross alone. For my guilt, he did penance. It is sufficient for me to be at peace!"

Herr Peder waved to the people.

"Now let's all sing," he cried with his dark voice, that was still a little deeper and more shaky than usual. "Herr Andreas, God's priest in Ravelunda and Fröjerum, who meets his Savior today, has asked that we all sing: 'He Shed His Precious Blood.' Because there is nothing better to die with, he says, than the gospel of our Savior's death and bloody atonement. So now we remove our hats and all sing."

He took up the hymn with a firm voice. His congregation joined in. They were a singing people here in the country, and now the new Lutheran songs had made a quick conquest. So the hymn was sung powerfully, and the priest's strong voice drowned out the noise. Or perhaps it became a little uncertain at the end. He stood with his hands folded hard and looked up into the clear, bright sky. Across from him stood the scrivener, who sang with a hoarse and struggling voice. Even he held his hands folded so hard that his knuckles were white.

When the hymn was finished, Herr Andreas lifted his hands as if he stood in a church and lifted his voice:

"*In manus tuas, Domine, commendo spiritum meum . . .*"[11]

It was the old response from Compline, perhaps the most spiritual and beloved of all the melodies in the daily hours. The old people had heard them innumerable times as the summer dusk flee over the churchyard or in the fall darkness fell to a close under the firmament. Herr Andreas knew that it was not just Herr Peder and his sexton, but certainly anyone down there in the crowd would be able to answer.

Then something unexpected happened. Herr Peder sent one of his raptured looks out over the crowd, first to the sexton and then to the congregational members. Then he made the response in Swedish:

"Lord, into your hands . . ."

The sexton fell in, and a few children followed, then came the women and the men with their base voices. This had one had been sung innumerable times in the church during these last years. It spread like fire over the crowd:

". . . I commend my spirit."

---

[11] Into your hands, Lord, I commend my spirit.

Herr Andreas looked at his brother in the office. His eyes fell. Then he continued in Latin.

"*Redemisti nos, Domine, Deus veritatis.*"[12]

He had sung this many thousands of times before. But never before had it been so filled with meaning as today. It seemed to him to be a miracle far above anything he could hope for that he today on the day of his death would meet God's redeeming faithfulness in this overwhelming way and be able to see what he had longed for most of all and most deeply despaired of: his own soul's salvation and the reestablishment of his church. In this hour, he was the world's happiest man. Above him, he had an open heaven. Around him, he had people who sang the holy offices. When the responsory was repeated for the third time, it came from all four corners.

"Lord, into your hands, I commend my Spirit."

Herr Peder called him back to reality.

"It is permitted to say something. But you know that it has to be short."

Herr Andreas took a couple of steps forward. There was a dead silence in the crowd. With a loud voice, he said:

"It was all very honorable of you, that I today die as a great sinner who for the sake of Jesus alone should hope in grace and mercy. It is also honorable of you that I, from my heart, forgive all my enemies high and low. And I beg you and all for forgiveness for the bloodshed and distress that I caused. It is my earnest desire that all that may remain of my possessions shall be distributed in Fröjerum and Ravelunda among those who have become widows and fatherless during the rebellion—regardless of which side their kin have fallen for. Herr Peder has promised to administer the distribution. And so I pray God to reward them all who wish our native home well from the heart."

While he still spoke, he loosened his collar and let the frock fall over his shoulders so that his torso was bare. He took two steps back, knelt over the bare spot in the grass with his bare neck. His emaciated body was white in the sun.

---

[12] You have redeemed us, Lord, faithful God.

The executioner had unsheathed the sword. The scrivener who up until now had been completely calm and almost happy had again become very pale. He turned away.

Even in the crowd, there was a little motion. An eerie mumble broke the dead silence. It began down in one corner, and it spread to the sides, it reached the ranks of the knechts in the middle of the place of execution. It grew into an audible grumble. Suddenly someone yelled loudly, from far within the gray mass:

"Release the priest!"

And it was answered by an echo from the other side:

"The priest is no traitor!"

It was like a spark in a powder keg. The peasants were used to speaking their minds loudly from the depths of the ranks here in the thingstead. Now it rained from all sides.

"Free him! He has done no wrong! He is a righteous priest. Let him loose!"

Now a stone came flying. With a muted sound, it hit against the armor plate outside a soft sweater. The horse under Herr Tönjes danced again. Lather ran in white streams from the bit. The reins were tight as bowstrings. The knight's face was shut and hard. It seemed that the order pressed against the back of his lips, ready to fly out.

He never found the time to say anything. The condemned man rose and lifted his weak white arms with the rattling chains.

"Madmen!" he shouted. "Be quiet! He who takes up the sword shall die by the sword!"

The alarm died down, and the knechts lowered their spears. The priest panted so that all his blue bruised and bloodshot ribs could be seen.

"Hear you, good people," he cried. "Today we shall do something great, something that builds up both Christ's church and the Kingdom of Sweden. You know what?"

They had become completely silent; all eyes were directed at him.

"We shall forgive. We, who all need so much forgiveness and receive so much forgiveness, we shall forgive everything for the sake of Christ. We shall rather suffer in the name of Jesus than fight for ourselves."

He breathed again deeply.

"Today, I only suffer for what my sins are worth. It is not only the king who has condemned me to death. God has done it long ago. But today, all has been forgiven for the sake of Jesus. Such is our God. Should we then not forgive? And ask each other for forgiveness? Now I will begin . . ."

He turned around and went over the hill to Herr Tönjes, who had managed to calm his horse again.

"Dear lord, I ask you sincerely to forgive that I met you with so little love and so much arrogance—and that I never really wished you well or sought your best. Forgive me!"

Herr Tönjes only nodded and waved averting with his hands. He was very red in the face. His hands fumbled before is eyes. So he let the visor fall down with a clang, no one would see his face any longer.

"Time is up," he said with a garbled voice. "Now, it must be done."

The prisoner went back into the ring and knelt again. The executioner stood in position at his side.

Suddenly the scrivener took a couple of steps forward and fell to his knees beside his brother. He was very pale and kept his hands folded hard.

"Thank you, Martin," said the priest. "In the stocks, at the Lord's Supper, and in the place of execution, you have always been with me. Now I go forward a bit. Hold fast to the faith and we will meet again."

The other looked up, and his pale face was completely calm. He bowed slowly, and Herr Andreas turned his head and looked over his shoulder.

"And now, brother executioner, you may do me this one last great service."

He shut his eyes and began to pray. His face looked up.

"Bow your head a little more, lord," said the executioner, "otherwise it won't do."

Slowly the condemned man bowed his head forward, still praying. Herr Peder, who stood there with tight lips and folded hands and looked on, thought to himself, that he saw his brother in the office bow his neck just as reverently and calmly before today. It was when he gave him the body and blood outside the church doors.

The executioner swung.

The crowd heard two thuds, first a short and hard then a softer one. The trumpeters blew loudly. The horses recoiled and there was a rustling of weapons. The peasants were silent. Many were on their knees. Others crossed themselves.

Herr Peder walked up quietly and put the dead man's head upright. Then he slowly sang the benediction over him. In the next minute, the trumpets blew the signal to fall in and the knechts drew up their halberds and arranged themselves to leave while the crowd pushed in from all sides.

Herr Peder went over to the knight, who still had his visor shut.

"What do you plan to do with the body, lord?"

"I have no orders concerning that matter," said Herr Tönjes hesitantly.

"May I answer for it?"

"Fine by me, then I don't have to worry about it. Thank you and farewell."

He turned his horse around. Just as he was about to go away, he turned one last time in the saddle.

"What do you plan to do with the body?"

"Take it to Fröjerum, and let it be buried inside the church with all honor," said the priest boldly.

The knight drew in his reins.

"Just don't let there be any rebellion or rioting with the matter," he said sharply.

"You don't have to worry, lord. I shall conduct the funeral myself and keep the funeral sermon so that there is not rioting and unrest anywhere—except perhaps in the consciences."

"What will your sermon be about then?"

"About that which Herr Andreas preached to us here: that we all need forgiveness and shall give forgiveness."

The knight turned his horse halfway. He sat straight in the saddle and looked down at Herr Peder through the helmet's eyeholes.

"If I could ever understand you, priests," he said. "Sometimes, you sound like you are His Majesty's most faithful servants. But there in the church, it was another tone that was just heard. It was very close to being a sermon of rebellion. Who do you really serve, lord?"

Herr Peder calmly looked up at the visor.

"God."

"But then what about the king? And the judge? And us?"

"We serve you for God's sake. You have your commission from God. But it is God and not you that we serve. Finally, it is God who may determine. We have only to obey his Word. Then it may be all or nothing."

The knight folded up his visor and gave the priest a long testing look.

"I understand that a priest must think so. It is all worthy of respect."

"More than that, Herr Tönjes," said the priest slowly and very firmly. "It is the only right way to live that there is on this earth—for noblemen, priests, freemen, and peasants. We all stand under God's word. Therefore, we only have two possibilities: The obedience of faith, or the condemnation of unbelief."

The knight shut his lips. His face was inscrutable.

"Perhaps," he said. Then he spurred his horse, tapped his hand to his helmet to say good-bye, and trotted toward the riders. In the next minute, they had already made their way through the crowd and set their course for the road.

Herr Peder took a deep breath. It smelled of horse, blood, and warm earth. He looked around among the peasants who shyly gathered around at the foot of the hill in delayed shock. He waved to some of them and gave his commands. Then he turned to the scrivener who still knelt at his brother's side. He didn't say anything but put his hand on his shoulder.

After a minute, the gravediggers came with the litter. Carefully they laid the dead man out properly and swept in his black frock. Slowly they walked up to the church again. It was now the warmest part of the day. The birds had quit singing. The canopy of oak leaves which already had some of the summer darkness in color stood completely still. The people in the poor gray entourage who came walking behind the litter were also quiet. A single trumpet signaled off in the distance, shiny and proud like a bright parade.

Herr Peder and the scrivener kept their hands folded. Only at the gate to the path did he lift his right hand and pointed down to the meadow.

"Peder," he said, "it is strange: today I have received back both heaven and earth . . . both the church and the kingdom."

The priest looked at him, puzzled.

"Yes, I mean I received back heaven when I was led to believe in the undeserved grace. Now heaven above is open to me, and I will never again barter with God, only thank him. But when I understood this forgiveness of sins, I also found peace on earth. Before, I bartered with men and left them because of their sins. Now I know that we all bear the same cross and that I am the greatest among sinners. Now I will gladly help and serve. Now I am glad to be able to sit like the others in the church pews. And now I believe that I will go back to my old place at the castle and do what good I can—and I can live every day in the forgiveness of sins."

He was quiet for a minute.

"Peder," he said, "isn't it strange that everything is so simple when one has the forgiveness of sins? Is it not the heart of the whole of our existence this atonement and the forgiveness of sins?"

Herr Peder smiled again for the first time after the execution.

"Yes," he said, "so it is. This is the heart of everything: the atonement and the forgiveness of sins."

CPSIA information can be obtained
at www.ICGtesting.com
Printed in the USA
LVHW010504080820
662366LV00006B/314